PENGUIN BOOKS

the cottage at rosella cove

Sandie Docker grew up in Coffs Harbour, and fell in love with reading when her father encouraged her to take up his passion for books. Sandie first decided to put pen to paper (yes, she writes everything the old-fashioned way before hitting a keyboard) while living in London. Now back in Sydney with her husband and daughter, she writes every day.

www.sandiedocker.com
@SandieDockerwriter

sandie
docker

the
cottage at
rosella cove

PENGUIN BOOKS

PENGUIN BOOKS

UK | USA | Canada | Ireland | Australia
India | New Zealand | South Africa | China

Penguin Books is part of the Penguin Random House group of companies
whose addresses can be found at global.penguinrandomhouse.com

Penguin
Random House
Australia

First published by Michael Joseph in 2019
This edition published by Penguin Books in 2020

Cover illustrations: (crimson rosellas) Anastasia Lembrik/Shutterstock.com;
(envelopes and seashells) Katy's Dreams/Shutterstock.com; (books) Elzza/Shutterstock.com
Cover design by Laura Thomas © Penguin Random House Pty Ltd
Typeset in Sabon by Midland Typesetters, Australia
Printed and bound in Australia by Griffin Press, an accredited
ISO AS/NZS 14001 Environmental Management Systems printer

A catalogue record for this
book is available from the
NATIONAL
LIBRARY   National Library of Australia
OF AUSTRALIA

ISBN 978 1 76089 985 1

penguin.com.au

For Karen

One

The gravel crunched beneath the tyres as Nicole slowed the beat-up Holden Barina on her approach to the cottage. Along the peninsula that spilled down the steep cliffs into the ocean below, the sun cast long shadows.

The cottage coming into view was smaller than she'd expected, but she supposed these things were hard to judge based on a few thumbnail pictures on the internet. Still, she was lucky to be here, to have somewhere to go, so she shouldn't complain.

She pulled up beside the broken picket gate, barely visible beneath the tangle of weeds that smothered the old fence. She wiped tears from her eyes. They still fell sporadically now, the four-hour drive doing little to dull her emotions. At least the shaking in her hands had stopped.

A cool breeze hit her bare arms and she hugged herself tightly. The taste of salt touched her lips.

The air was sharp and clean as she drew a deep breath and counted to ten. She shivered; something was not quite right. Then she recognised it. Quiet. No sirens. No traffic. No constant hum of the thousand indistinguishable sounds that surrounded you in the city. Just the breeze and the gentle crash of waves she couldn't see.

Nicole opened the boot and she stared at the contents of her life, stuffed into the tiny hatchback – one suitcase of clothes; one box that contained a knife, a spoon, a fork, a plate, a bowl and a couple of packets of food; one brand-new phone with new SIM; one laptop.

Deep breaths, she told herself.

She grabbed the suitcase and shoved the gate open, tearing off weeds to free it a little. If there was a path to the verandah, she couldn't see it. Dragging herself through the knee-length grass, she hoped there were no snakes. Were there any snakes in this part of the country? She had no idea. She'd never even heard of Rosella Cove until a few weeks ago.

She went up to the safety of the verandah and opened the door. It creaked loudly and as Nicole stepped into the doorway, the air from outside whooshed in. She started coughing and choking as billows of dust swirled around her. How long had it been since anyone had set foot inside this house?

She flicked on a light and took in her new home. *Home*. Such a foreign word.

Above her the ceiling was cracked and yellowed, pieces of plaster missing here, sagging there. The paint on the wall stretching away to her left was peeling. The stench that assaulted her nose – old, musty, some sort of caustic funk – was almost too much to bear.

As she took a few steps in, the floorboards beneath her groaned in protest.

There was a thud and a screech.

Nicole jumped, dropping her suitcase, and it opened, clothes spilling into the dust.

In the corner of the room that opened out from the hallway, a pair of small yellow eyes stared out at her, daring her to make a move.

Nicole screamed. The monster ran.

Nicole's chest pounded and she scooped her clothes back into the suitcase and ran outside.

Locked inside her car, she concentrated on her breathing – in, out, in, out. How on earth had it all gone so wrong? How had she ended up here?

She knew how. She just hadn't come to terms with it and wasn't sure she ever would. But she had to try. As hard as it was to accept, this was her new life now. For a little while at least.

September, Three Years Ago

'No peeking.' Mark's hand rested gently across Nicky's eyes. The warmth radiating from his body as he pressed against her back enveloped her, and he directed her towards the balcony of his fifth-floor apartment. *Their* apartment.

'What's this about?' She laughed.

'You'll see.'

A warm breeze hit her as they went outside. The rumble of the constant traffic below, the music of early morning.

'Okay,' he whispered in her ear. 'Open.'

On the small glass table in the middle of the balcony sat a laptop with a fat pink bow stuck to its top.

'Happy six-month-aversary.' His grin revealed dimples that gave her goosebumps. Man, she loved those dimples.

'I thought moving in together was our six-month-aversary present.' She hugged him tightly.

'It is. But this is just a little something extra. You can't keep using that dinosaur you call a computer. Not if you're going to be a serious writer.'

A serious writer. It was all she ever wanted to be. And she'd finally written something that looked like a manuscript, but she couldn't seem to find her flow to finish it. The story she'd been working on the last twelve months had stalled and she couldn't find her way out of the funk.

'You'll get there, princess.' He kissed the top of her head.

A tear slipped down Nicky's cheek. *You'll get there* – her mum's favourite phrase.

'Hey. It's okay.' Mark wiped the tear away. 'I know you miss your mum, but you've got me now.'

'I know.' She was so grateful for Mark, every day. But nothing, no one, could replace her mum. Joy and heartache fought within her – six months with Mark, six months without her mum.

'Why don't we head down to the park after breakfast and you can take your new toy and see if inspiration strikes?'

Mark cooked up a delicious meal of eggs Benedict and smoked salmon and made a thermos of hot chocolate for Nicky to take with her. In the shadows of the skyscrapers they wove their way through the grey streets of Sydney's CBD, past the businessmen in black suits, until they reached the green solace of Hyde Park. Middle-aged men rode their bikes at top speed along the paths and women in their activewear pushed expensive prams as they sipped on organic decaf soy lattes. Nicky had stopped going to the café on the corner of the park where the barista would frown down at her for ordering a full cream hot chocolate with extra marshmallows.

Moving in with Mark to the slick suburb of Surry Hills, thick with its fashionable cafés and bars and boutiques, was going to take some getting used to.

When they got to the middle of Hyde Park, Nicky set herself down on an old wooden bench under a large Moreton Bay fig. Dark green leaves dangled on grey branches hanging from the trunk, which melted into the ground in ribbons of tall, thick roots.

Mark kissed her goodbye, put his headphones in his ears and continued on through the park to his office on Macquarie Street. Their usual Friday morning ritual. Only today Nicky had her new laptop with her. Some days her fingers would float across her old keyboard creating flowing paragraphs, her mind liberated of clutter, free to compose unhindered. Other days her fingers would lie motionless beside her as she watched the passing ensemble of city-dwellers glide about their day, oblivious to her scrutiny. Then, later that evening, all the images and sounds and smells would transform in her mind. The old woman in her sunflower dress walking her tightly crimped toy poodle might become the nosey neighbour of her protagonist. The tall, well-built man shouting at his child not to run away might have just the right jawline or hairstyle her hero needed. The smell of vinegar on fish and chips as two black-clad teenagers strutted by might help set the scene of her fallen heroine's childhood home. Scenes that didn't make it into her current work were scribbled in notebooks under her bed, waiting for their story to be told.

Lately, though, inspiration had been conspicuously absent.

Nicky closed her eyes and took in three deep breaths. The sweet, sharp scent of freshly cut grass filled her head and when she refocused on the tide of humanity passing by her, her mind was clear. The tide of humanity. The tide of time. Was this the missing element to her story?

She flipped the new laptop open and her fingers darted across the keys. All background noise melted away until the only sound Nicky could hear was the tapping of the keyboard.

She stayed in the park till the cool afternoon breeze sent shivers up her back. Then she hurried home, stopping at the small supermarket one street over from their apartment on her way.

When Mark got home, Nicky was in the kitchen surrounded by potato peelings and torn basil and white fatty bits of chicken strewn across the bench.

'What happened here?' Mark lay his briefcase on the side table at the front door.

'I did it. I figured out how to fix my manuscript and I wrote all day. I finished it.'

'So you thought to celebrate you'd poison us?' Mark laughed and started clearing up the meal, if it could be called that, that Nicky had spent the last hour preparing. 'Nicky, I love you, but I thought we banned you from the kitchen.'

He put down the plates and wrapped her in a tight hug.

'I know. I was just so excited. I wanted to do something special for us.' Nicky looked up into his dark brown eyes, which crinkled around the edges as he held back more laughter. 'Okay.' She smiled. 'Maybe cooking wasn't the best idea.'

'No, but why don't we order in to celebrate instead?'

After dinner they sprawled on the couch, wrapped in each other's arms. Mark traced his fingers up and down Nicky's hip while Adele played softly in the background. 'Make You Love Me', the song they first kissed to, came on and they looked at each other and smiled.

'You are the most beautiful woman I've ever met.' He brushed her long black hair aside and kissed her freckled cheek.

No one had ever called her beautiful before.

'And I'm the luckiest woman in the world.' She rolled over and sat on top of his hips, running her fingers through his short black beard.

'Good.' He reached up and pulled her head towards his, kissing her long and hard.

Happiness surged through Nicky. Her life was more perfect than she ever could have imagined.

———

Nicole stretched, trying to loosen the crick in her neck. She'd slept the night in the car, too afraid to go back in the cottage in the dark and face whatever beast was residing in there.

She'd have to summon some courage from somewhere, though. There was no way she could spend another night in that cramped back seat.

Looking at the cottage in the stark morning light, she could see the decay the evening shadows had hidden.

Perched atop the peninsula, it sat all alone, a scar upon the green landscape. The corrugated roof was peeling off in sections, and its pale blue wooden exterior was covered in dirt so thick in places it almost looked like stucco. White – once white – posts separated the wrap-around verandah from the iron roof overhang, looking tired, as if they'd give way at any moment.

No wonder no one else had taken on the cottage. She knew six months free rent in exchange for light renovation had seemed too good to be true, but she had little choice. At least it was a roof over her head, despite the disrepair, and right now she needed that more than anything else.

'Okay, then,' she said aloud. She had a job to do.

Tiptoeing into the cottage, she listened for any sound that her creature housemate was inside. She peered into what she assumed was the living room. There, in the corner, a grey–brown lump was curled up tightly.

'Yah!' she screamed and the animal sat up, alert. It was the largest possum Nicole had ever seen and it didn't look too happy to see her.

She shouted and waved her arms about and chased the unwanted guest out the back door. There was a small hole in the screen and she guessed that was how it had been getting in. From the stench in the place, she guessed it had been making the living room its home for quite some time.

Nicole walked around the cottage, inspecting for any other holes that a stray animal could use as an entry point.

A sense of dread swelled through her as she took in the scope of work the cottage would need.

There was the kitchen – torn, mouldy wallpaper, chipped cupboards, a couple of less-than-safe looking power points. It was a big job. She traced her fingers over the faded blue laminate benchtop and wondered what stories hid beneath the scorch marks. A forgotten pot as a mother rushed outside to rescue a child from a grazed knee? A cigarette dropped and left to smoulder in the middle of an argument?

There were the walls in the hallway and two bedrooms that needed to be stripped, cleaned and repainted.

And the floors. What was beneath the decades of dust that covered the entire cottage?

She had no real desire to turn the house or garden into a thing of beauty and warmth. Beauty and warmth were distant concepts she no longer understood. But she was duty bound.

So what if she'd lied about her renovating experience on the application? They'd lied too – about the extent of work to be done. She should have guessed when she realised the arrangement came with a stipend 'to assist with the cost of renovations'. Stipend did not equal minor renovations. But, desperate people did desperate things. Hopefully this cottage would buy her enough time to figure out what to do next.

She'd have to be careful. The allowance wasn't unlimited and the money she'd saved wouldn't go far. Her freelance editing work would take care of her day-to-day needs, but wouldn't stretch beyond that. She'd have to do most of the work herself. Thank goodness for internet searches and how-to videos. But where to start?

She pulled out the small notebook she always carried in her handbag and started to write a list. She'd need some supplies. Going into town was not something she particularly wanted to do, but she didn't have any other options. She needed to fix the back screen door and at least give the place a thorough clean if she had any hope of sleeping inside tonight.

Nicole stood outside The Cove IGA, suddenly very conscious of her bedraggled appearance. In a town this size, a new face would certainly be noticed. Nicole only hoped she wouldn't be subjected to too much direct questioning. She knew that townspeople in these sorts of places traded in innuendo and stickybeaking. She could cope with that. Their intrusive personal probes, however, she wasn't looking forward to. Maybe the fact that she was only here for a few months meant there wouldn't be enough time for them to dig too deeply.

She took a long breath and tried to smooth her wrinkled shirt before stepping through the doors.

She wheeled her trolley through each aisle, picking up the staples: bread, margarine, pasta, sauces and double-choc Tim Tams. She noted the different brands of items and was surprised by the variety on offer in such a tiny place.

When she got to the register she was greeted by a young man.

'Afternoon, ma'am.' He nodded politely.

'Hi.' She cast her eyes down.

He rang up the total and gave Nicole her change and receipt.

She walked across the wide road lined with old buildings protected by overhanging awnings painted in different shades of pastel. There was a hairdresser, a bakery and a gift emporium where, according to the window display, you could find wares to amaze even the fussiest of recipients.

At the end of the long street was a park of manicured green grass dotted with dark wooden benches and tall bottlebrush trees that offered shade.

Nicole spotted the hardware store, Trevor's Tradies, and entered, taking her list out of her pocket. She moved quickly through the rows of shelves, grabbing only what was on her list.

'You must be the new resident of Ivy Wilson's cottage.' The volume of the overly cheery checkout woman's voice made Nicole drop her paint scrapers onto the counter.

The woman continued, her red curly hair bouncing with each emphatic nod. 'So nice someone's in there finally. You know, that place used to be the pride of the cove.'

Nicole forced a smile. The run-down cottage she'd stumbled across on the internet being the pride of anything was a strange concept.

'All it needs is some TLC.' The lady's smile was full of warmth. 'I can't believe they found anyone to rent it given the state it's in.'

'It does need some work,' Nicole said, nodding. 'Can you tell me where I can find mould remover?' She looked around.

'Aisle three.' The older lady at the next register butted in. Cheryl, as her bright yellow name tag indicated, waved her hand towards the back of the shop.

'Yes, well, you'll probably be needing that, won't you? That place has been shut up for so long now.' The redhead stuck her hand out. 'I'm Mandy, by the way. Welcome to Rosella Cove.'

Nicole shook her hand briefly. 'Nice to meet you.'

Mandy helped her load her things into the car, not stopping for breath as she offered up her son to help with the garden if Nicole needed it. That yard was in quite a state, after all.

Nicole thanked her for her help and drove off. In the rear-view mirror she could see Mandy watching her all the way up the long street.

Nicole moved slowly around the cottage. In the dappled afternoon light, she took in the sight before her. A thorough clean had certainly helped.

With the dust and mould washed away, she could now see what was in need of a simple cosmetic makeover – the laundry, hall and spare bedroom; and what was in need of serious repair – the kitchen, lounge room and fireplace, and verandah.

She pulled the small notebook out of her back jean pocket and made another list.

The items of furniture under the dust sheets, as few as they were, were in relatively good condition. Between that and the newly fixed door, she figured she was safe to stay the night inside. Safe enough, anyway.

With aching shoulders, and dust and who-knew-what in her hair, Nicole shuffled into the bedroom and flopped onto the old bed that came with the place. She buried her head in the pillow and contemplated her new life in all its uncertainty, and the life she'd lost, once so bright, now broken.

November, Three Years Ago

'Hey, Nicky,' Mark called as he came through the apartment door. 'I've got news.'

Nicky wiped away her tears and closed her emails. Another rejection. This one stung, though, just a little more than the others. She'd met this editor. She'd thought they'd hit it off. Was 'not right for our list at this time' the publishing equivalent of an 'it's not you, it's me' dating brush-off?

'Nicky?' Mark came into the darkened bedroom, flicking on the bright light. 'Is everything all right?'

Nicky stood up and turned into his embrace.

'Oh, Nicky. Another one?'

She choked back a sob.

'I did tell you not to get your hopes up.'

She stepped back.

'Not because you're not good enough. You're more than good enough. But this is a tough road. You tell me all the time how terrible the odds are, don't you?'

'I know.' She sighed. 'I just thought this time . . .'

'I know. But you just have to keep trying. I believe in you. You'll get there one day.'

Nicky forced a small smile.

'When you work hard enough, good things happen.' Mark moved back with his hands on his hips, a wide grin stretched across his face.

'You got it?' Nicky asked.

'Yep. You are now looking at the youngest partner at Gregory and McIntosh Solicitors.' He threw his arms open.

Nicky hugged him tightly. 'Congratulations. You've worked so hard for this. We should go out and celebrate.'

'Only if you feel up to it.'

Nicky swallowed hard. She didn't really feel up to it, but Mark had been working towards this promotion for so long; he deserved to go out and enjoy his success.

'Of course. Just give me a few minutes to get ready and we'll head.'

'Are you going to wear the blue dress?' Mark winked at her as she opened the cupboard. She pulled out the dress he'd bought her not long after they'd first met. Fitted, but not too tight, with off-the-shoulder cap sleeves, full length with a long split up one side.

At the whisky bar, the noise was so deafening it was hard to hear anyone speak. Most of Mark's colleagues were there and acknowledged her in greeting but didn't bother to make conversation. Some of Mark's friends had also managed to come after a quick round of texts.

Nicky kept an eye on the bar door while pretending to be interested in whatever the monotone secretary from the firm was telling her. Mark was holding court, receiving congratulatory pats on his back, and beaming from ear to ear. She was so proud of him, even if she had trouble mustering any real enthusiasm for the festivities around her.

Dressed in a tight black dress, her best friend, Jane, burst into the bar, her tall frame enabling Nicky to catch sight of her immediately. Jane pushed her way through the crowd and hugged Nicky when she got to her.

Jane bent slightly and whispered in her ear, 'You look like you'd rather be anywhere else.'

'No. It's okay. He's earned this,' she replied, looking fondly over at Mark.

'Maybe so. But I think we both could do with a drink.' She threw her long blonde plait over her shoulder.

They tucked themselves away in a dimly lit corner of the bar. It was marginally quieter than where the rest of their party was. The quilted leather benches were soft and comfortable, the large pillar candles in the middle of the dark wooden tables let off a gentle yellow glow.

'So, what's the downer?' Jane asked as she sipped on her single malt.

Nicky drank her water and told Jane about her latest rejection.

'Oh, bugger,' Jane sighed. 'Serving smashed avo on sourdough tomorrow to the tourists should make you feel better. Not.'

They clinked their glasses in toast of Nicky's weekend job. Monday to Wednesday she worked at an accounting firm, and weekends she waited tables in a little café down near The Rocks. It wasn't such a bad working life. Having Thursday and Friday as her weekend did mean she could tuck herself away and write without distraction. Though the downside of having a different weekend from the rest of the world was nights like tonight, when everyone else was partying hard and she had to be up at five for a six o'clock start.

Not that she was a stranger to early starts. Since she first started writing she'd got up at five-fifteen on the dot every workday to get an uninterrupted two hours writing done.

'Just think,' Jane continued, 'when you're super famous, and you will be – I know that for sure – you can look back on these days and laugh. You just have to hang in there.' She reached across the table and squeezed Nicky's hand, her tan in stark contrast to Nicky's pale skin. She had her mother's English complexion to thank for that.

Where would she be without Jane? She'd been her best friend for a decade now. A writer herself, unpublished too, Jane was the only one in Nicky's circle who truly understood what it was like.

'And when are *you* going to finish?' Nicky said, eager to turn the conversation away from her own failings.

Jane grinned. 'You can't rush perfection.' It was her standard answer whenever Nicky asked about her progress.

'No. But you can give it a little push along,' Nicky replied with a laugh.

Mark strode across the room, glass of whisky in one hand. He sat himself between the two women and put his drink down.

'How are we going, ladies?' He threw an arm round each one and pulled them towards him. 'Enjoying the evening?'

Nestled in his shoulder, Nicky drank in his musky scent. 'Not as much as you, it seems.' All night he'd worn the biggest grin, his dimples working their magic on everyone around him.

'Maybe we can work on that,' he whispered in her ear.

'Okay. That's my cue to leave.' Jane slipped out from under Mark's arm and stood up.

'So early?' Nicky rose, Mark's hand in the small of her back.

'We'll talk next week.' Jane hugged her tightly. 'Congratulations, Mark.'

'Thanks for coming,' he said. 'I reckon we might head off too. Just let me say goodbye, princess.' He kissed Nicky and went off to work the room one last time.

'Man, you're lucky.' Jane said, wistfully. 'Smart, rich, devastatingly handsome. And totally into you.'

Nicky smiled. She knew how lucky she was the second they'd met. His boss, Mr Gregory, had handled her mum's will. It wasn't the sort of thing the firm normally did, especially not for someone with as little to leave behind as Nicky's ageing mum. But it was a favour for an old friend, apparently. Nicky suspected they were once more than friends, but never asked. She didn't really want to know. When she came into the office to sign the paperwork, she was awestruck by the lawyer she'd run into in the foyer. Tears were falling down her face as she said her final goodbye to her mum. His kind offer of a handkerchief – who even used handkerchiefs anymore – and offer of a coffee melted her heart. She knew even then that he was the one she wanted to be with.

From across the bar he waved, indicating he was ready to go, and into the cold night air they stepped.

Snuggled together tightly in the back of the taxi, Mark ran his fingers through Nicky's long black hair.

'I've been thinking,' he whispered in her ear.

'I know what you're thinking.'

'Well, yes, that. You know what this dress does to me. But I was also thinking about your writing tonight.'

'Oh?' She wasn't expecting that.

'Now that I've made partner, I'll be bringing in more money. What if you wrote full time?'

'What? How?'

'Give up your jobs. Just for six months to see how it goes. You could write your next book. Go to conferences and festivals. Network. It will all help, won't it?'

'I . . . I guess it couldn't hurt. Having a second book would be good . . .' Nicky knew this was every writer's dream – the time and space to write full time. 'But I couldn't ask you to do that for me.'

'You're not asking. I'm offering.' He took her face in his hands. 'I just want to give you everything. At least think about it.'

He kissed her and she leaned into him, heat teasing every inch of her skin.

Two

*N*icole barely slept, alert to every noise – every hoot, creak, scuttle – in this strange place. She dragged herself out of bed just as the sun was rising and looked at the next task on her list. Clear out the kitchen. That was a big job. Maybe too big a job. Back at home – ouch. That word, 'home', really stung. Back in Sydney, whenever she was faced with a task she didn't want to do – edits that were giving her grief, research that wasn't inspiring her – she'd go for a long walk. It always worked. Surely here, so much closer to nature, it would be even more effective.

Making her way along the hillside that poked into the sapphire ocean, she drew in long breaths. Gentle fields of emerald grass surrounded her with tall strong eucalypts, their bark shedding as the turning season dictated; the forgotten cottage, *her* cottage, and its tangled mess of shrubs and long grass fell away behind her and somewhere down the long dirt road she'd come in on yesterday sat the town, with its own small beach to the south.

As the path before her dropped down a long slope to the

cove below, an earthy-grey drop of shimmering boulders of brown was gently caressed by the in and out of constant waves; Nicole came across a run-down boatshed perched on the edge of the peninsula. The panels of wood were cracked and the once-blue paint, possibly the same blue that coated the cottage, was now yellowed and flaked. The dirt splattering the bottom of the building made it hard to see where earth ended and building began. The decrepit planter boxes, suspended beneath grimy windows, were overgrown with weeds, and the surrounding grass reached as high as Nicole's knees. In the absence of human care, nature was slowly reclaiming her territory.

The only part of the property not touched by the ravages of time and neglect was a wooden bench nestled against the eastern wall. Nicole moved through a gap in the fallen picket fence, drawn to the bench. It wasn't new – scratches, marks and dents suggested its age. But the finish was that of a piece of furniture often oiled and looked after. There was a worn carving, initials, perhaps an 'I' and 'T' or maybe 'F', in the centre of the backrest. It looked as though no dirt or dust had ever touched the intricate letters. Nicole glanced around, searching for further indication of someone frequenting the place, but found none and she lowered herself on to the bench.

She was all alone.

How quickly and totally the life she loved had disappeared. Perhaps she'd wake tomorrow and find this had all been a dream, or a nightmare. But the vibrant life she once had seemed so very distant now. Perhaps *it* was the dream, never real to begin with.

Enough. Dwelling on the past would do her no good.

'What the hell are you doing here at my boatshed?' An old man with a weathered face rounded the building, his voice low and full of contempt.

'E . . . excuse me? Your boatshed?'

'Yeah, my boatshed. I live 'ere. What are you doing?'

'Oh, sorry. I had no idea . . .' Nicole stared at the bedraggled man before her holding a fishing rod and tackle.

'No idea is right.'

'Sorry. I was just admiring the view. Taking some time out. If I'd known someone lived here I certainly wouldn't have intruded.'

The old man seemed to be sizing her up as she spoke and she returned in kind. His brown corduroy pants were clean, but did have tears in them. His blue checked shirt also looked clean but was threadbare around the collar and elbows. His beard was long and grey, and curled in all directions at once. His blue eyes showed a hint of forgotten spark.

'You actually live here?' Nicole asked.

'Yeah, I do. And I don't like visitors.'

'Sorry. I'm Nicole.' She extended her hand but it was left midair until she withdrew it. 'I'm living in the cottage up the hill. I guess that makes us neighbours?'

'I know who you are.' The man grunted and placed his fishing gear on the ground. He folded his arms across his chest.

'Oh. Okay then,' Nicole said. 'I guess I'll be off.'

No answer.

She headed back up the path. Who was he and why was he living there?

Stop it.

How long had he been there?

It's none of your business.

She had no intention of taking any interest in anything or anyone ever again. Certainly not for the short time she was going to be here. She walked away.

Is he alone in there?

∽

Charlie watched the young woman until she was out of sight. He picked up his tackle box and dinner catch and touched the carved initials in the bench gently with two fingers. From the cove he'd seen her sitting there and he didn't like how it made him feel. No one had sat there for four decades. No one had the right to.

He looked up to the sky and pictured the green eyes he still missed so terribly. There was no point thinking of the past. There was new life in the cottage now. He pushed the long-buried memories from his mind and went inside.

Why hadn't she been afraid of him? Most other people were. Who did she think she was, destroying his peace like that? The locals had learned long ago to leave him to himself, but he knew instinctively she was different. Those blue eyes. There was something behind the sadness. He'd known it was a risk, his plan, but he had no other choice.

———

For the last few days Nicole had been debating where on earth to start the renovation. The kitchen needed the most amount of work, but probably wasn't the best place for a novice like her to start. She had to get her feet wet with something a little more manageable. Even fixing the walls seemed a rather daunting job.

She'd reordered her lists, prioritising each task from smallest to biggest.

Nicole stood in front of the fireplace. The plasterboard covering the opening was rotting. Well. No point putting it off. Today was the day she'd scheduled its demolition, and she always followed her schedule. She picked up the large mallet she'd bought and pulled a dust mask over her nose and mouth.

She wouldn't be able to restore the beautiful old fireplace on her own. That required specialist skills. And probably more money than she had. But she could at least strip it back and clean it up.

There were no specific instructions when she'd signed the rental paperwork as to how far she needed to take the renovation. 'Clean and repair to ensure the habitability of the cottage, with thoughtful restoration.' What did that even mean?

She swung the mallet and threw it forward into the sheet of plasterboard.

Crack.

A primal surge coursed through her. She swung again, frustration channelled into the mallet. She took another swing.

Crack.

Anger burst forth. She drew the mallet back, further this time.

Crack.

Tears streamed down her cheeks.

One more swing.

The mallet tore right through the board and hit the side of the fireplace, dislodging one of the bricks. It crashed to the hearth.

'Oh, shit.' She dropped the mallet.

She was pretty sure this didn't count as 'thoughtful restoration'.

She picked up the brick and tried to shove it back into the cavity it came from. But the next brick moved, too. With tentative hands, Nicole felt her way along edge of the fireplace. Four bricks moved beneath her gentle touch. The mortar that should have held them in place was missing.

One by one she removed the bricks, revealing a hole. With the torch on her phone for light, she leaned into the fireplace to get a better look.

Please, God, don't let there be any spiders in there. Or snakes.
Or even a possum.

Inside the hole there was a box and she pulled it out, brushing
the dust away. It was wooden, intricately carved with shells and
very old. The lid had a name etched deep into its surface. 'Ivy.'

Nicole gasped. 'Ivy Wilson's cottage', the lady in the hardware store had said. She gently opened the lid, revealing bundles
of envelopes bound with yellow ribbon. The thick parchment was
stained with the tarnish of age. As she went through the envelopes
she saw the same name on each one, Sergeant Thomas Wilson, and
a date.

She put the letters back in the box. Nothing good could come
of looking into the depths of someone's personal life.

There was a time when curiosity would have had her tearing
open the envelopes. But that curiosity had died along with her
previous life.

She carried the old wooden box down the hall and placed it in
one of the kitchen cupboards.

There was a loud knock on the door and Nicole jumped. Who
could it possibly be?

Perhaps she could pretend she wasn't home. Another knock. She
closed her eyes and took a deep breath. They weren't going away.

Opening the door just a crack, she saw the redhead from the
hardware store, Mandy or Maggie or something, with a broad smile
on her face and holding a casserole dish in outstretched hands.

Nicole frowned.

'Hi. It's Mandy, remember me?'

'Of course. Hello.'

'Just a little welcome warmth, for dinner tonight,' Mandy said.

Down by the fence two men hauled whipper snippers from the
back of a ute. One was a young man not long out of childhood,

with the same red curls as Mandy, wearing an old T-shirt and a pair of boardies. The other was a tall man, in his mid-thirties maybe.

'That's my boy, Jack, and Danny Temple. Danny's the town's handyman. I thought the two of them could make a start in the garden while we have a cuppa. What do you say?'

Mandy pushed past her and headed to the kitchen. From the overgrown lawn Danny nodded slightly in Nicole's direction and he and Jack went into the garden and started slashing the long grass. Nicole didn't quite know what to do. She ran after Mandy.

'I can't afford to pay them,' she blurted out as Mandy put the casserole in the small bar fridge that had come with the cottage.

Nicole had done a budget and she hadn't accounted for gardening work. The stipend that came with the rental deal wouldn't stretch that far.

'Oh, don't worry about that. The boys will do it for free and the town coffers can pay for any materials.'

Nicole frowned.

Mandy shook her head. 'Sorry, I should explain. It's Nicky, right?'

'Nicole.'

'Well, let me officially welcome you to Rosella Cove, Nicole. If there's anything you need, don't you hesitate to ask. Everyone's pretty friendly here. You'll see that for yourself soon enough. We had a town meeting once we heard about you renting this place and we agreed that to see this old girl sparkling back to her former beauty again, we'd help out a bit. Jack's doing landscaping at TAFE, so he's happy to get some experience, and Danny does a lot for the town.'

'That's . . .' Nicole really didn't know what to say. She knew country folk were generous, but this went beyond generous. Why would they help her, a perfect stranger, out like this? But, the scale of the job before her was far beyond her capabilities and she wasn't really in a position to turn away help. Especially free help. 'Thank you,' she said simply, deciding not to question it.

'Don't mention it.' Mandy moved about the kitchen as if it were her own and made two cups of tea.

They made their way out to the front verandah that wrapped around the whole house in a wide sweep of cedar protected by a corrugated iron overhang. The discoloured paint of the weathered supports which were possibly once white, was flaked so badly the slightest touch left confetti covering their hands. Mandy gave Nicole a run-down of the town – footy every second Saturday at the oval where they also held a market, the markets usually more successful than the footy team; trivia every month at the pub, she was most welcome to join in, Lord knew Mandy's team could do with an extra brain; art classes in the town hall . . .

Nicole listened to the happy lilt in Mandy's voice, feeling guilty she wasn't in the garden helping the guys. Not that her lending a hand would be considered help. She'd discovered long ago that her thumbs were definitely not green.

'He's a great worker, my boy.' Mandy looked in Jack's direction.

'Seems so.'

'A good kid, too. Not that he's a kid anymore. I was only just eighteen when I had him. I was going to study journalism, can you believe? But,' she shrugged, 'popped him out just after exams and here we all are two decades later.'

Mandy's openness made Nicole feel slightly more at ease. She'd forgotten that about country folk – their candour and lack of pretence. The friendships she'd made after moving to the city tended to be quite superficial. Most people seemed concerned about their square meterage, which private school they'd attended, their next promotion at work. At least in her corner of the city that's how it went.

The whirring of the whipper snippers stopped and Jack and Danny loaded piles of grass clippings into the back of the ute. The sweet smell of freshly cut grass floated on the light breeze and filled Nicole's nose.

'When we heard someone was moving into the cottage, I did a little snooping. One of my vices.' Mandy raised her hand to her chest in a gesture of apology. 'And once I found out your name, well, you're Nicole Miller the author, aren't you?'

There wasn't much point in lying. A quick Google search would turn up a picture of her author Facebook page, complete with photo. Nicole ran her fingers through her recently cropped hair. She tucked what she could behind her ear and it sat just below her chin.

'Oh, so you are? You look a little different from the photo in the back of *Tide*, but that's to be expected, I suppose.'

'Yes, well it was taken a little while back.' A few years, a dramatic haircut and a couple of extra kilos did make for altered appearance.

'How fabulous to have you here. Just wait till I tell everyone we've got a famous author living among us. Not that they'll believe me. Literary heathens, the lot of them.' She giggled, her cheeks puffing out with a wide grin.

Thick white clouds danced across the sky hiding the sun and Nicole shivered with the sudden drop in temperature.

'I just loved your first book,' Mandy continued. 'How come we haven't seen another?'

Nicole looked in her teacup. 'Oh . . . I guess I just got a bit . . . knocked off track.' She shrugged.

'Oh.' Mandy didn't look convinced.

Nicole braced herself. She really wasn't prepared to answer deeply personal questions. The pain was still too raw.

'Maybe the cove will help you get your writing mojo back,' Mandy said, and reached across to pat her hand.

'Maybe.' Nicole pulled her hand back, relieved Mandy didn't probe any further. If only it were that simple.

Surprisingly, Nicole didn't have to shift the conversation. The upcoming footy match was, apparently, very important, and Mandy filled her in on the rivalry between the cove and nearby Woodville and the various regular characters involved, including her husband, Trevor, who coached the team. Nicole found herself laughing out loud and relaxing even more.

When the guys finished clearing out the first section of the front yard, from the kitchen window to the letterbox, they packed up the ute and called out to Mandy.

'That's my cue to get out of your hair.' Mandy stacked the teacups and saucers. 'We'll chat soon, hey?'

In the fading afternoon light, Nicole watched them leave. It had been some time since she'd enjoyed a quiet cuppa with a friend. Not that Mandy was a friend. And there wouldn't really be time enough for her to become one. Shame. Nicole had forgotten how nice it could be to just sit and chat. Even if the other person did most of the chatting. A soft smile touched her lips.

Well, she'd taken the first and hopefully hardest step to rebuild her life. And that was something.

Wasn't it?

March, Two Years Ago

'To Nicky.' Mark raised his champagne glass in salute and the small group at the table followed his lead. It was fitting that they celebrated Nicky signing a publishing contract in the tiny Vietnamese restaurant she and Mark had been in when her agent, Di, had rung with the offer. Nicky looked at the faces smiling back at her. Jane could barely contain her excitement. Di filled up the champagne glasses once more and Mark's friend Robert patted him on the back.

'To great stories.' The cheer went up again. She'd done it. She was getting published. Well, *they'd* done it. It was as much Mark's success as hers. Without him none of this would have happened.

She listened as he told the story of how she'd collapsed into his arms when she got the book contract, his chest full, eyes beaming with pride. It didn't matter if he was exaggerating. She hadn't actually collapsed into his arms, but she had hugged him tightly. She hadn't actually cried for an hour, but she had shed a tear. Though he did deserve some credit. He was, after all, the reason her manuscript got in front of Di in the first place, using his connection to Robert, who happened to be Di's neighbour, and he was all too happy to share this in his speech.

'Sounds like we should be toasting Mark, too,' Jane called across the table and glasses were raised once more.

Over the steady din of the busy restaurant, Nicole fielded questions. Jane – when will the book be out? In about twelve months. Di – when will the next manuscript be ready? Nicky was working on it. Robert – how much was the advance? None of his business and a stern look from Mark.

The waitress, dressed in a deep blue áo dài tunic, bowed as she placed the bill on the table.

'Why don't we head to Currie's dessert bar?' Jane suggested.

'Great idea.' Nicky stood. She wasn't ready for the night to end just yet.

'Just a second.' Mark's voice cut through the excitement. 'There's one more thing.'

He got up from the table and dropped to one knee in front of her.

'Nicky.' From his pocket he produced the most beautiful ring Nicky had ever seen. 'Will you marry me?'

Cheers erupted from the table as Nicky nodded, unable to speak. Mark stood and picked her up, kissing her intently. They were swarmed by their friends coming in for pats on the back. Jane appeared at Nicky's side and wrapped her in a quick, tight embrace. 'I'm so happy for you,' she said. 'Everything is falling into place.'

Mark slipped between them, draping his arm around Nicky's shoulder. 'Did she show you the ring?' he asked Jane.

'Can't miss it,' Jane said warmly.

The sapphire-cut diamond sat large on Nicky's finger. Her cheeks went red as Jane held her hand up, admiring it once more.

'Maybe we should take a raincheck on Currie's,' Jane said. 'You two probably have other things you want to do tonight.'

'Oh, but . . .' Nicky looked up at Mark, who was gazing at her intently. She knew what that gaze meant. She turned back to her friend. 'Okay. But promise me we'll catch up properly soon.'

'Of course,' said Jane, and kissed her goodbye.

Mark trailed his fingers through Nicky's hair. 'Is she okay?'

'What do you mean?' Nicky said with a frown.

'I don't know. She seemed a bit . . . off.'

'Off?'

Mark nodded. 'Yeah. Just that look she gave you on the way out.'

Nicky had noticed the frown on Jane's face, but didn't really think much of it.

'She wouldn't be jealous, would she?' Mark asked.

'Of the book? No way.' Jane couldn't be jealous. She was almost as happy about it as Nicky was.

'Of that? Of us?' He shrugged.

Nicky stared at the door of the restaurant, as if she could still see Jane's silhouette weaving through the dark night outside. There was nothing about her best friend's behaviour that seemed odd. At least, she didn't think so. Maybe the wine had gone to Mark's head. Though, she did make a comment about Nicky not having time for old friends anymore now she was going to be famous. But that was just a joke. Surely.

Back at their flat Mark dragged Nicky into the bedroom.

'Come now, my fiancée. Show me how much you love me.'

Nicky liked the sound of that. His fiancée. She belonged somewhere now. With someone.

He kissed her strongly and they fell into bed.

In the dim light of the moon Nicky sat on the balcony wrapped tightly in a blanket. Mark had fallen asleep hours ago but she was still restless, the excitement of the night still buzzing through her. She pulled out her phone and looked at the last picture of her mother, taken in the nursing home, just after her seventy-seventh birthday.

It made Nicky's heart ache that her mother wouldn't see her get married. At thirty, Nicky wasn't exactly old, but her parents had had her so late in life. They were forty-seven and fifty-five when she was born, and by then they'd all but given up hope of having children. Nicky was their miracle baby and they were wonderful parents. But they weren't young and two years ago her dad had a heart attack. Then the following year her mum was diagnosed with cancer. And just like that, Nicky was alone in the world. No siblings. No family.

But now she had Mark.

His soft snoring floated through the apartment and she hugged her knees tight to her chest, savouring the sound.

She opened her Messenger app and typed out a quick note to Jane. She was sure there was nothing to Mark's earlier concerns, but Jane was the closest thing to family Nicky had after Mark, so it was better to be safe than sorry.

'Hey. Sorry about bailing tonight. Are you free next Thursday? Coffee?'

She looked at her screen and held her breath. No response.

Of course not. It was the middle of the night. Jane was probably sleeping. Nicky was worrying about nothing.

She climbed back into bed beside Mark and wrapped her arm around his chest. She would be up in a few hours for her early writing stint and really needed to get some sleep. Unaccustomed to wearing much jewellery, the ring on her finger felt heavy and strange and she stared at it in the dark, smiling until slumber finally came.

Three

icole stripped the last of the paint from the fireplace as the midday sun streamed through the old leadlight window in the living room, casting pools of rose, olive and lemon light across the cedar floorboards. She'd got up at five to clean the last of the dust from the windows throughout the cottage and then started on the next task on her list.

Danny had offered to restore the fireplace as a labour of love, a personal interest project, and Nicole had to get it prepared. The carved mantelpiece, aged and chipped, was supported by damaged columns and scrolls. The cracked tiles of the hearth lay dull, with life beneath waiting to be freed. In the middle of the lintel Nicole could see something carved into the stone.

Was it an insignia? She'd seen it some place before.

She ran into the kitchen and pulled out the old box she'd found hidden in the fireplace. There it was, the same lettering on the lid. And each envelope was sealed with the identical 'I&T' in wax.

She'd seen it elsewhere, too. On the bench outside the boat-shed. A spark of interest sizzled and Nicole shoved the box back in the cupboard. No. She couldn't read those letters. They were someone's private thoughts and she had no right.

Standing back in front of the hearth, Nicole tried to imagine it restored to its former glory. How many nights had Ivy sat in front of a warm fire, reading a book maybe, or knitting perhaps? Had she sat there alone? With the Thomas from the letters? With a brood of noisy children swirling around her feet?

She took a dustpan and brush and swept up the last remaining dirt, making sure she got right into the back corners of the fire box, thick with ash and tiny debris. The brush caught something heavy. Heavier than the piles of ash she'd been sweeping up. She fingered through the pile and pulled out a small piece of wood. It looked singed, but not burned. She turned it over in her hand. A spinning top perhaps?

A knock interrupted her contemplation and she ran into the kitchen and put the relic in the same cupboard as Ivy's letters before opening the door.

Danny stood on the other side of the screen in his King Gees, toolbox in hand. His well-defined jawline, warm smile and sandy-coloured hair were quite a combination. Tall and strongly built, he looked every bit ready for the work that lay ahead.

He'd brought Jack with him, who was going to do some work in the garden.

'Thanks for this.' Nicole let him in.

'No worries.'

Danny set to work in silence. His first task was to stabilise the chimney and flue. 'No point restoring this beautiful old girl,' he stroked the mantle, 'and having the lot come down on her.'

As he worked away, Nicole made a start on stripping the master bedroom's wallpaper. The old glue was stubborn to remove and it took her quite a while to find a good rhythm, and then once she did, she'd lose it again, battling with the old paper. If only stripping the wallpaper was all that was necessary. Her new best friend, Google, had given her detailed instructions on the washing and preparing of the walls after the paper had been removed before you even thought about slapping on some paint. She really wasn't looking forward to those steps.

As the afternoon sun began its slow descent, Nicole's shoulders started to ache. Stripping wallpaper was nowhere near as fun as it sounded. And it hadn't sounded like much fun. She decided there and then that she would never hang wallpaper anywhere, so no one coming after her would ever have to spend four hours trying to remove it from two walls.

'Excuse me, Nicole.' Danny stood in the bedroom doorway. 'I think I might call it a day.'

Nicole put down her scraper. 'Me too. Can I offer you a tea or coffee before you go? Maybe some water?' They'd worked all afternoon without a break.

He accepted a glass of cold water and they sat at the Formica dining table in the kitchen in awkward silence.

'So.' Nicole needed to say something. Anything. 'How do you know so much about repairing fireplaces?'

'Because of my dad, actually. It was a hobby of his back in England.'

Nicole thought she'd detected a slight accent. 'You're from England?'

Danny nodded. 'My family moved here when I was sixteen. My parents have gone back now, though.'

'But you stayed?'

'Yep.'

She waited for him to elaborate, but he wasn't forthcoming. She studied his face, trying to get a read on him. His eyes were soft, kind, but carried in them a touch of sadness.

'And you're a writer?' he asked, and Nicole got the distinct impression he was changing the subject.

'Yes.'

'Mandy told me.' He smiled. 'She was pretty excited about having a real writer among us.'

'And are you a reader?'

He shook his head. 'Not like Mandy. History and architecture are more my thing.'

'Have you ever tried historical fiction? Something like *Pillars of the Earth*?'

'I'll look it up,' he said, and smiled.

'Anyone home?' Mandy's light timbre rang through the cottage.

Nicole got up to let her in, but she was already walking down the hall.

'I just came to pick Jack up and thought I'd see if you wanted to come over for dinner tonight,' Mandy said, swanning past Nicole towards the kitchen.

'Oh, no, I couldn't intrude.' Nicole trailed after her, her mind racing to find a plausible excuse.

'Nonsense. What's one more mouth? Or two.' She looked to Danny sitting at the dining table. 'Even better.'

'That's very kind, but . . .' *Think, Nicole, think*.

'Unless you have something already prepared?' Mandy raised an eyebrow.

Nicole thought about the toast and jam she'd planned on having. 'Well, no. I don't.' She shook her head.

Danny rose from the table and leaned towards her. 'No point trying to fight her,' he whispered, and gathered his tools.

'It's settled, then!' Mandy pulled a notebook out of her purse, ripped a page off and scribbled on it. 'We'll see you at seven. Here's my address.' Then, just as quickly as she'd whirled into the cottage, she was gone again, leaving a stunned Nicole in her wake.

Nicole sat at the heavy wooden table that Mandy's husband, Trevor, had apparently built many years ago and took the last mouthful of velvety fish pie from her plate. It was the good china, Mandy had said, the wedding Wedgwood that only came out for special guests or occasions. The table was decorated with a crisp white tablecloth and maroon paper napkins. Pink, yellow and white roses, picked fresh from the front garden, adorned the centre of the table.

'How is everything?' Mandy asked with the smallest hint of nervousness in her voice.

'Oh, it's delicious, thank you.'

It reminded Nicole of her own mum's fish pie, the one out of the Country Women's Association cookbook that had been so well used the pages were falling out of their binding. In fact, the whole evening had reminded Nicole of the family dinners she used to enjoy. Mandy had taken control of the conversation, just like her own mum could, and did her best to fill Nicole in on the who's who around town, including all the local heroes and villains.

It may have been a different town from the one she grew up in, but the tales were the same. The evil local councilman who was always looking for the next big development to put the town on the map, willing to take any kind of kickback to line his own pocket. The resident greenies who chained themselves to the trees just outside of town and rallied the locals to stop said next big development – a resort, of course. The teacher at the small school whose dedication had seen more than one Year Twelve student make it into a top university degree, though their own personal life was never quite as successful. The florist who always donated her services when someone died as the poor family didn't need any more grief.

While his wife yakked on about small town musings, Trevor laughed, barely able to get an affirming 'ah-huh' in, even when asked a question. Jack sat quietly, putting away an amount of food Nicole found truly staggering, even for a young man. Danny seemed relaxed, like he was part of the family.

Family. Nicole had to fight to keep melancholy thoughts from swallowing her. She looked around the room at the pictures of Mandy and Trevor and Jack that adorned the walls in mix-matched frames.

'So, how do you like Ivy Wilson's cottage?' Trevor asked, as Mandy excused herself to prepare dessert. 'Fair bit of work to be done, hey?' He smiled warmly.

'For sure. But with Jack's help the garden at least isn't quite so daunting.'

Jack gave a corroborative grunt.

'Still,' Trevor continued, 'bloody big job to tackle on your own. Surely a good-looking sort like you has a fella waiting in the wings, hey?'

Nicole coughed. 'Well, ah . . .'

Jumping up and running from the room was probably a bit extreme, but that was all that came to her mind right then.

Thankfully, she didn't have to as Mandy came back in with a large pavlova bulging under the weight of cream and fruit piled on its delicate meringue crust. She whipped Jack's dinner plate away as he scooped up the last morsel of his fifth helping of fish pie.

'She's not doing it alone, Trevor,' Mandy said. 'She's got Danny helping.'

Nicole took another sip of wine. She wasn't supposed to be tackling this job on her own. She wasn't supposed to be here at all. She was supposed to be happily married by now, ensconced in her inner-city apartment writing her next bestseller. She fidgeted with her napkin.

Mandy sat down. 'Have you got some family or friends coming to help you with the renos?'

She scrambled to cover her truth. 'No. I . . . ah . . . felt, I guess, like . . . I wanted a personal project, I suppose.'

'You're a brave woman.' Trevor shook his head and then jumped as if he'd been kicked or pinched.

Nicole didn't feel brave. Not one bit.

'Bit of a strange situation, though.' Mandy served up the pavlova. 'Making you fix up the place. It's stayed empty all this time since the old girl died. No one knows why or how. Plenty of people sniffed around, made offers to the estate agent. But they were all turned down. Ivy had some big-shot Sydney lawyer taking care of things, apparently, and he wasn't quite so forthcoming with information as one of our own might have been.' She winked.

Smart lady, Nicole thought. *If you want to keep a secret in a small town, keep it elsewhere.*

'I reckon she's got cousins or something in Sydney that inherited it. Never had any kids of her own. I guess they're finally going to sell. Whoever they are.'

The temporary nature of Nicole's situation hit her again. Six months was all she had here and then the cottage would be sold.

'So, what do you make of our little corner of the world, Nicole?' Trevor asked, looking very pleased with himself that he got another question in.

'It's a beautiful spot,' she said, forcing a smile. 'And so peaceful.'

'You haven't met Charlie, then.' Jack gulped down a large portion of pavlova.

'Sorry?'

'Charlie. The crazy old guy who lives in the boatshed.'

So Charlie was his name.

'Now, now, Jack. He's not crazy. Just a bit of a loner.' Mandy shrugged.

'Bit?' Jack snorted. 'He hasn't spoken to anyone in what, a hundred years?'

Mandy shot her son a look and he quickly put another spoonful of pavlova into his mouth. 'Just saying.' He shrugged.

'Charlie moved here some forty-odd years ago, so Mum says. Or is it fifty? No, fifty.'

Mandy's grey eyes sparkled as she eased into her story. 'Kept to himself right from the beginning, they say. We were scared of him as kids . . .'

''Cause he's a crazy loner,' Jack said, spluttering cream onto his plate.

Both Mandy and Trevor clipped him over the top of his head.

'You know how kids can be. Case in point.' Mandy's steely glare silenced her son. 'But Charlie's never harmed anyone or anything. In fact quite the opposite . . .'

Mandy's words drifted off and a sad, wistful look crossed her face momentarily. Nicole wondered what memory she was holding back.

Mandy cleared her throat. 'He just stays out of the way, really.' Her focus was now back to the present. 'People have tried over the years to get to know him, but no one has ever managed.'

'Not even my wife. Not for a want of trying, mind you.' Trevor winked at Mandy, his eyes crinkling around the edges, his smile crooked.

'True,' she admitted. 'Like everyone else I went out of my way as a kid to spy on him. No one knows much about him at all. Where he came from, why he stayed. One day he just appeared and was living in the boatshed and has been there ever since. Never had any visitors, far as anyone knows.'

A spark of latent curiosity ignited and Nicole found herself desperate to know more about the old man and find out what lay beneath his gruff exterior. Would he have to leave too once the cottage sold? Or were they separate properties, divvied up at some point in their history? She hung on Mandy's every word.

'Comes into town once every three months or so for food and basic supplies and every morning heads off along the northern face. No one knows where he goes or why. Every now and then some brave kids try to follow him.' She looked pointedly at Jack. 'But he always sees them and scares them off.'

'Because he's a weirdo,' Jack mumbled.

'That's enough, Jack,' Danny said quietly. 'There's more to Charlie than you think.' The mood around the table shifted and silence fell.

'This is a lovely pav, Mandy.' Nicole changed the conversation.

'Thanks. The secret's in the cream. King Island,' she whispered.

Nicole offered to help with the dishes, but Mandy would have none of it. She kissed her husband on the top of his balding head. 'You can help, though.'

Nicole had insisted on walking home, citing fresh air and a need to stretch her legs. But what she really needed was some space. She hadn't had this much social interaction in, well, she couldn't remember how long.

It hadn't been unpleasant. Quite the opposite. But it had been overwhelming.

She could have gone straight home, but the thought of being surrounded by those stark bare walls wasn't exactly inviting.

In the distance the town lights twinkled as Nicole strolled along the headland. Moonlight bounced off the tall gum trees lining her path like sentries standing at attention, and quiet washed over her like a balm.

The boatshed rose before her, shrouded in darkness.

'I thought I told you to leave me alone.' Through the night, Charlie's voice rumbled towards her.

Nicole jumped. 'God, don't scare me like that.'

'Then don't snoop around where you're not wanted.'

'I wasn't snooping.'

'Then why are you here?' Charlie frowned.

'I was just out walking.'

'Well, I don't want you here.'

Nicole wouldn't have been surprised if Charlie stamped his foot next. 'I don't really want to be here, either, but I don't exactly have a choice.'

'We always have a choice.'

Was he right? Was there another road Nicole's life could have taken? 'Maybe. But not always much of one.'

The hardness around Charlie's eyes softened ever so slightly.

'Goodnight, Charlie.' Nicole smiled.

He grunted and walked away.

Charlie knew all about choices. He'd made some pretty catastrophic ones in his life. He only hoped his latest choice regarding the cottage wasn't going to end up in that category. He had to believe it wouldn't.

He lay awake on his old wooden bed and stared out the portal window to the indigo sky until it bled into morning. Some nights, sleep evaded him entirely. It was often better when it did. At least awake he could stop the images coming. The sounds.

Bright orange flames radiating heat that sucked the air from his lungs. Screams, desperate cries that pierced through the thick blanket of smoke.

At least awake he could force his thoughts away from his mistakes and towards the woman he'd silently loved, the warmth and kindness in her green eyes that had once gazed upon him without judgement, even though she knew the truth.

Four

It turned out flocked wallpaper was a lot harder to get off than regular wallpaper. Nicole reasserted her conviction that she would never be the perpetrator of such a crime against renovation. After she'd spent four days stripping out the main bedroom, living room and hallway, she'd figured tackling the spare room would come easy. She was wrong. She'd struggled all morning and was only now starting to make progress.

As she scraped a small piece off she noticed something underneath. Not the plain old walls she'd uncovered in other parts of the cottage, but something patterned. She scraped another jagged strip off the wall. Yes. Beneath the flocked terror was another layer of wallpaper.

Surely this constituted crimes against humanity.

Nicole ran her fingers over the pattern. Small toy soldiers and building blocks – wallpaper for a child's room.

But hadn't Mandy said Ivy never had children? And that no one had been in the property since her passing? It must be from an earlier owner, Nicole figured.

Pushing through exhaustion, she worked all day to reveal the whole room, careful not to damage the second layer of paper. She stood in the middle of the room and stared at the walls. She was in no doubt that this had once been a nursery.

Nicole opened her laptop and Googled wallpaper, trying to get a sense of the age of the children's pattern she'd uncovered. Thirty minutes of trawling through various websites left her no definitive answer, but from what she could tell, it was probably from the thirties or forties.

When did Ivy and Thomas arrive?

Questions swirled through Nicole's mind as she paced the kitchen floor. There were, potentially, answers right here within her grasp. Right inside that cupboard in the corner where she'd shoved Ivy's box.

She edged towards the cupboard door, and retreated back again. No. She couldn't.

Nicole wasn't sure if she believed in fate or signs. She wasn't sure what she believed in anymore at all. But she couldn't ignore the fact she'd found the box and that echoes of Ivy and Thomas seemed to be shadowing her – the initials carved into the bench, the ones over the fireplace.

Maybe she could just take a peek.

She pulled the box out of the cupboard and sat it on the table. She took a step back, then inched towards it again and sat down.

She pulled out the letters and undid the yellow ribbon that tied them together. She broke the wax seal of the first letter, the cracking sound sending a shudder of guilt through her as she ripped into this woman's private life.

11th January, 1941

My Dearest Tom,

Today I have sent you a telegram with the most wonderful news. I hope it reaches you safely. Perhaps it is silly of me to write as well. Given how long this letter takes to reach you, these words will not be news at all, but the brevity of a telegram simply cannot do for news like this.

As I write, I am two months along. Yes, my love. That night we spent in the boatshed before you shipped out. Do you remember it? I can never forget it myself. How you picked me up from the bench after our supper by the sea and carried me through the door, the way your hand reached beneath my petticoat and the warmth of your touch on my thigh. I loved staying there all night with you, staring up at the stars through the portal window.

I appear to have escaped the torture of morning sickness, though I am often tired. Every day I walk along the peninsula down to the cove and imagine you home, playing with our son – I am certain we are having a son – teaching him to fish. I picture the three of us running along the sand, splashing in the waves that tease our feet, collecting sea shells to lay on the mantle.

I wonder if he will have your handsome face. My hair perhaps.

Father is overjoyed with the news. Mother, it seems, is unmoved. Not even the thought of a grandchild is enough to soften that woman's contempt for your 'lack of breeding'. I suppose a child that carries a bloodline anything less than aristocratic is an affront to her. You should be thankful you have not yet met. Though I do wish she had at least let Father walk me down the aisle.

Maybe she will come round when our son is born, and then she will finally forgive me for marrying 'below my station'.

Maybe I hope too much.

If only she had given you a chance, she might have realised that breeding and money do not determine character and that there are more good people outside her circle than within.

Yes, I hope too much. Light and joy fill me, however, as I am sure you.

We must discuss names, my love. Thomas Junior is an obvious choice. I am not one to do the expected though, as well you know. We never would have danced that night three years ago if I did what was expected of me.

What do you think about Charles? After Father's favourite author. It is a strong name. Or Matthew? After your beloved grandfather. Something for you to ponder in those lonely moments between rest and battle.

My nights are a little less empty now, with our son growing inside me. You are here with me. A part of me. Though I miss you every moment of every day.

Stay safe, my dearest.

Ivy

Nicole fingered through the pile of letters to the end, just as she always skipped to the last few pages when reading a new novel. The first few letters were dated close together, the next becoming more sporadic until there were great gaps of time between each one. She didn't count them, but they were many, from this first in 1941 to the last in 1976.

She took out the next letter, but then put it back. She'd treat this like a book where she would pace herself out, reading only a little every evening. Mark always questioned how she was able to do it – how she could put it down each night. But to her it was easy. The quicker she read something, the quicker the joy would end. And she never wanted it to end. She had lots of practice drawing out a good book. Right up till the very last chapters, at least – and then she raced to the end.

Having brought no books with her, perhaps Ivy's letters could substitute.

As she re-read the letter, her own loneliness enveloped her and memories of a life now gone swallowed her.

November, Two Years Ago

The sun glinted off the ripples in the harbour as small boats and large ferries cut white lines through the water. Nicky looked out at the sails of the Opera House before them and watched the throng of people meander by, then turned back to the plate of pasta and glass of wine in front of her.

Jane had organised Sunday lunch with Nicky and Mark at one of the sun-kissed restaurants that lined the concourse of the Opera House so they could meet her new boyfriend, Miles. He was tall and lanky with a goatee, and couldn't keep his hands off her.

As the waiter cleared away the plates, Jane cleared her throat. 'Miles and I have something to tell you.' She beamed. 'We're getting married.'

Nicky jumped up from the table and threw her arms around her friend. 'Congratulations!'

'It won't be a big affair. No hoopla. Just a few friends at the registry office, maybe.'

'Do you have a date?' Nicky asked, sitting back down.

'Well, unlike you two slow pokes we're not going to take forever to set a date. We're planning on an early winter wedding. Maybe up north so it's warm.'

'Oh my gosh. That's so . . . well, congratulations.' Nicky raised her glass. 'This most definitely requires a toast.'

Nicky had so many questions. It had been a couple of months since they'd caught up properly – she'd been so busy with her edits they just hadn't found the time. A coffee here, a phone call there, was all they'd managed. So much had happened in between. They excused themselves and ducked to the bathroom, where Jane told her the whole story, from how she'd met Miles, to how she knew so quickly he was the one, to how soon they'd be moving in together. By the time they started heading back to the table, Nicky was satisfied Jane was in fact very much in love and happy, and the men were deep in conversation about some sort of financial investment strategy.

'Ah, here they are.' Miles grinned as Jane sat down beside him.

'We didn't think you were coming back,' Mark said.

'Ha, ha.' Jane took a sip of water. 'A good catch-up takes time. I hope your ears were burning, you boys.' She tapped Miles on the chest. Mark frowned.

As they finished off their drinks, the girls talked about their wedding plans, Jane's far more detailed and formed than Nicky's. Miles and Mark sat back and listened dutifully and when the bill came they split it. The afternoon sun began to sink behind the Harbour Bridge and they walked along the concourse, Nicky and Jane arm in arm.

'I've finished my manuscript,' Jane whispered in her ear.

'What? That's brilliant. Why didn't you tell me?' Nicky hugged her tightly.

Jane shrugged. 'You've been so busy. And I figured now you're a big-shot author, you might just laugh at me.'

Nicole stopped walking. 'I'm hardly a big-shot. And I would never laugh at you or your writing. I love you both.'

'Well, then. I was wondering, maybe, only if you have time. Would you take a look at it?'

Mark caught Nicky's eye and tapped on his watch, and she paused, trying to figure out what he meant.

'I mean, it's okay if you say no. I'll understand.' Jane's voice was soft.

'What? No. Of course I want to read it.' Her hesitation had given Jane the wrong idea. 'I can't wait.'

Jane let out a deep breath. 'Thank you. Just to tell me what you think. Nothing more.'

Nicky put her arm around Jane's shoulder and they continued along the concourse.

'Well, that was a bit of a shock.' Mark pulled Nicky closer to him in the back of the taxi.

'Yeah, but they seemed so happy, didn't they?' Nicky lay her head on his shoulder.

'I suppose.'

Nicky knew that tone of voice. 'What?' She lifted her head. 'What's wrong?'

'I don't know. I just kind of wonder why it's so out of the blue. You don't think . . . no. That's stupid.'

'What?'

'Well, I just wonder, with all your success and us getting engaged, maybe she's just looking to take some of the limelight.'

'Jane? No way. She's not like that. You saw them together. They are totally in love.' Her voice caught on the last word. It wasn't like Jane to be so impulsive.

Mark shrugged, but Nicky could see the doubt in his eyes. Doubt she was herself trying to ignore.

'I don't know. Just seems a bit odd.' He shrugged.

Nicky stroked his arm. 'I think it seems perfectly romantic. Does make you wonder, though.'

'What?'

'If we're ever going to set a date.'

Mark shuffled back in his seat. 'Is that what you two were talking about in the loo?'

'Among other things.'

Mark shook his head. 'We've talked about this. Once I'm firmly established as partner, then we can look at setting a date. Besides, we've got a lot going on with your book release. Don't you think we should wait till after then?'

They'd had this discussion before, Mark ever practical and wanting to wait till just the right time. Nicky was just so impatient for her life as Mrs Avery to start, for them to become the family she so desperately wanted.

'I know. You're right.' She shrugged.

'Hey, princess.' He cupped her chin in his hand. 'It won't be long. I promise. We'll get married, have lots of babies and be a family.'

Maybe Mark was right and they were better off waiting. As long as it wasn't too long. She didn't want to end up like her parents. No, it was fine. They were still young. Another six months, or twelve, wouldn't make a difference.

They had plenty of time.

———

Outside Trevor's Tradies, Nicole struggled to fit the ladder in the car. It wasn't a huge ladder, but even so, her tiny hatchback was no match for it. But she needed something taller than the little stepladder that had come with the cottage if she was going to have any chance of fixing the ceiling, which was the next job on her list.

'Do you need a hand?' Danny waved as he walked up the street.

'I appear to be losing this battle,' Nicole said with a laugh.

'You know, you can just borrow mine. Anytime.'

'It wasn't that expensive.'

Danny frowned.

Damn. She didn't want him to think she was some poor no-hoper. She was. But she didn't need others knowing it.

'I meant so you didn't have to steal someone else's car to get it back home.' His eyes were soft and gentle.

'Oh.'

'Tell you what.' He lifted the ladder with ease. 'You help me with something and I'll throw this on the ute and bring it out to the cottage.'

In the front seat of his ute were two boxes of books.

'We'll take one each,' he said.

'Okay. And where are we going?'

Danny pointed towards the grand old building that housed the post office. Nicole had noticed it the day she'd arrived with its brick and stone arched frontage and clock tower you could see from almost any point in the town centre. A heavily pregnant woman with blonde hair tied in a loose bun waved to Danny as she guided an old man outside and Danny put his box down and sprung up the three steps to help him navigate his descent.

'Thanks, Danny,' he whispered hoarsely and patted his shoulder. 'You're a good kid.'

The old man hobbled down the road and Danny watched him till he was sure he was steady on his feet.

'That's Bill Tucker. Ninety-four years old and still walks everywhere. They don't make them tough like that anymore. Let's get these inside.' He picked up his box.

Once inside, Nicole saw that the building opened up into two distinct sections. The post office to the right and through another set of doors, the library.

The blonde lady greeted them as they entered.

'Beautiful day, hey?' she said. 'Shame I'm stuck in here.'

'Sure is. Nicole, this is Jacqui.' He introduced the two women. 'How's the bump?'

Jacqui rubbed her protruding belly gently. 'Heavy and in the way. Not long now, though.' Her smile held little joy.

'The wager at the pub on the baby's name is heating up, you know? The sooner you put us all out of our misery, the better.'

Jacqui laughed. 'The sooner I put myself out of this misery, the better. Have a good one.' She waved as she headed into the post office.

Danny filled Nicole in on the bets the whole town were taking on what Jacqui and Jason would name their fifth child.

What had started out as a friendly bet one night between George Russo, the pub owner, and Trevor took on a life of its own and once the pool reached five hundred dollars, George suggested donating the money to the preschool refurbishment and the entire population of the town got behind the idea. Three thousand dollars had been raised so far.

Danny steered Nicole to the left as the glass doors to the library slid open. The delicious smell of the books hit her and for a moment she stopped, closed her eyes and drank it in. She hadn't seen any sort of bookshop in town. Not that she could afford such luxuries. She wasn't surprised Rosella Cove didn't have one. Most small towns these days had lost theirs. She hadn't even thought to ask anyone if there was a library. That didn't surprise her, either. The not asking. She hadn't exactly had too many coherent thoughts lately.

A gentle cough from Danny brought her back to the present and she set the box down on the counter in front of them.

'It's not big. But it's got a half-decent selection. What it does boast, though, is the best in modern technology and terrific Wi-Fi. And a pretty good local history collection.'

Nicole walked around the shelves and computers. It was a pretty good set-up. No rival for her local back in Sydney, of course, but impressive for what it was.

A woman came out from the back office and stood behind the counter. 'Hey, Danny. I see you've brought in more history books to donate.'

Danny lifted one of the boxes onto the counter.

Nicole recognised the lady. It was the older woman from the hardware store. Cheryl.

'Hi, Nicole. Nice to see you again.'

'Cheryl.' Nicole gave a little wave. 'I thought you worked at Trevor's.'

'Three days a week I do. I volunteer two days a week here. You need to fill this out,' she said, pushing over some papers, 'and I'll set you up with a borrowing card.'

Even though she wasn't going to be in Rosella Cove for very long, the thought of six whole months without a book was one Nicole couldn't bear. She signed the application and Cheryl issued her with a card straightaway.

'Tada. You're now a fully fledged library member with access to all that we have.'

'Did you want to get something now?' Danny asked.

No. She wanted to come back when she was alone and could

take all the time in the world to peruse the shelves. Not that it would take long, she thought, looking around the small space. But, still.

'Okay, let's get that ladder of yours home.'

Danny dropped the ladder just inside the front door of the cottage and left Nicole to her tasks for the day. Now that the walls were stripped, she had to clean them. All her research told her that if she didn't prepare the walls properly before painting them, the paint wouldn't stick right and in a few years it would be peeling off.

She did think about trying to get away with that. It wasn't like she was going to be here when anyone discovered her shortcut. But there was still so much wallpaper glue on the walls, and she was pretty sure someone would notice if she just painted over the top of that, so she may as well do the job right.

After three hours of painstaking washing and scraping and scrubbing, Nicole was regretting her decision not to take a shortcut. Maybe she could've got away with it – she could have passed the lumps and bumps off as some sort of modern take on stucco. Still, having the ladder meant it was easier to reach the top of the walls. Why hadn't she thought to get one earlier?

The ache in her shoulders soon became too much to bear and she finally decided to put her tools down and take a long, hot shower.

Afterwards, under soft lamplight, Nicole curled up on the old floral sofa in the living room. With her dressing-gown wrapped tightly around her, she ticked off her to-do list for the day. Buy ladder, check. Finish cleaning the walls, check. Read Ivy's next letter.

Nicole sipped on her cup of tea and broke the wax seal of the next envelope. A tingle of excitement bubbled through her.

19th March, 1941

My Dearest Tom,

Your gift arrived today and with it a swelling of joy in my heart. Our little one will have the spinning top his father crafted from the branch of an olive tree so far from home.

Nicole ran into the kitchen and took the spinning top out of the cupboard. Was this it? Any lingering doubts she had about reading a stranger's thoughts dissolved. This was going to be her next great read.

In answer to your question, yes, I suppose we must consider the possibility you suggest, and I do believe that if I am indeed carrying a girl, you would spoil her rotten. I am certain it is a boy, and will still try to steer you towards Charles, but I will indulge you. Briefly. How do you feel about the name Charlotte?

I have placed the spinning top on the mantle above the fireplace, next to the picture of you. Right as I placed it there, I felt the baby move for the very first time. I believe he recognised his father.

When I travelled to see Father in Sydney last week, I found the most delightful wallpaper – pink and blue panels with little toy soldiers and bouncing balls and blocks in red and blue and green. I have begun work on the nursery, hanging two walls already and I shall complete the third today. It is keeping me busy and distracted from thinking about the atrocities you are surely surrounded by. I pretend each day you are here beside me, helping me ready the room for our little arrival.

There are whispers that Japan's threat closer to home is escalating and troops may be recalled. Perhaps, my love, you will be on home soil sooner than expected, even if not home with me.

Oh, my. Your son just gave me an almighty kick. He knows I am writing to you and says hello.

I walked into town today and encountered Joan Wetherby. I have tried, as you wished, to make friends with your old chum, but it seems she has no desire to let me in. I was standing outside the post office chatting idly with young Lucy Falcon, the woman who moved into the yellow house on Cove Road just before you shipped out. Joan sauntered up beside us, greeting Lucy, ignoring me. That woman has always been cold towards me, but never before has she completely forgotten her manners. She did not even ask after you.

Oh dear, your son is restless tonight. Perhaps he did not like the vegetable soup I made for dinner. I thought it quite delicious. We have not faced the harsh rations here that inflict our English sisters, and I had all manner of vegetable to make use of.

My love, I must cut this short. Evening melts into night and I wish to take a walk in the moonlight like we did when you were here.

Stay safe, my darling.

Ivy

Nicole folded the letter carefully and slipped it back into its envelope.

She reached for the next one. No. With her old life now gone, routine and order were all Nicole had left to hang on to. The days were easy enough to fill with tasks, but the nights were excruciating in their loneliness. Metering out Ivy's letters went some way to easing those dark hours.

She pulled out her notebook and started making scratchy marks. Ivy. Tom. The nursery. The baby. Around her words she doodled pictures – ivy leaves on a vine, a spinning top. Random thoughts and half-ideas.

Five

February, Last Year

The end of the signing line was finally in sight. It was the last of Nicky's author talks. As much as she loved them, the schedule had been gruelling, and she was relieved this was the end.

She kept checking the crowd all night to see if Jane had turned up.

'She didn't come?' Mark appeared beside her.

Nicky shook her head. It was her own fault. Jane had sent through her manuscript before Christmas, but with all the preparation for her book launch, Nicky just hadn't got to it.

She'd apologised. More than once. But now it was getting embarrassing. She hadn't texted Jane in weeks, shame stopping her each time.

No wonder Jane didn't come.

'I did tell you not to get your hopes up.'

He had. More than once. Nicky played moments from the last few months over and over in her mind. Was Mark right? Had she just not seen the signs of jealousy? One of his greatest assets as a lawyer was being able to read people. Maybe he saw the truth about Jane that Nicky had refused to accept. She didn't want to believe it, but the evidence was there. Maybe Jane wasn't the friend she thought she was.

As the event wound up, Nicky and a small cohort headed out for dinner to celebrate. It was the newest restaurant in Sydney, a fusion of east and west cuisine that was served in miniature portions on oversized black plates. Mark was very pleased with himself that he'd been able to pull a few strings and get them a table. Her agent, Di, was there, of course, and Mark. A couple of Mark's colleagues. The librarian from the event. Despite the cheery group surrounding her, Nicky felt empty, and a little alone.

Di clinked her glass and everyone turned to her. 'I think tonight is a wonderful chance to share some news that I received today. Nicky, you've won the Jackman Literary Award! I'm so proud of you.'

Mark led a chorus of cheers and Nicky's heart swelled. Never in her wildest dreams did she think she'd get such recognition for *Tide*. A waiter brought glasses of Champagne for everyone and Mark hugged her tightly.

It was the greatest moment of her career so far, and all she wanted was to tell Jane. She skulled her glass and ordered another drink from a passing waiter.

'Don't you think that's enough?' Mark whispered in her ear.

'Not really.' She drank it quickly.

'Well, I was thinking we'd celebrate some more when we got home.' He ran his finger down her spine.

She shrugged him off and pulled her phone out to send a text to her best friend, to share her latest news. But how would she react? Would she see it as Nicky showing off? The first contact

Nicky makes in two months and it's to tell her about a prize she'd won?

She put her phone away.

Later that night, back at the apartment, Nicky and Mark got ready for bed, changing into their pyjamas, folding down the doona.

'So?' Mark asked. 'What are you going to do with all that money?'

'It's not that much.' Nicky shrugged.

'But add it to your advance and it isn't too bad.'

No, it wasn't too bad at all. Nicky rearranged her pillows so she could sit up a bit. 'I suppose I should pay you back for keeping me these last few months.'

'Oh, Nicky.' He laughed and climbed into bed beside her. 'There's no paying back for that. We're together. We share things. Everything. Me taking care of things the last few months wasn't a loan you have to pay back.' He took her hand and rubbed it gently, kissing her palm and twirling her engagement ring around her finger.

Nicky leaned over and kissed him. 'I love you.'

'I love you, too. Now what do you think? Are you going to splurge on something you've always wanted? Like a piano?'

Nicky laughed. She'd never wanted a piano.

'Or a whole new wardrobe? Or put it away so you can buy a weekend house on the water one day?'

Nicky laughed again. 'I think you're adding more zeros to the amount than are actually there.'

'True.' He nodded. 'Though it wouldn't be impossible.'

'How?'

'What I bring in is enough for us to live off, and then some. If we were smart . . . I don't know, it could be doable.'

Nicky thought about it. If they were smart, maybe they could have it all. 'I suppose we could keep living off your income. Put mine away and any extra you get. How long do you think until we could afford something like that?'

Mark shook his head. 'I don't know. A couple of years and we'd have a decent deposit. We'd have to keep it separate, though. It's too easy to spend money without realising it.'

'Why don't we set up a joint account then? Just for the savings.'

'I suppose we could. Gregory's got an excellent financial adviser. He always seems to be getting good interest rates. I could look into if you like.'

Nicky smiled and nestled into his shoulder. It wasn't long before Mark's rhythmic snoring told her he was asleep. She rolled and over and picked up her phone.

'Hi Jane,' she tapped out the beginnings of a message, but every opening she could think of sounded so lame.

'Sorry I haven't been touch.'

Delete.

'I know I've been slack.'

Delete.

'Guess what?'

Delete.

Nicky put the phone away. She would read Jane's manuscript first and then she'd be able to contact her friend with a guilt-free heart.

————

Nicole could hear the commotion from up the street – an announcement was being made over the loudspeaker, followed by a piercing screech at the end as the mic was turned off. She heard the buzzing of distant chatter and car horns beeping. The smell of a sausage sizzle met her nostrils as she approached the playing field and she closed her eyes and paused to drink it all in. It was a comforting aroma that could transport her instantly to her childhood.

Rugby league wasn't exactly Nicole's favourite sport, but she just couldn't face washing and scrubbing any more walls, where old memories were too easily conjured. Besides, she figured being invisible was easy enough in a large crowd distracted by the spectacle in front of them. She'd be gone once the lease ran out, so really there wasn't any harm in surface level friendships to pass the time.

'Hey, Nicole!' shouted Trevor from the sideline as he put his team through a last minute warm-up.

Danny, dressed in a cove jersey with the number one on his back, nodded in her direction.

She waved back to them, suddenly conscious of how conspicuous she was, wearing her floral shirt and jeans; she was the only person there not clad in Rosella Cove's black and white or Woodville's blue and yellow.

Around the oval locals and visitors, distinct in their opposing colours, sat on picnic blankets and stood in small groups. When the starting horn sounded, an almighty cheer rose up from the many spectators.

She made her way over to the hill, where Mandy greeted her with a hug and poured her a coffee from the thermos at her feet. This early-round match against their arch rivals was going to be tough, apparently, and an extra supporter was very welcome.

Nicole looked around the crowd, watching the faces turn from anguish to delight to disbelief as try-saving tackles were made, field goals scored and penalties given, and she realised she was smiling. The noise from the crowd, in particular the screaming from Cheryl and Jim, the plumber Mandy had arranged to fix Nicole's shower, made it almost impossible to have a conversation, and for that she was thankful.

Once upon a time, people-watching was her favourite activity. She hadn't done it for so long now and as she watched the crowd around her, she could feel a familiar pull.

Her heart warmed at the sheer joy on the face of the little boy from Woodville in a replica Wolves' jersey watching his dad cross the line, and she laughed at the old grandma wrapped from head to toe in the Rosella Cove Rangers' black and white stripes cursing the ref who was bloody blind and might move a damn sight quicker if he borrowed her Zimmer frame.

Nicole's mind was taking in everything and she could feel the fuzzy outlines of potential scenes and book characters starting to form. These old habits that had led to her becoming a writer were resurfacing after so long dormant, that it thrilled and terrified her in equal measure. Could she write again? Did she want to?

At the half-time horn, the Rangers were down a try. Nicole followed Mandy and Jack to the sausage sizzle line and got herself a banger with onions in a slice of home-brand white bread. Jack went and found the team to lend his dad some moral support as he tried to rally the troops, and Mandy steered Nicole towards the market stalls.

There were padded, lace-covered coathangers and knitted bears, granny-square afghans and toilet-roll dollies, apple teacakes and chocolate rough slices. There was a stall selling children's wooden toys, and one with jewellery made from beads of garish colour and stones so big Nicole wondered whose hand or neck would be strong enough to hold them.

Another stall was selling garden ornaments made from recycled materials that Nicole lingered briefly at, wondering if perhaps the copper and tyre brolga would look good in her front yard when it was eventually finished. If it was ever finished. Not that she could afford such extras. And Jacqui, the pregnant woman from the post office, was selling artwork – mostly pretty, albeit generic-looking, landscapes. But she also had a few abstract pieces that caught Nicole's eye.

'Nicole! Good to see you again,' said Jacqui. 'You like these ones, do you?' she gestured to the abstract pieces Nicole was admiring. 'I'd be more than happy to show you a few more like it sometime. I keep them back at my garage studio – they tend to be a little too out-there for the market crowd.'

'That would be great, thanks, Jacqui.' Nicole tried a warm smile, wondering if Jacqui could read her mind, which was calculating exactly how much money she didn't have to spend on art.

Sitting back on the picnic blankets on the hill in their viewing area as the game continued, Nicole realised she was finding the excitement running through the crowd somewhat infectious, though she was loath to admit it to herself. The cheers gained volume and frenzy as the clock ticked into the final few minutes. The teams were tied – eighteen points each. In the last few seconds a field goal from Danny put the Rangers in front and the cheer from the home crowd as the horn sounded the end of the match was so loud Nicole had to cover her ears.

A group of boys aged between six and sixteen, all dressed in Rangers uniforms, encircled Danny.

'He coaches a few of the junior sides,' Mandy said to Nicole. 'He's brilliant with them.'

The boys clambered to pat their hero on his back. Danny picked up the smallest of the boys, Jason Junior – Jacqui's eldest – and sat him on his shoulder for the extended victory lap, which the crowd lapped up. Trevor gathered them all in for a big group hug before jogging over to his wife for a big kiss.

Mandy leaned over to Nicole. 'They'll be celebrating with a schooner or three down at The Royal,' she said.

Rowdy footy players and beer was not an enticing combination for Nicole. It was time to slip back into obscurity and attack those waiting walls, but Trevor grabbed her by the hand.

'Not so fast, you.' He flung his arm around her shoulder. 'Our lucky charm is coming, too.'

Nicole frowned. 'Your what?'

'This is the first time in years we've beaten those buggers. And the only thing that's different is you.' He slapped her on the back.

Mandy leaned in wrapping her in a protective embrace. 'I'll make sure she gets there.' She pushed her husband back towards his team.

'I'm afraid you've done it now, Nicole.' She frowned, though Nicole caught the twinkle in her eye.

'Done what?'

'They're very superstitious, this lot. When they lost the grand final four years ago they blamed the fact that Danny Temple didn't wear his lucky socks. Got blown off the line in a storm. Though the boys will tell you Woodville stole them. Without the socks, they just couldn't win. Been on a losing streak ever since. Danny almost got kicked off the team. Would have lost the captaincy too if it weren't for the fact that it was the anniversary of his grand-dad dying and everyone felt sorry for him. If they reckon this win is down to your presence, then . . .'

She shrugged.

'. . . well, I'm afraid you're the new lucky socks. Better clear your Saturdays for the rest of the season.'

Nicole stared at Mandy with wide eyes. No, no, no. This was not part of the plan.

Mandy gently directed her down the street. 'It'll be all right, Nicole.'

The Royal stood proudly on the corner of High Street and Sydney Road, the main intersection, and the pub was the physical and spiritual centre of the town. It was a place where birthdays and anniversaries were celebrated. Families came by for quiet Sunday brunches, and nearly every fundraising event for the local school or footy team or bowls trip was held there. It was also one of the oldest buildings in town. Its red bricks stood strong against the weather of time, according to Mandy, who was giving Nicole a full run-down of the hotel's history as she walked her to a quiet booth up the back.

George Russo had taken over the pub around forty years earlier and every few years or so thereafter he would reinvent the restaurant. There was the Italian theme at first, which was not surprising, given George had come straight from Naples to the cove. Then there was the Chinese era, self-taught from cookbooks, and after that was the short-lived Tapas phase that the locals didn't take too kindly to. Nicole tuned out for a while and when she refocused, Mandy was up to the current flavour of the month, Thai.

'Of course, he always keeps his famous penne carbonara on the menu. He's no fool.' Mandy shook her head.

'Of course.'

Nicole leaned back into the green leather bench seat, no doubt a remnant from the Irish refurbishment Mandy had mentioned at some point in her spiel. On the walls were photos of the Rangers over the years, and old black and white pictures of George's home city, with narrow streets and tall stone buildings.

The double front doors burst open with such force that Nicole was surprised the glass panels didn't shatter, and a shouty, tuneless version of 'We are the Champions' erupted into the relative quiet. The boys had arrived.

Much to everyone's apparent shock, the first round was on George. He even poured himself a schooner and everyone raised their glasses in cheers, toasting the team's surprising success.

Danny and his winning goal were celebrated first, and he skulled a beer as the men sang the team song. Trevor was next, downing a schooner in one fluid movement.

Nicole saw Trevor making eye contact with her from across the room and pointing her out. Mandy shook her head in warning, but the boys took no notice. Danny and another player swooped over and lifted a stunned Nicole onto their shoulders. They carried her to the bar, plonking her on top.

'To our lucky mascot!' Trevor shouted as he handed her a schooner.

Terror gripped Nicole as the boys started singing the team song again. She'd never skulled a beer in her life, rarely drank the stuff. As the song got louder and she looked at the expectant and joyous faces beaming up at her, she knew she had no choice but follow tradition.

The song reached its climax and she took a deep breath, downing the amber fluid dutifully, screwing up her face in disgusted triumph after the last gulp.

Trevor helped her off the bar. With hearty pats on the back, she retreated to the safety of the booth, where Mandy was waiting with a kind expression on her face.

'Are they always this rowdy when they win?' Nicole asked, a little breathless.

'It's been so long I can hardly remember,' Mandy laughed.

Nicole waited until Mandy excused herself to go to the bathroom and then made a sneaky exit out the back entrance.

She sucked in great gulps of evening air as she walked down the quiet street and up towards the path leading to her cottage. It wasn't the beer itself that had upset her, though that would probably come back to haunt her later. It was the feeling of having no choice in the matter.

The long, slender trunks of the gums that lined the road shone with a pale silver glow. The ocean beside her reflected the lunar light in blinking slivers. Three wisps of cloud cloaked the edge of the moon creating an eerie glow to the sleeping sky.

As she passed the boatshed she noticed a light on in one of the portal windows. Nicole stopped in her path and gazed at it.

She found herself wondering about the hermit life Charlie seemed to lead. What did he do with all that time alone? Did he read? Did he have a television in there? Did he piece together puzzles? Did he sit and stare at the wall for hours at a time, like she sometimes did?

Was she going to remain alone like Charlie had been for the last fifty years? Maybe it was better that way. Maybe Charlie was perfectly happy. She could find a hobby. Take up knitting once the renovations were done, or crochet. She could get herself some cats. She didn't particularly like cats, but that's what lonely old women had, right?

'Oi!' A shout interrupted her tumbling thoughts. 'What do you think you're looking at?'

'Just admiring the view.'

Charlie limped up the path from the cove towards her.

'This time of night? Ain't safe.'

'No. I might run into an angry old hermit,' she replied, feigning fear. 'I want to clear my head. The beach seemed like a good spot for that.'

Charlie grunted.

'Seems you thought so too.' Nicole raised her eyebrow.

He grumbled as he opened the old wooden door to the boat-shed.

Nicole tried to peek inside, but Charlie only opened the door just enough to squeeze through and shut it very quickly.

''Night,' she called as she continued down to the beach.

∽

Inside, Charlie had a good view from his northern window as Nicole paced up and down the sand quickly. What was she doing down there? Clearing her head, yeah right. He knew why people went down to beaches at night. But he didn't want to relive old memories.

Charlie was relieved when she finally passed his boatshed an hour later as she headed back up the path towards the cottage. He wondered what someone so young could have weighing so heavily on their shoulders. Though, as he thought about it, he probably wasn't much older than her when his life fell to pieces.

He only hoped she'd get the job done he'd brought her here to do.

———

Nicole walked into the unlit cottage and slipped her shoes off. She switched on the lamp in the living room, settled into the couch and pulled out Ivy's next letter.

14th April, 1941

My Dearest Tom,

I have failed you.

Please forgive me. I was not strong enough to hold on to our precious little boy. Yes, my love, he was a boy. But I lost him. Dr Johnson tried to save him, but could not. There was so much blood.

I have spent the last few weeks in Woodville Hospital. They do not know what caused this. 'Mother Nature's way', they said. Her way to what? I cannot help feeling as though my body was not enough for him. To want to stay, or to want to survive.

Father brought me home today. Mother had the nursery redecorated before my release. And I cannot find the spinning top you sent. Mother said it is better not to have reminders. That it will be easier to move forward as if it never happened.

But it did happen. How will you ever forgive me?

Please do. I ask this of you, knowing it is something I cannot do myself.

Please say you still love me and that I will remain forever yours.

Ivy

Nicole let the tears flow as she clutched her stomach. Poor Ivy. Suffering such loss with Tom on the other side of the world. She couldn't stop reading there and swallowed hard as she broke her ritual.

She pulled out the next letter – a yellow envelope bordered in thick garish red with URGENT TELEGRAM emblazoned on the front. Carefully she opened it. It was dated the day after Ivy's letter. The yellow paper, slightly torn at the edges and wrinkled as if screwed up into a ball and flattened again, bore typed words, screaming in capital letters.

'REGRET TO INFORM YOU THAT YOUR HUSBAND
SGT T WILSON IS REPORTED MISSING IN ACTION AS
A RESULT OF AIR ACTION LETTER TO FOLLOW
MINISTER FOR THE ARMY 2 13 PM'

Nicole dropped the telegram into her lap. Oh, Ivy. How cruel and unfair.

Doubling over, she rested her hands on her knees and tried to stop the crying. To lose a child and have Tom go missing in one go. To lose everything.

Six

Just as dawn broke over the water, Nicole hauled herself out of bed. It was amazing how tired she was, and yet sleep had evaded her most of the night; how she couldn't turn off the thousand thoughts that ran through her mind. She put the kettle on.

Trevor and Danny would be by this morning to help put shelves up in the living room. Given the celebrations yesterday, she figured they wouldn't be here early. In fact, they might not turn up at all.

Nicole sat in the wicker chair on the verandah sipping her coffee slowly as the sun pushed its way through the sky. Ivy's box sat on the small table, though she dared not open it.

She couldn't face the next letter. She wasn't sure she wanted to. Nothing good could come of looking into the depths of someone's personal life. There, only pain lived. Her earlier instinct of trepidation had been right. She walked back inside picking up the box, and took it into the kitchen, where she placed it back in the cupboard.

Her heart ached and dark, sad thoughts threatened to intrude. She had to keep busy. Yes, that's what she had to do.

She pottered around the cottage, sweeping and wiping away dirt. No matter how often she cleaned, everything seemed permanently covered in a thin veil of dust.

An hour later a knock on the door signalled the unlikely arrival of Trevor and Danny.

Trevor looked as if he'd rather have been in bed and she suggested as much.

'Not worth the grief,' he grumbled as he slumped his way past her.

Jack was with them too, standing behind his old man. 'He tried to get out of it, but Mum wouldn't have it. Went on about his word being his bond or something and not letting friends down.' He shrugged and placed his iPod earphones in his ears and headed back down to the front garden. With all the grass cut back, today he was going to focus on removing weeds.

Danny shrugged, flashing her a smile from his green eyes, and went into the living room to set up his tools.

Nicole led Trevor into the kitchen and fixed him a strong coffee before checking to see if Danny wanted a drink.

'No. Thank you. But with Trevor out of action, I might need some help.'

Nicole frowned. Yes, she was getting pretty good at stripping paint and wallpaper, and putting a mallet through plasterboard, but beyond that her DIY prowess had not yet progressed. She couldn't actually build anything.

Her 'help' consisted of handing Danny tools, the names of which she learned as they went, and passing screws as he put in place shelves on each side of the fireplace.

'This is going to look awesome when it's finished. It might take us a while to source the right tiles for the hearth, but we'll get there,' Danny said, after they'd been working together for nearly two hours. He took a step back and admired their work. 'And when you fill these with books,' he tapped one of the shelves, 'wow.'

Filling those shelves with books was something she would never get to do – no money, no time and she hadn't brought any of her own with her.

'Uh-oh. You're frowning.' Danny's shoulders slumped. 'Have I done something wrong?'

'No. Of course not. It . . .'

Her breathing quickened. Thanks to Ivy's letters her emotions were far too close to the surface. Danny's expression was full of warmth, drawing the words from her, though she tried to keep them in.

'. . . It's just, I didn't bring any of my books with me. Not even my favourite, *Anne of Green Gables*. I . . . it got ruined. Before I came here.'

'That is an awfully sad face for a ruined book.'

'It was my all-time favourite.'

Danny reached out and touched her shoulder gently. Heat pulsed down Nicole's spine and she stepped back. What was that?

Danny cleared his throat. 'Why don't we see how Trevor's doing? I reckon Mandy'll be along shortly to check on him.' They went into the kitchen together, where Trevor was slumped over on his forearms at the table, asleep.

Nicole grinned. Danny was probably right. They ought to get Trevor up.

'Trev.' Danny shook the man gently.

Trevor sat up, panic across his face.

As if on cue, Mandy called out from the front door and Nicole heard her footsteps up the hallway.

'You left without saying goodbye last night,' Mandy said, and Nicole thought she detected a hint of hurt feeling beneath Mandy's usual friendly tone. 'I hope they behaved today,' she said to Nicole, looking from Trevor to Danny. 'This one still backs up all right after a night on the grog.' She patted Danny on the shoulder. 'But this one?' She looked down her nose at Trevor. 'He still thinks he's twenty.'

'No, they were great.' Nicole smiled. 'We got through it all today.'

'Excellent. You boys run off then and let Nicole and I have some girl talk. Poor thing probably needs a break from the two of you. Shall I pop the kettle on?'

The quiet beauty of the early afternoon sun slowly dropping behind the tall eucalyptus trees in the distance, was punctuated by Mandy's infectious laugh. She recounted events from the night after Nicole had left the pub.

'You missed a doozy.'

'Sounds like it,' Nicole said.

'I understand why you left, though. Cove people can be a little full on if you're not used to them. Especially when it comes to their footy, and especially when they have their first win in years.'

'It wasn't bad,' Nicole said. 'Just a bit intense.'

'Intense is one way to put it!' Mandy turned to face her, looking serious all of a sudden. 'So, what exactly brings you to our little corner of the world, Nicole? Don't get me wrong, I love this place, but it's a bit out of left field for someone like you, I'd say.'

'Someone like me?'

'A celebrity. Don't they normally go to Bora Bora, or Paris? Or Byron Bay even?'

Nicole laughed. 'I'm hardly a celebrity.'

'Sure you are! You wrote that amazing book,' Mandy said. 'And in my eyes that makes you a celebrity.'

Nicole grimaced.

'Oh, you don't have to say anything. I'm just glad you're here. Maybe we can run a piece in the *Cove Chronicle* about our brush with fame.'

Nicole dropped her teacup and it hit the saucer with a loud clang. 'No. Please don't.'

Mandy raised an eyebrow. 'Not if you don't want to. Of course.'

Nicole knew she had to change the subject and a thought came to her. 'I was wondering if you could help me with something.'

'Anything,' Mandy said quickly.

'How much do you know about Ivy Wilson?'

'Ivy?' Mandy looked surprised. 'Not a lot more than I told you about that night at dinner.'

'Oh, that's right. I just wondered . . .' how could she get round this without giving too much away, '. . . if there was any more to her story. The real estate agent I signed the lease with gave away nothing. What's the deal exactly with Ivy?'

'Hmm. Let me think. She moved here in the late 1930s as a young bride. She came from money in Sydney, I think. Story goes that she married someone her parents didn't approve of. I don't know what happened to him. She died in the early eighties, no, mid-seventies, but I was only a kid. I have sketchy memories of these picnics she used to hold, though they're pretty legendary with folks around town.'

Mandy poured herself more tea and shadows from the distant gums stretched out across the land as the sun began to drop.

'Mum used to tell stories of this beautiful old place. No one really knows what happened after she died. She'd hired lawyers from Sydney, like I said at dinner. Plenty of people have sniffed around over the years, made offers on the place. But they were all turned away.'

Nicole wished she could get out her notebook and start writing down the questions pinging around her head. What had happened to Tom? To Ivy? Why had the house stayed empty so long? Why had it never been sold? And how did Charlie fit in?

'Why the interest?' Mandy asked, interrupting her thoughts.

'Every time I meet someone and they find out I'm living here, people talk about her. She must have been really something.'

'I can ask Mum what she knows. Her lucid days are few and far between, but next time she's good I can ask.'

'It's no big deal.' Nicole suddenly felt guilty for keeping Ivy's letters from Mandy. She knew Mandy could help her unravel this mystery faster, but she was still ashamed at having pried.

'Nah, it's fine. When Mum's on form, she likes to talk about the good-ol' days. You could come with me if you like.'

'Oh. No. I couldn't impose.' A faint yearning stirred inside Nicole. There was that curiosity again. 'Thank you. But no. And don't you bother her with it, either.'

'It would be fine,' Mandy insisted, but Nicole shook her head. 'Okay, then,' she continued. 'But if you ever change your mind, you let me know.'

Nicole spent the rest of the afternoon alone, scraping peeling paint from the ceiling in the hallway. Afterward she took an evening stroll along the peninsula down towards South Beach. The opposite direction of the boatshed. She didn't think she could cope with being challenged by Charlie.

As the road wound round the bend back towards the cottage, Nicole was struck by the beauty of the indigo sky fading to pale blue then into a peach that deepened to fire orange at the horizon. The black silhouettes of the scratchy branches and leaves of the gum trees surrounding her looked as if they had been painted there.

For the first time that day she felt peace.

When she reached the cottage she crawled into bed exhausted and ticked off today's list. Bookshelves, check. Make a start on ceilings, a weary check. Ivy's next letter. She hesitated.

She wasn't sure if she could take that kind of emotion tonight. But she did want to see if Ivy was all right.

She took a deep breath and opened the carved wooden box. Unlike the first few letters, there was no stamp on this envelope.

25th October, 1941

My Dearest Tom,

No news has reached me yet as to your fate. So I must believe that is a good sign. I am sorry it has taken me so long to write to you again. But with nowhere to send my correspondence and the grief of losing our child, I simply have not been able to put pen to paper. The unrelenting pain that consumed me the first few months after that dark, dark week now comes in waves that overwhelm me without any warning and then subside to a dull ache around my heart.

Mother would think it quite ridiculous that I write to you like this. However, I fear gravely that should I not correspond with you, then I give up hope. And that I cannot afford to do.

Mother says I must face the reality of your 'situation' and prepare myself for unwelcome news which might yet come. I do believe that woman has no compassion in her whatsoever. She is far too practical for emotion.

She is right, of course. But I will not give up, though the more time that passes, the harder it becomes.

I have left the house today for the first time since your news reached me, as I felt duty-bound to visit with Lucy Falcon. She called on me many times these last six months with a plate of food, a posy of flowers, an offer to chat, only to have me shoo her away. News reached us yesterday of her husband Henry's passing, another casualty of this infernal war. He is the second we have now lost from our tiny community. Colonel Bridges first and now Lucy's husband.

It was a brief visit. She was trying to be stoic, bless her, but I could see the pain in her eyes. No matter how hard we try to hide our feelings, our eyes give us away should anyone care to look. Thankfully, most people do not bother.

I shall call on her again soon.

Joan visited me once during my, what shall we call it? Isolation. She left a basket of flowers on the doorstep, but did not come in.

The sun was so warm on my back today as I walked home along the peninsula. It was a balm I did not know I needed. I went to the cove, in part, I admit, to avoid seeing Mother. She has decided to stay with me until I 'recover my senses'. I sat on the sand just out of reach of the waves, tracing my fingers around the pippy shells that washed up with yesterday's storm.

I inhaled as the ocean exhaled its salty breath. It was as if I was breathing for the first time in six months. What is it about the sea that calms a troubled soul?

It is our anniversary next week, my love. I will mark it as we always did, with a picnic by the boatshed. I shall have to find a distraction for Mother, but I will think of something. I will bring a basket of your favourite food and sit on the bench you so beautifully crafted all those years ago. I will look for you in the waves, my dearest.

I cannot promise not to cry, but I will endeavour to think only of the days we had together and how very much you always made me feel loved. I shall hold steadfast to the hope that you will be returned soon. Until then I shall continue to write.

Forever yours,

Ivy

Seven

The heritage-listed Federation homestead that housed Rosella Cove's elderly and those who needed full-time care stood proud on a large blanket of green grass. Inside, high ceilings and lavish leadlight windows created a sense of grandeur and joy. It was a week since Mandy had suggested bringing Nicole along to meet her mother in order to find out more about Ivy. And this morning Mandy had turned up on the cottage verandah, insisting it would be okay for Nicole to come with her.

They stood in the foyer, and Nicole spun round to take it all in. 'This is a stunning building.'

'It's the least we can give them,' Mandy whispered.

She led Nicole through to a spacious garden out the back where the twenty or so residents could enjoy the sun. There they found Carole, Mandy's mum, sitting on a wrought-iron bench under a dripping jacaranda tree at the rear of the garden.

'Mum, this is Nicole. She's new to town.'

Carole nodded, her thinning grey hair catching in wisps on

the gentle breeze. She went back to the conversation she was having with herself, soft mumblings which mainly consisted of gossip from around the nursing home. Nicole didn't know whether to find it hilarious or scandalous.

Apparently someone named Fred Appleton had tried to hit on Carole during bingo, right in front of Mrs Appleton, who he'd clean forgotten he was married to.

'He suggested we go to Fiji, you know,' Carole confessed. 'But how can I leave my babies behind?' She smiled and patted Mandy's hand. 'Who's this, then?' Carole looked at Nicole.

'Hi. I'm Nicole. I'm living in Ivy Wilson's cottage.'

'Really? Where is Ivy, then? Is she with you?'

'She's gone, Mum. Remember?' Mandy's shoulders slumped.

'We must be due another picnic. Will she be back soon?'

Nicole glanced at the ground. Despite the age of her parents when they passed, they'd been spared the horror of diminishing faculties – their bodies had given up well before their minds. She had never spent time with someone in Carole's condition. It was far more confronting than she'd have imagined.

'He won't be there, will he?' Carole grabbed Nicole's arm. 'There's something about him.'

'Who, Carole?' Nicole asked.

A soft, purple bell fell from the branch above and landed on Carole's shoulder. She turned her head to look at it as if studying its fragile form for botanical detail, or trying to read tiny lettering printed on its delicate flute. Then she carefully lifted it from its resting place, laid it beside her and stared ahead with altered eyes.

Silence settled over the three of them.

Mandy took her mother's hand and smiled lovingly at her. She kissed her on the forehead.

'That's it for the day,' she whispered to Nicole.

'I'll be back tomorrow, Mum.' She adjusted the blanket over Carole's legs and Nicole followed her out of the home.

'Sorry. We didn't really get much information about Ivy. Come back for a cuppa,' Mandy suggested, 'and I'll dig out some old photos.'

Nicole went back to Mandy's house with her, where they found Trevor stretched out on the banana lounge on the back patio. Jack was sprawled across the lounge with the TV on full bore. Mandy waved hello to her son as she turned the TV volume down, receiving barely a nod in response.

'Mandy?' Nicole stopped as they walked into Mandy's kitchen. 'I'm sorry. It must be so hard, watching your mum, well, I . . .' She reached and touched Mandy's arm.

'Nothing to be sorry for.' Mandy sighed. 'Believe it or not, that was one of her better days.'

'How do you do it? Find the strength?'

'She's my mum,' Mandy replied with a shrug.

A stab of pain hit Nicole's chest. What she wouldn't give to have her own mother back again.

'It's okay. Really. I enjoy the trips down memory lane. It was hard at first, but we're used to it now. Come. Sit down.'

Nicole was all but plonked into the kitchen chair as Mandy fussed about, putting on a pot of tea and telling her all about how Carole was diagnosed with early-onset dementia. Nicole's heart went out to her as Mandy described the day Carole had walked out the front door and up the street completely naked. Thankfully, Charlie had found her at the cove and brought her home, knocking on their front door, silently returning Carole into their care. Mandy's gratitude was not just for her mum's safe return, but also for knowing Charlie wouldn't speak a word of her mother's undignified demise. Nicole wondered if this was the memory that had choked Mandy up at dinner when she was talking about Charlie that night.

Nicole poured milk into her tea and stirred absentmindedly as she contemplated Mandy's stories about Carole and Charlie.

'You said that night at your place that Charlie's been here about fifty years, right?'

Mandy nodded. 'Something like that.'

So many questions ran through Nicole's head. She was losing her battle to quell her curiosity. 'Was that before or after Ivy died?'

'Before. A bit before the picnics started, I think,' Mandy said. 'Let me see.' She pulled an old shoebox out of the cupboard. 'I have some photos from when I was a kid. Maybe there'll be something useful in here.' She pulled out a silly baby picture of herself with a nappy on her head, and a faded photo of her with friends, all of them covered from head to toe in mud. She'd been about ten, apparently, and she told Nicole how the rain just didn't seem to stop that summer. Then she pulled out a Polaroid with muted colours and handed it to Nicole.

Nicole looked at it closely. There was a group of kids running round the edges of a picnic blanket laid out on a lawn. Even in this tired old picture the blue and white painted exterior of the cottage was striking.

'That's me.' Mandy pointed to a little girl with tight red ringlets sitting with two others, surrounded by dolls, on a picnic blanket laid out on the lawn. A young boy kicked a soccer ball next to them. They were all about three or four, Nicole guessed.

'That's Trevor.' Mandy pointed to the boy.

An old lady stood in the left of the photo, watching the children with a contented look across her face.

'Is this Ivy?' Nicole asked.

'Yes. I don't remember much about the picnics, but that's her for sure.'

Ivy's grey hair was long and wild. Nicole, for some reason, had pictured it neat. She wore a flowing gypsy skirt and peasant blouse in bright blue. This didn't fit with the Ivy of well-tailored clothes and prim and proper manners that she'd imagined from the letters. The woman wore no shoes, and her bare feet peeked out from under the layers of her skirt.

In the background of the photo, where the blurred gum trees stood tall, she thought she could make out the dark shadow of a man leaning against one of the trunks.

Could that be . . .? Nicole could no longer fight the persistent curiosity bubbling inside. She did, however, manage to fight the urge to pull out her notebook and write down the thousand questions flashing through her mind.

'Here's another one of Ivy.' Mandy handed Nicole a photo. Ivy was obviously in it by accident; she was clearly passing by while Mandy's mum was in the main part of the frame fussing over Mandy and her two brothers standing outside the post office in town.

'We were heading to someone's birthday or something in that one, I think,' Mandy offered as Nicole studied the picture. 'Dad was trying to get a family shot, but apparently we weren't being all that cooperative.'

Nicole was transfixed by the image.

'I hope these help. From what I remember the picnics were held once a month after the Sunday service. The whole town would go. I was only a baby when they started.'

Nicole reached across and patted Mandy's arm. 'Thanks for this. It's brilliant.'

'As I said, I hope they help.' Mandy shrugged. She started drumming her fingers on the side of her chair and tapping her foot.

Nicole continued to scrutinise the photos.

'Okay, Nicole. Time to spill the beans,' Mandy blurted out.

'Sorry?'

'This interest in Ivy Wilson? It's got nothing to do with the house. Something else is going on. If I knew what you were looking for maybe I could be better help. Otherwise I don't know what needle I'm searching for in the bloomin' haystack.'

Nicole looked Mandy in the eye. 'There's . . .' She wanted to tell Mandy the truth about the letters, talk it over and find out more, but she wasn't sure what it all added up to yet.

'If you're researching for another book, maybe I could help. That would be so much fun.' Mandy's eyes lit up. 'Oh, please say yes. I can just see myself as a research assistant to a famous author.'

Nicole held back a laugh. Even the most famous writers she knew did their own research. Mandy's view of authors was charming, if not entirely correct.

'Oh, no. It's nothing like that.' Nicole's curiosity may have been piqued, but writing again was another matter entirely. 'It's just . . .'

No. It had nothing to do with waiting to see what it added up to. The actual truth of it was she just wanted to keep Ivy all to herself. To have a friend no one else knew about, something no one else could touch or tarnish.

'I have to go.' Nicole dropped the photos and Mandy looked at her with wide eyes.

'I appreciate your help.' Nicole stuttered and ran out the door, leaving her fledgling friendship behind.

Friendships were such fragile things.

June, Last Year

Nicky nestled into the couch, legs tucked under, to doodle in her notebook. She scribbled words down, trying to find an idea for her next book that she was sure was somewhere in her mind. She just couldn't find it. Mark was in the shower. They'd had sex as soon as he'd got home from work, but Nicky had been distracted the whole time. She was still distracted now.

She'd finally read Jane's manuscript, six embarrassingly long months after her friend had given it to her. And it was good. Really good. She'd sent her a text yesterday to tell her so, two of them actually, but there had been no reply.

Maybe Jane was angry with her, despite the glowing feedback. Nicky couldn't blame her. With each week that had gone by since Christmas, her shame at being such a bad friend had grown, and her courage to make contact had shrunk.

And with each week that had gone by without Jane calling or texting her either, it was harder to break the silence.

But surely now Nicky had read the manuscript and reached out, her old friend would respond.

She sent another text and waited.

No response.

What if something had happened to Jane? No, Miles would have got in touch if that were so.

Jane wasn't on any social media. She hated the whole idea of it. So Nicky couldn't her look her up. But maybe Miles was. Why hadn't she thought of that before? She flipped open her laptop.

A quick search was all it took to find him on Facebook and Nicky sat there, staring at the screen, silent tears falling down her cheeks.

'Nicky? Is everything okay?' Mark came up behind her, wrapped in a towel. 'Oh, Nicky.' He put his arm round her shoulder.

She couldn't believe what she saw. There, looking gloriously happy, was a photo of a beaming Jane, barefoot on the sand in tropical Queensland, a flowing wedding dress, standing next to Miles as he planted a kiss on her cheek. It was posted a week ago.

Jane had got married. Without her.

'It's okay.' Mark embraced her tightly.

'I just . . . How could she . . . I don't understand. I mean, I know we haven't been close lately, but she's my best friend.'

At least she *was*.

Mark crouched on the floor, his hands on Nicky's knees, his eyes level with hers.

'I hate to say this, but maybe she isn't the friend you thought. She didn't come to any of your events. She hasn't answered your texts. She's always been jealous of you. You're better off without her.'

'No.' Nicky shook her head. Even if Jane was a little bit jealous, surely she wouldn't . . . But she stared at the bright aqua hues of the perfectly clear ocean and the powder-white sand – the evidence was there in front of her.

Jane hadn't wanted Nicky at her wedding.

'It's okay. Let it out. It's not nice finding out people aren't who you think they are,' Mark said, wrapping her in his arms.

Nicky did let it out. In great big ugly sobs as Mark tried to soothe her, stroking her hair, whispering into her ear.

'I love you, princess. I'll never let you down like this. Come to bed, hey?'

Nicky shook her head. 'I just need to . . .' She didn't know what she needed. She closed her laptop and tossed it to the other side of the couch. 'I'm okay. I'll be in in a minute,' she said, squeezing Mark's hand.

He kissed the top of her forehead and headed to bed.

Nicky lay on the couch, silent tears falling down her cheeks. As the hours ticked by, sorrow swelled and subsided at random intervals and sleep didn't come.

At five in the morning she crawled across the couch and turned on her laptop. She opened a new document and started typing half-sentences that went nowhere.

She knew nothing she wrote that morning would be worth keeping, but she found some small comfort in the ritual.

———

Nicole spent the afternoon scraping the living room ceiling, but it did little to quell her guilt. She wasn't proud of her behaviour that morning. Mandy had done nothing but extend a hand of friendship, and Nicole had responded rather rudely. She'd have to think of a way to apologise. Flowers? No. Not the right sentiment. What did her mum used to do when she was trying to mend a bridge?

She baked. Now that was something Mandy would probably appreciate. But Nicole's skills in the kitchen were questionable at best. There must be something basic she could make. Like choc-chip cookies. How hard could those be?

The next morning she'd give it a crack. If it failed, no one would know and she'd fall back on the flowers option.

As the night grew cold, she curled up on the sofa under a blanket in front of her empty bookshelves, and read over her notebook where she'd jotted down the questions that had come to her that morning looking at photos of Ivy. It was getting harder not to skip ahead with Ivy's letters. But the routine was comforting and it was almost as if she was checking in with a friend at the end of the day. Nicole missed having someone to check in with. In her lonely life, these snippets of light were worth holding on to a little longer.

2nd November, 1941

My Dearest Tom,

The sun was so warm today, my love. The morning began as it often does in late spring, crisp and cool, and melted into a warm bright day with clear blue skies and a gentle breeze. The sea was such a beautiful deep shade of turquoise and I found it soothing as ever to watch the gentle, rhythmic ripples. Had you been here, I know you would have loved removing your shoes to feel the warm grass between your toes. So, my dearest, I did so in your stead and I must admit I giggled like a schoolgirl as I danced our wedding waltz barefoot around the headland.

Perhaps I shall never wear shoes again. What would Mother have to say about that?

Nicole thought back to Mandy's photos, with Ivy barefoot in each one, and smiled to herself.

As fate would have it, I had no need to send her on an errand today as the CWA required her services. You know how she cannot refuse being needed. She tried to take me with her but I feigned illness.

Mother was out of the house by ten, which gave me ample time to ready our anniversary picnic. Naturally, I prepared far too much food. Even when you were here I would make too much. Imagine the excess today with only one mouth to feed! Still, the seagulls did not complain.

I found myself talking to them as I would you while they squawked and scavenged around me. They were not very good listeners.

I could not bring myself to enter the boatshed, my darling. I made it as far as placing my hand on the doorknob, but before I could turn it open, images of that night before you left for war flooded my mind. Oh, what I would not give to have another night in the boatshed with you.

So, I remained outside today, eating our anniversary lunch with the seagulls. I miss you so, my darling.

On a far brighter note, Father has been asked to present a series of summer talks at the university in Sydney. If he accepts, he will be gone for at least a month and he plans to take Mother with him. She is saying, of course, that she cannot possibly leave me in this state. 'Not until the child stops wallowing in permanent grey and pulls herself together,' I heard her say. 'The child'? Honestly!

Perhaps I will wear the red floral dress you bought me for my birthday a few years ago so she is convinced she can leave me here. Then I will have my peace back. I blame you entirely, Thomas Wilson. Until you went missing she was perfectly content to leave me be, even with you so far from home. But since you refuse to be found, she has been smothering me. She will not let me out of her sight and she fusses and barks instructions and has even, can you believe it, started looking for potential suitors for me. Just in case the worst should come to pass.

Yes, I think I will have to fool her into going with Father.

Happy Anniversary, my love.

I will bring more cheer when next I write, but for now I cannot disguise how desperately I miss you and how wretchedly my whole being aches each day that passes with no news.

My days are empty and nights bitter without you here with me.
You must return to me soon.

Forever yours,

Ivy

Eight

The first attempt at chocolate-chip cookie dough ended up in the bin. How could flour, sugar and butter taste so bad? She'd followed the recipe, hadn't she? She looked again at the app on her phone. One cup of flour. Check. One hundred and twenty-five grams of butter. Check. One cup of sugar. Che— Hang on. She picked up the canister of sugar and tasted its contents. Argh. Salt. No wonder.

'Damn it.' She threw the tea towel onto the table.

'Anyone home?' A familiar voice trilled down the hallway.

Nicole went over to the front door. 'Come in.'

Mandy reached up to wipe the butter out of Nicole's hair. 'Oh my. What's happened here?'

'I was trying to bake. For you, actually. To say sorry for running out on you yesterday.'

'Oh, Nicole. No need for that.' Mandy shook her head. 'It was an emotional day for both of us. What did you make?'

Nicole frowned.

'Oh.' Mandy steered Nicole to the kitchen. 'Oh,' she said again, taking in the mess. 'Just as well I brought these with me.'

She held up the Tupperware container she had with her. It was filled with lamingtons.

After cleaning up the kitchen, they went out to the verandah. Nicole brought a pot of tea and mugs, while Mandy carried a plate piled high with her lamingtons.

'These are delicious,' Nicole said, grabbing one – her second – and stuffing her mouth as they sat down.

'A bit of a specialty of mine,' Mandy said. 'Once you've got the sponge right, the secret's in the consistency of the icing.' She winked.

'I'll take your word for it. Not much of a domestic goddess here. As you saw. Baking never was my strong point.'

'Happy to show you someday.'

'I may just take you up on that.' Nicole smiled warmly.

They finished their lamingtons in silence and Nicole worked up the courage to explain herself. She knew it wasn't necessary, but she owed Mandy something. Just, how could she explain anything, without explaining everything?

'I, ah, really did want to say sorry.' She took a deep breath.

Mandy's expression was soft and warm. 'Honey, you don't need to explain yourself to me. I suspect there's a whole lot more going on with you than a bit of an interest in a woman who's been dead for a few decades.'

Nicole raised an eyebrow.

'I read people. It's a gift of mine. Besides, no one with their life totally together would have taken this renovation deal.' She laughed gently.

Nicole's life was certainly not together.

'Look. It's not my place to pry, but if you ever feel like talking about it, you always have me. If not, well, we've plenty of other excitement to keep us busy round here. This afternoon's match, for example . . .'

Nicole laughed out loud.

'You will join us, won't you?' Mandy asked.

'Well, I am the lucky socks,' Nicole replied with a shrug. 'What choice do I have?' She grinned.

'Attagirl.' Mandy chuckled.

'Carn, Rangers!' screamed a man standing right behind Nicole on the hill. The deafening cheer went up from the crowd as Danny crossed over the try line, extending their lead beyond the reach of the soon-to-be beaten Giants of neighbouring town Glensdale, some hundred clicks south of the cove. Some of the Giants supporters, unable to watch their team lose, started packing up their deckchairs and picnic blankets to head back to their homes. Nicole had never heard of the town, but she knew it would be a sad place to be tonight.

'Never were a loyal crowd, that lot.' Cheryl shook her head.

'That's one sure thing about the cove,' Mandy said. 'No matter how far down we're beaten, we stick by our boys to the end.'

She waved to Trevor, who looked up from the sideline with a triumphant grin across his face.

'No matter how bloody embarrassing it is,' Mandy whispered in Nicole's ear.

When the boys came off at full time, met with cheers and pats on the backs, they headed straight for Nicole.

Surrounding her in a happy huddle, they cheered. 'Three cheers for Nicole. Hurrah, hurrah, hurrah.'

Danny lingered as the rest of the players went to join their families.

'Thanks for coming today. As far as that lot are concerned you're our official lucky charm now.' He winked. 'Not sure they would have gone into the game confident if you weren't here. Come celebrate with us at the pub, hey?'

Nicole nodded.

Down at The Royal, Trevor handed Nicole and Mandy a glass of wine each. The whole team raised their glasses in salute with a chant of 'Rangers rule, Rangers rule', until they both raised their own in response.

'Hurrah!' came the collective shout.

From the jukebox in the corner, Nicole heard the first few bars of 'Brown-Eyed Girl' ring out. Trevor gave Mandy a cheeky grin and danced towards her. As one, the crowd parted and he took Mandy by the hands, leading her to the middle of the room.

As Nicole watched the couple that had caught everyone's attention, Danny made his way over to her. He'd gone home and changed into dark jeans, a grey T-shirt and black leather jacket. Nicole couldn't help but notice he cut a rather dashing silhouette. How had he managed that so quickly?

'Cute, aren't they?' he said as he edged beside her.

'Yeah, they make a pretty good case for the true love fanatics.'

'Not a believer?'

'A love agnostic, shall we say?' She gave a half-smile then became suddenly very aware of Danny's warm body beside her. She knew she had to change the conversation, retreat, but how? Before she could get too flustered, Danny saved her from an awkward attempt at small talk.

'So, how are you liking life at the cove?'

'It's very different from Sydney, but I can't complain about how welcoming everyone has been.'

'Yeah, we're a friendly lot. Bit strange sometimes.' He laughed, nodding his head towards George trying to remove one of the young boys hanging upside down from the ancient bar top.

'Well, weird isn't restricted to the country.' Nicole shrugged.

'No. Never really spent much time in the city myself, but I reckon you've got your fair share of crazy there.'

'True.'

'Have you got much writing done since you've been here? Mandy's hoping you will write her into your next book, I think.' Danny turned his body ever so slightly towards Nicole and bent to speak close enough to her ear for her to hear above the crowd. He smelled of orange and cinnamon.

She coughed. 'Oh. Um. I'm not really . . .'

'You're not writing?'

'No.'

'Why?'

'I'm not sure I've got anything else to say.' She had been filling up her notebook with questions and thoughts, yes. But she was still a long way off finding inspiration to actually write.

'Maybe all you need is time.'

'Time?' Nicole frowned.

'Joseph Heller took thirteen years to get his second book out after *Catch-22*.'

Nicole laughed. 'And no one can remember the name of it.'

'Maybe not. But that's the only literary reference I have, I'm afraid.' Danny grinned.

Nicole stared into his green eyes and felt her cheeks flush.

'But I guess if writing is no longer your thing, you could take up flipping houses.'

'Doing what to houses?'

'Flipping them. Buying cheap, renovating and then selling for a profit.'

Nicole shook her head. 'I think you're overestimating my renovation abilities there.' And my budget, she thought.

'Well, unlike literature, this is an area I do know something about, and for a rookie renovator, what you've achieved so far is pretty impressive.' A smile spread across his face and Nicole was rendered speechless.

'You okay?' he asked, touching her forearm.

'Yeah.' She scrambled to change the topic. 'They're just so cute.' She looked at Mandy and Trevor, who were wrapping up their performance.

'Shall we outdo them?' His eyes were bright with daring.

'Not possible. That would be like competing with —'

'Fred and Ginger?'

Nicole nodded.

'Perhaps not, then.' Danny winked. 'Can I get you another drink? You've hardly touched that one.'

'No, I'm done for the night.' The last thing she needed right now was alcohol to cloud her judgement.

'Water? Squash? Cup of tea?'

He was looking so earnestly at her. She couldn't keep rebuffing. 'I could do with a water, I guess.'

She watched him as he walked to the bar and let out a long sigh.

'Oh boy, that song is going to kill me one of these days,' Mandy said as she appeared at Nicole's side.

'If it's any consolation, you looked great.'

'Much consolation, indeed.' Mandy fanned her cheeks with her hands.

'There you go, ladies.' Danny returned with two glasses of water. 'Compliments of the winning captain.'

'Last of the big spenders, this one.' Mandy laughed.

'But you love me anyway.' Danny gave her a kiss on the cheek.

'True.'

'I'll leave you ladies to it, then.' He slipped back through the crowd and rejoined his teammates seamlessly.

Nicole coughed and moved her attention back to Mandy. 'You've done that dance a few times, I take it?'

'More than a few. It's kind of our song.' She grinned. 'Every time it plays Trev takes me for a spin like we're teenagers again.'

'Hang on,' Nicole said. 'You have blue eyes.'

'Yep.'

'Then how come . . .'

'Well, Trevor believed for years the words were "bright-eyed girl" and when we first started going out he'd sing it to me. I didn't have the heart to correct him. He was so darn cute and it was only when he decided that it should be our wedding song and went looking for a copy of it that he realised.'

'Oh no.' Nicole raised her hand to her chest.

'Bless his cotton socks, he was so upset. But I still thought of it as our song, you know, and in the end we did it anyway. During the wedding dance everybody shouted out "bright" whenever "brown" was sung. It turned out to be pretty special.' She smiled fondly.

Someone put another song on the jukebox and pockets of friends started singing when the chorus of 'What's My Scene' started.

Happy noise filled the pub and Nicole was glad there was no more chance to talk.

She leaned in closer to Mandy's ear. 'I might call it a night.'

'Are you sure?'

Nicole nodded.

'Why don't I pop round on Wednesday and give you your first cooking lesson? I'm off work.'

'Sounds great.'

'Done. Night.' Mandy gave Nicole a parting kiss on the cheek.

Lying in bed, Nicole tossed and turned. She could still feel the touch of Danny's hand on her arm, still feel his warm breath in her ear. But it was too soon. She wasn't ready for this.

Anyway, maybe she was misreading the whole situation. Why would someone like Danny be interested in her? If there was one thing she'd learned from her previous life, it was that feelings couldn't be trusted.

Ever.

August, Last Year

Nicky had a mission.

If she'd learned anything these past few months since her spectacularly silent fallout with Jane, it was what she really wanted. And what she really wanted was to finally get married to Mark.

Every time she tried to raise the topic of setting a date, he deflected with one excuse or another. He was working on a big case; one of the partners had taken extended leave; he wanted time to just enjoy being a couple before the drama that came with organising a wedding; didn't she think she should get her second book finished before the distraction of a wedding took over their lives. Every time he made his case he was logical and intelligent and convincing.

But when did logic come into love? It certainly didn't for Nicky.

She knew she wasn't going to best him in an argument. There was no point even trying that route. She had to find another way.

As she sat under her Moreton Bay fig in Hyde Park, she watched the people walking by, wondering how each one of them would handle the predicament she found herself in. The old man walking his terrier might take a pragmatic approach and decide that the marriage didn't matter as long as they were together. The young woman jogging past her, iPhone strapped to her upper arm, might issue an ultimatum. The middle-aged woman dressed in a grey skirt-suit talking into an earpiece might just go ahead and organise the wedding regardless and simply tell the groom to turn up on the day.

Nicky chuckled to herself. Perhaps that was not the best approach to take. She knew she had to do something to shake Mark out of his complacency. But what?

A woman pushing a pram stopped and sat beside her on the bench. Carefully she lifted her baby out and sat him in her lap. She bounced him gently as he looked with wide eyes out onto the world passing before him.

Nicky felt a soft tug at her heart. They had talked about children. Often. They'd discussed having three or four and how they couldn't wait to start their family.

Could she just let nature take its course? Let fate decide?

No. As desperate as she was to marry Mark, she couldn't get pregnant to force his hand. That wouldn't be fair.

What she could do, maybe, was use it as leverage in a discussion. Appeal to his paternal instincts. Given her family history if they wanted three or four kids, then it might not be wise to wait too long. Maybe this avenue was the one that could win her the argument.

She spent the rest of the day preparing the perfect evening. The apartment was immaculate. She bought fresh flowers for the table and ordered in Mark's favourite meal, including dessert, from the little Portuguese bistro round the block. For the finishing touch she decided to wear her blue dress – his favourite.

She was surprised by her own eloquence and poise as she made her case to Mark. He dug in to his lemon meringue pie, and then sat back and listened to her reasoning.

'So, that's what tonight is all about, then?' He crossed his arms in front of his chest. 'Impressive argument, counsellor. How about this? In twelve months, I'll have been partner long enough to be firmly entrenched, you'll have had plenty of time to finish your next book, and we should be in a position then to get married.'

'So, we're setting the date? Twelve months from today?'

'Looks like it.'

She ran around the table and hugged him tightly. 'Oh, I can't wait to be Mrs Avery and have little Marks running around the place.'

Nicky hadn't slept so well in months. With the issue of the wedding date sorted, she'd slipped into a deep sleep and every morning for the last week, she'd needed her alarm to wake her up at five. She sat at her computer, the morning sun filtering through the window warming her back. Despite a week of blissful sleep, for the last few days the words remained stuck somewhere in her mind, inaccessible. She knew what was wrong. She couldn't stop thinking about wedding plans. And wedding plans meant thinking about the bridal party. And that meant thinking about Jane.

She hadn't tried to make contact with her friend since seeing the photo of her and Miles on Facebook, but whenever she thought about her own wedding, she couldn't help but want Jane by her side. Maybe this was the olive branch they needed.

Her hands shook as she pulled out her phone.

'Jane, I think . . .'

Delete.

'Hey, Jane, just thought . . .'

Delete.

Argh. The right words were not easy to find. Maybe there were no right words. Maybe there were just honest words.

'Jane. I miss you. If I upset you, I'm sorry. I didn't mean to. Mark and I have set a date and I really want you to be part of my wedding. Please respond.'

With the text sent, Nicky felt a sense of relief.

The words flowed more easily then and by the afternoon she felt she had a handle on the beginning of her new manuscript. She made a cuppa and sat on the balcony of the apartment looking out to the street below. A fire engine screamed past, people rushed along the footpath with their heads down, taxis beeped their horns.

Mark would be pleased with her writing progress today. Every morning as he left for work he'd say it was a great day to write. Every night he'd come home and ask how she did. When she moaned she had writer's block he'd say, 'If you didn't dwell so much on the block, you might be able to shake it off.' When she scowled at him in response he'd embrace her. 'I just know how talented you are and I can't wait to read your next book.'

She really needed to think of a way to thank him. He believed in her. Her writing. It was only a month till his birthday and she wanted to get him something wonderful.

After an hour searching the net for unique gifts, everything seemed just a little bit naff. Then it hit her. A holiday. A mini weekend getaway somewhere romantic, somewhere exclusive.

She researched locations and hotels and in the end decided on the stunning mountain lodge overlooking a valley in the Blue Mountains. It was a lot more than she would normally be comfortable spending, but she had to make this birthday special. It wouldn't hurt to dip into their savings a little.

Her phone beeped with a text and her heart soared with the hope it might be Jane.

But it was Mark. His late meeting tonight had been cancelled. He was going to grab a quick drink at the office and be home earlier than expected.

Well, at least that was something.

She turned back to the computer screen and clicked the 'book' button for the hotel. Yes, this was just what they both needed.

At the checkout page her debit card was declined. Strange. There should be more than enough to cover it. She tried again. Nope.

She flicked through her diary, looking for her internet banking details. She never used it. She had the debit card for day-to-day expenses and all their bills were set up to be direct payments. What did she need with internet banking?

When she found the login and password, disguised as a phone number, she loaded the bank's site. The little red circle spun round as she waited and then she pulled up their joint account.

She frowned. Maybe she was looking at the wrong page. No. She was in the right section. But that couldn't be right. There should have been something in the vicinity of twenty thousand dollars in there. But she looked at the screen trying to compute the information in front of her.

The balance of the account was only five hundred dollars. Where had their money gone?

Nicky tried ringing Mark for the fourth time. No answer. She sent another text and tried to make it sound more urgent without sounding too panicky. The news had been full of stories lately about cybercrimes and identity theft. She felt sick in her stomach at the thought.

After what felt like hours, he finally arrived home.

'Honey, something terrible's happened. Someone's hacked into our account and taken our money.' She ran up to him.

'What are you talking about?'

'I wanted to do something nice for your birthday . . .' her words spilled forth desperately as she tried to calm her fear. 'We need to call the bank.'

Mark sat down on the sofa and patted the cushion next to him. Nicky lowered herself beside him. Why was he being so calm about this?

'Nicky, our money is perfectly safe. I transferred it into a high-interest bearing account. So we can get that deposit sooner. We only keep enough in that account now for daily expenses.'

'What? When did that happen?'

He patted her knee. 'When we first discussed your prize money. I told you Gregory had a financial adviser. He said this was the best way to do it.'

Nicky racked her brain, trying to recall the discussion they first had about it. All she could remember, though, was leaving it up to Mark to organise.

He frowned. 'The high-interest account isn't locked. We can transfer money back anytime we like.'

'How do I do that?'

'Well, we have to go through the financial adviser. But with a bit of notice he can do it. There's plenty of money in my account to pay for a holiday though.'

'Oh. But I wanted to do this for you. Use my money.'

Mark took her hands in his. 'Nicky, you seem to keep forgetting we're engaged. There's no mine or yours. It's all ours.'

Nicky shrugged. It wasn't quite the same.

'Why don't we talk to the adviser tomorrow and transfer some money out? We'll lose a bit of interest, but we'll make it back up in the long run.'

'No. That doesn't make any sense.' She shook her head. There was no point losing interest.

Mark told her how touched he was that she would think to do this for him, and suggested they book the holiday anyway, using money from his everyday account and treat it like a pre-wedding honeymoon.

This wasn't what she'd been going for, but the thought of getting away together was too enticing and she agreed. Next year she'd come up with a better plan for his birthday.

The following Friday Nicky stood at the bar at Mark's firm's party while he worked the room. She looked around at the familiar yet distant faces. She knew the names of some and had been to dinner once or twice with a couple of them. The rest she wouldn't have known if they were employees or clients or random people off the street. And none of them made an effort to talk to her.

The two gentlemen in grey suits next to her were talking about some case they were working on. She tried to listen in. Anything would have been better than the silence she was trapped in. But they were speaking so low, she couldn't make out a word.

She ordered another drink. Never a big drinker, Mark's work dos always saw her indulge a little more than usual, just to help her get through the long boring hours.

'Excuse me?' A young man, mid-twenties maybe, came up beside her. 'I can't help but notice you here on your own.'

'Oh. Hi. Just keeping out of the way. Too much shop talk for me.'

'I know what you mean.'

The young man was a client of the firm. Or rather his family was, and he was there to 'represent', he said. He was a sweet man, and had Nicky laughing before long. It was a welcome change from the rest of the night.

'And who are you with tonight? You're clearly not a lawyer.'

Nicky took that as a compliment and smiled. 'My fiancé.' She pointed over to Mark.

'Ah. Avery the Assassin.'

Nicky had heard the nickname before. Every case that went to court, he won. Most opposing counsel tried to settle before it got that far.

Mark slipped his way through the press of people towards them. 'How's your night?' He put his arm around her waist and pulled her in tightly. 'Having a lovely chat, were we?'

Nicky turned back to the young man, but he'd gone. 'Seemed like a nice enough guy.'

Mark shook his head. 'Just goes to show you never can tell. He's after his family's money and will do anything to get it. Nasty man, really.'

'But he seemed so nice.'

Mark raised an eyebrow. 'If you weren't so naïve, maybe you'd see people for who they are. Look what happened with Jane.'

Ouch. That nerve was still raw.

'What do you say we head home?'

Nicky was relieved. She wasn't sure how much more of this party she could take.

*

The next day, in the early light of morning, Nicky woke and got ready for the day. Today she was determined to attack the writer's block that had been plaguing her. But first she needed to tidy the kitchen. Twice. Then she rearranged the pantry and went to put the washing on. The apartment was never so spotless as when she was struggling to write.

Just after ten, with no new words written, but lots of 'essential' research done on the net, Nicky started making Mark's breakfast. The smell of bacon would rouse him for sure.

He padded into the kitchen, already dressed.

'Sorry, Nicky. I've got to go catch up on some paperwork in the office.' He kissed her on the forehead.

'Wait . . . I —'

But he was out the door before she could get her words out.

Nicky sat at the dining table looking about the perfectly clean apartment. Ever since she'd given up her job at the café, Saturday mornings were always reserved for a slow breakfast and not getting dressed till lunchtime. She would get a couple of hours writing done, would make Mark breakfast and then they'd while away the day together.

She fiddled with the placemats in the middle of the table. She rearranged the cushions on the couch.

She checked her phone. A week and no response from Jane.

Well, she guessed she had her answer then. Jane wanted nothing more to do with her. Her heart felt heavy.

The only family Nicky had left now was Mark.

The clock ticked loudly on the wall.

Nine

Memory was a funny thing. Sometimes it hit you when you least expected it to. Sometimes it came when you were perfectly prepared. Sometimes it came in fleeting snapshots, a face here, a feeling there, never quite revealing the complete picture. Sometimes the whole sorry saga played out in your mind and nothing you could do could stop it.

Sometimes Nicole just wished she could forget.

No one was due to come and help her today, and for that she was thankful. Mostly. How was it that she could want so desperately to be alone, yet at the same time fear loneliness?

If only there was a way to be alone, without actually being alone.

Perhaps there was.

She prepared a thermos of hot chocolate. It was a risk, she knew. But she weighed it up and decided it was worth taking.

A gentle breeze rustled the gum leaves overhead as she meandered down the sloping hill towards the boatshed. The sea was impossibly blue and still, and the early morning showed promise of a warm autumn day to follow once the crisp air was heated by the rising sun.

She approached the boatshed. Oh, this was madness. What was she doing?

'Charlie?' As she called out his name, apprehension rose in her. Yes, he was a safer option for company than Mandy, with all her questions and insight. And he was certainly safer than Danny, with his green eyes and heat-inducing touch. But seriously? This was what she was reduced to now?

Chances were he'd simply scream at her to go away.

'You're back.' He grumbled as he opened the wooden door to the boatshed.

'Yes. I wondered maybe . . . if you would like . . .'

His expression was unreadable. Come out with it and ask, or run away – her two options.

'. . . I brought hot chocolate.' She held up her thermos and smiled what must have been a ridiculous grin.

Charlie threw his arms open in an arc, inviting her into his grounds.

Nicole hesitated, only a moment, then moved through the gap in the fence. Charlie motioned to the eastern side of the boatshed.

The wooden bench glowed golden brown in the morning sun.

'No!'

Nicole dropped her thermos.

'You don't get to sit there.'

He reached beside the bench and pulled out an old, collapsible deckchair. The blue and white striped canvas was stained and the wood faded, but it looked sturdy enough.

To her surprise, Charlie ducked back inside and pulled out another deckchair for himself and placed it a few feet away from hers. Why would he so lovingly care for a bench that he didn't sit on? She could ask him, she supposed, but people didn't go round taking care of a piece of furniture when everything else around was decaying. Not unless there was something deeply significant going on. And it was far too early to be digging into personal stuff. Another question for her notebook.

'Would you like some?' She picked up the thermos.

'Hot chocolate tastes like mud.'

'Still,' she persevered. 'Better than the cookies I tried to make.'

'Humph,' came the response.

They sat in silence, Nicole unsure where she could go with this impossible man. In the end, she resorted to cheap clichés.

'It's a beautiful day, don't you think?'

A single nod in answer.

'Do the winters get cold here?' she asked.

A slight shake of the head.

'I've heard midsummer can be brutal.'

This was met with a shrug.

'Seems like a nice place.'

Another shrug.

'How long have you lived at Rosella Cove?'

'Long enough.'

Nicole smiled. She'd finally got an answer out of him. 'Friendly neighbours.'

'Humph.'

Perhaps she saw the slightest twitch at the edge of Charlie's mouth, but she couldn't be sure. She took a big sip of hot chocolate as she watched the seagulls gliding on the breeze.

She stole brief glances to her right as she drank, noting in Charlie what would have been a quite imposing physical presence in his younger days. His large hands and broad shoulders suggested he'd been a strong man once. Beneath his wild beard Nicole could see a once-handsome face and she wondered how he could end up so totally alone in the world. How did *anyone* end up so totally alone in the world?

Charlie rose.

Nicole got up too, taking his lead that the morning was over.

'Stay,' he said and she sat back down.

He returned some minutes later carrying a tattered box with him in one hand and a small, portable table in the other, then sat down.

'You play?' He laid a brown Scrabble board on the tray table between them, its edges ragged and torn.

'Sure.'

'You any good?' Charlie looked her directly in the eye.

'I'm not bad,' she answered honestly.

Her dad had been a huge fan of the game and they'd often played. She couldn't imagine Charlie being anywhere near as good as her father, though.

She picked up her seven yellowed tiles with faded lettering. X, q, e, t, two s's, and an a. She ran through the possibilities in her mind, discarding the shorter easier ones – axe, set, tea – looking for harder ones. Texas was there – what a shame proper nouns weren't allowed. Qats was possible, but she wasn't sure Charlie would be familiar with the Arabian plant and she didn't want to get in a fight. She decided to let him lead the way instead of starting the traditional way of drawing tiles.

'Age before beauty,' she suggested.

'I'm definitely the former, but you?' He looked her up and down.

Was that a quip? Well, that was something. 'Right then.' Nicole flexed her fingers. 'Gloves are officially off.' She grinned.

A few minutes in it became obvious to Nicole that she should not have underestimated Charlie. She wished she'd used qats when she'd had the chance.

'L, e, a, r, n,' Nicole spelled out her fifth word. 'Five points, double word score. Did you know that up until the nineteenth century it was perfectly acceptable to say 'he learned me how to read'?' She added her points to her score.

'Hogwash.' Charlie stared at his tiles.

'True story.'

He ignored her.

'j, o, v, i, a, l,' Charlie placed his tiles on the board. 'Sixteen points, triple on the j, thirty-two.'

'You would be jovial about that.' Nicole shook her head as she added up his running total.

'From the Latin jovialis, of Jupiter, the planet said to exert a happy influence.'

Nicole stared at Charlie.

'Problem?'

'I'm just a bit surprised you know that.'

'Why?'

'I just . . . no reason, I guess.' She had no answer. Charlie could have been anybody before he'd ended up here. A professor, a carpenter, a scientist, a footy player.

She searched the board for possible openings.

The sun reached higher in the sky, casting small shadows across the ever more crowded board and Nicole knew she was in trouble.

'Hanged, another eleven points,' Nicole announced, but it wasn't enough. 'Well, I take my hat off to you, Charlie. Good win.' She helped him pack away the game. As Charlie lifted the board, it tore some more.

'You're not too bad yourself,' he conceded. 'Thought you might be all right at this.'

'Really?'

Charlie shrugged.

'So how is it you can read me so well after one meeting?'

He raised an eyebrow.

'Okay, a couple of accidental bumping-intos.'

'Practice.'

Nicole looked at him, her brow furrowed.

'The less you're seen, the more you see.' He shrugged again.

'Ah, he's a poet and a philosopher.' Nicole exaggerated a bow as she got up.

'Humph.' Charlie shook his head as he pushed past her.

'Maybe I'll see you next week,' Nicole said, as Charlie waited outside his door for her to pass.

He didn't say another word.

Back at the house, Nicole started sanding the floorboards in the living room with the sanding and polishing machine thing she'd hired from Trevor's. As she made the soothing circular motions around the room, she replayed the few hours she'd just spent with Charlie.

By most people's standards the morning would have been considered a disaster, but she'd found Charlie's quiet, prickly company quite comforting. Exactly what she'd been hoping for. Now what did that say about her?

She stifled a laugh.

She was happily having non-conversations with an irate hermit, and her most intimate relationship was with a mysterious woman who'd been dead for four decades. It was not exactly the life she'd imagined for herself, but here she was.

Halfway around the large room she dropped the handle of the sanding and polishing machine thing and crouched down to turn the power off. She could feel the laughter bubbling up inside and, given Trevor's strict safety instructions, she thought this would be the best option.

She sat on the floor and allowed the laughter to escape her lips freely. Tears began to roll down her cheeks and she wiped them away between chuckles, shaking her head.

'Life rarely goes according to plan.' Mark's voice sounded in her head.

'Well, you sure got that right,' Nicole said out loud with a laugh.

She lay back on the floor with her arms flung out to the side. Eventually, she regained composure and stood up, brushing the last rogue tear away.

'What a mess.' She sighed loudly and turned the machine on again.

By eight o'clock Nicole had finished sanding the floors in the living room and fell into bed exhausted without having dinner. She rubbed her temples, then her aching shoulders. She closed her eyes and it wasn't long before she fell into the deepest sleep she'd had since her life turned upside down. She wasn't fitful. She didn't have strange, fragmented dreams where her life played out before her as she sat watching, silently screaming. She didn't wake at one, or at three, or at five. She simply slept.

And slept.

ㅤㅤㅤㅤㅤㅤㅤㅤ⁓

Charlie shuffled around the boatshed in the dark. That woman was so perplexing. He shook his head. Why would she bother to sit there half the morning then not even probe him with the annoying questions he'd been expecting? He'd waited for her to deafen him with endless pointless chatter, or purge her own life story as the lonely are wont to do, especially to strangers.

Not that he minded, of course. In fact, he was relieved not to have to listen to her waffle. But it was confusing. People were usually predictable. It was their only saving grace. They see an old man who lives alone and keeps to himself, they taunt him and treat him like a freak show exhibit. They see an old man who lives alone and keeps to himself, they suspect him of whatever unsolved crimes have been committed in the area.

Charlie could predict their callousness and judgement, and therefore shield himself from them.

Not that he was above judgement. That time would come one day, and when it did he'd accept his fate without fuss. But until then, he was sentenced to this shadow life.

He pottered about the boatshed, trying to shake the uneasy feeling Nicole's presence caused in him. He'd wanted this, after all. But he hadn't anticipated being so put out by her unpredictable behaviour – it was making him very uncomfortable.

Perhaps she'd have all the questions for him next time she came to visit. This morning was a Trojan horse visit, to convince him to let his guard down. Well, he wouldn't allow that.

He sat on the end of his dusty old bed, surrounded by the shelving he used to divide the open space inside the boatshed. In his hand he held a photo. He had set things in motion now. And once you did that, there was no turning back. It was time to be a man. For the first time in his life.

He knew what he had to do. He just hoped he had the strength to follow it through. Courage could be a bastard of a thing to find. Especially for a coward like himself.

He took one last look at the photo. The young woman stared back at him, her dark eyes warm and trusting. Misplaced trust she would regret. The boy in her lap laughed, his blue eyes dancing, piercing through Charlie's guilty heart. He flipped the photo over. Maybe some pasts were too painful to face.

———

Nicole hummed along to the radio as she tidied the kitchen in anticipation of Mandy's arrival, dancing as she went. Maybe it was the fact she'd actually slept properly for the last three nights. Maybe it was the calm that had come over her since that morning she played Scrabble with Charlie at the beginning of the week. All she knew was she felt lighter than she had in months.

Finally the kitchen was spotless for Nicole's first cooking lesson – as spotless as it could be in its state of disrepair. Trevor had fixed the oven so it was usable, though it would still need replacing. Nicole had been avoiding a full kitchen refit, but with the rest of the cottage now taking shape, she couldn't put it off any longer. The renovation in this room would start in two weeks.

'Yoo-hoo!' Mandy's voice called out, right on time.

'In here,' she answered.

'Are you ready to start our first baking lesson?' Mandy asked, waving a cookbook at Nicole.

Nicole shrugged. 'Are you sure we shouldn't wait till the new kitchen is in?'

Mandy shook her head. 'There's no time like the present. And we're starting pretty basic, so a basic kitchen will do just fine. Though I bet you can't wait till this is all spic and span.'

It wasn't really something Nicole was fussed about one way or another. It was the room she used least in the cottage. Even the gorgeous new kitchen she'd acquired in Sydney from moving in with Mark had barely seen her cook.

But normal people liked nice kitchens and the renovation wouldn't be complete without a total overhaul of this room.

'Well, yes,' she lied. 'Then maybe I can down tools for a bit and take a break from the reno. Just for a few days.'

'Picking up a bit of lingo from Trev and Danny there, I hear.' Mandy laughed.

'Apparently. Next thing you know I'll be walking round with builders' crack.' Nicole realised her rudeness immediately. 'Sorry, I didn't mean . . .'

'Don't be silly. It's a stereotype for a reason. And between you and me, I've had to tell that husband of mine to pull up his King Gees more than once.'

Mandy opened her book, a diary stuffed full of handwritten recipes and magazine cut-outs, to the Anzac biscuit page. 'As I said, I thought we'd start with something basic and work our way up.'

'I didn't think you'd need instructions.' Nicole raised an eyebrow.

'I don't. I've made these so many times I could make them in my sleep. You, on the other hand, are a different matter.'

'True.'

'Put this on,' Mandy said, and handed her an apron.

'Nigella doesn't wear one.'

'Well, when you become a domestic goddess, you can wear whatever you like. Cook in a bikini for all I care. Until then, trust me.'

She thrust the apron into Nicole's hands. She also handed her a small box neatly wrapped and tied with a white ribbon. 'I thought you could use these.'

Nicole opened the gift. Inside was a set of measuring cups. She let out a laugh. 'Thanks.'

Turned out Mandy was right about the apron. Nicole was covered in flour and coconut by the time the trays made it into the oven. Together they cleaned up the mess she'd made on the bench and washed up the dishes.

'How'd you get to be such a good cook?' Nicole asked as they put the kettle on, anticipating the warm biscuits that would come out shortly.

'Mum taught me. She was tops.'

'My mum tried to teach me, but I wasn't interested. I always had my head in a book.'

'It's never too late to learn.'

'From her it is.'

Mandy stopped pouring the hot water into the teacups.

'My mum died three and a half years ago,' Nicole explained.

'Oh, I'm so sorry.' Mandy laid a gentle hand on Nicole's arm.

'Thanks. Dad was already gone, a year before that. It took a long while to adjust to the fact they weren't there anymore. Especially Mum. I'm still not sure I have.' She shrugged.

Mandy nodded. 'My dad died when I was twenty. I still miss him every day. It's kind of like, I don't know . . .'

'Like the whole world shifted slightly left, but you stayed put.'

Mandy squeezed her hand. In silence they drank their tea and waited.

The timer dinged.

'Are we ready?' Nicole asked, pleased the shrill chime had interrupted them. She pulled out the baking tray. 'They look okay,' she said.

'They look great.'

'Today the humble cookie, tomorrow soufflés and crème brûlée.' Nicole flicked her tea towel in a flourish and both women burst out laughing.

'So, Nicole,' Mandy said, when they both calmed down. 'I was wondering if you might like to come to trivia next Thursday night.'

Nicole winced at the thought, but tried to cover it up with a nonchalant expression. Going to the football was one thing, but trivia was much more intimate. She'd have to have conversations with strangers. She wasn't ready for that.

'Look, no pressure. But we are a fun team. It's me and Cheryl – you remember her from the hardware store, Jacqui from the post office and Danny.'

It was a very small group, but at least they weren't total strangers. Maybe she could handle this.

'We used to have one more, but the Telford girl's gone off to uni, so you'd be making up numbers and really helping us out. Only if you want to, of course. Like I said, we do have a lot of fun.' She stopped, a pleading, hopeful look in her eyes. Nicole felt her resolve waning.

'What do you say?'

After Mandy left, Nicole sanded the hallway and then cleaned up the dust. So much dust! If she ever renovated another house, this would be one job she'd want to pay someone to do. She didn't have the money for that now though. The stipend was thin and she had to do as much as she could herself.

She took a long hot shower, washing dust out of her hair and curled up on the sofa for her nightly dose of Ivy.

12th December, 1941
My Dearest Tom,
Today I spent the afternoon with Lucy. She made tea, even though I insisted there was no need, and she fussed about terribly.

I took some lamington cakes with me. Though, as I suspected, she did not touch them. Why is it we think food and tea will make everything all right again? What could possibly make this situation all right again?

Lucy wore that vacantly brave expression we all wear when we have to keep on going even though we feel dead inside. I know that expression very well.

You have been missing now for so long, my love, it is hard to maintain hope. There was a story in the papers a few weeks ago of a soldier being found in a tiny village in France, two years after he was separated from his platoon. He had no memory of who he was and it was only chance that another division was passing by and stopped to take water that they found him.

Whether it is a tale of truth, I do not know. But chance and hope are all that I have to hang on to.

Just before I took my leave of Lucy and our uneasy silence, I reached out and took her hand in mine. She must have seen something familiar in me, a mirror of her own feelings perhaps, because her bottom lip began to tremble. I cradled her cheek in my other hand and her tears burst forth.

We held each other tightly and sobbed into each other's shoulders. I do not know for how long. I do know that when we both regained our composure our silence was no longer awkward, but comforting. It is strange how close you can feel to someone without exchanging words. I believe now, in each other's company, neither of us need put on the brave face we do with others to protect those around us from our grief.

She walked me to her porch and squeezed my hands as I left. Despite the heavy emotion of the afternoon, I felt somehow lighter as I walked down her path and out her gate. Even encountering Joan Wetherby did little to dim the only ray of brightness I have had recently. Naturally she was incapable of anything more than forced civility. I have never understood why that woman has always been so ill-tempered towards me. Towards everyone. The only kindness she has ever shown me is the time she left me flowers just after you went missing.

I must say goodnight, my sweet; ensure I have enough sleep to enable me to face another dark day without you. Wherever you are, I hope you can feel my unyielding love.

Forever yours,

Ivy

Ten

The following Thursday Nicole found herself stepping through The Royal's doors, wondering how she had let Mandy talk her into it.

Her pulse quickened and her chest tightened. Nope. She couldn't do it. She stopped and turned back round, hoping to get out of there before anyone saw her. The doors opened, as if by magic, offering her her freedom.

In walked Danny Temple.

'Thank God I'm not the only one who's late.' He smiled at Nicole, who stood frozen in terror.

'Ready?' Danny gently put his arm around her shoulder just long enough to steer her to the tables.

Everyone else in the group had already arrived and paired up into teams.

'I'm going to the bar,' Danny said to Nicole. 'What'll you have?'

'A lemon squash, please.'

He winked and turned away.

'So glad you could make it.' Mandy grinned broadly. 'You know everyone.'

Cheryl and Jacqui smiled at her.

'How are you travelling, Jacqui?' Nicole said. The poor woman looked so tired.

'Ready to offload this,' she replied, rubbing her bulging tummy. 'But,' a smile spread across her face, 'not long now. And with any luck, the boys will have paved the way, so to speak, and she'll slip right out.'

'So to speak.' Nicole grimaced.

Mandy smiled. 'Keep your legs crossed there, Jacqui.'

George brought over a bowl of wedges with sour cream and chilli sauce – a trivia night staple apparently. 'Jason will be starting the questions in one minute,' he said.

Jacqui grabbed Nicole's arm. 'We might just be starting something else. Now.'

Everyone looked at Jacqui, not quite comprehending what she'd said.

'She's coming.' She tapped her tummy.

Everyone stood up, chattering at once, trying to figure out what to do.

Jason, Jacqui's husband, who was about to jump on the microphone with his first question, saw what was happening and raced over.

'Here we go!' he called out as everyone cheered, grinning broadly as he escorted his wife out of the pub.

'Phone us,' called Mandy after them. 'Good luck.'

'A round on the house,' announced George. 'And all bets are closed.'

A cheer went up from the patrons and the trivia crew took their seats.

'Welcome to trivia night,' Cheryl said. 'Where anything can happen.'

*

No Trivia Master meant no trivia, but no one in the pub seemed concerned. They all hung about waiting on news from the hospital and George kept the drinks flowing. Less than half an hour later, Mandy's mobile rang. Danny helped her stand on the table so all the pub could hear her.

'A girl . . .'

'We knew that,' came a voice somewhere from behind.

'Three point two kilos. Both well . . .'

'And?' shouted several people from around the room.

'Drum roll, please,' she requested, and Danny, Trevor and Cheryl tapped the table.

'Amy Jewel! The prize goes to . . . me.' She took a deep bow as the winner of the wager.

There were cheers and groans and lots of clapping, and George produced the prize bottle of bubbles.

'Add a couple more bottles,' said Mandy, handing George some money. 'A glass for everyone.'

Only cheers were heard that time.

'That's the name she used to call her dolls when we were little,' Mandy whispered in Nicole's ear as she sat back down. Nicole laughed.

At the end of the night Nicole strolled back to the cottage alone. It was a beautiful evening, though cooler outside than she was expecting. The sky was oily black and the stars blinked brightly, sending secret coded messages to each other across the universe. Nicole breathed in the fresh, crisp air as a gentle breeze tugged at the loose tendrils of hair around her face. It still surprised her how different the air tasted here, so clean and light.

A rustle in the shadows of the streetlights made her jump.

'Sorry.' It was Danny. He was sitting in the gutter. 'I didn't mean to frighten you.'

Nicole relaxed. 'Too much to drink?'

'Not enough,' he mumbled.

'Isn't tonight supposed to be about celebrating?'

'For some.' Danny stood up.

He didn't wobble or stumble, so Nicole figured that he wasn't drunk.

'You're right.' He shook his head. 'You're right. Celebrate!'

'Are you okay?'

'Yep,' he said. 'Just being a miserable sod. Sorry.'

He strode off into the dark and Nicole continued on her way home, the happy glow of the night now a little dulled.

She'd never seen Danny look so miserable. And there was nothing about the night that she could tell that could have upset anyone. But then, as she knew well, no one really knew what went on behind people's perfect facades.

August, Last Year

Large bunches of colourful blossoms adorned the kitchen bench and the dining table. It was Mark's birthday, yet he was buying Nicky flowers. They were guilt flowers, she knew, for all the late nights he'd been putting in at the office. Still, they were beautiful.

Thankfully their weekend away was tomorrow. Just in time. They needed a chance to reconnect.

She bent over the instructions that supposedly told her how to put together her new desk. Another guilt present. She'd been wanting a new desk for ages, asking Mark for the money, but he'd always resisted. Now here it was. If only she could make head or tail of the confusing pictures that made up the instructions.

After two hours wrangling wood pieces and allen keys and

plastic plugs, Nicky won the battle of the desk and stood back to admire her handiwork. For someone who'd never put anything together in her life, she was pretty impressed with herself. The left leg was a little wonky, and she had screws and an oddly shaped piece of wood left over, but she was more than willing to ignore that fact.

Mark's key turned in the door. He'd come home early so they could get up to the mountains before dark.

'Hey.' He hugged her, and handed her a small pink box wrapped in a silver ribbon.

'What's this?'

'Just a little something for my love.'

Inside the box was a delicate diamond bracelet. 'It's beautiful.' Nicky smiled as Mark secured it to her wrist. 'Thank you.'

'Is this it?' Mark indicated the desk.

'Yep. Proud of me?'

Mark nodded. 'Is that the same desk you showed me you were going to get?'

Nicky had thought if she saved a little on the desk, then she could afford some special lingerie for the weekend.

Mark frowned. 'I think I like the other one better, but it's your desk, I suppose.'

'I can take it back,' she said.

He shook his head. 'As I said, it's your desk. Let's get on the road before it gets too late.'

They drove in silence and by the time they got to the winding mountain road an hour later the sun had begun to set.

'Can't be far now,' Nicole said, trying to break the quiet.

Mark reached over and took her hand. 'Twenty minutes.'

They turned off the road and drove down a long tree-lined driveway. In the clearing ahead was a stone and wood lodge nestled among tall mountain blue gums.

The hotel was even better than the pictures and as soon as they entered their room Nicky could feel the tension release from her body. Standing in front of the large windows, she looked out across the valley covered in eucalypts. The last rays of sunlight bathed the valley in a soft pink glow, and the only noise was the birds in the trees starting their evening song.

From behind her Mark wrapped his arms around her waist, propping his chin on her shoulder. 'It's beautiful. Thank you for organising this.' He kissed her neck. 'Let's get changed and head to dinner.'

Nicky slipped into her new black dress, especially bought for the occasion, and smoothed the fabric over her waist.

She twirled around in front of Mark.

'Stunning.' He smiled and extended his hand, and together they headed down to the restaurant.

The small dining room was lit by candles and fairy lights, and the tables were covered in white tablecloths with thick gold linen napkins folded into lotus flowers. The menu highlighted local ingredients, and everything sounded delicious.

Mark was telling Nicky about his latest case, as much as he was able to given the binds of confidentiality, and Nicky gave him an update on her manuscript. It was going painfully slowly, but she was starting to feel the story taking shape.

'That's good. When do you think it might be finished?'

Nicky shrugged. 'I don't know. Maybe the first draft by the wedding.'

'It will be great for you to get another book published. It'll do your self-esteem some good. Can't be easy coming up blank like you have been. You wouldn't want to be a one-book wonder.'

Nicky tilted her head. She wanted to get angry at him. Except he was right. It really hadn't been easy. She'd been struggling to get a handle on her next book for months now.

'You know I believe in you, princess. But if you don't believe in yourself, my faith won't mean anything.'

The waiter brought dessert – a decadent concoction of meringue and mousse and chocolate and raspberries that looked like a piece of art too good to eat. But Nicky did eat it and it was delicious. She ate half of Mark's, too.

They headed back to their room and Nicky ducked into the bathroom to change into the black lace lingerie set she'd bought. She felt a dull ache to the left of her stomach. Perhaps she shouldn't have stolen half of Mark's dessert.

She checked herself in the mirror, making sure she'd squeezed into the tiny pieces of lingerie completely.

Oh, God. A sharp pain made her double over, clutching her belly. She tried to stand, but wasn't able. The pain got worse.

'Mark!' she screeched.

He came rushing into the bathroom. She reached out her hand and everything went dark.

Eleven

25th January, 1942

My Dearest Tom,

What a joyful day it is, my love. Father has taken the post at the University of Sydney and I'm relieved that Mother has gone with him. It took quite the effort and some considerable acting skills I must say, to convince her I was 'well enough', as she put it, to be left alone. Well enough? As though I am suffering some kind of medical affliction!

You should have seen the performance I gave. I believe Ms Garbo herself would have been impressed. Naturally, I eased into the role of normality. Too big a turnaround too quickly would only have resulted in suspicion. I joined Mother on a few home visits first, accompanied her into town, and helped her in the garden. One step at a time.

It was my return to church at Christmas that ultimately swayed her. The depth to which I had to push my sorrow was almost too great as I sat in our pew without you. Father Anthony seemed genuinely happy to have me return to his flock at last, and I could not tell him that I doubted my return would be permanent. I am yet to resolve my anger with a God that deemed his need for our little one was greater than ours and he refuses yet to answer my prayers for your safe return. Nor can I bear to hear 'Amazing Grace' without conjuring thoughts of you holding my hand the way you always did when we sang it together. I am far from found, my darling.

However, I must endure this cruel pain. I overheard Mother asking, no, ordering, Father Anthony to keep her informed of my health. I wonder for how long I shall have to maintain my religious pretence.

I even attended the CWA's annual Christmas Fair. It was a more subdued version of the usual scene of wild children running from pony to slide and back again, and overly sweet jams in gingham-topped jars. But the battle of the sponges was centre stage again and caused this year's scandal. Joan Wetherby was mortified to lose her title to young Mrs Li – you can imagine the outrage that burned across her pale, pointed face. I do fear for Father Anthony's safety now, as he was the judge in question. Always was a man of impeccable taste, I say. The wood chop was a rather sobering affair with so few young men competing. Another reminder of the war.

It might surprise you that I did not enter my lamington cakes this year, but then, it may not. I told Mother I certainly would. I shall simply tell her I did not place, though she will not believe it. The only thing I have ever done to make her proud is winning that ribbon every year.

The entire town is trying so hard to continue as usual, and I wonder how many of our neighbours are pretending their lives are happy and normal. I doubt many can see through my own facade. Except Lucy. We share our unhappy bond wordlessly, but I know we understand each other's pain.

There are still days, I am ashamed to admit, that I do not rise until midday and days I do not leave the house at all. Not even to venture in to the garden. You would be disappointed with how I am wallowing so. I am not proud.

These days are less and less frequent, however, and I have decided I will make the garden my focus. I will tend the plants and flowers as you always did, in preparation for your return.

I will leave you now, my darling. I think of you each passing moment.

Forever yours,

Ivy

PS The talk of the fair was Bernie Telford's proposal to split from Woodville Football Club once the war is over. He apparently had a fight with the President of the club. I thought of you when I heard the whispers and knew you would like to know.

Nicole re-read last night's letter. She wondered if anyone remembered how the rivalry with Woodville began. Or was it one of those tales that got bent and twisted with time until no one knew exactly how it started, but they were all adamant it was for a good reason?

She knew she was delaying the start to her day. She was meant to be tackling the next job on her renovation list. The kitchen. Over the last week she'd finished sourcing reclaimed cabinetry and the new kitchen would be arriving tomorrow. Today she had to strip the old cabinetry out.

She pushed up the sleeves of her plaster-splatted tracksuit jumper and checked her list for the fourth time to make sure she had the order of tasks straight in her head. Danny would be around soon to help, but she wanted to get as much done as she could on her own.

With her trusty old sledgehammer she broke up the laminate benchtop into manageable-sized pieces and lay the sections in the corner of the room. She lifted the last piece of bench up but buckled under the weight of it.

'Shit,' she shouted as she fell to the floor.

'You okay in there?' Danny came rushing into the kitchen. 'What the hell are you trying to do?'

He lifted the piece of bench off her easily and placed it on the floor with the others. 'Are you hurt?'

'I don't think so.' Nicole felt her vital extremities.

Danny helped her to her feet.

'I was about to knock on the door when I heard you scream. Were you seriously trying to do this on your own?'

Nicole looked at the floor.

'Why?'

'I can't afford to pay someone to do it.' Her voice cracked.

'I meant why not wait till I got here?' He rubbed her shoulder. 'Did you forget I was coming?'

Nicole shrugged. 'No. I . . . just . . . well, you've done so much to help already. I don't want to take advantage of you.'

'Haven't you figured it out yet? We're pretty good at chipping in around here, helping out our mates.' Danny shook his head. 'Let's knock this over together.'

Three hours of hard work later, Nicole and Danny sat on the verandah, looking out at the front garden, which was now dressed with top soil thanks to Jack and ready for the next stage. Turf. Nicole poured them each a glass of icy cold lemonade.

'Thank you for your help today,' she said.

'Any time. Next time though, wait for backup. Save us both on Deep Heat in the long run.' He rubbed his back.

Nicole laughed. 'Sorry.'

'Nah. I'm the one who's sorry. That's why I came over early. I was a bit rude to you after trivia.' He stared out into the yard.

'You obviously had something on your mind.'

'Yeah. Something.' He nodded, his gaze distant.

The writer in Nicole wanted to ask questions. Was he in love with Jacqui? That didn't seem right. Jason? No, she hadn't picked up that vibe. Not that that meant anything. The way he sat now, staring into the distance, told her there was something more to his late-night abruptness.

She fought back the urge to ask more questions and stayed quiet.

'So, is this what you thought you were signing up for when you took on this place?' Danny indicated the cottage behind them.

'Not quite.'

'Well, as I said before, you're doing an amazing job.' Danny smiled as he looked into her eyes, holding her gaze. 'Anyway.' He coughed and shook his head. 'I've taken up enough of your day.' He stood. 'I should head before you kick me out.'

'Are you kidding? I owe you big-time after today.'

Nicole stood and walked him to the step.

'What time are the boys from Woodville coming over to install the new kitchen?'

Nicole averted her gaze.

Danny grabbed her by the shoulders. 'You're kidding me. Do you honestly think you can do a job like that on your own? No one can.'

'Not the electrical stuff. I've got someone coming to do that.' A quote for five grand just for labour would have chewed up most of what was left of the money from the lawyers for the renovation and that meant she had no choice but to install the cupboards herself. She had no idea what she was going to do about the tiles for the splashback, though.

Danny dropped his grip and shook his head. 'Give me a minute.' He pulled out his phone.

'Danny, please. Don't. I can't let you do this for me.'

He tapped away on the screen. 'Then don't think of it as for you.' He turned and looked her in the eye. 'This place means a lot to a lot of people around here. We all just want to see it back at its best.'

Danny's phone pinged. Three times. 'There you go. Tomorrow you'll have a crew of burly footballers here to help you install your kitchen.' He turned abruptly and strode down the front garden path.

'Wait. Where are you going?'

But he didn't turn back.

Nicole watched him head out the gate. Then she saw that further down the path, Charlie was struggling with his grocery bag. In a few bounding steps Danny was beside him, taking his load. Together they walked towards the boatshed. Danny turned around and waved goodbye to Nicole, who was both miffed by his sudden departure and touched by his kindness.

Charlie took his bags off Danny and pushed open the old door to the boatshed. It creaked loudly, as it had done for years. He would oil the hinges again, but it would make little difference.

'Thank you,' he said softly as Danny headed back up the path. He was a good boy, the Temple kid.

The row of daddy-long-legs guarding the entry were momentarily disturbed by the rush of fresh air as Charlie closed the door quickly behind him. He manoeuvred round the boxes piled awkwardly on top of each other, careful not to touch their dusty surfaces. He removed his shoes at the inner line of busted plastic milk crates that sat just beyond the barrier of cardboard.

His fingers lightly trailed along the bookshelf that separated the entrance from the rest of the room, rising and falling over the bumpy spines of the books – some near vertical, most at varying angles of horizontal. He paused briefly, reached to the shelf above his shoulder and pulled out the only dust-free novel, gently caressing its front and back to ensure it remained clean and then carefully returned it to its place.

He lowered his tired aching body in his armchair in the far corner of the room, surrounded by dust sheets that hid long-forgotten treasures. He cursed the pain that invaded his every bone and muscle. He knew he was old, he didn't need constant reminding.

His simple wooden bed lay to his left against a clean white wall, and in the corner next to that stood a small fridge, a sink, a simple hob and a few shelves stacked with tins. His basic bathroom, a toilet and tiny shower, was behind him.

A picture of a barefoot woman in a flowing gypsy skirt midtwirl in a patch of grass hung above his bed, the only sign of life in his little corner of order among the decaying chaos that surrounded him. He smiled at Ivy in greeting as he did every time he came inside.

Charlie looked out the portal window at his small view of the perfect blue ocean, framed by dirt and salt that clouded the edges of the round glass. The bus trip to Woodville and back had taken its toll, but he couldn't do what needed to be done here. He couldn't give idle tongues any fodder.

He wasn't sure how the first part of his plan was going to work out, but at least something was happening with the cottage. And now that the next part of his plan was in motion, he only hoped there would be some redemption, even it wasn't for him.

Twelve

*T*he first day of the kitchen installation was going well. As far as Nicole could tell anyway. Danny had turned up early in the morning with a Matt and Greg from the football team and they got stuck straight in.

Nicole tried to be of use to them – she handed them tools, helped hold pieces of wood in place – but in the end she was just in the way. They didn't say anything to that effect, but she could tell.

The best thing she could do for them was make herself scarce.

She wandered around the garden, perhaps there was something there she could do. No. Jack had that completely under control. Section by section he was turning the mess of shrubs and grass and weeds into something that looked presentable. He would have some good photos for his TAFE portfolio soon. Not having to pay for the kitchen installation meant Nicole could use the stipend to buy the turf, and it wouldn't be long now till that could be laid and Jack could start putting in some plants.

She went out to the front gate to look at the cottage in its entirety. The inside might well be coming along nicely, and the yard, but there was still the exterior. How on earth was she going to tackle that? Would she even have enough time? Her first couple of months at the cove had gone by so fast. It wouldn't be long now till her lease was up. She wondered if there was any option to extend it. Probably not, if they wanted it sold.

Nicole's stomach tightened at the thought of having to move on after her time here. She'd have to start looking for a house-sit soon, she guessed. Line something up so she had somewhere to go.

Staring at the cottage was not exactly doing wonders for her mood, so she turned around and headed down the peninsula.

As she passed the boatshed she saw Charlie sitting on one of the deckchairs, looking out at the sea.

'Morning,' she called.

He turned around and nodded in greeting.

'I've been kicked out while they do the kitchen.' She laughed.

'So you thought you'd come and annoy me?'

Nicole shrugged. 'Or go for a walk.'

'You do that a lot. Walk.' Charlie got up and pulled out the other deckchair, motioning for her to sit, then went into the boatshed.

He returned a few seconds later with his Scrabble board, and lifted it up to show her, raising an eyebrow.

'Why not?' Nicole smiled.

The morning passed in gentle silence. Every now and then Charlie would sprout a fact prompted by a word played – shrew, eleven points, eat eighty per cent of their own body weight a day – and Nicole would try to counter with the next move. Wattle, thirteen points, genus acacia.

As they packed up the game, Nicole tripped on the deckchair.

'Stumble, thirteen points, you lose.' The hint of a smile touched Charlie's lips.

'Ha, ha.' Nicole smiled. 'You think you're very funny, don't you?'

He shrugged.

By the time Nicole got home, the guys were gone and Danny had left her a note. They'd be back 'each day for the rest of the week to finish the job. Leave the electrician to me. There's a temporary stovetop set up in the living room.'

Nicole would have to find a way to thank Danny and his friends. This old cottage really must have meant an awful lot to the people of the cove for everyone to give their time and energy so freely. Another question for her notebook. Another letter to read to bring Nicole one step closer to uncovering this story.

10th June, 1943

My Dearest Tom,

It would appear that I must continue going to church. Father Anthony's scrutiny is proving more than troublesome to shake and when he is not watching me, his wife is. Between the two of them, they are as bad as having Mother here herself! Father Anthony is over every second day and Peggy every other.

I can now say with absolute authority that he did not marry her for her culinary skill. If she continues to so generously ply me with her sour casseroles and dry, hard roasts, I may be forced to commit a quite unchristian act. At least the goannas just beyond the tree line along the path to the boatshed do not seem to mind her cooking. I keep expecting to find one lying in the sun with its rigid claws reaching helplessly towards heaven. But they are as tough as they look, I suppose.

Oh, but I am being most wicked. She is only trying to do her wifely and Godly duty. I am too ungrateful. If Father Anthony knew my thoughts, he would no longer be so welcoming of my presence in church. You were always the better of the two of us, my darling. I fear my innate flaws show more easily without you here to temper them.

I am loath to admit, but it has crossed my mind, that perhaps Father Anthony has done a deal with the devil herself. In exchange for his spying, she loosens her notoriously tight purse strings. It would not be the first time Mother has used her money to get what she wants.

Listen to me once again. Is my soul irrevocably lost?

So, to Sunday service I must dutifully trudge each week. If Mother were to hear anything negative, she would no doubt return, and I fear how much worse she would be should that come to pass.

Lucy sat beside me last Sunday, and I must confess it did lift my miserable spirits somewhat to have her there. I hope she joins me next week and I have told her so.

We are developing quite a strong friendship, which I do find rather strange. Though I should not, given our shared circumstance. Do you remember when she and her Henry, God rest, first came to town? She was quite reluctant to join our community. Mind you, I was not as welcoming as I perhaps should have been. I am sure you would tell me I made no greater effort as I was threatened by her beauty, and you might be right. None of that now matters. Events have conspired to bring us together.

She is now the only person in town I can be honest with. Be myself with. Lucy and I have lunched with Colonel Bridges' wife as the three war victims of the cove, but she is so much older than Lucy and me, and that creates some distance.

I am ever thankful for Lucy's friendship. It is a most lonely existence I lead now waiting for news of your fate, my dear, and Lucy is fast becoming my one tether to this cold world.

It is, again, late. I write at night as I often feel crippled with sadness when I sign off and this way I am able to head straight to bed. I must to bed now, my darling.

Forever yours,

Ivy

Over the week the new kitchen slowly took shape and Nicole busied herself with smaller jobs around the cottage – stripping back and replacing skirting boards, starting the undercoat on the walls.

When the last tile of the kitchen splashback went in on Wednesday morning she stood in the middle of the room and took it all in. The reclaimed whitewashed wooden cupboards looked so pretty beneath the stripped and varnished oak benchtop, and the black subway tiles a friend of Trevor's had saved for her from a pub renovation in Woodville set just the right tone.

'Thank you.' Her voice was barely a whisper as she looked at Danny and Matt and Greg, standing with their hands in their pockets, waiting for her validation. 'It's . . . perfect.' She excused herself quickly.

Hiding in the living room, she tried to compose herself by going over her lists, which she'd stuck on the wall. The kitchen was perfect, and the cottage was now starting to feel like a home. Except it never could be home. Not for her. Once the renovations were done, she'd be kicked out. She'd never get to truly enjoy the beautiful kitchen the footy boys had made for her. Not for very long, anyway. She wiped away her tears.

'Excuse me, Nicole,' Danny said as he came into the living room. 'We're all packed up in there and the boys have headed off.'

Nicole turned. 'How will I ever thank them? Thank you?'

'They didn't do it for the thanks.' Danny shrugged. 'It's just mates helping mates.'

He noticed the lists behind her.

'Creating your own wallpaper?'

Nicole cringed. There were a lot of lists.

'I've never seen anything like this before.' He whistled. 'You're either the most organised person in the world, or borderline crazy.'

'Take your pick.' Nicole smiled.

'Everything categorised and prioritised. Man, do you need a hobby, or a job, or a dog, or something.'

'This is my hobby.' She grinned. 'And I'm allergic to dogs. And I have a job, sort of.'

Danny raised an eyebrow.

'I do a little freelance editing. Speaking of jobs, how is it you're able to be here picking me to pieces? Don't you have other jobs around town to work on?'

He shrugged. 'They come and go.'

It was Nicole's turn to raise an eyebrow.

'It's not really my job-job. I just help out a bit here and there.'

'So do you have a job-job?'

'I can't believe the local grapevine hasn't filled you in on that already.' He put his hands on his hips and studied her lists. 'I can help with this. And this. And these.' He pointed to a number of tasks.

'I try not to get involved in gossip,' Nicole said.

'In a town like this involvement isn't really optional. I'll have to speak to the powers that be and let them know their system is failing.'

'Well, yes, we can't have that now, can we?'

'Indeed.' He seemed to hesitate.

Nicole shifted her weight from side to side.

'I really should let you get back to it then.' Danny backed out of the room.

'Wait.' Nicole caught up with him. 'Thank you. Really.' She could feel her eyes welling up again. Damn.

He reached out and touched her arm. 'Any time.'

The next morning Nicole continued painting the first layer of undercoat on the walls and by late afternoon she had two rooms completed. She stretched out her aching shoulders. If only there was a bath in the cottage. Oh well, a cuppa and then flopping into bed sounded just as good.

'Anyone home?' Mandy's voice called from the verandah and Nicole let out a long sigh.

'Hi, Mandy.' She forced a smile. She really just wanted to go to bed early.

'I thought we might christen this gorgeous new kitchen of yours.' She held out two shopping bags of food. 'Danny said it came up a treat, but he wasn't sure you were completely happy with it.'

What? Oh. She'd hoped he hadn't seen her crying.

'It is stunning,' she said to Mandy. 'Take a look.'

They went into the kitchen and Mandy gasped. 'It is. So why aren't you dancing a jig?'

'I'm just exhausted.' It wasn't entirely a lie. She was actually exhausted.

Mandy's face fell. 'Oh. All right then. Maybe it's best we do this another time.'

'Would you mind?'

'Of course not.'

Nicole didn't want to upset Mandy. The woman had been nothing but kind to her. 'What about tomorrow?'

Mandy's smile sparkled. 'Tomorrow it is.'

After Mandy left, Nicole curled up on the sofa with a cup of tea. As she lay Ivy's box in her lap, a sharp trill echoed through the large room. She looked at her phone. A Sydney number she didn't recognise. All her editing work came through email, and only Mandy and Danny had her new number. It must be a call centre. Certainly not worth answering when she had other, more interesting things to focus her attention on.

She opened Ivy's box and reached for the next letter, stopping as she fingered through the envelopes at the blaring red and yellow of another telegram. February, 1944.

Nicole held her breath.

'I DEEPLY REGRET TO INFORM YOU THAT YOUR HUSBAND SGT T WILSON PREVIOUSLY REPORTED MISSING IN ACTION IS NOW REPORTED KILLED IN ACTION DEEPEST CONDOLENCES LETTER TO FOLLOW MINISTER FOR THE ARMY 4 45 PM'

Tears streamed down Nicole's face. No! No, no, no. It couldn't end like this. Oh, Ivy.

To hell with her schedule and rationing. Nicole ripped open the next letter.

16th July, 1944
My Dearest Tom,
Life without you makes no sense. I have tried so hard to be stoic.
I have endeavoured to come to terms with your loss and continue on, as life dictates I must. But I simply cannot let you go.

I have cried more than I thought possible these past few months and I have cursed God and screamed into my pillow at night. News of your passing should not have come as a surprise to me with you missing for so long, but I always held out hope. Always.

Now, that hope is gone. Now you are gone. And I am lost. What am I to do without you?

It is your birthday today. Happy Birthday, my darling. You are now thirty-eight, though you will not have aged a day. You will forever be the handsome young man all the girls swooned over and I shall go grey and get wrinkles. In years to come, when I show a photo of my husband, people will no doubt look twice at me trying to place the dashing next to the dashed and not quite making us fit. No matter. I will have the precious memories of when we did fit together beautifully, and I shall hold fast to them.

I planted a rosebush to mark the occasion. I hope I can nurture it to full bloom. Lucy made a delicious sponge cake to honour you and we blew out a candle for you. She spent the day with me, which I was concerned I would find hard to bear. I had been hoping to spend the day alone by the boatshed. However, it appears that on such a difficult day her company was a comfort to me.

She does not force idle chatter, nor entertain salacious rumours, yet we manage to spend hours in conversation. She is quite the learned mind and we have had many a discussion on religion and philosophy.

We do not discuss the war, though the papers report on nothing else it seems. The Allies have the upper hand, but I fear the swift end is not as nigh as the press wish us to believe, though I wish it were for the wives sitting at home waiting for the day Lucy and I will never see.

I know I should cease these letters now you have left this world, but to do so would mean you are entirely lost to me forever. That the last piece of you I hold will disappear. And that is a burden

I simply could not bear. It is silly, I know, my way to hold on to you
a little longer. Yet hold on I must.

Happy birthday, my love. You are with me always.

Forever yours,

Ivy

Nicole's heart ached. She returned the letter to its box and switched off the light allowing darkness to hide her sorrow.

Rolling over to her left side, she hugged the spare pillow and closed her eyes tightly. A picture of Mandy and Trevor dancing in the pub floated through her mind. They danced out the front doors and onto the footy field. They danced past her atop Danny Temple's shoulders. His green eyes flashed a smile at her as they spun away. They danced around her new kitchen, through her half-finished garden that was littered with Ivy's letters, and past the boatshed where Charlie watched on, a frown on his face. From beside the boatshed a figure shrouded in black walked towards her, sending a shiver up her spine.

August, Last Year

Nicky's throat hurt. And her eyes wouldn't open.

She could hear the quiet, repetitive beeping of a machine. She could feel something on her hand, pinching, uncomfortable, annoying. She could smell disinfectant.

She was in a hospital.

She blinked as she adjusted to the bright light.

Mark was sitting in the chair by the window staring out into the early morning. Nicky closed her eyes. Images flashed through her mind. An ambulance. A jolting ride. Strange faces above hers, studying her. Blackness. Blurred light. A friendly face then blackness once more.

She groaned.

'Nicky?' Mark's familiar voice. 'Are you awake?'

She opened her eyes and saw the concern across his face.

'Oh, thank God. You gave us such a scare.'

She cleared her throat. 'What happened?'

He sat on the bed beside her and explained that she'd ruptured her fallopian tube and was rushed to hospital.

'How?'

'Apparently you had an ectopic pregnancy. Why didn't you tell me you were pregnant?'

She shook her head. 'I didn't know.'

Mark called for the doctor and an old man came in, wearing a calm, reassuring expression across his face that medical types often had when delivering bad news. The damage to her tube was so great they had had to remove it.

'But that's why Mother Nature gives us two of things.' He smiled, an attempt, she guessed, to make her feel better. His words came at her in a blur. Risk of reoccurrence. Blah, blah, blah. Specialist in Sydney. Blah, blah, blah. He finally left the room.

Nicky turned to Mark. 'When can we go home?'

A week later Nicky sat in the specialist's suite in Darlinghurst, squeezing her hands. She'd had ultrasounds and a laparoscopy, just to make sure everything was okay for when they wanted to have a baby, and they were waiting on the results. Mark paced the elegant waiting room.

Inside the consultation room the specialist asked them to take a seat. She was a tall woman with a kind face and her demeanour immediately put Nicky at ease. She talked about each test, what it was designed to do, what it told her, what Nicky's tests said specifically.

'There is significant obstruction of your remaining fallopian tube, a malformation from birth, it seems. The chances of you falling pregnant without assistance are very slim . . .'

Nicky reached out for Mark's hand. He didn't return her squeeze. The doctor continued to detail Nicky's situation and Nicky tried to focus on her words.

The ride home was silent. Nicky and Mark sat far apart from each other in the back of the taxi. Mark's head was bent down over his phone the whole time.

When they got home Nicky ordered in dinner, not that she felt like eating, but it was something to do. Maybe it would bring Mark back to her, make him talk to her as they sat at the dining table. When the food arrived she took out the plates and cutlery and set the table. Mark still wasn't talking.

She pushed her curry around the plate, barely taking a bite, watching him intently as he put forkful after forkful in his mouth, his eyes lowered to the table the entire time.

'Mark. Please talk to me.'

He looked up.

'Please. We need to discuss this.'

'What more is there to say?'

'We haven't said anything. About how we're feeling. About what our options are. Talk to me, Mark.'

Mark got up from the table and cleared his plate away. 'Are you finished?' He took her plate too.

'Mark, please,' she said, and grabbed his arm.

'There's nothing to say, Nicky.'

'There's plenty to say. We have options. Maybe not great options, but still. Options.'

Mark turned and faced her, his face a storm cloud of emotion. 'I'm not growing my baby in a test tube. That's just not right. You can't give me children, Nicky. And I don't know what that means for us.' He turned and walked away.

It was his pain talking. She got that. She was hurting too.

He just needed some time to process things. They both did. It was all such a shock. How could either of them think straight at the moment?

She'd make an appointment for them to see a psychologist in a couple of weeks. Once they'd had some time to digest all the information. And then they could start to think about how they were going to navigate the new landscape of their life. They just needed time.

Thirteen

Mandy watched as Nicole carefully folded the egg whites into the cheese. 'That's it. Nice and gently. We don't want to knock the air out.'

'Like the mousse.' Nicole smiled.

'Yes, well, no need to relive that one.' Mandy shook her head. 'Can you believe how far you've come?'

Nicole laughed. She may have come a long way, but it hadn't been easy. Poor Mandy had continued the weekly lessons for the last month, patiently sharing her culinary knowledge with Nicole. It had taken her three goes to get the mousse to set properly, the cheesecake had the texture of rubber, the lamb roast landed on the floor with a loud thud when she took it out of the oven, and it was more than a little embarrassing when Jim and Danny turned up after someone called the Rural Fire Service, reporting smoke billowing from the cottage. Nicole had set the casserole too high and she and Mandy had got distracted chatting on the verandah. They were the butt of every joke at The Royal for some time afterward.

Still, ever so slowly, Nicole was getting the hang of it. Her chicken parmigiana had turned out quite well and the caramel slice had been delicious. Even Charlie had enjoyed that one.

And here she was attempting a soufflé. Mandy kept reassuring her it was easier than most people thought, but Nicole wasn't convinced.

'Secret's in the prep of the ramekins,' Mandy said. She'd given Nicole a set as a gift a few weeks earlier.

Nicole poured the mixture into the ceramic moulds that sat on a tray, which she slowly lifted into the oven.

'See, nothing to it.' Mandy grinned.

'Don't jinx me.' Nicole still didn't believe jinxes, but there was no point tempting fate. 'We'll know in thirty minutes if there was nothing to it.'

'Twenty minutes.' Mandy corrected her and set the timer. 'I'd better go. See you at trivia at seven.' Mandy called as she headed off to see her mum in the home. 'Let me know how these turn out.'

Nicole was nervous as she pulled the tray out of the oven twenty minutes later, but the soufflé had turned out okay. Nicole happily dug into one and decided that, other than perhaps being a little bit heavier than they should be, they weren't too bad at all. Jane would have loved them, her favourite dessert. Sadness wrapped itself around Nicole's heart. She missed her friend all the time.

She finished off a second one, and with her tummy full and no desire to do any renovations, she pulled out Ivy's next letter, the date catching her eye.

16th August, 1945
My Dearest Tom,
The war is over.

The Americans have exacted retribution on the Japanese and they have surrendered. The papers are full of victorious stories and it is as if the entire nation has had a few pints and is dancing in the street. The joy is palpable.

Unfortunately it comes too late for so many, and painfully so for those of us who lost love ones so close to the end. News of Samuel's death reached us three days ago. Mrs Bridges has shut her door and answers to no one. To lose the colonel was hard enough on her, though she stayed strong. To lose her son in the same war! I cannot imagine the poor woman's grief. That only leaves young William Tucker to come back to us. Only one from eleven.

The very soul of our community bleeds even while it rejoices.

Father Anthony is planning a special service for when William returns. A thanks for his safe homecoming and a memorial for you and the others. I do not know how I will get through it, even with Lucy by my side.

I must confess, a feeling of 'what now' has wafted over me since the marvellous news of the surrender reached us. Even those without loved ones serving have been in a state of limbo, holding their breath till it was safe to exhale once more. And now they will expel their air of uncertainty and continue their lives, their daily routine no longer marred by tragic news or ration cuts. For them, things will become normal again, over time, perhaps, and perhaps a different kind of normal, but it will happen.

I, however, fear I will not know normal again. You were my normal. Before you, I was a spoiled, lost little girl suffocating under Mother's tyranny. Then you came along and set me free, showed me what life could be. What it should be. I never breathed before you entered my life. How shall I breathe now you are gone?

The war has been a kind of distraction until now, I suppose, from your disappearance, from our lost little boy, from your death. Something to think about each day other than my own sorrow. Now it is over and all that is left is grief.

How I am to find any sort of future without you here?

Tonight before I sleep, I shall raise a glass of wine – do you remember the bottle we put aside the night you proposed? – toast the end of the war. I need to search for a new beginning.

I miss you, my dear, so very, very much. May the world now know peace so that your sacrifice was not in vain.

Forever yours,

Ivy

She read the letter again, letting the sadness and joy wash over her in turn. One line in particular stuck with her.

For them, things will become normal again, over time, perhaps, and perhaps a different kind of normal, but it will happen.

A different kind of normal. Nicole never would have guessed making soufflé and going to trivia nights would be her normal. But look where she was.

She checked her watch. Damn it. She was going to be late.

Ten minutes late wasn't too bad, she figured as she rushed into the pub. She took quick stock and discovered she'd only missed three questions. And two of them were about sport, so that wasn't too bad.

Danny went to get her a drink and Jason asked the next question.

'Which novel, a story within a story, won the 2002 Man Booker Prize?'

'Not fair,' shouted Cheryl and she pointed to Nicole. 'They have an unfair advantage.'

'Pipe down,' Jason grumbled. 'There are questions here for everyone.'

Danny returned with drinks and looked at the answer Nicole had written, and shrugged.

'Was it any good?' he asked as he sat down.

Life of Pi was one of those books that tended to polarise readers. 'Not one of my favourites,' she admitted.

Danny nodded. 'I saw the movie. Man, the loneliness of that boy!'

There was something in his tone that caught Nicole's ear. Something . . . sad.

'Would you two stop talking? You've missed the next question.'

'Sorry, Mandy.' Danny grinned and looked at Nicole.

Oops, she mouthed back to him. She took a potato wedge from the bowl in the centre of the table. It was cold. That would teach her for coming late.

That night it was Cheryl's team that took home the prize – a bottle of red wine – and she didn't mind one bit showing it off to the group as they all sat together after the game.

'So, how's Jack's little quest going?' Cheryl leaned across the table, her breasts threatening to spill from her shirt.

Mandy shook her head. 'He won't tell us anything. He won't even admit he has a crush on Katie Lewis. He's just like his father. It took Trev eighteen months to work up the courage to ask me out.'

'It's true,' Trevor said sheepishly, hanging his head. Everyone laughed.

'And I'm pretty sure Katie feels the same way about him, but they're both too scared to do anything about it.'

'Aw, how sweet,' said Jacqui, rocking a sleeping Amy in her arms. The only way she could make it tonight was if she brought the baby with her, and she was determined to get out of the house. 'I'm sure they'll figure it out.'

'If I had my way . . .' Mandy raised her finger.

'If you had your way, Fate and Destiny would be out of a job and the entire cove would be under your control.' Cheryl laughed.

'And the world would be a better place for it,' Mandy retorted, and raised her glass in salute.

Gentle conversation fell over the group, and Nicole observed her friends with a sense of contentment. She had no idea this had been missing in her life. This extension of warmth and connection they all seemed to share. For so long it had just been her and Mark, isolated within their own relationship, no one else close. And when that life ended, there was nothing, no one.

Nicole skirted around the edges of this friend group, afraid to get too close, to touch it, want it and then have to leave one day not too far away.

Jacqui left first to race home, complaining that her mother always said she was happy to babysit, but always looked pointedly at her watch whenever Jacqui and Jason returned. This was the first time they'd convinced her to watch the boys since Amy was born and Jacqui didn't want to risk alienating her.

Cheryl joined Jim at the bar, and Mandy kissed Nicole goodbye on the cheek and headed off to visit with Carole.

And then Nicole was alone with Danny.

'I'll walk you out.'

He led her to the doors of the pub and Nicole braced herself against the cold night air. He put his arm round her shoulder, briefly rubbing it, and removed it once they were walking up the street.

'I can walk with you if you like. Bit of protection.'

Nicole laughed. 'It's not Kings Cross in the nineties. I think I'll be okay.'

'Well, no, it surely isn't. We haven't had a drug-related stabbing in at least a few days.' He grinned. 'But you obviously haven't heard of the Cove Pirate.'

Nicole stopped walking and turned to look Danny directly in the eye.

'This ought to be good.' She smiled. 'Out with it then.'

'Well.' Danny lowered his voice and started walking, not breaking eye contact, drawing Nicole along in his path. 'Legend has it that on nights exactly like tonight, when celebration is afoot . . .'

'Afoot?'

'Yes, afoot.' He grinned. 'When celebration is a-*foot*,' he emphasised the word, 'the Dread Pirate . . . Pete, most fearsome in his time, wanders the streets of the cove looking for his lost love.'

'Dread Pirate Pete?' Nicole raised an eyebrow.

'Well, he wasn't fearsome for his name, though his name did strike fear in the heart of any who heard it.'

'I'll have to take your word for that.'

'It was his insatiable appetite for pretty young ladies that frightened all who were unlucky enough to know his name.'

'Really?' Nicole couldn't help but giggle. 'Sounds like most young men I know.'

'You misunderstand me, dear lady. Appetite,' he said. 'Ap-pe-tite.' He smacked his lips together.

'Oh, I see.' Nicole feigned sombreness.

'His count was near a hundred when one day, he landed here, on South Beach, and came to feast on the young ladies of the town. He came across a young lass, like yourself, walking, just like you do now, and he had his mind fixed on what he'd do with her. But then . . .' he paused dramatically.

'But then?' Nicole had to play along now.

'Just as he was about to raise his sword to her, she asked how the day's sailing had been, can you believe?'

'I barely dare.' She gasped, raising her hand to her chest in feigned shock.

'She didn't scream or cry, but kept a straight face. He answered and then she asked another question. And another and another, each question more interesting than the last. Before he realised it, the dawn was about to break and his heart had been stolen. Never before had he felt love,' Danny paused, 'nor would he again.'

'Oh, do go on.' Nicole grinned.

'The young girl's father happened by, right as the lass was stealing Pete's heart, and realised just who was sitting beside his beloved daughter. He picked up the pirate's own sword, which was on the ground in the dirt, and charged him, piercing him right through the gut. The Dread Pirate Pete was killed just as he was about to declare his love for the maiden and carry her away on his ship so they could wed.'

'How terribly tragic.' She raised her hand to her chest in mock drama.

'To this day,' Danny continued, 'on nights exactly like this, exactly as it was a hundred years ago, with the night sky so dark and fluid, the ghost of the Dread Pirate Pete wanders the streets of the cove, looking for his lost love, so he can finally sail away with her.'

'Wow. For someone who doesn't read, you sure can spin a yarn.' Nicole's smile broadened.

'Mock me at your own peril. The story is true as I'm standing here.' He stopped dead in front of her and her momentum forced her to stumble into him, her hands to his chest.

'Well, then, maybe you're right.' She stepped back, her cheeks flushed. 'Perhaps I should have an escort. We're halfway there already, so you may as well stick around.'

'It's the only wise thing to do.' He put his hand on his chest.

'If you're ever looking for a book deal, I've got a lot of contacts in the world of fiction,' Nicole said teasingly.

'Fiction?' Danny raised his voice. 'Fiction?! I should leave you to him.'

'Now don't do that. After an effort like that you should at least see it through.'

'It worked though, didn't it?' Danny winked.

'I guess it did,' Nicole replied with a laugh.

They talked right up till they reached Nicole's door, and she had to admit, she didn't entirely dislike the company.

'Thanks for walking me home.'

They stopped on her front verandah. Danny brushed her fringe to the side and his green eyes looked into hers.

Nicole could feel the heat rising over her skin as Danny's hand lingered against her neck and she drew in a sharp breath.

'Sorry,' she said, casting her eyes down.

'Is everything okay, Nicole?'

She nodded. 'Of course.' She shoved her hands into her coat pocket. She didn't dare look into his eyes.

'Right, then.' He cleared his throat and gave her shoulder a quick squeeze. 'Goodnight.' He headed back down the steps and out the gate.

As she entered the cottage, she knew she somehow had to put out the heat that enveloped her. Maybe Ivy could help with that.

15th December, 1946

My Dearest Tom,

The festive season is upon us and you will never believe what Lucy has me doing. We are making decorative angels to give away at the church's Christmas stall next week. We are using all manner of objects to make them – gumnuts and leaves, newspapers and fabric scraps, cleaned-out tin cans – whatever we can scrounge. I never considered myself at all creative, as you are well aware, but Lucy has a real gift. I mostly help her with gluing and tying things under her direction. I am not sure I am of any help, but she never complains. And the hours we spend together creating them are such fun.

It is a hard time for both of us and I suspect the choice of crafting angels and not stars or baubles is her not-so-subtle way of helping me through my grief. She sees right through me and knows that I have not yet come to terms with losing you. I try not to analyse things too deeply, though, because I know that if I did, I would come to the conclusion that Lucy also realises I still carry the burden of our angel baby much too heavily around my heart. And that is something I much prefer to keep deeply buried.

Mother and Father have joined me at the cove for the holidays and it is a relief to have our activity as an excuse to be gone from the house for hours at a time. Mother thinks it is trivial, a waste of time. She also insists that if I must continue to make the 'ridiculous things', then I should be selling them rather than giving them away, even though she is adamant they are not worth a half-penny.

Lucy and I know, however, how a simple gesture at this time of year can lift a damaged spirit, especially after all our little town has lost. I hope our angels, meagre as they are, will spread at least a bit of cheer this year.

I am trying to ignore Mother as best I can. She does not like me going about in bare feet and insists I wear shoes in her presence. It feels strange now, but I oblige her for the sake of peace. Thankfully she and Father will not be here long, as Mother has plans to spend time in Melbourne with some of her new university friends over the summer. Father speaks at night of his students and lectures. He seems very happy. I shall miss his quiet company once they are gone.

It is yet another holiday without you. Will these ever get easier? The birthdays, anniversaries, Christmases? So many people have told me time heals as though that is supposed to be a comfort. They never say how much time, though, do they? And what if healing means forgetting you? I do not ever intend to stop thinking about you.

There have been whispers of bringing back the Spring Dance, now that we are no longer at war. It will of course be one more celebration to remind me you are not here. I remember so clearly that night at the Spring Dance where we met. The horror on Mother's face as we danced, how devastatingly handsome you were, how nervous I was. But, it may not ever happen. Not if Joan Wetherby has any hand in the matter. She is vehemently against the idea of bringing the dance back. Says dances are folly and nothing but trouble. Did she not enjoy them when you were at school together? I wish I had known you then.

I shall not linger long, my love. Lucy entrusted me to finish two angels on my own tonight and their little wings are beside me waiting to be attached. They are quite endearing, these angels, I must admit. Mrs Li has been very generous and gifted us some beautiful paper to use on the wings. They are covered in a red and gold pattern that shimmers under candlelight. Perhaps these wings will help a lost soul's dreams take flight, or give hope to one who has lost theirs. Is that not what Christmas is about? Hope.

I miss you, my dearest, so very much.

Forever yours,

Ivy

With each letter Nicole fell in love a little more with Ivy, the same way she'd fall for characters in a book. Only this wasn't a novel. It was real life. Ivy's real life. A life Nicole wished she could be part of, instead of having to live vicariously through decades-old words.

If only she could step through the parchment and back in time and leave her own world behind. No Mark, no pain, no heartache.

No Dread Pirate Pete or Danny. She smiled, her cheeks flushing again at the memory of their walk home.

Stop that. Stop that right now.

Fourteen

Danny arrived on time the next morning, ready to help Nicole put up the cornices. Or at least she thought he had. But instead of his usual work clothes he was wearing a very casual outfit and a mischievous smile.

'How do you feel about playing hooky today?' Danny asked as he strode down the hall.

'Er . . .'

He grabbed Nicole's shoulders and steered her towards the door.

'But —'

'But nothing. Your lists will be there when you get back.'

He pushed her through to the verandah.

A yelp of protest died in her throat as she felt the morning sun bathe her face in sunlight. By the time they got to his car and Danny had opened the door for her, she couldn't deny being outside was a much nicer prospect than renovations.

They stopped at a red light – it was the only set of lights in town. Mandy walked past on the opposite side of the road and waved at

Danny before noticing Nicole in the passenger seat. She smiled and gave Nicole a cheeky little wave as Danny opened his window. The light turned green, but he didn't move. Nicole was surprised when the car behind didn't beep, but simply moved round them.

'Hey, you two. Where are you off to?' Mandy walked over to Nicole's window and leaned in.

'Thought I might show Nicole here the tracks.'

'Bit of a rough ride.' Mandy looked at Nicole. 'But the tried and true thing to do for fun round here. Enjoy.' She looked back to Danny. 'Be careful. The top track hasn't dried out properly from the last rain.'

Nicole frowned.

'You'll be perfectly fine.' Mandy assured her. 'No better driver than Danny. Have fun.' She smiled and watched them pull gently away as Danny eased on to the accelerator.

As they passed an old man hobbling along the pavement, Danny slowed down. It was the same old man he'd helped outside the post office that day during Nicole's first month in town.

'How ya doing, Bill?' he called out.

Bill nodded and smiled.

'You have to love that man,' Danny said. 'He's a stalwart of the footy club, and our only returned war vet.'

'Oh.' Nicole turned around to get a better look at Ivy's William Tucker. 'I know,' she said absently.

'You've met?'

'Sort of.' Nicole watched the figure from Ivy's life fade as they drove on. 'He's been at the games, right?'

'Every one of them.'

'So where exactly are we heading?' Nicole asked.

'Best place in the cove. You'll love it.' He smiled broadly at her and she relaxed some more.

Leaving the sealed roads of civilisation five minutes out of town, the gentle up and down of the bumpy dirt track was a fitting setting as Nicole listened to Danny tell stories of what he and his mates used to get up to in the bush around them when they were teenagers. Trapping goanna, collecting fallen branches and building forts, climbing the tall trees and jumping down beside unsuspecting bushwalkers, frightening them silly.

They turned a corner and her grip on the doorhandle tightened as the track (she assumed they were still following a track, though she couldn't see one) got rougher and rougher.

'You might want to hang on now, Nicole,' Danny said. 'It's going to start getting bumpy from here. We're taking a little side trip off the tracks.'

'Off the tracks?' She looked at him with wide eyes.

He simply shot her his confident, cheeky grin and winked.

She giggled as they jerked and jolted and slid and spun. It was either giggle or cry and she didn't want to show any fear.

Moving between excitement and terror with each impact, she looked over to Danny a few times and he appeared calm and in control, which was at least somewhat comforting. But the fact that he was silent for the first time since leaving the cottage both reassured her and worried her at the same time.

And then, seemingly in the middle of nowhere, Danny stopped the vehicle and beeped the horn. Nicole took a few deep breaths and looked around.

'I don't mean to be disrespectful, but how is this,' she circled her hands, 'the best place in the cove?'

She looked around again in case she'd missed something. Nope. Trees, shrubs, twigs, dirt. The same scenery they'd been driving through for the past twenty minutes – only thicker beyond this clearing.

'Well, we're not there yet. The rest of the way is by foot.'

Danny got out of the car and went round the other side to open Nicole's door.

'Come on. Just a little walk past there.' He pointed to what was possibly the largest tree Nicole had ever seen.

'I believe I've seen this movie.' Nicole stayed put. 'It doesn't end well for my character.'

Reaching out his hand, Danny laughed. 'You're safe – I'm not a murderer.'

'Said every murderer ever.'

'Besides.' He smiled. 'You're Mandy's friend and she and Trev are like family to me. You don't mess with family.'

Nicole took his hand.

They walked for fifteen minutes, Danny with such purpose that Nicole could only assume he knew exactly where he was going. To her it all looked the same. Then they came to another clearing and Nicole stopped to look around.

'This is amazing,' she gasped.

'Pretty cool, huh?' Danny whispered in her ear and stood beside her.

Stretched out below them was the entire town – the clock tower of the post office reaching tall in the centre, the wide main street lined with buildings whose awnings formed a pastel rainbow, the houses clustered in pockets around the town centre, the peninsula jutting into the ocean.

'That's . . .' Nicole pointed to the north.

'Yep. Your place.'

It looked tiny from where they were, but it was clearly identifiable, perched alone on the northern bulge of coastline. Nicole could also make out the boatshed and the stretch of sand below it.

The deep blue of the sea bled into the green border of bush and trees that gave way to the white and grey and orange of the town that sat like a pin cushion on the soft quilt laid out below her.

She turned to Danny and smiled. 'Thank you.'

He winked. 'Come and sit down,' he said, pointing to a granite boulder in the middle of the clearing.

As she was taking her seat, Nicole thought she'd caught a glimpse of a familiar figure disappearing down a thin track off to the side. She started.

'Don't worry,' Danny said. 'That's just Charlie.'

'Charlie?'

'Yeah. The guy that lives in the boatshed. Not that you've probably met him. Keeps to himself good and proper.'

'We've met.'

'You have? Well, don't let him scare you. That,' he pointed to a thin opening in the scrub that was barely visible, 'is the other, less fun way to get up here.' He smiled. 'This is a fair way off the known tracks and Charlie and I are the only ones who know about this spot. Far as I can tell, anyway. Well, and now you. It's Charlie's spot, really. He comes here all the time. Or he used to, though not so much anymore. But we have an understanding. That's why I tooted before. In case he was up here, to let him know I was coming. As long as I don't do it too often, he doesn't mind. At least I don't think he does.'

So, this is where Charlie comes.

'I first stumbled, literally, on this place after Grandpa died.' Danny sat beside her, looking at the town below. 'We were close, Grandpa and I. It was the day of his funeral. I was upset and I ran off into the bush one day. Found this.' He spread his hands. 'Tripped right over this.' He patted the boulder.

'I sat here and bawled my eyes out. Don't tell the boys. I even decided I was going to build a hut and live up here and never go back to town.' He gave Nicole an embarrassed grin. 'Trouble was, some other hermit already had it staked out.' He laughed. 'Charlie found me here. When I saw him, I thought I was in deep shit. We all heard the rumours about the crazy old fella in the boatshed. We even helped spread them. I thought he was going to eat me or something.'

Nicole laughed, unable to help herself.

'I know, stupid, hey? He didn't, obviously. Didn't even say a word to me. But I remember the look in his eye. He knew about Grandpa, for sure. I reckon he knows more about what goes on in this town than anyone else, you know?'

Nicole smiled wryly. She didn't doubt it. She remembered Charlie's words to her: 'The less you're seen, the more you see.'

'I'm sorry.' Nicole took Danny's hand and squeezed.

He squeezed back and didn't let go. 'Thanks. Anyway, Charlie said nothing. He sat just behind the tree line over there, looking out for me I suppose. Come dusk he got up and waved his hand for me to follow and he led me back to town. Just as well too, 'cause I had no idea how I'd got here or how to get back, and I doubt I could have built a sturdy enough hut to sleep in for the night.'

Nicole let out a little chuckle and Danny smiled at her.

'I tried to find my way back a few times after that, but never managed. Then, one day I followed Charlie. Like every kid before and after me, I'd tried to follow him many times and learn his deep dark secrets. And like every other kid, I'd failed. But, that day he let me and led me here. I soon learned the way on my own. As I got older I figured out the four-wheel-drive route and I warn Charlie when I'm coming. Truth be told, it's as much for my sake as his. Sometimes he still freaks me out a bit.'

Nicole laughed out loud.

'I came up here a lot too after my gir—'

Nicole turned towards him and saw pain in his eyes.

'Well,' he shrugged, 'let's just say there was a time in my life when I really needed to come up here a lot.'

'So why did you bring me here?' Nicole asked.

'It always seemed like a good spot for lost souls.' He shrugged. 'Thought maybe it might be some comfort to you.'

Nicole could feel tears welling.

'It's all right.' Danny put his arm around her and she rested her head on his shoulder. 'You'll find your path again. We all do.'

The return run was faster, scarier and more fun. Nicole found herself laughing out loud as they careered downhill back to town. It probably helped that she was more relaxed, having not been dismembered and scattered through the forest.

Danny dropped her home and walked her to the door.

'Thank you. Today was . . . I haven't felt so . . . in such . . .' She coughed, gathering herself. 'Thank you.'

'Anytime you want to go back, you just let me know.'

He kissed her on the cheek and heat teased her skin as she watched him walk down the path.

She closed the door behind her, unwanted memories forcing their way forward.

September, Last Year

Time, it seemed, was not Nicky's friend.

With each passing week, Mark's stubbornness grew.

He didn't go to therapy with her. Apparently, he didn't need some stranger telling him how he felt about things. But he didn't have any better solutions. His preference was to carry on as if nothing had happened. The only thing he did do was push back their wedding plans. Nicky had been through a lot, after all, and Mark was concerned about what the stress of planning their big day would do to her. She needed time to recover properly, and he would be as patient as she needed.

One night over dinner, when she tried once more to bring up their situation, he groaned heavily. 'We've been over this, Nicky. There's no point rushing into things. If you don't take the time to heal properly, emotionally, then where will you be?'

Was he right? Did she need more time to heal, emotionally?

She'd kept trying to write, but to no avail. She'd tried to read. But no book could hold her attention for more than a few pages. She'd even tried to learn to cook. But every recipe turned to disaster. She'd padded around the apartment aimlessly, day after day. Everything she did was tainted with the pain she was carrying in her heart.

But could she let the pain go as Mark seemed to have done so easily?

She stopped therapy after her third session and started visiting her Moreton Bay fig every day. She took her laptop with her and instead of trying to work on her next novel, she decided to try writing about her surroundings – people, pets, trees, detailing the private moments that passed before her.

The third week after she started her daily pilgrimage to the park, she decided not to sit on her bench and wandered the tree-lined paths that crisscrossed the manicured grass, exploring parts of the green oasis she rarely visited. In one little corner of the park a small group of middle-aged men and women practised tai chi, led by a tiny Chinese woman dressed in a wine-red velour tracksuit. Around another bend, four artists had set up easels and were painting the scene before them, supervised by an octogenarian in a baggy linen suit, who was encouraging them with gentle words. A group of schoolchildren straggled past her in loud excitement as their teachers tried to wrangle them into groups and finish whatever worksheet they were supposed to be doing.

All around her people were learning. People were teaching.

An idea started to form in her mind. A half-baked idea, maybe. But the spark was enough to cling on to and she raced home to start exploring it further.

When Mark came home that night, her half-baked idea had turned in to a plan and she was bursting to tell him all about it.

He walked into the dining room with a large chocolate bouquet. 'Hey, princess. Thought this might cheer you up a bit.' He kissed the top of her head and poured himself a glass of wine to have with dinner.

'I have some news.' She sat down beside him.

'Oh?'

'Well, I've been doing a lot of thinking and . . .' she put the proposal she'd been working on all afternoon in front of him. A proposal for a course at the writers' centre that she would teach. 'What do you think? I have to get the expression of interest in this week if I'm going to be considered for next semester's program.'

Mark read the pages. 'So you'd be teaching every Wednesday? For eight weeks?'

'Yes. I just thought . . .'

Mark stood up. 'Even though we agreed you wouldn't go back to work?'

'Yes, but . . .'

'Am I not enough for you?' He frowned.

'What?'

'Well, it seems to me like you're desperate to fill your life with things other than me.'

Nicky stared at him, not comprehending.

'You're still hanging on to the idea of having children. I saw the IVF brochure in your drawer. I was going to ignore it, but now you've forced me to bring it up.'

Nicky felt her face go hot from shame. She had gone behind his back.

'And now this. What else am I supposed to think other than I'm not enough for you?'

Nicky didn't know what this was, and she scrambled to form a coherent response.

'Well?' Mark asked.

'I just thought maybe it might be fun. Give me something to do other than sit around here and stare at my computer screen.'

Mark shook his head and retreated into silence.

'Mark, please. You won't talk to me about our options for having children, you won't talk to me about this. What's going on?'

'You want to talk? Then let's talk.' He took her hands. 'I don't want to have a child in a test tube and I don't want to raise someone else's kid, so adoption is out of the question. Do you ever stop for one minute and think about my feelings in this? No. It's all about you. And now you come at me with this idea that will take you even further away from me and you wonder why I'm not thrilled. I never thought of you as selfish before, Nicky, but I'm starting to wonder if you even love me at all.' His face fell, forlorn.

'Of course I love you.'

'Then why aren't I enough for you?'

Mark walked out of the apartment and Nicky couldn't move. How had they ended up here? So far away from each other? She collapsed on the floor.

Early the next morning as Mark snored, fast asleep, Nicky stood at her open cupboard and took out a pair of jeans and a couple of T-shirts and packed them into her small overnight bag. She'd feigned sleep when he came home just after one, smelling of red wine and she lay there all night, going over and over the conversation they'd had. She needed to get away. Just for a day or two. After everything that had happened lately, she needed to get some perspective. Just a couple of days to clear her head. Refocus. Deal with all these emotions she'd been bottling up.

Mark wouldn't be thrilled. But surely he'd see the value once she came back fresh and happy and devoted once more.

But where would she go?

She stopped packing. She had no money for a hotel. Not a decent one, anyway. She tiptoed to her desk and turned her laptop on. There was usually a few hundred dollars in their joint account.

She opened the bank balance.

One hundred dollars. That wouldn't be enough for one night anywhere near here. Shouldn't there be more than that? Last time she checked, which was only yesterday when she did the online grocery shopping, there was five hundred in the account.

She clicked on the transaction history. At nine thirty last night, the rest of the money had been withdrawn. Mark had drunk it all away.

'Nicky?' Mark's groggy voice came from the bedroom. 'Come back to bed.'

Nicky stayed right where she was.

Fifteen

*N*icole sanded back the peeling layers of decades-old paint from the window frame in the spare room, revealing the bare wood beneath. She went over it gently with some fine sandpaper and then a soft cloth. Opening the tin of primer, she dipped her brush in and made her first, slow, precise strokes.

Were her memories possibly now false, ruined by pain, and therefore not to be trusted? Was the Mark who supported her writing career the real Mark? Or was the real Mark the man who'd damaged her so badly? Which version of the past was correct? The past she'd thought she had in the heady mist of happier days, or the past she now remembered? Were the first deep layers of memories of a first love true? Was the middle layer of choking grime always there beneath the surface? Did the top layers of anguish simply tarnish any memory connected to Mark, or was the pain the clear varnish that enabled complete transparency and clarity?

She wiped the tiny white splatters of paint from the window glass with a damp cloth.

A constant shadow of self-doubt and questioning now clung to her every waking moment. A lack of certainty of the history she thought was hers. A lack of trust in her own thoughts and feelings.

Nicole crossed 'prep & prime window' off her list.

That was the worst part of all in this whole sorry situation – that she could no longer trust herself. Would that trust ever come back? How did you go about finding yourself after getting so completely lost?

Ivy had done it, hadn't she? Nicole cleaned up, made herself some afternoon tea and opened the next letter.

6th February, 1948

My Dearest Tom,

I have found myself in the dubious position of leading the ladies at the CWA. That Lucy Falcon has a lot to answer for, putting my name forward like that. Still, the choice was myself or Joan Wetherby, so you can see why I could not refuse.

My first order of business is to organise a fundraiser. We are in desperate need of an extension to the hall. I am not sure how best to go about it, though. It will still be some time before a full recovery from the effects of the war can be declared. How do I ask people to give when they have so little?

I shall discuss it with Lucy on Sunday when she comes for dinner. It has become a regular event now, a roast with Lucy. We take turns hosting. Occasionally we invite others to join us. This week it is only the two of us, however. And it is her turn to cook. She has quite a talent.

Her home is lovely, though one thing I find quite odd is that there is not a single picture of Henry in the place. Not on display at least. It is as if he never existed. My photos of you are jammed so tight on the mantle above the fire. I must admit though, for months

I would pass your face and have to close my eyes. Maybe she simply has them in her bedroom, so she is surrounded by him during those dark, lonely hours that, for me at least, are still so terribly hard to endure.

No doubt Joan Wetherby will express her ideas for the fundraiser at the next meeting. When I suggested we could make the Spring Dance our fundraising event she shouted at me. Actually raised her voice in front of everyone there and accused me of selfish motives. What selfish motives could I possibly have?

I have asked Father Anthony's wife, Peggy, to sit on the committee. I believe she will add some much needed temperance to the discussions. Joan would never upset her publicly, though what she says behind her back is downright sinful. Is it unchristian of me to use the innocent wife of our beloved spiritual leader for my own means?

William Tucker has decided to take a wife. Do you remember young Iris Telford? She was an ungainly, tall, thin stick of a teenager when you left. Well, she has grown into her looks quite stylishly, I must say, and William is smitten beyond words. She is warm and caring and perfectly suited to his quiet nature.

The entire town is abuzz with excitement. Something so lovely to look forward to. Iris has asked Mrs Li to make her wedding dress, which upset Joan. The spiteful woman took it upon herself to speak to Grandma Telford about the 'unseemly matter', not for a moment considering that the Matriarch would actually approve of the arrangement. Joan forgets that the Telfords are the Telfords for a reason and they are astute business people with tight purse strings. Mrs Li's work is impeccable and she charges only what she must.

Why Joan would want to destroy this joyous occasion, I do not know. Perhaps she simply cannot stand to see others happy.

*Do you remember the kerfuffle she created right before our
wedding? Of course you do – it almost ruined our beautiful day.
I will not allow her to interfere in these nuptials.*

*William smiles constantly nowadays. It is a nice change to see
him happy. I believe he carries the burden of being our only returned
soldier quite heavily around his heart.*

*I must to bed, my dearest. I would ask you to wish me dreams of
inspiring fundraising events, but I only ever dream of you.*

Forever yours,

Ivy

Nicole could imagine Ivy running the CWA. It would have been
a sight to behold. And the fights with Joan? She could see them
clearly in her head. Her own mum had had a nemesis when she
was on the Country Women's Association, though Nicole had
long forgotten the woman's name. It would be somewhere in the
minutes of the old meetings.

Minutes? Maybe . . . no, she couldn't be so lucky.

At nine o'clock the next morning she grabbed her bag and ran
out the door.

Danny was right. The local history section of the cove library
was, indeed, impressive. Someone had scanned and digitised all
the CWA minutes dating back to the 1920s. Many of the pages
were hard to read, some impossible. But they were all there.

Nicole searched for the right dates. 1948. There was Ivy's
name. CWA President.

She made a copy of the minutes for the rest of that year.

What else had Ivy mentioned in the letter? Something about a
dance. Maybe there was mention of that in the newspapers.

Nicole didn't know which gods to thank, but the newspapers
had all been digitally preserved, too.

'The library's going to close soon,' Cheryl said, putting a gentle hand on her shoulder. She'd have to come another day.

'Cheryl, who copied all these documents? It must have taken forever.'

'Volunteers from the local history society. We're a small bunch, but dedicated. Would you be interested in joining us? We could always do with new members.'

Under other circumstances, she might have been tempted. For a town broadly aware of her living situation, they seemed to quickly forget how temporary it was.

'I'll think about it,' she said, with a polite nod. There was no point making a big deal out of reminding people she wasn't sticking around.

She quickly photocopied the newspaper clipping she'd found that mentioned a spring dance. There was a photo of a group of young men and women dressed in their best outfits, big smiles on their faces. She recognised Ivy, the smile the same as the woman in Mandy's photos. Here she was looking at Ivy's past. A happy past, it seemed. Unlike her own.

October, Last Year

For the next two weeks Mark was a model fiancé – coming home early, taking Nicky out to dinner, bringing her chocolates, listening with interest as she described the vignettes of her day.

That Saturday night they sat down to a feast of Indian curries that Mark had prepared. When they'd finished eating he presented her with a gift. A pair of diamond earrings that matched the bracelet he'd bought before. They were stunning.

And they left Nicky feeling cold.

'What?' He frowned. 'You're upset with me again? Seriously, Nicky. I just can't win with you, can I? No matter what I do, you get upset with me.'

She raised her eyes to meet him.

'Is this still about you being barren?'

'I'm not barren.'

'Oh, Nicky. Don't go nitpicking over semantics. Barren, infertile, reproductively challenged. Whatever. I thought you'd moved past this.'

Silence filled the room. Nicky slowly rose and walked towards the front door.

'Where are you going?'

Nowhere. There was nowhere for her to go. No friends to go to. No money to take her anywhere. No choice. But she couldn't stay there.

She walked out into the night.

Wandering the streets of Surry Hills, surrounded by restaurants and bars throbbing with happy people, Nicky had never felt so alone. How had she ended up here, with this as her life? She was a strong, intelligent woman. Yet here she was. Not so strong and intelligent after all.

Two young men stumbled out of a small bar and nearly knocked her over.

'Sorry, lady.' They threw their arms around each other and continued on down the street.

Maybe this was just a rough patch. Lord knew Mark hadn't dealt with his emotions after her emergency surgery. And despite his protestations that she was enough on her own, she suspected he was upset that they couldn't have children. That *she* couldn't. At least not naturally. Grief could do funny things. Maybe he was just trying to find his way round his.

Maybe.

She walked past a buzzing late-night café where a young woman sat perched on a stool outside playing a soft, lilting folk song, as the people listening to her drank their soy lattes. Nicky stopped for a moment. The girl had a beautiful voice.

Mark did love her. Of that she had no doubt. He just didn't know how to deal with what had happened.

She didn't, either.

She wound her way back to her apartment. Maybe he'd be asleep already and she could just sneak in and sleep on the couch – look at things with a clear head in the morning.

There were no lights on. A good sign.

But sitting in the dark on the sofa, Mark was waiting for her. He fell to his knees as she crossed the room, and buried his forehead into her waist.

'Princess. I was out of line. I'll never be such a jerk again. You can't leave me. Not ever.'

Nicky stood still.

Mark lifted his head and looked at her with tear-soaked eyes. 'I'm sorry.'

They were two words she'd never heard come out of his mouth before.

Nicky took Mark's face in her hands. 'Never again.'

'I promise.' He stood and kissed her softly on the forehead. Then he drew her in for a tight hug.

Sixteen

Nicole walked along the path to the boatshed. Morning rays of light bounced off the ocean and rosellas danced between the trees in flashes of bright colour.

Sleep had come in fits and starts last night. Memories plagued her, and she had tossed and turned, and her body felt heavy today. When she reached the boatshed she saw Charlie waiting for her and her mood lifted a little. He greeted her with his customary nod.

'I'm feeling lucky today, Charlie,' she said as she sat on her canvas chair.

'Not lucky enough,' he grumbled back.

'I came pretty close the other week, you have to admit.'

'Not close enough.'

'We'll see.' Nicole arranged her tiles and started watching Charlie carefully for any clues he had good letters – a touch of his nose, running his thumb along his forefinger.

'Kilt. Triple word score.' She had the upper hand now.

'In the mid-1700s tartan was banned by the British government,' Charlie said, not looking up from the board, studying his next move.

'Is that so?' Nicole had decided that Charlie must have either been a professor in his previous life, or game-show host – his breadth of knowledge so vast. One day she might just ask him.

He was even quieter than usual today. Not that she minded. She was just grateful he now accepted their weekly game as a given.

He put down his next word in silence.

She countered.

The sun moved across the sky.

He said no more.

'Oh, yes!' Nicole shouted. 'And that's the game, old man.'

'No one likes a bad winner,' Charlie mumbled.

'No one likes to lose.' She grinned.

Charlie packed up the Scrabble game and took the box and table into the boatshed. Nicole folded the chairs and carried them to the door, leaning them against the dirt-spattered wall. She headed up the path and when she got to the gum tree that encroached the track just before the hill's rise, she stopped and turned.

He never noticed, but she always watched him walk down the cove and up the North Face, every Sunday after their game. Except last Sunday. He'd stayed in the boatshed that day and when she popped by on Monday under the pretence of sharing a coffee, he wasn't there.

'I had to go away', was the only explanation he offered when she asked him about it.

At least Ivy was more forthcoming with details about her life. Sometimes too many details and the vignettes became a blur that Nicole could not recall. Mostly though, the letters stayed with her and she could recite them by heart.

8th April, 1950

My Dearest Tom,

Our Easter markets were a resounding success. So successful we have now decided to charge a minimal amount so we can replenish our stock and make more for Christmas. We will donate any profit beyond our supplies back to the church.

Lucy tried to show me how to make bunny rabbits with wool and rags, but the ears were always lopsided. She is much better at them, and her rabbits are very popular with the children.

Angus Lewis spent some time chatting to us at the stall. I assumed he was interested in Lucy for more than her artistic talents. I was wrong.

He called on me yesterday, most unexpectedly, to make his intentions clear. I found myself in need of sitting down. I even poured a stiff sherry.

He is a perfectly amiable man, as you well know, and despite him being some years my senior, we have always enjoyed a warm friendship. But, for him to court me? I am simply not interested. His wife, Katherine, passed I think eight months ago, and he is lonely. That I can most sympathetically understand. But I am not the solution to his problem.

I cannot imagine being in the arms of another man, my darling, and I am now so used to being alone I am quite set in my ways. I told him as much; the latter, not the former. I do have some sense of compassion. He said he was willing to wait for me to come round to the idea. And I believe him, Thomas. The man had a look of determination I have rarely seen and I feel he will be more than persistent in his attempts to woo me. What am I to do?

Lucy suggested I should reconsider my rejection, but she is mad. She still holds hope I have a hidden artistic talent to discover, so, clearly we cannot trust her judgement. Always the optimist, my sweet Lucy.

I have decided to redecorate the cottage. I feel that I am drifting though my life with no real purpose and perhaps this is a project that will help. I need some more colour in my life, though I am sure Mother will disagree. She and Father have bought a new apartment in Sydney, closer to the university. Mother's letters continue to describe her social engagements mostly, but every now and again Father puts pen to paper and he seems happier than I can remember him ever being. He writes fondly of his students and enthusiastically of his work. He never mentions Mother's parties or soirees.

It is late, once more, and I must to bed. I will need all the strength I can muster to keep Angus Lewis at bay, I fear. Wish me luck.

Forever yours,

Ivy

Charlie knew Nicole had been frustrated losing to him so many times before today. It had been a few weeks since she'd tasted victory. He'd thought about letting her win, holding back. He didn't want her to get so perturbed that she'd stop coming. Not that he was overly thrilled to have her there. But he was kind of getting used to her.

He was grateful she never forced idle chatter, never asked him anything personal. If a word was played and an interesting conversation came out of it then so be it. She told him once that part of the Sistine Chapel had to be repainted because of mould. 'Chapel', thirteen points. Often they passed the morning in comfortable silence. Her calm company brought back memories he hadn't realised he'd missed.

If only she'd stop forcing her cooking attempts down his throat. She'd brought scones today. They weren't bad, he supposed. She was definitely improving, though why she insisted on using him as her guinea pig was beyond him. Perhaps it was because he wouldn't be missed if she accidentally poisoned him.

He forged his way through the bush and up the steep mountain path until he reached his spot. He didn't know how much longer he'd be able to make the trek, each time now harder than the last.

He lowered himself on to the cold rock and stared at the two small buildings in the distance, the deep blue ocean their solid, still backdrop. For some reason, being so far away helped him feel close. Close to Ivy once more, his guardian angel so long ago taken from him.

He'd found his rock not long after that awful night on the beach. He'd been a scared young man then, sitting among the trees, no noise save the wind blowing through the leaves. The image of her wet, limp body haunting his thoughts, wondering why he'd been the one to find her, where it would lead him.

He'd looked down the valley that day at the tiny town below him dwarfed by the emerald green and sapphire embrace of nature and felt comfort for the first time in a long time.

Dappled sunlight filtered through the leaves and cast shadows across the grass in front of him.

He needed that comfort again today.

Of course he'd known travelling to Sydney would be hard, but nothing could have prepared him for what he saw. He'd watched from afar, too scared, too ashamed to make himself known. All that trouble to find his son and he couldn't take the last step. Coward. All his life a coward.

Charlie saw the young man playing a ball game in his front yard with a little boy. His own grandson?

He'd watched for nearly an hour. The little boy, about ten years old Charlie guessed, had stretched his dad's shirt over his head.

Bile had risen in Charlie's throat and he'd had to fight to keep it down as he saw the scars covering his son's torso. So red and vivid, even from where he stood hidden.

Guilt coursed through every fibre of his body as images of that woeful night flashed in his mind.

Seventeen

Mesmerised, Nicole watched on as Danny replaced the last of the cracked tiles of the fireplace hearth. He'd finally managed to find some gorgeous reclaimed originals from a wrecking yard in Perth. And it was worth the two-week wait to get them shipped over.

'It's stunning,' Nicole exclaimed, as Danny backed away from the hearth.

'Not too shabby, hey?'

She hugged him tightly.

'Dinner's ready,' Mandy called from the kitchen. 'Come on in, boys.'

'Smells great,' Danny said as he sat down at the table, flecks of dirt still splattered on the tops of his hands despite the fact he'd washed up.

Jack took his boots off at the front door and came inside, followed by his father.

'I thought you were here to help me.' He slapped Trevor on the shoulder. 'Knocked off half an hour ago, the bludger.'

'You had it under control.' Trevor smiled. 'I did the hard part, fixing the gate for you.'

'Wash your hands and sit down,' Mandy said to her son.

It was Mandy's idea to have a mini working bee and to make use of Nicole's new kitchen. No point a kitchen that large going to waste. Thankfully, Mandy did most of the cooking. Nicole played the role of sous-chef.

'I can't thank you guys enough for this,' Nicole said, sitting next to Mandy. 'Everything's looking, well, it's starting to look like a real home.'

'What are friends for?' Trevor winked. 'Besides, we'll all get our payback in due course. We're planning to put an extension on soon, hey, love?' He smiled at Mandy.

'And I reckon my place would look great rendered,' Danny said.

'And I've got a TAFE assignment for design that could use a spare pair of hands,' Jack added. 'On second thoughts, maybe you could just do my written reports for a semester.'

They all laughed.

'Oh, I see,' Nicole said with a grin. 'That's how it is, then. No such thing as a free lunch round here.'

'That's right.' Mandy shook her head. 'But there is such a thing as a free dinner, so quit the banter and dig in.'

She placed the casserole dish in the middle of the table and started serving up.

Nicole looked around the table surrounded by people with whom she shared no blood connection, no history. People a few months ago she didn't even want to get to know. A group of strangers brought into her life by chance and circumstance.

Jack belched loudly. Trevor clipped him over the head.

'I can't help it,' Jack said, pleading his innocence.

'Appreciation of a good meal.' Danny patted Nicole's hand and let it linger just a second.

'What are our chances against the Badgers this weekend?' Nicole asked, hoping the blush in her cheeks went unnoticed.

Bringing up a Rangers game was guaranteed to set this lot off on a long discussion.

A wave of melancholy drifted over Nicole as she listened to the gentle chatter. Finally she felt these people were becoming genuine friends, but with each renovation task completed, Nicole inched closer to the cottage being finished. Closer to her lease ending. And then what?

After they finished dessert, Trevor helped Jack put away the gardening gear, and Mandy packed the dishes she'd brought with her in their car.

Danny pulled a small parcel out from under his coat as he slipped it on. 'I thought you might like this.' He handed her the gift.

'What's this for?'

Danny shrugged. 'Just because. A little something to help you fill those shelves now the fireplace is finished. But you can't open it yet.'

'Why not?' Nicole frowned.

'It needs to be opened at just the right time.'

'Oh?' Nicole raised an eyebrow. 'And when will that be?'

Danny winked. 'You'll know.'

Nicole stood on the verandah watching her guests leave. Trevor and Mandy hand in hand, Danny with his arm round a squirming Jack's shoulder. They were a picture-perfect family. Nicole sighed.

November, Last Year

Sunday passed in a blur of breakfast in bed, pyjamas, hot choco-lates in bed, black and white movies, and laying in each other's arms. Monday morning saw Mark head to the office early, and then every night that week he was late home. It should have been an opportunity for Nicky to write, but no words came, loneliness consuming her a little more each night.

On Friday morning she cooked Mark bacon and eggs for break-fast. He came out of the bedroom and smiled. 'Smells delicious. But I'll have to take a raincheck. Got an early meeting.'

He left the apartment without saying goodbye.

Nicky refused to be stuck home alone so took herself around the boutiques a couple of blocks away. Not that she would buy anything. Not that she could.

She stopped in front of a new pop-up shop with baby clothes hanging from a miniature aqua clothesline in the window. Sorrow swelled within her.

She'd tried to push her desire for children from her heart. She really had. But the pain was still inside her, eating away at her.

She put her hand up to the window, imagining how soft the lemon and grey onesie would be to touch. A wave of sorrow hit her, swelling though every inch of her. She struggled for breath.

A woman in the shop turned to look at a cot and Nicole rec-ognised her profile. There was Jane, heavily pregnant, picking out nursery furniture.

Nicky spun around and ran off down the street as rain started to fall.

Back in the safety of the apartment, she crawled under the covers of her doona. Complete and utter sadness consumed her.

Anger, regret, confusion swirled inside her and she clasped the side of her head with both hands, silently screaming in her mind.

A deep breath.

Another.

She pulled out her phone and made an appointment with the therapist.

After three sessions of therapy, it was obvious the doctor wasn't going to be able help much without Mark's involvement. Nicky tried to get him to come along. She tried to make him understand she needed his help.

'You don't have to understand *why* I'm feeling like this,' she pleaded with him in the dining room after dinner one night. 'But can't you understand that I am, and that I need your support?'

'No.' He got up from the table opening and closing his hands, pacing in front of the bookcase. 'There is nothing to understand. We can't have children. We can't change it. End of story. Move on with life.' He reached to the bookcase, sweeping his arm across the shelves, knocking a pile of books to the floor. He picked up her beloved copy of *Anne of Green Gables*, tore pages from their binding and threw the book across the room in frustration. 'Can't you understand how I feel? How much pressure are you going to keep putting on me to be someone I'm not?'

Mark stormed out of the apartment and Nicky picked up her book and sobbed into the ruined pages.

Eighteen

*N*icole sifted through the church bulletins in the library collection searching for anything that might mention Ivy. Or Joan, or Lucy – any connection to Ivy at all. Like the CWA records, so much of it was hard to read. There was scant detail – a mention here, a reference there. Still, it was fun trawling through the past, even if it wasn't turning up much. She'd been chipping away at her renovation lists all morning and the change in pace was most welcome.

Going through the church records, Nicole's focus had been on any marriage notifications. She'd got up to 1953 with no luck. Ivy's letter that morning perhaps was a foretelling of what was further to come. Though she hoped not.

23rd July, 1952

My Dearest Tom,

Angus Lewis is a man of great perseverance. I have not once given him any encouragement, yet he persists in his futile pursuit of me.

I have been subtle and gentle in my rejection of his advances, and blunt and forthright also. Nothing works.

Lucy is of no help. She continues to try to change my mind and, I am sure, offers Angus hope behind my back. I cannot blame the poor man. When one is no longer in one's twenties, the options narrow. And in a town like this, they are limited to begin with. Lucy, being a few years younger than I, is perhaps too young for him. Mrs Bridges, far too many years his senior, and Peggy's sister, Grace, is newly engaged to a man from Sydney. Ruling out children, the elderly and the already married, I guess it leaves me. His only choice. I am sure if there were any other suitably available women, he would not look in my direction at all.

Of course Joan has weighed in on the matter. It is not proper for a woman to be without a husband, she insists. What will people say? What kind of example am I setting for the young ladies of the town? Though I am sure in her mind they were rhetorical questions, I did however answer.

'I suspect the young girls of town could not care less whether I am single or married, and if they did then I am glad I am showing them it is perfectly fine to be independent of a man. Far better to be without a man than with the wrong one.'

I know, my love, it was wicked of me to say such a thing to her. Anyone with half a brain can see her marriage was never one of sunshine and rainbows. Not that any of us would dare say such a thing directly.

Father came to visit last weekend. On his own. Imagine my joy. Mother had some crucial engagement she simply could not get out of. He has never come to see me alone before. Never been allowed to. I wonder why he was not pressed to attend whatever social event she found so important. Perhaps it had nothing to do with the university and therefore his tweed learnedness was of no use to her.

Whatever the reason, I am glad for it. I cannot remember the last time Father and I had such a chance to talk.

He looks ten years younger when he speaks of his studies but appears very weary when Mother comes up in conversation. I stopped bringing her up within the first half-hour of his visit.

We spoke of a great many things, but what surprised me were his questions of you. What you were like as a man, as a husband; what your interests were. Everything there was to know about you. I showed him the pictures taken that summer before you left. He commented on how strong and handsome you looked. I was inclined to agree. You would have got on exceptionally well, had you been allowed to meet. I shall never forgive Mother for keeping the people I love apart.

I sought Father's counsel on the Angus Lewis issue. 'Your mother would have a fit if she knew you were turning down a perfectly acceptable suitor,' he said. 'Should we tell her?' He had to hold back a laugh. He told me he could tell that I would not be happy with Angus and that I am not to underestimate the need for happiness in a relationship. He held my hand as we sat on the verandah.

With Father's words to strengthen my resolve, I shall find a way to let Angus down gently. You have ruined me, Thomas Wilson, for all other men. There will only ever be you.

Until next time.

Forever yours,

Ivy

PS I must tell you that they have begun expanding the schoolhouse this week. There seems to be an explosion of new families coming to the cove and children are springing forth everywhere. Our quiet little corner of the world will never be the same again, I fear.

Nicole felt a little sad for Ivy. She'd been quietly hoping Angus would win her over in the end. It somehow didn't seem right for Ivy to end up all alone. She would check more records tomorrow. She would keep reading the letters. Something – intuition, understanding narrative arcs, blind hope, perhaps – told her that Ivy's story was far from over.

Nicole left the library and enjoyed the warm afternoon sun on her back as she walked up Wilson's Road, and a gentle breeze kissed her face. As the cottage came into view a shadow moved across the verandah and Nicole stopped.

Charlie spun round when he heard the noise behind him.

'Oh,' Nicole breathed out. 'You nearly gave me a heart attack. What brings you by?'

He didn't mean to snoop. But when she wasn't here, he thought he'd take the opportunity to see how the work was coming along. The garden was acceptable. What he could see of the interior through the windows was satisfactory too. He didn't know much about design, but what he saw was neat and clean and the broken fragments of Ivy's house were being repaired. Lovingly so, it seemed. Ivy would be happy to see the fireplace restored so beautifully. He was anxious to see the cottage finished, to gaze once again at the welcoming blue and white jewel set on its green and floral carpet.

There was no way Nicole could know of his vested interest in her work and there was no need to tell her yet. Besides, there was other, more pressing business he needed help with.

'I was just looking for you. I have a favour to ask.'

'Of course.'

'If I give you some mail, will you post it for me? Next week maybe?'

She nodded, a frown across her face.

Nicole didn't know it yet, but she was pivotal to his plan working out. He had a debt to pay, a memory to uphold, and he needed her help to do it.

Nineteen

The parcel Nicole had been waiting for arrived the next morning. She put her tools down and opened it. Perfect. She hoped he'd like it.

Outside Danny's door she raised her hand to knock.

Was that music coming from inside? She leaned closer to the door.

Through the thick wooden door she could make out someone singing out of tune to 'Flame Trees'.

Before she had a chance to knock, the door swung open and Danny stepped out, stopping mid-lyric when he saw who was on his doorstep. He smiled sheepishly.

'Hey, Nicole. I was just heading out. To what do I owe this pleasure?'

Nicole swallowed her laugh. 'Oh, I was just passing by and thought I heard Barnsey singing, so . . .'

'You criticise Chisel, and I'll have to run you out of town.' He smiled.

'I love Cold Chisel. No, I actually came by . . .'

'Come in,' he interrupted her. 'Where are my manners?'

'I thought you were leaving?'

'I wasn't going anywhere special. Come in.'

'I wanted to give you this, to say thank y—'

All coherent thought abandoned Nicole as she entered Danny's home and saw the bookshelf in front of her. No. Bookshelf wasn't an adequate description. It didn't even come close.

'Oh . . . my,' she whispered.

A great curved wall of books swept across the open entrance. The entire wall was shelved, and each shelf was filled with history texts and coffee table books of the world's beautiful architecture.

She stepped forward.

Intermittently, the rows of books were interrupted by a statue or carving or a knick-knack. In the middle of the bookcase was a picture of Danny, aged perhaps ten, sitting in the lap of a beautiful woman.

Danny stood behind Nicole as she reverently inched towards his collection. Behind the wall was a staircase that led to the second floor of the house and the shelf upon shelf of books rose with the sweeping curve. In her wildest dreams Nicole couldn't have imagined a more glorious bookcase, only hers would be filled with novels.

'So, history and architecture aren't just a hobby of yours?' She turned to Danny.

'No. I have a degree. In both.' He smiled.

'In both?'

'It was my grandfather's influence. He used to take me all round Europe and expound on all the great cathedrals and castles and palaces.'

'I can't believe this collection,' she said, looking up along the shelves.

Between *The History of Prussia* and *Gaudí: The Construction of Dreams* sat a book that didn't fit in with the rest. She looked more closely. It was a copy of *Tide*.

Her cheeks flushed and, she moved her eyes further along so he couldn't follow where she'd been looking.

'This is truly impressive. No wonder you get all the history questions at Trivia Night right.'

Danny invited her to sit on the sofa. Around the room Nicole saw intricately woven wall-hangings and photos of fishing villages and ornate temples, and pictures of what she assumed was a school, with children playing soccer in the dirt. If Danny took the photos himself, he was a very good photographer.

Her gaze stopped on a photo of Danny outside the school surrounded by a bunch of barefoot children, their grins beaming. The name of the school was written in two languages, though the English was mostly obscured by Danny's head. There were dozens of photos of the same school on every wall.

'I'm in awe,' she said. 'I might have to rent this space from you as my own personal library if I ever need to do any research.'

'You're always welcome,' he said. 'Free of charge, even. But, that's not what you came over for, is it? Books?'

'Actually, yes,' Nicole said. 'I came to give you this. A thank you.' She held out the gift she'd brought, but suddenly felt foolish. *Pillars of the Earth* would pale in comparison to the texts they were surrounded by.

'There's no need to thank me.' Danny put the gift down and looked deeply into Nicole's eyes. 'Is everything all right?'

Danny's steady gaze unsettled her more than she was prepared for. 'Yes.'

'Good.' He leaned closer to her, the distance between them suddenly very small.

He reached his hand up and touched her cheek.

Nicole's breathing quickened. The force of the pull towards him was nothing she'd ever experienced before. Such physical desire – thrilling, frightening. He moved his hand behind her head. She couldn't move. She wasn't sure she wanted to. Gently he pulled her towards him, his soft lips tasting hers.

A strange sensation, a wonderful sensation, shuddered up between her hips as Danny drew her closer.

She raised her hands to his chest and felt his heart pounding. Just like hers. She gasped.

He slowed his kisses, ever so slightly, and she pulled back, breathing heavily.

Danny leaned forward and gently she pressed her fingers into his lips, stopping his advance.

'I didn't mean to . . .' He had trouble catching his breath.

'It's okay.' Nicole smiled. 'I just think maybe we need to take this slowly.' She reached out and squeezed his hand.

'I can do slow.' He turned her hand over and kissed her palm. 'Pancakes?'

Nicole frowned.

Danny hauled himself off the sofa. 'Pancakes are slow. Ish. And I haven't had breakfast yet. Will you join me?'

They moved around his kitchen, cracking eggs, pouring milk, whisking batter. Each time their hands touched, Nicole felt the heat tingle over her skin.

'Here,' Danny said. 'Add this.' He handed her some cinnamon.

She took the spice jar from him and he held her hand in his for just a moment.

'It just adds a little something.'

The first pancake came out of the pan looking a bit sad and Nicole frowned. 'Did I do something wrong?'

Danny laughed. 'Nah. The first one is always a dud. Dud-looking, anyway. But here, taste it.' He scooped a forkful of the pancake up and held it to Nicole's lips.

'Oh wow. That is good.'

After pancakes Nicole perused Danny's collection once more.

'These pictures are amazing.' Nicole picked up the photo of Danny with the grinning kids. 'Where is this?'

'Bangladesh. Those kids are amazing.' His eyes lit up. 'They're why I keep going back.'

'Keep going back?'

'I go every year.'

'In your work holidays? Actually you haven't told me yet what your job-job is.'

'Ahh,' he said. 'The grapevine still broken, I see.'

'I guess.' Nicole looked at him.

'When Grandpa died he left me a bit of money in a trust. When I came of age, it became mine. I invested wisely.' He shrugged.

'So there is no job-job?' Nicole raised an eyebrow.

'Not in the traditional sense.'

'So, in a drug-lord-mafia-hired-killer sense?' Nicole asked.

Danny laughed. 'I'm sure that would be a lot more interesting, but no. It was a fair bit of money and I trade on the stock market for my real job.'

'Uh huh. And what about your two degrees? Don't you get bored filling your days with other people's odd jobs?'

'You'd be surprised.' He shrugged. 'But I only do that part of the year.'

'Why's that?'

'When I go to Bangladesh every year, it's for a few months at a time. I help out a school over there.'

'Wow.'

'Keeps me out of trouble.' He winked.

'And I reckon that takes some doing,' Nicole said with a grin.

He stroked her hair.

'Those kids deserve a break. And if I'm in a position to give it to them . . .' As his voice trailed off, a fleeting moment of sadness flickered in his eyes. He bent his head ever so slightly.

Nicole's cheeks warmed as he kissed her softly. She lingered there in his embrace a moment and then pulled back. 'I think I've taken up enough of your day. Weren't you on your way out when I intruded?'

'Damn. Yes.' He furrowed his brow. 'I really should go. But what about your present? I haven't opened it.'

'Oh, no. Don't open it while I'm here. I'd be too embarrassed.'

'Okay.' He kissed her again, briefly, and led her out the door.

As she walked home, the sense of bliss that had settled over Nicole slowly dissolved into fear. It wasn't long now till her lease would be up, but she wasn't worried that she would have to leave. She was worried that she might just want to stay.

December, Last Year

Over the past month Mark continued on as if nothing had happened. Nicky stopped her therapy sessions. There was no point.

It was time to go.

She made an appointment for the morning with Mark's financial adviser so she could get her book money back. She'd leave Mark whatever interest they'd earned.

*

That evening Nicky sat on the sofa and waited for Mark to come home.

As he let himself in the door, she pulled herself upright and took a deep breath.

'Hey, gorgeous.' Mark greeted her and she didn't answer. 'Oh no. What's wrong now?' He rolled his eyes.

'Is there something you need to tell me?'

'No.' He frowned.

'I went to see the financial adviser today.' She kept her voice even.

'Oh.' Mark moved to the kitchen and poured himself a whisky. 'You have to understand, princess, that sometimes investing is a risky business.'

'It's all gone. All of it.'

He drank his glass in one sip. 'Well, yes. But we can save up again.'

Nicky counted to five, focusing on her breathing. 'You weren't even going to tell me?'

'There was no need.' He shrugged.

Nicole stood.

'Hey, why were you trying to access the money anyway? Is there something *you* need to tell *me*?'

Oh, no, no. She wasn't going to let him turn this around. 'Don't. Don't you even! How could you do this to me? To us?'

Mark tried to talk his way out it – the investment had been risky but if it had paid off, wow-wee; he'd lost a lot of his own money in the deal too; didn't she realise he was only doing it for her.

Was this her fault? Wait. No. Realisation slowly seeped into Nicky's soul, their whole relationship coming into focus – the blaming, the second guessing, the oh-so-subtle manipulation that led to constant self-doubt. She fought the urge to scream.

'Oh, Nicky.' He wrapped his arms around her shaking body. 'We'll be okay. We'll get through this.'

Mark released his embrace and made a quick dinner, which they ate in silence. He slunk off to bed shortly after and Nicky started making a plan.

She wouldn't just leave. She'd disappear. Somewhere he couldn't find her.

She pulled out one of her notebooks and started making a list.

New phone – prepaid.

Accommodation – rental? House-sit?

Food. Petrol. Money.

Money? Editing?

Money? Bank account.

New email address.

Change passwords.

Each task she would need in order to get out of there.

Money was obviously the biggest problem. It was going to take some time to get together enough so she could leave. First order of business – set herself up as a freelance editor.

Twenty

Nicole tried to stop thoughts of Danny, memories of Mark flooding her mind, by drowning in Ivy's words.

5th April, 1957
My Dearest Tom,
I have taken a job.

I am working for Father Anthony, doing his accounts, basic clerical work. Joan has made her feelings on the matter quite clear. Is that not a surprise? I ran into her at the shops the other day and, according to her royal righteousness, it is beneath a woman of my breeding to even consider a job and the whole fabric of society is at risk of unravelling if women get it into their heads they are better off working rather than staying at home raising families. Apparently once men returned from the war, women had no right to stay in the workforce.

You will be very proud to know I walked away without responding. Mostly because I was afraid I would reveal my own truth. That I needed something to drag me out of the melancholy that has plagued me recently.

Lucy has recognised my shift in mood and is perhaps thinking of all the little things that remind her of Henry. She has had a most extraordinary idea. A ridiculous idea. She is determined we take a holiday to Italy. I always assumed our mutual loneliness would claim my mind first, but it would appear I was wrong. She is talking nonsense, of course, but she seems quite determined to drag me to Italy. What on earth would I do in Italy?

Neither of us speaks Italian. I have never left Australia. Even when Mother and Father went back to England briefly when I was just a girl, they left me at home with Nanny Celia.

As it happens, Lucy's family are even wealthier than Mother's. Mother will not be pleased to hear this. And Lucy has money put away for emergencies.

She has decided to declare our lonely situation an emergency and this is her solution.

I cannot go to Italy!

She has the entire trip planned. She has family over there and we are to stay with them. And, you will not believe this, we shall be undertaking an art course. An art course! You well know I can articulate the history and technique of any given masterpiece, but to actually produce art, or anything resembling it? You would have thought that she would have learned from our Angel experience. Apparently not. A friend of her cousin runs the course and she has been corresponding with him in order to secure our places.

She has even taken it upon herself to arrange time off for me. My arrangement with Father Anthony is rather flexible.

If I were to agree, if, we would go during the European summer. But what would become of the cottage, of the boatshed? I did raise this issue with Lucy, believing it would end the idea, but she had a *plan for that too. Another cousin of hers, just arrived from Ireland, or some such story, would love to house-sit. How many cousins does this woman have?*

It is madness, is it not? Me, in Italy, doing art courses!

Though, I have to say the pictures Lucy showed me were beautiful. And she is so excited it is hard not to get swept up in her enthusiasm. I do not wish to disappoint her. And it might be nice to have something to look forward to.

There are elements to the idea that sound fun. Eating genuine Italian food in small trattoria; going to the museums; seeing the Ponte Vecchio.

Maybe I should go. It cannot hurt, can it?

I am sitting on our bench as I write this. The sky is a lovely shade of blue and the sun is warm. Autumn again, my love. I can feel you sitting here beside me, watching the ocean. Your toes are playing in the grass and the gentle breeze teases your brown curls. You are so content. So distant.

I know what you would say. You would tell me it was high time I enjoyed myself and an adventure was just what I needed. A wild, crazy adventure.

Yes, my dearest, perhaps I will head to Italy. Wish me luck.

Forever yours,

Ivy

It was no good. Not even Ivy could save Nicole from Mark intruding every thought she had. Kissing Danny had released all the emotions she'd been bottling up for so long now; it had forced her memories to the front of her mind.

Oh God, this is what Mark had reduced her to. His lasting legacy no matter what Nicole did, no matter what she could ever do. He'd always be there in her head.

March, This Year

For the last three months Nicky had shut down, withdrawing from Mark, turning off her emotions. And he hadn't even noticed. At what point had she lost herself? The ectopic pregnancy? Before that? The months since?

All she knew was that she no longer existed, and the only way to live again was to leave.

She kept her freelance editing work secret and slowly she'd saved some money. All she had to do now was find somewhere to live.

Nicky opened her laptop and scrolled through a house-sitting website. It was a good option. No cost, moving every couple of months. Trouble was, none of them were available immediately. She'd have to hang on a bit longer. God, she didn't know how long she could keep this up.

She clicked on the next listing. 'Unique property, available now.' She read the post, her enthusiasm waning as the details emerged. Free rent. But there was a catch: 'some renovation needed'. Damn.

Her shoulders slumped.

She sent an email to the agent anyway. It couldn't hurt. From the pictures it looked like it only needed a lick of paint. She might be able to manage that.

They responded three days later, saying all the paperwork was ready and she could have the keys once she signed, but she told them she had to think about it. Who was she trying to kid, thinking she could renovate anything? The whole sorry situation she found herself in was already pathetic. She didn't need to add ridiculous as well.

Two nights later Mark came home from work, a large bunch of roses in hand.

'I think it's time we reset the wedding date,' he said. 'What do you think about June?' He kissed her on the top of the head and she frowned at him.

'What now?' He threw his hands up in defeat.

Nicky wondered if there was even the slightest chance of saving this relationship. 'You still want to marry me?'

'Of course I do.'

'And children?'

He shook his head. 'I'm going to bed. Let me know tomorrow if June works for you.'

In the morning Mark kissed her on the forehead as if nothing had happened, as if nothing had changed. For him it hadn't.

But it had for her. She could not live like this anymore.

Nicky rang the number to see if the rent-free cottage at Rosella Cove was still available.

She packed a suitcase full of clothes and looked around the apartment. Other than her laptop, everything belonged to him. She grabbed a plate and some cutlery from the drawers and turned her back on home.

She swung by a solicitor's office to pick up a key to the cottage and got into her old car and headed to Rosella Cove.

Back at Mark's apartment, in the very middle of the clear dining table, she'd left her engagement ring with a simple note.

'It's over. Goodbye.'

Twenty-one

*N*icole walked around the cottage, taking in the scope of what she'd already achieved. Everything was stripped back, plaster repaired or replaced, new cornice and skirtings, bookshelves, window frames ready. The fireplace was fully restored. Okay, she couldn't take much credit for that. And the kitchen was complete – credit also not hers. The floors were fully sanded and polished – she was definitely going to take credit for that. All that remained to do in the other rooms to finish them off was a couple of coats of fresh paint.

She just had to pick a colour and apply it to her clean fresh walls. All of them. No small job. Today's task was to finish the undercoat. By late afternoon she could tick the spare bedroom and hallway off her list. As the last shards of evening light filtered through the bay window in the living room, Nicole lifted Ivy's next letter back out of the box. Her old friend's life was coming together, which was more than she could say for her own mess.

2nd July, 1957

My Dearest Tom,

It will come as no surprise to learn that I have failed miserably in my efforts to become a Renaissance artist, though I must admit the attempt has been more fun than I imagined it would be. I have laughed more in these past few weeks than I have in ever so long.

Lucy is also glowing, though I suspect it has more to do with our rather dashing young teacher, Fabricio, than our stunning surroundings or the sun that has kissed our skin with brown. His passion for art is quite infectious. And while I clearly have no talent, his gentle humour even has Old Dowager Kendle smiling when she thinks no one is watching. She is one of the other students here, and she has done her best to break our spirits with her pious attitude and scathing criticisms of our work, but she has not succeeded. How can any of us take note of her bitterness when we are immersed each day in such sweet beauty? Max, a rather loud Texan, who at first meeting you would never think would be interested in art, has even abandoned trying to turn her round. He is perhaps the most talented artist amongst us.

Fabricio has politely suggested I might wish to try another creative avenue and has a friend who teaches sculpture in the evenings. Do you think I could be any worse at that than I am at painting?

So, I am continuing with my art lessons in the morning, mostly for the company, and then I wander through the shops and cafés in the afternoon. Sometimes I find a tiny museum to explore on my own while Lucy and Fabricio visit art galleries. She says they are only friends. He is married, after all. I believe she is concealing the truth of her feelings from me. But who am I to judge? If she is happy, I am happy.

From Monday I will begin the sculpture class at night. We may yet unleash a hidden talent.

Please stop laughing.

I must remember to thank Lucy for dragging me here. We are already talking about a trip for next summer.

I have included a photo of Lucy and I with our latest paintings.

I miss you, my love.

Forever yours,

Ivy

Nicole ran her fingers around the edge of the small black and white image.

Lucy had a gentle smile and dark hair cropped around her ears. She held up a portrait and Nicole could just make out the hint of mischief in the eyes of the subject. Was this Fabricio? Nicole smiled.

Ivy's smile was broad and her hair was wild and whipped around her face and neck. Her painting, a landscape, was lopsided with the perspective completely askew.

The two women looked so happy.

Nicole's phone pinged to life, echoing in the silence.

The same Sydney number as before? Damn call centres. Maybe, if she answered it she could tell them, in no uncertain terms, to leave her alone. She looked at the flashing screen. Should she?

No.

She picked up the handset and pushed the green button.

'Hello.'

'Nicky, princess?'

His voice shot through her ear and her heart leaped against her chest. She hung up, threw the phone across the room and ran out the front door.

Behind her she could hear the phone ring again as she ran down the path as fast as she could.

By the time she saw Charlie it was too late and as she tried to stop from colliding with him she slipped on the loose dirt beneath her bare feet and crashed to the ground.

'What the hell?' Charlie shouted at her. 'Are you deliberately trying to run me down, you lunatic?'

Nicole didn't answer. Her torso heaved, her sobbing becoming louder.

Charlie knelt beside her and softly put his arms round her.

'Come on, now. This is no place to burst into hysterics.' He gently rose, pulled her to standing, and led her to the side of the boatshed where the deckchairs were.

'Sit.'

Nicole obeyed and took a tissue to blow her nose. Her nose always ran excessively when she cried. 'Nicky's Niagara Nose', Mark called it.

Mark! She sobbed again.

Charlie sat beside her in silence.

'I should've gone overseas.' Nicole spluttered through sobs.

Her hands were shaking.

'What's this about?' Charlie asked.

Nicole shook her head. 'I have to leave.' She couldn't face him. Not after everything that had happened.

'What?'

'I have to go. I have to leave town.' If he'd found her number, it was only a matter of time before he tracked her down. One thing Mark wasn't lacking in was cunning and determination.

Charlie put his hand on Nicole's shoulder as she tried to stand up. 'Stop. Breathe.'

She shook her head, more vigorously. He didn't understand. 'I can't. I have to . . .'

'Stop.' Charlie looked her in the eye. 'I know a little about running. It isn't the answer.'

'But . . .' Nicole sucked in deep breaths.

'You have friends here. Whatever this is about, they can help you.'

No. They couldn't. They wouldn't. Friends she'd known for life had abandoned her. Why would friends she'd known five minutes stand by her?

'I get it.' Charlie shook his head. 'It's easy to turn the world away. But once you do, there's no turning back. No matter how you wish you could. And whatever romantic notion you might have about this kind of life,' he spread his arms to encompass the boatshed, 'this ain't romantic at all and the pain never stops. Never. Running isn't the answer.'

'I can't . . .' Nicole ran up the path, casting long shadows in the dusk.

She returned home and curled up on the sofa. Pain throbbed at her temples. The evening was quiet bar a few possums scuttling about in the trees outside. The only light in the house came from the dim side lamp next to her.

She hadn't turned the phone back on, hadn't answered her door when Mandy dropped by, instead cowering in silence in the dark, pretending she wasn't home.

Was Charlie right? Would her new friends stand by her?

If she ran, would Mark simply find her again?

Confusion, doubt and anger swirled around her head and she rubbed her temples. She jumped up from her seat and dashed around, gathering only the important things, throwing them into the suitcase she kept under her bed.

She rushed through the living room and stopped in front of the bookcases. Danny's gift sat there, alone on the shelf.

'You'll know when the time is right.' His words echoed in her mind.

She pulled at the ribbon.

A single tear fell as she looked at a brand-new copy of *Anne of Green Gables*.

She'd only mentioned it once in passing when he was building the shelves and he'd remembered. He'd remembered such a small detail. A detail so significant to her.

She slid to the floor and pulled her knees up in a tight hug.

Charlie bumped into the dusty box labelled 'kitchen' and rubbed his throbbing hip. Stupid old thing. He should have thrown it out years ago. Thrown all of them out years ago. But he couldn't bring himself to do it. He'd always held out hope that one day these relics of a time so long ago would be useful once more, cherished once more. But today it seemed that hope was fading.

He'd seen the fear in Nicole's eyes. The girl was going to run. He didn't know what from, or where to, but he knew what that resolve looked like. He had his own selfish reasons for needing her to stick around. He had a promise to fulfil and he needed her to finish what she'd started with the cottage.

But there was something else. Something that surprised him. His heart broke for her when she sobbed like that, feelings welling inside him. He thought he was done with feelings, but all he wanted to do when she cried in his arms was protect her, make things right.

He closed the boatshed door behind him and trudged over the peninsula and through town.

Twenty-two

Nicole rocked back and forth on her bed, cradling Ivy's box. Moonlight shone through the window, the only light she needed to escape into Ivy's letters, to stop her tumbling thoughts.

10th July, 1957 . . . It would appear Fabricio was right about me trying sculpture. Even I can see we are a better fit. I may even produce something worth keeping before our time here in Italy is done. No laughing . . .

Nicole sighed.

If she fled again, could she take Ivy with her? Then again, it didn't seem right to take her from her home.

She opened another letter.

30th July, 1957 . . . I caught Lucy kissing Fabricio behind the ruins today. I was looking for inspiration for my latest assignment, but this was not quite what I had in mind. I did not reveal myself and have not told Lucy I saw them. She will tell me if and when she is ready. Did I mention he is married? . . .

And another.

August 15th, 1957 . . . We leave fair Tuscany in a few days and I must say I am apprehensive to return home. I have felt so . . . so light since being here, and I fear the heaviness I left behind will reclaim me once we are back. Though, I do return with a new hobby, a new passion, perhaps, and maybe that will be enough to buoy my spirits.

Lucy is very sad. She and Fabricio seem to have become quite close, despite the years (and spouse) between them. At first I thought it was merely a harmless flirtation, but I believe it has grown into something more substantial . . .

And another.

17th October, 1957 . . . I have sold my first sculpture. It is an angel, standing serenely, looking to the sky. Mrs Hays bought her for her daughter Carole and she suggested I make more and sell them at the Christmas stall this year. I am flirting with the idea.

When I sculpt, I am at peace. I am returned to Italy. I am calm.

I shall not charge much, mind you. Just enough to cover the materials. Joan has voiced her disapproval . . .

'Nicole? Are you home?' Danny's deep voice shattered the silence.

He couldn't really be there. It was just her imagination.

'Nicole?' he shouted again.

She stood on wobbly legs and shuffled to the front door.

'What are you doing here?'

Danny smiled. 'Charlie was worried about you.'

'Charlie?'

'He asked me to come and see you. You look awful.'

With that, Nicole broke down and Danny caught her in his arms.

Nicole had no idea how much time had passed. All she knew was she'd sobbed into Danny's shoulder endlessly and he didn't budge. He didn't complain. He didn't force her to tell him what was wrong. He just held her until her tears subsided.

'Is there anything I can do?' Danny asked, leaning back.

'It's just . . .'

He waited.

He pulled her closer and his lips hovered close above hers.

Nicole's heart began to beat faster and her stomach tightened. Desire coursed through her and she put her hand on his strong chest, felt his heart pounding against her fingers.

But then fear seized her and she swallowed hard. 'I . . . I'm sorry.' She pushed him away gently. 'I can't.'

'Whoever he was he really hurt you, didn't he?'

Nicole nodded.

'Maybe if you let me in, Nicole . . .' Danny's eyes pleaded. 'Whatever he did, I'm not him.'

'No. You're not. And it scares me. When you're close to me, when you touch me . . .'

'I frighten you?' He frowned.

'No. Not you. The feelings you stir in me.'

'Isn't that a good thing?' He smiled.

Nicole ran her fingers through her hair. How could he possibly understand? She had to make him see.

'Breathe, Nicole. Just talk to me. It's just you and me.' He took her hand in his.

She sucked in a deep breath. It wasn't just the two of them, though. Mark was there, always there, and now he had her number. She could not face him, dredge up all those wretched emotions, and relive the past. But if she stayed here he'd find her and she'd have to.

Danny took a deep breath. 'Whenever you're ready, I'm here to listen. But can you promise me one thing?' He looked at the suitcase at the door. 'Don't do anything rash. Not until you've talked to someone. It doesn't have to be me. Mandy is there. Anyone. Please just stay, Nicole. Not for me. For you. This is your home now.'

He held her tightly. How could she leave?

Twenty-three

The gums were completely stripped bare of their flaking skins, revealing a smooth, pale grey layer that shone in the sunlight. Scores of them stretched before Nicole like ghostly statues left scattered, uncared for. Their spindly branches reached out in all directions grasping for intangible love. The green leaves, like elongated tear drops, swayed ever so slightly in the gentle breeze. She could hear rosellas tweeting to each other from the foliage, and caught glimpses of bright red and blue and green darting from tree to tree. The sound of the ocean crashing in the distance reached her ears in waves and the smell of grass filled her nose.

As Nicole walked to the boatshed, she breathed deeply. In and out.

When she arrived, the small collapsible table and chairs were set up with the Scrabble board in place. She sat down and pushed and trailed the tiles across the board while she waited.

'Wasn't sure you were still around,' Charlie grumbled as he emerged from the boatshed.

Nicole looked at him and smiled.

They played in silence. Nicole studied Charlie as they made words and kept score. She could tell when he had good letters, his left eye would crinkle ever so slightly at the edge, almost as if he were about to wink. When he was about to place a word across a triple score, his thin lips tightened just a little. Needing extra time to figure out his next move, his thick, wrinkled forefinger on his thick wrinkled left hand tapped the table.

There was no banter. None of their usual one-upmanship of meanings or origins of words. No interesting anecdotes. But it was peaceful and for that Nicole was grateful.

Charlie won once again and Nicole congratulated him with an extended hand, which he took, grasping it firmly as he would another man's.

'Thank you, Charlie,' she said, but didn't let go. 'I don't know if you were right. About not running. But I am going to think it through.'

'I haven't got much right in this life, my girl.' He shook his head.

'Well, there's a first time for everything.' She smiled.

'Keep that phrase for if you ever beat me by more than a small margin,' he said, packing away the board.

'When, not if.'

'Let's not get carried away.'

'Thank you also for sending Danny round. It helped. Talking to someone.' Not that she'd told him anything. But it had given her pause. And she knew that if she ran, Mark would just find her again. There had to be another way.

Charlie shrugged. He headed to the door of the boatshed, but turned before going in.

'I don't know what any of this is about, young lady. But I do know one thing. If you want whoever this is out of your life, running doesn't work. You've got to stand up for yourself.'

Nicole stared at Charlie. How could he possibly know?

The less you're seen, the more you see.

How much did he see?

On the way back to the cottage Nicole took in a deep breath of warm air and allowed herself to smile and walk with her shoulders back. She had Charlie, and in the topsy-turvy world that was now her reality, that was at least something.

She had Charlie and Danny and Mandy and Ivy. And in this reality, where she'd lost everything else, that amounted to a big something.

2nd January, 1953

My Dearest Tom,

The Christmas stall was a great success. I sold all bar three of my sculptures. It will not be long before every house in the cove has an Ivy Wilson original on their mantlepiece or side table. Of course, once that happens my artistic career will be over with no new buyers, but that is the lot of a suffering artist, is it not? Yes, you are allowed to laugh.

Lucy has been receiving letters from Fabricio, although she continues to insist there is nothing to it beyond friendship. But, you and I know differently, my love. I wonder if their 'friendship' will be renewed when we return to Tuscany later this year. Yes, my dear, we have decided that as widows of means we are perfectly within our rights to flit over to Italy as often as we wish. Or perhaps we might go to Spain or France. We have discussed this also. Our tickets for June are already purchased. We are going to stop first in London for the coronation of Elizabeth.

Father Anthony is thrilled with the news and has given us the specific task of taking in two or three churches during our time away – places he has always wanted to go. Naturally, the first on his list is the Duomo in Florence. We did, of course, go there last time, its sage and pink beauty glorious, but he has a distant relative there, a clerk or some such he wishes us to look in on.

We are happy to oblige.

Of course, having Father Anthony's blessing for our trip also helps keep Mother's tongue in check. I am not as selfless as I pretend. She does not approve of two single ladies of breeding gallivanting around the world without a chaperone. She certainly would not approve of Lucy's friendship with Fabricio, but she is none the wiser on that count. But what can she say if we are on a mission for Father Anthony?

Mother and Father have joined me again for the holiday season. Father's wit seems to have slowed somewhat in the past twelve months and Mother is pressing him to retire. She has her building now and a wing of the library, so perhaps she feels she has got all she can out of his situation.

In our quiet times alone I encourage Father to continue working for as long he wishes. He is a happy man ensconced in academia.

It may not surprise you to learn that Mr Wetherby is no longer in the family home. He is back with his parents. Joan is telling everyone who will listen that it is due to the ill health of his mother, but the entire town knows that the sour woman has kicked him out. Not that he is not deserving – the wretched scoundrel is the worst of men. Why she married him so quickly I have never understood.

Almost the whole of the cove heard the raging argument that preceded the separation, though we act as if we did not.

I saw her yesterday, though she pretended not to notice me. Beneath her usual cantankerous expression I believe I saw genuine sadness. Perhaps it were a trick of light, but her cheeks appeared moist. My heart did reach out to her, even if I did not.

The New Year's fireworks down on South Beach were lovely once again. They are getting bigger every year.

Take care, my darling. Till next I write.

Forever yours,

Ivy

∼

Sitting in his worn-out chair, Charlie felt every day of every year of his eighty-odd years on Earth pressing on him. He'd forgotten how draining being connected with someone could be, especially at his age, especially with the young whose every up and down in life is a drama of Odyssean proportions.

Still, he was glad she'd stuck around. It showed she had character, and character was what he needed her to have. And playing Scrabble with her took his mind back to more pleasant days.

He could still picture Ivy sitting on the bench, him sitting opposite. He often let her win, holding back words that would give him a high score. It was the least he could do for the woman who'd shown a perfect stranger such open kindness. After that stormy evening on the beach, the cloud thick, black and rumbling in anger, the sea grey and violent, she could have simply thanked him or given him a small reward and sent him on his way. She could have ignored him. She could have called the police. But she gave a dishevelled young man shelter. She asked no questions of him; who he was, where he'd come from, how he'd come to be on that damp stretch of sand that day.

She'd saved him. A waste, most people would say, to save a man so he could live alone with his guilt and pain, decade after decade. But that wouldn't be the harshest thing they could say.

Pulling out his copy of *David Copperfield*, the cover clean and cared for, he opened it up at the first chapter. He'd read it so many times the words were part of him, the story part of his memory. If only all his memories were so well written.

The opening lines sang in his head and he disappeared into Dickens's world. 'Whether I shall turn out to be the hero of my own life, or whether that station will be held by anybody else, these pages must show.'

All Charlie knew was that he was no hero. Of his life or anyone else's. But he could still do something right. The appointment tomorrow with the lawyer in Sydney would enable him to. He hoped.

Twenty-four

Trivia was still half an hour away. Nicole paced the empty rooms of the cottage, read through her lists, checked her phone.

No further messages. Maybe Mark had given up. Nicole blocked his number.

The minutes ticked by, her thoughts drifting to the fact that Danny would be there. His green eyes haunted her, stirring feelings she'd rather remain un-stirred.

With too many untamed thoughts raging through her mind – Mark, Danny, Mark – Nicole turned to Ivy's words to soothe her soul.

She pulled out a postcard stamped July 1959. They were always stamped and franked, sent, but none of them were addressed to a person, just to the cottage. If the postman read them, which surely he would have, it would have appeared as though Ivy was simply sending home pretty reminders of her trips – not writing to her husband who'd been dead fifteen years.

We journeyed to Positano today with Fabricio. I was certain we would not survive the precariously winding roads. But it was well worth the angst. We are staying with a friend of Fabricio for a week and tomorrow plan to go to the Collegiate Church of Santa Maria Assunta. They have an icon of a black Madonna – what will Father Anthony say?

The picture on the front does not do justice.

Perhaps Ivy wanted to feel connected to Tom while she was so far away from home. Perhaps she wanted to pretend, briefly, there was someone back in Rosella Cove who wanted to know what she was doing on the other side of the world, and eagerly awaited her return. Perhaps it was simply habit now, part of her routine, to write to Tom.

The next letter brought a smile to Nicole's face.

15th October, 1960

My Dearest Tom,

You simply will not believe what has happened. Fabricio is here. His wife has passed away and he has finally declared his love for Lucy. I am, in some respects, most relieved as I had thought perhaps he had been mistreating Lucy's affection for him, that she was merely a convenient annual affair. But, I suppose I was wrong. He is here. With Lucy. And yesterday he proposed. Proposed! She said yes.

I should be much happier than I am.

Of course I am glad my dearest friend has found love again after such loss. And she is ever so happy. But, and I know it is desperately selfish of me to say it, she and I have been the closest of friends for so long now, I cannot bear the thought of someone stealing her away from me.

Lucy talks of adventures the three of us will have together now he is here, but I am not naïve enough to believe her. I know how things will be once they are married. And so it ought to be, too.

He stays in the boatshed. Naturally, he could not stay with Lucy, despite how the world views such things these days. Oh, I am starting to feel my age. Still, there are morals one must stand by and rather than see Fabricio waste his money staying at The Royal, I offered him the boatshed.

We have borrowed a bed from the Tuckers and have made the space comfortable enough. He shall not be there long. They plan to marry as soon as is practical.

Naturally, Joan Wetherby has been protesting quite loudly around town that a widow of my standing should not allow a strange man to take up residence on my property. She even raised the issue at the last CWA meeting, can you believe? Suggesting my actions were condemning the entire town to moral degradation. Said I never did give due respect to the relationship between a man and woman, and that I have gone completely mad as is evidenced by the fact I continue to refuse to wear shoes to our meetings. I have had my fill of that woman.

I resigned. Needless to say I shall not be winning any ribbons at the next fair for my baking.

Father's health worsens. He has stopped lecturing now and he and Mother spend their time in their apartment. I visit often and even suggested to Father I move there while he is so ill. He laughed and asked if I was trying to kill him faster. You see, it seems Mother is around him far more when I am there than when I am not and the peace of her absence is what is keeping him going. I write to him every week and he is still able to read my letters for himself and takes great joy in them.

Lucy has a cousin in Kingsford who has offered to put me up for as long as I need should it come to that.

I must go. Fabricio will be here shortly to cook dinner for Lucy and me. One of his many talents. He is actually quite a wonderful fellow. I wonder if he has a cousin we could impose upon to take on Joan and whisk her back to Italy?

Missing you dearly,

Forever yours,

Ivy

PS The Rangers play their first grand final next week – against the Wolves. The entire town is abuzz and we all plan to attend. Even me.

Nicole folded the letter and put it back. She looked at her phone. Damn. She was late for trivia. Again.

When Nicole got to The Royal, the others were sitting there, chatting quietly. Jason had held off on the questions at the behest of Mandy and a promise of a tray of lamingtons. But the second Nicole walked in, he started.

'Which Greek goddess has the symbol of the moon, or the deer?'

Nicole looked to Mandy who stared back at her with a blank expression. She turned to Danny. He smiled and gently brushed her thigh with his hand. That was no help. And it made her blush. He wrote down the answer: 'Artemis'.

As the questions rolled out, Danny got up to refresh everyone's drinks. He placed a hand on Nicole's shoulder as he passed and squeezed gently. It was a simple gesture, but a powerful one.

A table of German backpackers passing through town won the game, much to Cheryl's distress, but Danny bought her a glass of her favourite wine and she was placated. She sat quietly in the corner, chatting with Jacqui.

'Hey, Nicole.' Mandy interrupted the quiet conversation of the table. 'Before you got here tonight, we were talking about all the painting you still have to do.'

'Oh, please. Don't remind me.' Nicole rolled her eyes. Painting, the one thing she thought she could do before starting this crazy project, was now the thing she dreaded most.

'Well, we were thinking, how about a painting bee? Get that job knocked over,' Jacqui suggested and, before Nicole could answer, she and Cheryl got to work making plans for a fortnight's time.

As the group disbanded Danny leaned in to Nicole. 'Shall I walk you home?'

Nicole was torn.

'Just a walk.' He grinned.

'That would be nice.'

She and Danny stood on the verandah, saying nothing, looking into each other's eyes. There was a calmness to the moment, a gentle stillness that made Nicole feel alive.

'Goodnight, Nicole.' Danny leaned down to kiss her on the cheek.

She lifted her head slightly and his lips caught hers. He kissed her softly, sending warmth radiating through Nicole's entire body.

'Goodnight,' she breathed.

Nicole pushed open the door to the cottage. She'd forgotten to leave a light on and in the blackness she couldn't see. A few steps in she stubbed her toe and yelped. It was her suitcase, left at the door.

She wheeled it to her bedroom, and unpacked it.

Twenty-five

The next day Nicole spent the morning going through her Ivy folder that she kept under her bed.

Inside was the photo Mandy had given her (she should probably give it back), and the newspaper clippings and church bulletin copies she'd dug up from the library so far. She looked back at the *Cove Chronicle*'s article about the dance, the faces in the yellowed photograph known to her now. Joan was easy to spot, her steely glare the only unhappy visage in shot. Tom and Ivy, the targets of her scowl, looking as if they had touched the stars, stood just to the right. A young Bill Tucker standing off to the side, looking at the older men as if they were his heroes, was instantly recognisable, his stance and gaze unchanged after all these years.

An idea teased her thoughts and Nicole took out the large leather-bound notebook from the bottom drawer beside her bed and wrote more questions.

Who was the boy off to the left with the pointy face looking as if he owned the world? Why would Ivy be at this dance, if she was from Sydney?

Was there something here for Nicole? Something she could perhaps turn into a . . . No. This was for personal interest only. Ivy's letters were simply a way to pass time. A hobby.

She opened the next piece of her hobby.

28th December, 1961

My Dearest Tom,

Father is gone. Thankfully I was with him when he passed. Mother had insisted after Christmas that I return home to the cove. But, I could see Father was far more ill than she wished me to believe, so I stayed.

Father's passing was quiet, his breathing slowing as I held his hand. Mother was inconsolable. You know, I have never paused to consider the possibility that deep down she did love him.

The funeral was elegant and sombre. The university choir sang 'Amazing Grace', which was lovely. Father's contemporaries and his students made a point of speaking to me afterward, all of them praising his work and dedication. I felt most proud.

Mother and I parted after the funeral, the coldness between us still. Perhaps she has never forgiven me for marrying you. Perhaps she has never forgiven me for having to share Father with me. Perhaps I will never know.

I have Father's copy of David Copperfield *with me now. I took it without Mother knowing, but her approval is something I no longer need. There is freedom in that thought. I figured she would only sell it anyway. It must be worth a small fortune now. And I could not let that happen. It was his favourite and it needs to stay where it is loved.*

I cry each night knowing I have lost him. I hope the two of you find each other in heaven and become the friends I always knew you could have been if not for Mother's censure. Take care of him for me, darling. As Father Anthony said, 'A good soul has left our Earthly world.'

Lucy and Fabricio have now only two months till they marry. He has been waiting until his family were able to travel here for the celebration. They will arrive next month. I must say he has made the boatshed comfortable for himself since arriving. He is quite the handyman and he now has basic wash facilities in there. Father Anthony has ensured some of the church donations were filtered his way – a chair and a bookcase and a few smaller items, like a teapot and cups. I think the bookcase may have been Joan Wetherby's. Father Anthony always insists on anonymity when it comes to such charity. Joan would have palpitations if she knew what has become of it. Perhaps I should tell her.

Fabricio has given the entire boatshed a fresh coat of paint, inside and out. It certainly needed it and it looks quite inviting.

I have not entered many times over the years. Only on the odd occasion to clean. It is good to see it used once more. Though I will be happy to have our bench back once he is moved in with Lucy. I miss my Sunday mornings sitting there, looking for you in the waves. I have no family left now and I fear what will become of me once Lucy is married and has a new family to call her own.

Take care, my dearest. Watch over Father.

Forever yours,

Ivy

PS Lucy manned our Christmas stall while I was in Sydney with Father. She sold every one of my sculptures. William Tucker is the new coach of The Rangers and he bought one of my angels for his Iris, who was so taken with it she has convinced him to invite me to set up a small table at all their home games. We will see how it goes.

Twenty-six

With a black and white scarf around her neck, Nicole walked down to the oval, Mandy waving when she saw her coming.

'Well, look at you,' she said. 'A true convert at last.'

She tugged on the tassels hanging from the end of Nicole's Rangers scarf and grinned.

'When in Rome . . .' Nicole shrugged and smiled. 'So what are our chances?' She nodded towards the middle of the field where the two teams were warming up.

'Yet to beat them. Riverton have been champs three years in a row. But we've never had our lucky charm on the sideline when we've played them either.'

'Oh, no pressure then.' Nicole laughed, fanning her face with her hands.

'None at all.' Mandy smiled. 'You can handle it,' she whispered in her ear and wrapped her arm around Nicole's back.

'Maybe.' Nicole hugged Mandy back. Maybe she could.

Nicole found herself cheering out loud as the Rangers scored the first points of the match when Danny went over the line. And she found herself clutching at her scarf in despair as Riverton pulled ahead just before half-time. When the hooter blew, her shoulders fell and she realised how tense she'd been.

'Let's grab a sanger,' Mandy suggested.

The smell of barbecuing onions filled Nicole's nose as they walked through the market.

'Hey,' she said. 'How long have the markets been here? At the footy match?'

'Gosh, forever I think.' Mandy shrugged her shoulders. 'Certainly all of my life, at least. Maybe longer. Why?'

'Just curious. I've never really seen it before. Just wondering how it started.'

Was her hunch right?

'Cheryl might know,' Mandy suggested, as they arrived at the line for the sausage sandwiches.

'Back in the early sixties.' Cheryl put onions on Nicole's bread and Jim served up a fat, split sausage. 'A couple of CWA women, I think, set up a stall one day and it grew from there. I was pretty young, so my memory, well, you know . . .'

'Cute then, cute now,' Jim chimed in, and Mandy and Nicole smiled. 'Sauce?' he asked.

As they moved past the stalls, Nicole felt like she was moving through the past and present simultaneously. She pictured Ivy and Lucy standing behind their angels and sculptures, right there where Jacqui sat, perhaps. Maybe the following year Mrs Li joined them with her sponge cakes, there where the cake stall now sat. The year after that, Joan Wetherby with her lamingtons, or lamington cakes as they'd have called them, in direct competition, her table set up opposite, her gaze across the grass steely. Nicole stepped through time and imagined the number of stalls increasing each year, the advantage of fresh, out-of-town blood to sell to each fortnight dawning on people, until it grew to the eclectic crowd it was today. In her mind the two worlds blended into a perfect collage of then and now.

With five minutes to go, the Rangers were down five points. Both sides of the crowd were screaming and cheering loudly, waving scarves and handmade pom-poms. Not a single person remained seated. Nicole's arm began to throb and she realised Mandy's hand was buried deep into her flesh.

The referee blew a penalty against Riverton, ten out from touch, and the Rams supporters booed and hissed fiercely.

There was no point going for a field goal. It wouldn't be enough. Danny looked over to Nicole.

With a pump of her fist she mouthed, 'Come on.' Beside her, Mandy held her breath.

Danny winked and flashed a cheeky grin. He tapped the ball, faked a pass, wrong-footed the fattest Riverton player who was in his way and dived towards the line.

A deafening cheer erupted as the ref blew his whistle and indicated 'try'.

A conversion would win the game.

The Rangers supporters went quiet as Danny lined up for the kick. The Riverton crowd jeered and heckled.

Mandy smiled. 'He never misses these.'

Danny's shoulders rose and fell. Step, shuffle, step, kick.

A cheer went up around the spectators – the Rams spectators.

Danny had missed. His posse of mini-me Rangers surrounded him as he came off the field, consoling him with pats on the back. The littlest Ranger, Jason Junior wrapped him in a tight hug.

The atmosphere in The Royal was subdued to say the least. Small groups of players and supporters gathered in quiet conversations and George poured a steady stream of ale.

Nicole looked over to Danny, who was moving around the pub patting his players on the back. He smiled across to her and warmth flowed through her.

'Given we lost, you two seem pretty happy with yourselves.' Mandy returned from the bar with a couple of wines. 'Or is that *with each other?*'

Nicole couldn't help but grin.

'When?'

'The other day. It was just a kiss.' Nicole's pulse started racing just thinking about it. Them. Three kisses.

'A kiss?' Mandy had to cover her mouth to stop from screaming. Then she threw her arms around Nicole. 'I want to know everything.'

Nicole didn't tell her everything, but enough to satisfy her curiosity. 'And then we talked all morning. About absolutely everything.'

'He told you about Caitlyn?'

'Caitlyn?'

'His ex.'

'No. Is there something to tell?'

'It isn't really my place to say anything.'

Nicole gave her look.

'Okay, well, I have put my foot in it, I suppose. He and Caitlyn had a pretty nasty break-up, about two years ago now, and he never really got over it. We all thought they were going to get married. But turns out she didn't want kids. And he can't wait to be a dad. They just couldn't get past it.'

Nicole's mind started spinning. He can't wait to be a dad. She clutched her stomach.

'It wasn't long after that that he started going to Bangladesh regularly,' Mandy continued. 'He sure loves those kids.'

A shout went up from the other side of the pub and the juke-box started playing. Mandy and Trevor's song started and in a flash Mandy was being whisked onto the dance floor.

Nicole left the pub quickly. Halfway home she stopped to catch her breath. No, this wasn't fair. At all.

Inside the cottage she slumped into the couch and hung her head.

There was a light knock on the door.

'Nicole? It's Danny. Are you okay?'

Maybe if she stayed silent, he'd go away.

'Nicole? What's wrong?'

Nicole walked to the front door, opening it only slightly.

'Hey.' Danny frowned.

'I'm just really tired,' she lied.

'Have I done something wrong?'

Oh, God. He was doubting himself. He'd done everything right. This was all on her.

'No. Of course not.'

'You know, Nicole, when you're not being straight with me, your left eye crinkles ever so slightly.'

She drew in a deep breath. 'It's nothing. I just need to take things a bit slower.' *Like screeching to a sudden halt.*

'Okay. That's fine. But if we've got any hope of turning this into something, and I think maybe this could be something, we have to be completely open with each other. Tell me if there's something wrong.'

Nicole knew he was right. This was her chance to tell him about Mark, what had brought her here, about her inability to have children. Everything. But she just couldn't bring herself to do it.

He'd broken up with Caitlyn because she didn't want kids. How would he react if she told him she couldn't have kids?

'I'm just trying to work some things out. It's fine. Really.'

She could see from his expression he didn't buy it, but he was too much of a gentleman to push her too hard. He took her hands and leaned in to kiss her on the cheek, catching the corner of her mouth.

She turned her head slightly and caught the fullness of his lips.

The realisation this could go no further hit her hard. Danny said goodnight and walked off down the path.

Of course he wanted children. Why wouldn't he? Tears filled her eyes. Even if Nicole could find a solution to her living arrangements, even if Danny was as genuine and wonderful as he seemed, even if she could put all her insecurities and Mark-inflicted issues aside, there was one thing she couldn't change, couldn't control.

It was the one thing Danny wanted. The one thing she couldn't give him.

Nicole lay in bed and closed her eyes, but sleep evaded her.

She couldn't run. She couldn't stay. She was trapped in the in-between.

A life lost that wouldn't let her go. A life found that she couldn't hang on to.

She rolled over and pulled out Ivy's box from the bedside table. Her one comfort.

2nd February, 1962

My Dearest Tom,

Lucy's wedding was beautiful. There was no pomp and ceremony, which Joan felt necessary to point out continually. She was only invited because Lucy felt sorry for her, and, let us be honest, in a town like this such an omission would have been keenly felt. Still, Joan's sourness could not dampen the day.

Father Anthony blessed the union in a simple service, one I thought was appropriate given the age and circumstance of the bride and groom, despite what Whinging Wetherby says. It was, of course, nothing compared to her glamorous event, but no wedding ever was or will be as she still feels the need to point out, three decades and one divorce later.

We had a sumptuous feast back at the cottage afterward. The entire town was here, my love. The front yard was awash with colour – vases filled with pink and orange roses from the garden atop borrowed tables of all shapes and sizes draped in white linen cloth, green salads and red pasta sauces on display in clear bowls, powder blue and lilac sugared almonds sprinkled on loaned porcelain plates decorated with floral sprays.

It was kaleidoscopic, not the sort of party you could imagine me at the helm of, I am sure, but it was quite perfect. So wonderfully perfect.

Lucy and Fabricio looked terribly happy and any doubt I had about the two of them has been washed away. I do believe they are meant to be together. They will honeymoon in France and Spain and I will join them late in the northern summer in Florence. I fear this may be my last trip to Tuscany. I have no desire to play the role of desperate-widow-friend being accommodated out of a sense of pity.

Perhaps I should see some of Australia next year. Take The Ghan maybe, visit Ayers Rock, go to Perth. I will miss my annual art classes though. I have so enjoyed them. But they will not be the same now. Perhaps I can travel through Europe on my own instead. These days it is not as unacceptable as it once was for a woman to travel alone.

Can you see me as the eccentric old lady travelling the world with my beaten-up brown suitcase, sipping tea alone in a Parisian café, or wandering the Victoria and Albert babbling to myself?

I am so happy for Lucy. I truly am. To grow old alone is not an easy fate to endure. But, I must not dwell. These are happy days.

At next week's match, Peggy is joining me on my stall with her baked offerings. Father Anthony is talking about retirement, though I doubt it will ever happen and I think she is worried she will cease to exist should he follow through and they are no longer our spiritual leaders. She is looking for another way to reach out to her flock, I suppose. I did not have the heart to tell her that her cakes and biscuits may just drive her flock away. In all these years the poor woman has not learned to cook.

It will be nice to have some company, though, and I owe Father Anthony for the kindness he has always shown. Father Anthony is well loved. Yes, her cakes will certainly sell, though I cannot say with any confidence they will be eaten.

For now that is all. Take care, my dearest.

Forever yours,

Ivy

PS I have included a photo of Lucy's wedding. You can see how happy they are!

Nicole looked at the picture. Lucy and Fabricio were arm in arm, Fabricio wearing a simple grey suit and Lucy looking serene and beautiful in a soft blue kaftan. Beside Lucy stood Ivy in a bright floral dress that reached to her toes. Her bare toes. On the grass lay a pair of slippers, rejected.

Nicole couldn't help grinning. At least someone was getting their happily ever after.

As she returned the envelope to the box, she noticed the next one was very thin. Really thin. She pulled it out and gasped.

23rd March, 1967
My Dearest Tom,
She is leaving. Lucy and Fabricio are moving to Italy. To be near his family. She is leaving. They have only another two weeks before they fly. I did not think she would really do it, really go.

She is leaving me.

Now I have truly lost everything dear to me. What is there left? What have I now?

Nothing.

Ivy

Twenty-seven

Nicole stared out her bedroom window, willing the sun to rise. She'd given up on sleep hours ago and now she waited for dawn to release her from the torture that had gripped her all night. She usually looked forward to Sunday mornings – no renovation tasks scheduled, her weekly game of Scrabble with Charlie mid-morning. But this morning was tainted with images she conjured every time she closed her eyes.

She couldn't leave Ivy there like that last night, so sad, so wretched after news of Lucy's leaving. She had to read one more letter and make sure her friend was okay. But that one more letter had burned words into her mind that had kept her awake; that she would never forget.

The first rays of sunshine filtered into her room and she got out of bed. She went into the kitchen and started making chocolate-chip cookies, using Mandy's never-fail recipe. Charlie would groan, no doubt, about the repetition of her old favourite. He'd been enjoying her weekly experiments that constituted their morning tea. But today was not the day to try something new.

She wiped down the kitchen and checked her watch. How on earth was she going to pass the next few hours until she could get to Charlie?

She had so many questions. Maybe she should write them down. But where did she start?

She was desperate to know and he'd have the answers. But she couldn't rush into it. She couldn't blurt them out and expect answers on the spot. Even if there was time and gentleness enough to broach it with him, there was no guarantee he'd tell her what she wanted to know.

How would she be able to sit across from him and not ask about that night on the beach?

Tick-tock, the minutes plodded by.

She baked another batch of cookies. She cleaned up.

Tick-tock.

Finally the time came. She took in three long breaths and headed to the boatshed.

Nicole slowed her steps as she approached but she couldn't slow her racing mind.

Charlie was waiting for her, the Scrabble board set up, two cups of tea cooling on their saucers.

'Morning,' he greeted her.

'Morning.' Nicole smiled weakly.

'You look terrible. What's wrong?'

'I didn't sleep well, is all.'

Couldn't stop reading that damn letter.

How was it you came to be walking on the beach that night? she wanted to ask. Did you realise what Ivy was doing there? Of course you would have. It would have been plain as day. No silly questions. Charlie wouldn't answer silly questions. It would be the end of the conversation if it ever got started.

She laid out her tiles and scored eleven points with 'join'. She didn't see that she could have made 'enjoys' for sixteen.

The bigger question, of course, was how to start the conversation with Charlie in the first place. If she came straight out with it, she'd have to explain not only the fact she knew such intimate details of his first meeting with Ivy, but also how she did. She wasn't sure how he'd react to that.

But, if she led with a vague, general 'how'd you come to be living in the boatshed?' she'd be met with an equally vague and general response.

She stared at the letters on the yellowed tiles sitting before her, which now appeared as random black scratches. They made no sense at all.

Charlie had taken no pleasure in their game. Nicole was clearly somewhere else today. He'd kept an eye on the tiles she'd put out, as he always did, and she was clearly not on form. The 'y' she so casually discarded early on could have been held onto for much better use with a later move. Same with the 'k' three turns after that. It didn't even seem that she was looking at the letters she was using, let alone the words he'd placed on the board and how she could use them to her advantage.

What had her so distracted now? And why did it have to make his Sunday morning so sour? It was the only part of the week he looked forward to.

He took no pleasure in winning today. Not like that.

He watched her walk up the path as she left, and once again

questioned all his choices that led her here. It was too late now, though. The wheels were in motion for the custodian of what remained of his wasted and wretched life and of Ivy's legacy.

———

As Nicole headed home she recalled the letter, the words etched in her mind.

14th May, 1968
My Dearest Tom,
I have let you down. I have not been as strong as you asked of me when you shipped out. I gave up. Lucy leaving was more than I could bear, the utter loneliness that consumed me, intolerable. I find it curious now that such a relatively small event was what broke me. I survived losing you, and our angel. I have crafted a quiet life for myself these past twenty-odd years. Yet somehow the simple act of Lucy leaving reignited the burden of loneliness I did not realise I have been carrying all these years. The proverbial straw to break my back. My spirit.

I am ashamed to tell you what I did, but who else can I confess to? Father Anthony would be so disappointed in me. And if Mother ever found out . . . I cannot bear to think. Besides, God will judge me in His own way, in His own time. But I must confess to you. Perhaps it will help.

Two nights ago I walked down the path, past the boatshed, to the cove. It was just a walk. I had no plan. The waves were crashing so heavily. We have had terrible storms this past week. I stood on the sand, barefoot, staring into the pounding black. I felt so desperately alone. Alone and wretched and empty. The waves called to me.

I walked into the water. And once the water hit my ankles it pulled me towards its cold embrace. I walked in even further. Perhaps I was looking for that sense of calm I have so often felt beside the water. Perhaps there was no conscious sense of anything at all. Just slipping in to a state of nothingness.

The thundering stopped in my ears and the waves crashed around my hips. I knew I would not return to shore. I did not fight the pull. I did not kick or thrash my arms about. I was calm. So very calm.

I saw your loving face, so clearly, as the ocean took me under.

A rush of noise lifted me to the surface and I gasped for air. There was a voice, detached, distant. I felt myself being carried. I was cold and soaked. There was sand beneath my body. The waves tried to grab my ankles as I lay there, begging me to return. Oh, how I wanted to return. But the voice kept calling. He would not let me go. It went dark after that.

I woke in the boatshed atop Fabricio's old bed. The sun was pouring through the portal window.

There was a man there. In his thirties, perhaps? It is quite hard to tell. He made me drink tea and promised to fix the door he kicked in. He said nothing else.

I uttered no thanks, no explanation. I was too embarrassed to admit what had happened. Too exhausted to offer a lie as an excuse. I said nothing.

Did you send him to save me?

He is not from around here, or any town close by, that is certain. Something about him reads city, though I do not know from which one he comes. He has asked me no questions and I will return in kind.

He is in the boatshed still. I told him he was welcome to stay for as long as he needs. He carries no possessions, save the worn and dirty clothes on his back. I know not why he was passing that night, or where he was heading. He said he will stay until he fixes the door and then move on.

You will think me careless, I know, inviting a stranger to stay. But I had to offer him kindness, shelter, for what he did. And if you did send him, then I know I must look after him. There must be some purpose to him finding me, saving me.

I am full of shame and guilt. Can you forgive me?

This strange man who rescued me is intriguing. His face is covered in dirt and he wears a perpetual scowl but I detect a gentleness in his spirit. I do not fear him, though perhaps I should.

Time alone will tell.

Time. So often we speak of Time as a friend – how it heals our wounds, how it is on our side, how our happiest moments are the times of our life. Yet Time is also our enemy. We waste so much of it and can never go back to fix the mistakes or relive the joy. We wear the scars of Time across our face. Time claims each one of us in the end. It is the herald of death.

Time . . . I know I have spent too much of it alone. I know that I have wished, still wish, perhaps, my Time here to end. I do not know how Time-to-come will pass or what I am supposed to do with it.

Evening comes again. Time eternal. I have allowed him to stay in the boatshed these past two nights. It was the least I could do. There is a light on in there now. I have offered him supper, but he declined.

I have learned his name is Charlie. The irony of this was not lost on me and I had to hold back long buried tears for our lost little one.

Am I to look after this angel you sent? Will he stay?

Forgive me, my love, and help me find the strength I need for whatever is next to come.

Forever yours,

Ivy

Twenty-eight

Exhaustion washed over Nicole as she dozed in the wicker chair in the afternoon sun that flooded the verandah. It had been a very big day. After she returned from her Scrabble game with Charlie she finished applying the last of the undercoat to the hallway and cleaned up the rest of the cottage.

The sound of crunching gravel alerted her to someone's arrival and sat up straight as she saw Mandy's ute pull up.

'Hi,' called Mandy from the fence. 'Look at you there basking in the sun.'

'Hey.' Nicole waved. 'To what do I owe this pleasure?'

'I wanted to say sorry about the way I blurted out the Caitlyn thing at the pub, Nicole.'

'It's okay. I'm glad you told me.'

'Thank goodness.' Mandy raised a hand to her chest. 'He's a good man, you know.'

Nicole sighed.

'Okay, spill.' Mandy sat herself down on the other wicker chair and turned to face Nicole directly. 'What's the problem?'

'Nothing gets past you, does it, Mandy?'

'Not a lot.'

How much could she tell Mandy? It might be good to get it off her chest. Some of it, anyway. Would Mandy judge her?

'There's a guy. In my past. He . . . I . . .' No. She couldn't do it. 'And then there's this place and the lease . . .'

Nicole threw her hands in the air. Oh, what was the point of any it?

'Hmmm.' Mandy tilted her head to the side. 'You haven't given me a lot to go on. But let's see what I can do with it anyway.' Her smile was gentle and warm. 'Okay. The easy one first. When the lease runs out here, you can rent somewhere else. There are a few rooms in town. If worst comes to worst, there's always a spare room at our place. Even if it's just for a little while, till you figure out what you want to do. How'd I do with that one?'

A gentle breeze pushed through the gum leaves across the path, shifting shadows in a delicate dance. 'Pretty good.' A short-term, interim plan, but a least a plan.

'But that's not really the problem, is it?' Mandy shook her head.

Not the insurmountable one, thought Nicole.

Mandy got up and paced the verandah. 'This guy in your past? If he's definitely in the past, maybe it's time to leave him there. I don't know if you and Danny have a future, but wouldn't it be fun to find out?'

Nicole laughed. Yes. It would probably be a lot of fun. But that wasn't really the point.

'I've known Danny since he was a pimple-faced kid.' Mandy reached out and touched Nicole's arm gently. 'He's one of the good ones.'

Nicole nodded. 'I gathered that.' That was why she couldn't hurt him with the truth about her inability to have children.

Mandy crouched down beside Nicole. 'I know trusting someone can be hard, if you've been hurt before, but you'll never know if Danny's worth it unless you try.'

Trust wasn't the issue. Not trust of Danny, anyway. Not really. It was really whether she could trust herself again; whether she was willing to show all of herself, dirty truth and all, to someone else.

'So I'm two for two?' Mandy stood proud.

'Yep.'

'Then why aren't you smiling?' Mandy put her hands on her hips.

'What if . . .' Be brave, Nicole. A simple question. 'What if the guy from my past won't leave me in the past?'

'Easy.' Mandy wrapped her in hug. 'Then he's just a bully and together we'll bloomin' well make him. Bullies only respond to strength.'

Nicole let out a tiny laugh. It sounded so very simple. 'How is it you're so wise?'

'Natural gift, my dear. Now come inside and fix me a snack. I'm starving.'

Nicole threw together a quick chicken salad and they sat in the kitchen and Mandy went through the plans for the painting bee Jacqui had suggested last trivia night – who would bring what to eat, which tasks were allocated to whom, who'd bring what equipment. Nicole wanted to make a list, but Mandy put a gentle hand on her shoulder.

'We'll all turn up next Sunday and it will just work out.'

They tidied up their dinner mess and Mandy bade her farewell. 'Have you told Danny any of what you told me?'

Nicole shook her head.

'Maybe you should.'

To what end, though?

Nicole couldn't think about that right now. All she wanted was to find out what happened next with Ivy and Charlie.

16th December, 1968

My Dearest Tom,

Charlie remains in the boatshed. He has fixed the door and started on fixing up other bits and pieces – one of the window frames, the planter box at the entrance. He has offered to paint the cottage verandah and I have accepted. It is flaking and while I am sure I could manage the task (you would be impressed with the skills I have been forced to acquire from living alone!), I must admit I welcomed having an excuse to keep him here longer.

He has not been one for talking and is not a joyous soul spreading warmth – oh, how I miss Lucy. But, I have grown somewhat accustomed to his quiet company.

I have begun bringing him tea each morning and we often sit together, without speaking, on the bench you made me. We sip Earl Grey, and watch the waves. I find myself looking forward to those silent moments, the part of the day I feel I am no longer alone in the world.

Last week we came to an agreement, and it seems his stay will be indefinite.

The seed of a thought germinated in Nicole's mind. Did Charlie have something to do with the cottage and the rental agreement?

It was not intentional, on either side I believe, but it came to pass last Sunday and quite by accident I suggested he stay, and quite surprisingly he agreed. To be honest, I think he was as shocked by his acceptance as I was by my invitation.

We were finishing a game of Scrabble – he is a formidable opponent – and I asked him outright how long he thought he would be staying. He said he did not know.

'Do you have anywhere else to go?' I asked.

He shook his head. 'There is nowhere for a man like me,' was his answer.

How I wanted to know more! What horrible burden could a man so young be carrying to have lost his place completely in the world? My curiosity finally got the better of me, and so I asked.

'Tell me, Charlie,' I said. 'What was it that led you here? We are friends, if not in a conventional fashion, and I shall not judge.'

I could see in his eyes he wished to tell me but was scared to do so. Like a child who knows they have done something wrong and wants to confess but is afraid of his parents' wrath.

Nothing could have prepared me for his answer, my love, nothing in this world. I promised him I would never tell a soul and so I will not, not even you. He has taken a great risk in my knowing and I dare not betray his trust. My hands are shaking even now.

I will tell you that I have removed all traces of alcohol from the cottage. Even my cooking sherry – what will become of my Christmas trifle this year? But while his story is indeed horrific and sad, I trust he is no threat. I am, perhaps, being a foolish old woman, but if you had seen his eyes, you would agree with me.

Perhaps.

As he finished his story, my heart broke and, apparently, all sense left me.

'Would you like to stay here?' I asked and he looked at me as if he could not quite believe I had said it. He whispered yes and I felt overcome by a brief wash of doubt, wishing I could take it back.

Then I saw the tears falling down his cheeks and I realised I had done the right thing.

'My poor child,' I told him, 'this is your home as long as you wish.'

Before I emptied all the alcohol (do not fear – I gave your whisky away to William Tucker when he returned all those years ago; it did not go down the drain), I poured myself a large glass of wine and wondered if I would live to regret my rashness.

In the days that have followed I have seen a lighter side to my new tenant. He has even smiled. It is a sad smile, but he is ever so handsome when he allows it to grace his face. Some days he goes out fishing and just yesterday he gave me his catch for dinner. He even told me how best to prepare it.

He has agreed to be my handyman in exchange for board in the boatshed, and I have asked Father Anthony to send as many odd jobs for the church his way as is reasonable. I cannot see Charlie holding down a regular job (too many questions would be asked), and the man must eat. If Father Anthony was concerned, he did not show it. He simply made reference to 'all God's children'. That man is one of His true blessings.

Peggy's health is deteriorating, yet he still finds the strength to care for others. There is an apple teacake in the oven as I write this, that I will take over when I visit tomorrow.

Joan Wetherby has had more than enough to say on the matter. She accuses me of keeping a 'strange vagabond in the boatshed, a madman or criminal with surely dishonourable intentions'.

I finally lost control of my temper when she said this. I told her I preferred the company of a would-be crazed murderer who minded his own business to that of a mean-spirited, unchristian, busy-body who would rather spend her time spreading vicious rumours than caring for her fellow man.

I will ask God's forgiveness next Sunday for my outburst, many pews away from Mrs Wetherby.

If I am not murdered in my sleep before then, of course.

Perhaps I should not joke about such things.

Her only response, other than a shrill intake of breath, was to say, 'I can't believe he ever chose you.'

I have no idea what goes through that woman's mind sometimes, other than an awful lot of hot air.

Best I finish off this letter before I reveal too many of my evil thoughts.

I miss you, my darling. God willing I have not made a mistake allowing Charlie to stay. A new adventure in my twilight.

Forever yours,

Ivy

PS Mother has taken ill. I shall visit her next week. We remain as distant as ever. Perhaps I should have made more of an effort with her.

Whatever Charlie's secret was, it was big. Big enough for Ivy to get rid of all the alcohol in her house. Yet he'd found the courage to share it with her. Perhaps, maybe, if Nicole was brave, she could share her past with Danny.

Twenty-nine

The following Friday Nicole ambled down the path towards the small cove just beyond the boatshed, trying to draw on the peace from her surroundings. The evening sky was dark blue, the air warm. The waves lapped the sand softly, rhythmically.

She stretched out her legs as she sat on the sand, letting the water tickle her toes. The light breeze teased a few strands of hair out from her loose ponytail and a small flock of seagulls came to investigate if she had anything for them. She offered no bounty and they squawked their way back down the shore.

She concentrated on her breathing, trying to keep it in time with the water rolling in. All week she'd managed to avoid Danny, courage failing her miserably. And he'd respected her request to slow things down. Tomorrow's football game was an away match, so she had one more day's reprieve until she would have to face him at the painting bee.

'You ain't dressed for swimming,' Charlie barked from behind, making Nicole jump.

'Just as well I'm not planning on going in, then.' She smiled weakly as she turned to greet him. 'Did you catch anything?' She looked at the rod and tackle in his hands.

'Humph.' He shook his head as he came up and sat down in the sand next to her. 'What's got you so riled up?'

'Excuse me?' Nicole thought she'd been doing a good job pretending to be calm.

'Your cheeks are flushed and your finger there's tapping at a hundred miles an hour.' He looked to her left hand, which was indeed tapping against her thigh furiously.

Nicole laughed.

It had started during her HSC, the pinkie on her left hand tapping during the exams. She'd been so desperate to do well. And ever since, whenever anything of great importance was looming and Nicole's nerves were frayed, her little finger tapped. Her university exams, her first job interview, the day she submitted her manuscript to her agent.

'Well, girl?' Charlie said gruffly.

'I'm just trying to work through some things.'

'Bugs me to say this, but you're a smart kid . . .'

Nicole smiled.

'. . . you'll figure it out.'

'Oh, that's helpful.' Nicole raised her eyebrows.

'It's all you get.' Charlie grunted as he stood up.

Nicole stood too and Charlie looked at her strangely.

'What are you doing?' he asked.

'Thought I'd walk back with you.'

'Why?'

'Why not?'

They walked to the boatshed in silence. As Charlie veered off, Nicole stood on the path and watched him open his door.

He turned around to look at her.

'I can get into my own place, you know.'

'At your age,' Nicole spread her hands open in front of herself, 'one can never be too careful.'

'Bugger off home,' Charlie barked.

'Have a lovely day.' Nicole bowed extravagantly and started towards the cottage.

'Oi,' shouted Charlie.

Nicole walked back towards him. He held out a big yellow envelope.

'This is the letter you asked me about the other week?'

He nodded. 'Can you send it?'

'Of course.'

He handed it to her and took her hand. Looking straight into her eyes, he asked, 'Are you happy here?'

Nicole shrugged her shoulders. 'I guess.'

Charlie shook his head. 'Don't guess. Know.'

He turned and closed the door to the boatshed.

It was a simple question – was she happy here – but Nicole knew it was an important one. So much depended on its answer.

⁂

A hint of a smile crossed Charlie's face as he watched her go. Once she was out of sight, he moved round the boatshed slowly to the bench. He sat on the left side, as he always did, and conjured an image of Ivy sitting beside him – her wild hair blowing in the breeze, her bare feet tracing abstract shapes in the dirt, her warm green eyes smiling at him as they always did. He was now the same age as she was back then, thereabouts anyway, and the irony of that wasn't lost on him.

He wanted to reach out and touch Ivy's cheek, the same way he'd wanted to back then, but couldn't. She would never have seen him as anything other than a soul to save, and he'd accepted that. He would never have touched her so. Never dared. And not because of their difference in age, though that was significant enough, but because he wasn't worthy of her love. He knew how lucky he'd been to have her care for him in any way at all. That was enough and more than he was due. Men like him didn't get second chances. Especially not with women as special as Ivy.

'She's looking after the place just fine,' he said to the ethereal image beside him. 'She's got your feistiness about her.'

He shook his head and smiled.

'She's doing up the cottage real good so far as I can tell and it won't be long before she'll be able to fix this place up, too,' he waved his hand at the boatshed behind him.

'I'm sorry I let you down, but I'm setting it right now.'

He turned his head to the water and watched the waves.

'I've just got to see one more thing through.'

He turned back to look at Ivy, but saw only the wooden seat beside him.

———

The morning of the painting bee arrived and with it Nicole's nerves. Soon everyone would be here, including Danny.

A familiar yodel sounded from the front door. Mandy and Trevor had arrived.

They brought with them brushes and rollers, as arranged, and bowls and plates of salads and sandwiches. Many bowls and plates.

'Painting's hungry work,' Mandy said as she distributed the food among the shelves in the fridge and across the bench space.

Jack walked in carrying an esky and Mandy directed him to put it on the floor next to the fridge.

'Dad reckons it's not a real painting bee without beer.'

'Too right,' Trevor said, and winked.

'Righto.' Danny's booming voice announced his arrival. 'The cavalry is here. Let's get to work,' he said, placing a six pack on the table.

He stepped towards Nicole and it was all she could do not to collapse into his arms. She stopped herself – not until he knew the whole truth.

She couldn't lead him on like this – it wasn't fair. He didn't have all the essential information.

He reached his hand out and brushed her hair aside. 'Is everything okay?' He asked, frowning. 'I've kind of missed you this week.'

Oh, God. He didn't deserve this. 'Yes. Everything's fine. Just a little overwhelmed.'

'Ah, don't be. We do this stuff all the time. We've got you covered.' He winked and went to pick up his paintbrush and move to his allocated position.

'I thought you'd be half done by now,' Jim said as he and Cheryl walked in carrying a salad and apple crumble.

'Wouldn't want to start the fun without you,' called Danny.

Trevor assigned everyone their jobs and, before too long, shades of Rain Cloud and Powder Puff were making their way across the walls.

Three hours into the bee, the first coat done in the living room and hallway, a voice called through the front door. 'Anyone home?'

'Come in, Jacqui!' Mandy shouted from the living room.

'Hope you don't mind,' she said, turning to Nicole, 'I said they could stop by for lunch.'

Nicole must have looked terrified at the thought, because Mandy continued quickly. 'Not the whole clan. Just Jacqui and Jason and the baby. Lord knows what little Joshua would do to the place with all this paint lying around.'

Nicole put her brush down and went up the hall to greet the latest arrivals and took the fruit salad from Jason and popped it in the now very full fridge.

Jacqui held out baby Amy for Nicole to have a hold.

'Oh, no. Babies and I don't get on,' Nicole protested. But it was in vain, as Jacqui shoved Amy into her arms, leaving her no option but to hold on to the soft, pink bundle.

'See,' Jacqui said, 'you're a natural.'

Nicole held Amy in the crook of her arm, petrified. Her terror gave way to heartache as she held the tiny bundle.

She looked down at the large, dark eyes staring back at her.

Nicole was mesmerised and they locked eyes and for a moment she was enchanted. Then Amy burped. And then she vomited. Right onto Nicole's shirt.

'Oh, I'm so sorry,' said Jacqui, wiping the milky liquid with a towel she had been carrying.

'Pretty much the standard reaction I entice from little ones,' Nicole said, grinning. 'Lucky I'm in my painting gear.'

Danny walked in. 'What's that awful smell?'

'Me, I'm afraid,' Nicole said. 'I'll go change.'

She handed Amy to Danny and his fingers brushed against her arm.

'Did Aunty Nicole make you sick?' He cuddled the baby. 'She's quite nice once you get to know her.' He gave Nicole a cheeky grin.

'Watch it,' Nicole warned, 'or you might just find this shirt makes it into the back seat of your car before I have a chance to wash it. Windows up, hot day . . .'

'Wouldn't be the first lady's shirt lost on his back seat.' Jacqui laughed.

Danny shot her a look.

'I'm going to get changed.' Nicole walked out, shaking her head, her happy facade falling once she was out of sight.

When she returned Mandy suggested they set up the lunch tables outside. 'It's such a beautiful day.'

'I don't have any tables or chairs out there yet,' Nicole said, frowning.

'That's all right,' Trevor chimed in. 'We brought some with. We'll get set up, hey?'

Everyone headed out the front. Except Danny.

'I'll bring the good stuff,' he said, moving to the esky.

'And I'll . . .' Nicole raised her arms feeling quite useless.

'Rustle up some glasses?' Danny suggested.

'Yes.'

As he bent down to pick up the esky, he stopped and stood back up letting out a long, slow whistle. 'They've bred.' He read each new list on the side of the fridge. 'Man, you really do need a new hobby.'

Nicole grimaced.

'Of course, you are excelling magnificently at this one.' He tapped the side of the fridge. 'So, why mess with things?'

'What can I say?' She smiled. 'I like a bit of order, and a list never hurt anyone.'

'I don't know. I wrote a list once. Got me in a whole heap of trouble.'

'I don't think I want to know.' Nicole laughed.

'Probably best you don't.' A look of mock seriousness fell across his face.

'Well, my boring lists are the product of a chaotic mind and the need for some stability,' Nicole said.

'I think it's cute.'

'Cute? I've been called many things before, but cute isn't usually one of them.'

'I said your *lists* were cute, not you.' He smiled, closing the gap between them.

Nicole's cheeks burned.

'But, if I were to pick some adjectives to describe you, stubborn might come to mind.'

'Stubborn?'

'Have you forgotten the benchtop incident?'

Nicole shook her head and tried to move away, finding herself pressed against the kitchen bench, with no route of escape.

'Mysterious,' Danny continued.

'I'm very flattered.' Nicole smiled nervously.

Danny leaned in and whispered, 'Intelligent, talented, beautiful.'

He raised his hand and brushed her right cheek gently with his thumb.

Nicole could feel his warm breath on her face. He kissed her and as she wrapped her arms around his neck, his kiss intensified.

'What's taking so long with those darn drinks, hey?' Trevor burst into the kitchen.

Danny practically jumped back, and Nicole turned and busied herself with the glasses by the sink that all of a sudden needed rinsing.

'Hold your horses, mate.' Danny bent down and picked up the esky. 'Good things come . . .'

'Good things are in that there blue box,' Trevor said.

The men headed outside.

Nicole stayed back for a moment to collect herself. She had to put the brakes on this. They couldn't take things any further until she told him the truth about her past.

The sun shone warmly down on the motley crew gathered on Nicole's front lawn. There was enough food to feed the entire cove. It was laid out across the two trestle tables Trevor and Mandy had brought. The sweet aroma wafting off the mini pork and pumpkin sausage rolls filled Nicole's nose, and she couldn't wait to try them. The tuna salad was an explosion of fresh pink fish and green spinach and yellow capsicum. But the dish Nicole really wanted to try was the fluffy white coconut cream cake that sat in the middle of the spread.

The painting bee volunteers sat around the tables on a mix of wooden fold-up chairs and plastic moulded stools, chattering in between munches. Everyone except Nicole.

She looked at the happy, animated faces around her. She caught snippets of tales and idle gossip, heard giggles and guffaws. She felt a sense of warmth and contentment unlike anything she'd ever known.

A light breeze rustled the gum leaves overhead. Cheryl served everyone a second helping of her famous spinach and pine nut salad as she continued to discuss with Danny the trip she was planning to Paris later in the year. Danny recommended a few smaller, boutique museums Cheryl might be interested in, and his favourite gallery.

Beneath the table Danny's hand found Nicole's and he squeezed it gently.

Jacqui cradled a sleeping Amy in her arms as she talked tactics with Jack for the upcoming match against Woodville. Jason and Mandy compared notes on the previous evening's episode of *Let's Cook*, both lamenting not only the producers' need to insert ad breaks at the most inopportune times, but also their penchant for spending the first five minutes back from commercial breaks recapping what they had just seen.

Nicole took a sip of water and sighed.

Mandy, sitting beside her, leaned in.

'Are you okay?' she whispered and Nicole realised a tear was running down her cheek.

She nodded. She was okay. For the moment.

She was beginning to realise how lucky she was to have ended up here, knowing what loneliness could do; lucky she had this lot to care for her. And it seemed they really did care. It was almost like a family.

Family. The definition had changed quite dramatically for Nicole over the years. Growing up, the concept had been simple. Family was blood. Family was everything. When her parents died, family was Jane. Then came Mark. Her new family. A duo to protect and hold tightly to, and family became all about love and hope for the future. And then it turned to dust and Nicole stopped believing in the notion altogether. Could this be her new family?

She only hoped she had the strength to hold onto them.

There was one person missing still, though: Charlie. She would have liked him there. Maybe one day he'd feel comfortable enough to join them, just like he must have done when Ivy was around. Maybe once Nicole learned more about his history with Ivy, she'd be able to crack his defences properly. Maybe.

Laughter and chatter filled her garden, smiles filled the air. Yes, with this crew around her she would be okay. She would finish Ivy's story. She would break down Charlie's walls. She would figure out what her next move was. She would find a way to tell Danny the truth.

Under the table he ran his fingers along her leg, sending a shiver up her spine. She should have stopped him, but she couldn't. She enjoyed his touch. And once she told him her secret, he may never want to touch her again. Today she would take whatever came her way.

And tomorrow she'd tell him everything.

When lunch was over, everyone made a team effort to cover up all the food and carry the containers back into the kitchen and divvy them up among the cooler bags Mandy had brought them in. Cheryl and Jim started putting the first coat on the second bedroom. Mandy had sent Jack home to finish a TAFE assignment due the next day that he hadn't even started, and Lord help him if she got home and found he hadn't knocked it over. Nicole was putting the second coat on the living room with Trevor and Danny and Mandy.

'Can you hand me that cloth please, Nicole?' asked Danny.

Nicole reached down and threw the rag to him.

'Coming up a treat, isn't it?' He smiled, as he wiped some Rain Cloud from his hand. 'We'll be finished in no time.'

'If you can get more paint on the walls than yourself.' Nicole laughed.

'Picking on the slave labour,' he said, threatening her with his paint-soaked roller.

'Don't you even think about it.' She backed up.

'Wouldn't dream of it.' He winked.

Thank goodness they weren't alone, distance a little easier to maintain.

As the afternoon fell, the last lick of paint went on, and they started cleaning up. Jim and Cheryl took charge of washing out the brushes and rollers, Mandy folded up the drop sheets. Danny packed the paint away. Within minutes they were all done, each with a cooler bag of leftovers to take home.

Nicole hugged Cheryl at the door. 'Thank you.'

'What are mates for?' Trevor gave her a kiss on the cheek and jumped down the verandah steps.

'Act your age,' Mandy called after her husband, embracing Nicole before following him.

Danny was the last to leave. He lingered at the front door making small talk, clearly not wanting to go.

She didn't want him to leave, either. But she was exhausted. And if he stayed she'd have to tell him everything now. But she still didn't know how to do it.

'Would you . . . maybe we could have a picnic tomorrow?' she suggested. She had to get this over and done with. 'We can make a dent in all those leftovers.'

Danny laughed. 'Sounds like a plan.'

He kissed her softly on the cheek and walked off into the dusk.

It was amazing the difference the finished paint job made to the place. A mix of joy and sadness washed over her. It was like home. But once the outside was finished, she'd have to find somewhere else to live. Even if that was in Rosella Cove, it wouldn't be Ivy's cottage.

The thought was daunting, but she knew she'd be okay. Nothing could ever be as hard as starting over after she left Mark. Nothing could ever be as hard as leaving Mark.

This was just a fork in the road.

There was still twenty minutes of daylight left, so Nicole went for a walk along the peninsula. It was her favourite time of day – she loved the way the soft light bounced off the trees, bathing everything around in a pale yellow glow, the scores of rosellas flitting from tree to tree to find their evening rest spot. She loved the sense it gave that one day was behind you and another one, a fresh one, was just around the corner.

She passed the boatshed on the way back home and saw Charlie's light on. She sighed at the thought of him in there all alone.

Coming up the path, Nicole could hear music wafting on the breeze from the cottage. Which was strange, given she didn't own a stereo. Maybe Danny couldn't wait for their picnic.

She quickened her step, but as she reached the verandah she realised what the music was, and stopped dead.

No. No, no, no. She tried to run but fear filled her feet with lead.

Adele's husky tones wafted through the door, familiar lyrics assaulting her ears.

Thirty

'Oh, Nicky.' Mark burst through the cottage door and ran down the verandah steps. He threw his arms around her. 'I'm so glad I found you. I've been worried sick about you, princess.'

Nicole stiffened in his embrace.

Mark released his hold. 'It must have been so frightening for you, having a breakdown like that. But I'm here now. It'll be okay.'

'What?' Nicole shook her head, trying to turn her brain on.

Mark was here. And he was happy to see her. Not angry. Happy.

He pulled her inside the cottage.

'What . . . What are you doing here?' Nicole found her voice. A little shaky, but actual words.

'I've come to take you home, princess.' He embraced her again.

'What?'

He patted her head. 'We can get you some help. Deal with whatever it was that caused your breakdown and then everything will be okay again.'

'You think . . .'

'I think you're very lucky I found you. It wasn't easy, you know. But none of that matters now. What matters,' he kissed her again, seemingly oblivious to the fact she wasn't kissing him back, 'what matters is I found you and I love you and I'm never letting you go again.'

Nicole's mind was blank. What? How? She had to think. But she couldn't.

Inside her head she was shouting. Inside her mind she was racing down the street to seek refuge with her friends.

But she didn't make a sound. She didn't budge.

Mark sat himself on the sofa. 'Come. Sit.'

She couldn't move.

'Nicky, don't you think you should offer your fiancé more welcome than that? I've come a long way to find you.'

She sat beside him. 'Fiancé . . .' she said.

'That's right.' He stroked her leg. 'Remember? We made a promise to each other.' He pulled her engagement ring out of his pocket and slipped it on her finger. 'I know we have some problems, but surely we can work them out.'

Nicole started to shake.

'It's okay, Nicky. I'm here now. I can't imagine what you've been through. This must be quite a shock. Let me make it better now.'

'How did you find me?'

He shook his head. 'It wasn't easy. But I found your editing website. I tracked down one of the authors you'd worked with and I convinced them I needed to make contact with you, desperately. Once I had your email address, I used the one of the firm's private investigators. It cost me a lot of money, but it's worth it to have you back.'

*

In the dark, Nicole lay stiffly in bed. Behind her Mark lay snoring, his hand resting on her hip.

He hadn't tried anything, just wanted to lay beside her. He'd cried and told her he'd missed her so. He hadn't been able to sleep properly since she'd left. If she could just lay next to him a little while – surely she owed him that after abandoning him the way she did.

Nicole didn't dare move all night and in the early light of morning she slipped out of bed. She paced around the cottage, confused and angry at herself. This new life she thought she'd forged for herself was over. Mark was back.

There was no point trying to outrun her past, forget the pain. It would always be with her, haunt her, defeat her.

Tears fell down her cheeks. She knew she had to stop them. If he heard her, he'd come out.

She reached beneath the sofa and pulled out Ivy's box.

30th March, 1970

My Dearest Tom,

Peggy passed away last week. Father Anthony is remaining stoic, but inside I know he is broken. I see it in his eyes when he believes no one is looking.

I have cooked dinner for him, drunk tea with him, sat in silence with him. But that can hardly soothe his soul. Then again, I suppose for a man such as Father Anthony, his soul is God's to soothe, not mine. Still, it cannot hurt to let him know how very much he is loved and how sorry I am for his loss.

I asked Charlie what I should do. I seem to ask his opinion on most things these days. His mind is much younger and quicker than mine and he often sees things in a light that I do not. I am frequently reminded there is more than a generational gap between us.

My privileged upbringing and his terrible past force us into different perspectives on many of life's conundrums. He usually has a far simpler and more effective solution than I can conjure. I am constantly feeling proud of him and wish it were a pride I could share with you.

How one mistake can so easily ruin a life, many lives, hardly seems fair. If anyone deserves forgiveness it is Charlie. I have suggested that if he sought it, it may yet come. But, he is insistent it is too late and much better this way anyway. I am not sure I agree, but on this he will not hear me. I believe the forgiveness he truly needs is that which comes from within and I fear this may never come.

I wish I could take his pain and carry his burden on my old shoulders so that he can live the potential I know is inside him. What this young man could achieve if circumstances were different! However, they are not, as he points out regularly.

In the end, I organised a lunch for Father Anthony yesterday with a few of those closest to him – William Tucker and Iris, Mrs Li, young Carole. (Poor thing needed a pick-me-up. She has got her hands full with toddler number three and her husband is away). Father Anthony accepted my invitation graciously and asked if he could bring along a couple of the Sunday School kids whose parents were going to be late picking them up. Really, you would think given the circumstances they could have cancelled whatever was going to keep them away and pick the kids up on time. As if the poor man needed that. But some people only think of themselves, I suppose. I wonder how they would feel if the situation were reversed? I said yes, naturally. I could handle a few extra mouths, if it meant getting Father Anthony there.

Charlie helped me set up the yard yesterday. He moved the two trestle tables I use for my stall into position and set all the chairs up *for me. He borrowed some extras from the church storeroom. I cut some hydrangeas from the garden and some roses, and placed them on the tables with the violets. It was not quite as pretty as Lucy's wedding, but it was lovely just the same.*

Charlie did not join us, though I asked him to.

I made the pasta salad Fabricio taught me and sliced up some cold roast lamb. We had fruit salad and cream for dessert.

Father Anthony seemed to take comfort in the afternoon and squeezed me tightly in thanks afterward.

Apparently the Sunday School kids had such a great time they have been bragging to their friends who now stop me in the street and ask when it will be their turn to come over and have a picnic.

The children are so persistent that I have suggested to Father Anthony he might like to bring all of them over for a picnic next month. He thought it a lovely idea.

Charlie has finished his repairs to the boatshed and it is now, without a doubt, his home. I do hope he stays. Every now and then I see a look in his eyes and I worry he will take off. But, perhaps he is merely remembering his past.

The past haunts us all, I guess.

This is where he belongs and I tell him as such constantly. He simply shrugs.

I have decided to close my stall and only sculpt to order now. I have not the energy for it anymore. But you should see the markets now! Every manner of ware can be found: old, new, useful and ridiculously impractical. They will not miss my table of figurines.

Forever yours,

Ivy

PS I have just received a call to say Mother has passed away. I was with her only a fortnight ago. Perhaps I should have stayed.

Though I doubt she would have wished it. We found a gentle ease this past year, but never a closeness. And now we never will. I should have done more, for now it is too late.

No, Ivy. No, it wasn't fair that one mistake could so easily ruin a life. None of any of this was fair.

Nicole rocked back and forth, Ivy's words running through her head.

'*The forgiveness he truly needs is that which comes from within.*'

Forgiveness. And strength.

'Well, Nicole,' she whispered into the empty morning, 'what are you going to do about it then?'

Thirty-one

$\mathcal{N}$icole let the hot water wash over her, easing her tired muscles.

She stepped out of the shower and pulled on her clothes. Voices floated down the hallway.

'Who are you?' Danny's tone had an edge.

'I'm Nicky's fiancé.'

Nicole swore to herself and ran down the hall. 'Danny?' She called. 'Danny, wait.' She slid to a stop in front of the door.

'Is this why you've been pushing me away?' Danny's face was a storm cloud of hurt.

'Wait. Let me explain.'

'No. I think I've got the full picture.' He turned and strode down the verandah steps and away from Nicole.

She pushed past Mark back into the cottage. Oh, God, now she'd lost Danny too.

'So this is what you've been up to while I've been frantic with worry back at home? How could you do this to me, Nicky?'

'Please don't.'

'Don't?' Mark paced in front of her. 'Nicky, we're engaged.'

Nicole shook her head. 'No. I left, remember?'

'Without even giving me a say. That doesn't count. But apparently not much does with you. What? Were you planning on playing happy families with *him*? Does he even know that happy families isn't an option for you?'

Nicole took a deep breath.

'He doesn't, does he? What do you think he'll do when he finds out that you're barren?'

'I'm . . . not . . . barren.'

'Do you think he'll love you despite your failings? That's me, princess. I love you, despite all your failings. No other man could ever love you if he knew the truth about you.'

No. It wasn't true. If she just explained things to Danny, he'd . . . maybe . . .

'You're only half a woman, Nicky. Who else is ever going to love you but me?'

Nicole slumped into the sofa.

'You know I'm right. The only person in this world who truly cares about you is me. I wouldn't have come all this way, worked so hard to find you, if I didn't. You know it's the truth.'

So many words swirling through her mind. Maybe he was right. Her time here at the cove was nearly up, and look how quickly Danny had fled when Mark answered the door. He didn't even want to listen.

Nicole sat there, no words, no movements.

'Oh, Nicky.' Mark put his arm around her.

Familiar comfort washed over her. Had she been kidding herself this whole time? Mark did love her. In his way. Would anyone else? Would Danny?

'Come home with me, Nicky, and we'll be a family. Just the two of us.'

Just the two of them. Just her. Just Mark.

'Have you thought any more about adoption, or IVF?' she asked quietly.

Mark rolled his eyes. 'Really? Are we going to revisit that again?'

The significance of Charlie's question that day – was she happy here – was very clear to her now.

Yes, she was. And that's what mattered. It didn't matter if Danny would accept her or not. It would hurt, certainly. It would possibly break her heart if what she felt for him was as strong as she thought it was. But there was so much more to this than that. There was Charlie and Mandy and Ivy, and this quirky little town that had crept its way into her heart. She couldn't go back to such a narrow life as just the two of them. No matter what happened from here, *that* was no longer her life.

'I think I'd like you to leave,' she whispered.

Mark stared at her.

'Please leave.' Her voice got a little stronger.

'You can't kick me out. I'm your fiancé.'

'No, Mark.' She shook her head. 'Our engagement was over long ago. Please leave.' She pointed to the front door.

'But you belong with me.'

She shook her head. 'No. I don't.' She didn't know exactly where she belonged. Here at Rosella Cove? With Danny? But she knew now, without doubt, it wasn't with Mark.

'Okay. I'll look into adoption, if it will make you happy. Just . . .'

Nicole raised her hand. 'Stop, Mark. This is actually so much bigger than that. I am not the same person I was when we met. We are not the same. I don't want a life with you. It's over.'

Mark stared at her. 'No. I won't accept this.'

Nicole was getting weary now and she raised her voice. 'Mark. Stop. This is finished. We are finished. Leave. Now.'

Mark stood where he was, his mouth open, no words coming out.

'I said now.' She opened the front door.

'You can't do this to me, Nicky. If you don't come back with me, I'll —'

Nicole could the feel the anger rising inside her. 'You'll what? Take all my money? You've done that. You'll destroy my self-esteem? You've done that, too.' She raised her voice. 'Tell me, Mark, what can you possibly do to me?'

He looked at her with steely eyes. 'This isn't over, Nicky. I'll . . .'

Nicole held his stare, her resolve unwavering. 'The only way I'll come back to Sydney with you, Mark, is if you kidnap me. And I don't think your ego wants me that badly you'll commit a felony. Think about what that would do to your career.'

Time stopped as they stared at each other before Mark broke the silence.

'You'll be back. I know you will. But just you watch out. By the time you come to your senses, I might not be there waiting for you.' He stormed out the door and Nicole let out a long sigh and slid to the floor.

'Nicole? Are you there?' Mandy called, coming up the steps of the verandah.

Nicole let out a groan.

Mandy let herself in and threw herself on the floor beside Nicole.

'What is going on? I ran into Danny in town and he was like a raging bull. When I asked him what was wrong, he just grunted "ask Nicole". Did you two have a f—'

Nicole burst into tears and Mandy wrapped her in a tight embrace.

Nicole told Mandy the whole story. Everything about Mark, about what had brought her to Rosella Cove. Hearing it out loud, she saw with renewed eyes, the picture as a whole. She finished finally, and dropped her head into her hands.

'Oh, honey. I knew something was up, but I wasn't expecting that.'

'Sorry.'

'Don't be. I just can't believe you've been carrying around this burden all on your own.'

'Oh, Mandy, when he held me in his arms last night . . . It would have been so easy to slip back into "us". What if he always has that hold over me? What if I can't do this whole "life" thing on my own?'

Mandy helped her to her feet and guided her to the kitchen where she put the kettle on. 'I get that. I do. But let me ask you this.' She stood in front of Nicole. 'Look at this house, what you've accomplished, how you've embraced the cove, how it's embraced you. Are you even the same person now as you were six months ago?'

A lot had happened since she'd fled Sydney.

'No.' Of course she wasn't.

'Okay. So what if you allow the new you, the paint-brush-wielding-football-cheering-lucky-socks you, to accept what happened. That's all. Acknowledge that it hurt, know that it was a terrible point in your life, recognise that it changed you, but don't allow it any power over you now. Send it back to the past where it belongs. Let the new you take control of your own destiny. Whatever it is the new you wants that destiny to be.'

Nicole reached out and hugged her. 'You really should be a psychologist. Or at least a bartender.'

'I'll see if George has any openings. I am multi-talented.' She laughed and waved her phone at Nicole.

There was a knock on the door.

'What did you . . . how . . .'

'Multi-talented.' She smiled and hugged Nicole, whispering in her ear. 'Don't underestimate him. I have no idea how he'll he take the news, but I know he deserves a chance to figure it out himself.'

Nicole walked her to the door. Mandy squeezed her hand gently, slipping past Danny.

Danny waited.

'Please. Come in.'

He looked impatient and didn't meet her eyes.

Standing on opposite sides of the hallway, the tension between them was palpable.

'I'm sorry I didn't tell you about Mark,' Nicole started.

He shrugged. 'You don't owe me.'

'No. I don't. But I want to tell you. If you're okay hearing it?'

Danny leaned against the wall.

Telling her story twice in such a short amount of time was draining. But she didn't leave anything out. What was the point of keeping secrets now?

He took a step towards her. 'I knew you were dealing with something, but I kind of figured it was just your average break-up story. I didn't know there was . . . more.'

Nicole cast her eyes down. She had no idea how telling him about her fertility challenges would change things between them, but she'd had to be completely honest with him.

'I'm sorry,' she whispered, 'that I didn't tell you sooner.'

When Nicole lifted her eyes to his she was met with his kind face, looking right back at her.

'You have nothing to be sorry for. It's not like I've been exactly forthcoming about my past either.'

'What a pair.' Nicole managed a smile.

Danny turned slightly and held his hand out towards the living room. 'May I?'

They moved to the sofa and sat down, a cushion between them.

'I had a girlfriend . . .'

'Caitlyn.'

'How do you . . .?'

Nicole tilted her head. 'Mandy mentioned something.' She shared what she'd been told.

'That's why you were withdrawn that night. Mandy, Mandy, Mandy. Her heart is always in the right place. But . . .' He shook his head. 'Anyway. Here's the full story. She's the reason I stayed here when my parents went back to England. Caitlyn, not Mandy.' He allowed himself a little grin.

'I was head over heels, we were together forever and I had plans to marry her. I thought everything was great. We'd sit around and talk about our future, about how many kids we were going to have . . .' his voice caught in his throat, and he detailed their time together. It wasn't easy for Nicole to hear, but her story couldn't have been easy for him either.

'Then one day, out of the blue, she said she was leaving me. That she never actually wanted kids. Turns out, she'd just been stringing me along, pretending to want kids. She had her eyes on Grandpa's money. But she fell in love with a bloke from Woodville and couldn't keep up the pretence anymore. So, she dumped me. Just like that.'

Nicole reached across the sofa and touched his arm briefly. He pulled away slightly.

'A year later they were married. And she got pregnant. I didn't take it too well.'

Nicole swallowed deeply.

'When I saw Mark here, with you . . . and I had no idea what was going on. I just saw red. Sorry.'

'I guess we both could've handled things differently.'

He shrugged.

Nicole took a deep breath. She had to ask. She had to know. 'So, what do we do from here?'

'To be honest, I don't know. This is a lot to take in.' He stared across the room. 'For both of us.'

Yes it was. She turned her head away from him, shame blooming in her chest.

'What if . . .' Danny's voice was soft, tentative, and Nicole turned back towards him. 'What if we start again?' Danny held out his hand, which she took. 'Hi. I'm Danny Temple. I love history, I play footy and I do odd jobs around town.'

'I'm Nicole Miller. I write books, I cook badly and have recently got out of a less-than-healthy relationship.'

'Nice to meet you.' Danny's grin spread across his face.

Thirty-two

In the warmth of the midday sun Nicole carried a small fallen branch of gum, waving the leaves slowly above her head. A childhood spent fending off diving magpies had taught her well – with glorious spring days comes swooping season.

As she approached the boatshed she let the branch drop, sure she was safe. The door was ajar. Stepping over the fallen picket gate, she moved towards Ivy's bench.

It was empty.

She went back to the front door of the boatshed and knocked.

No answer.

She called out Charlie's name.

No answer.

She pushed the old wooden door and it creaked open.

'Charlie?'

No answer.

Past the dusty boxes she shuffled, whispering his name. When she got to the bookcase she could see Charlie lying in his bed and she moved quickly to his side.

The rise and fall of his chest told her he was still breathing. She reached out and touched his hand.

'Can't a man sleep in peace?' he grumbled, his voice weak.

'The door was open. I was worried.'

'What rot. I'm perfectly fine.' He tried to sit up.

Nicole leaned her weight in to help lift him.

'Don't need your help.' He coughed.

'Clearly,' she said. 'I'm going to go get the doctor. I'll be right back.'

She turned to leave, but Charlie grabbed her arm.

'No. Just fix me a cuppa.'

'Charlie, you need more than —'

'Fix me a cuppa, or leave me the hell alone.'

He pointed to his small sink and the rusting kettle.

Nicole didn't want to leave him alone, so she boiled the water. Charlie took his cup with shaking hands and Nicole pulled the only chair in the room up to his bed.

'What's going on?'

'I'm old, is all.' Charlie barked and started coughing again.

'I really think you should see someone.' Nicole frowned.

'Why? So they can take me away and shut me up in some sterile room with a bunch of sick strangers who'll infect me?'

'Charlie, I'm your friend. The closest thing to one you've got, anyway, as far as I can tell. Let me help you.'

'If you are my friend, then you'll do as I bloody well ask.'

Nicole looked into his eyes. There was no fear, though there was weariness.

'Stop fussing,' Charlie grumbled. 'I thought I could rely on you not to get soppy.'

She smiled weakly.

'Besides,' Charlie said. 'If you knew who I really was, you wouldn't be wasting your energy.'

'I may not know who you were, but I reckon I know who you are.'

'Humph.'

Charlie pointed to the floor and Nicole saw the Scrabble box.

'Now that wouldn't be fair, taking advantage of you like this.' She forced a smile.

'You wish.'

Charlie tried to stand up and Nicole reached out her arms to help.

He pushed her away.

'Okay, okay.' She backed off. Slightly. 'Just trying to help.'

'Just answering the call of nature.' He steadied himself on his feet. 'Been managing that on my own for more than seventy years. Don't need no help now.'

Watching him closely, Nicole hovered not too far from the bathroom door, trying to look like she wasn't waiting for him.

'So?' He crawled back into bed. 'Are you going to set this thing up, or not?'

He pushed the board towards her.

Nicole stayed with Charlie all afternoon and into the night as he drifted in and out of sleep after their game. Through the portal window the morning sun began to rise and Nicole shifted in the armchair, her shoulders stiff.

'Haven't you got somewhere else to be?' Charlie's voice, heavy, broke the silence.

'Not today.'

'Other people to annoy?' He sat up with considerable effort.

She shook her head. 'Nope. Just you.'

'You didn't stay all bloody night, did you?'

'I just wanted to make sure you were okay.' The wheezing from his chest, the coughing all night, had concerned her.

'Of course I am. I don't need a babysitter.'

'You do look better this morning.'

'Of course I do. Go wait outside. I've got something to give you, but you're not bloody watching me get dressed.'

Nicole hovered by the door to the boatshed, listening for any signs of a fall, or anything wrong at all.

'Good God.' Charlie pushed her aside as he opened the door. 'Give a man some room.'

Nicole backed off.

'Here.' He pulled an envelope out of his back pocket. It was the same size and shape as the envelope he'd given her to post a few days ago. 'I need you to post this for me.'

It was addressed to the same Mr A.W. Dixon in Sydney as the first envelope and the name seemed vaguely familiar to Nicole, but she couldn't place it.

'Today.'

'Soon as the post office opens.' Nicole touched his arm in reassurance.

'You can leave now.'

'I don't know. Maybe I should stay for the day.' Nicole smiled.

'God save me.' Charlie shook his head. He glanced at the envelope in Nicole's hands.

'All right, I'll head off, then. This thing won't post itself!' She waved it in the air.

'Thank you.'

'I'll see you tomorrow.'

'Tomorrow?' Charlie furrowed his wrinkled brow. 'Have I got to put up with you tomorrow, too?'

'Afraid so.' Nicole smiled sweetly. 'Lucky you.'

She kissed him on the cheek.

'Anything I can do before I go, Charlie?'

'Promise you won't be back before next Sunday.' A smile broke through his grumpy facade.

'I don't make promises I can't keep.' She waved as she headed up the path.

It was still another half-hour before the post office opened, so Nicole walked back up the path to the cottage. She sat on the verandah with Ivy's box.

15th January, 1973
My Dearest Tom,
I have spent the last few days sleeping on an armchair in the boatshed and my back is so terribly sore. As is my neck. I find it painful to sit here and write, though I feel compelled to keep going.

I went down there on Thursday morning for our usual chat, and a cup of tea, but I was not prepared for what I found.

Charlie was not waiting for me on your bench, which was strange, and I heard a noise coming from inside the boatshed. I walked round to the door and it was ajar. I had not noticed that when I arrived. I called out his name and was met with an incoherent mumble. I was most concerned, so I went inside.

He has done quite a good job in there, I must say. Some shelving as you enter, a little kitchenette. I would prefer a splash of colour, but you men are different. Somewhat sparse but rather neat and tidy. Then I came to the bed.

Atop, Charlie was lying in his underwear only, surrounded by maybe a dozen bottles. I did not count, though I did note there was whisky and rum and wine amongst them. All empty, bar the vodka bottle in his hand.

I removed it promptly and poured it down the sink. He tried to protest but was so inebriated he was unable to even raise his arm.

I cleaned up the mess around him and got a washer and bucket of soapy water to clean him up. The stench! I have never smelled anything quite like it.

Once he was tidied, I pulled his covers tight and he fell asleep immediately. Or perhaps he fell unconscious. Either way, I was not able to leave him alone.

So, I pulled the old armchair next to his bed and settled in.

On day two he became quite agitated and demanded to know where his drink was. When I told him it was gone, he screamed at me and threw his bed linen at my head. Luckily it was soft furnishings as I am not as nimble and quick-of-reflex as I once was.

I will confess, my dearest, that I was quite frightened. I have never seen such anger and I certainly felt like fleeing. I do not know why I stayed.

That is a lie. Of course I know. I owed him. I owed him for that night on the beach. I owed him for the years of companionship that have kept me going. Besides, what have I at this stage of my fading life to lose?

I could not abandon him.

On day three he was silent and still, just lying there. I remained silent also, simply watching. He refused to eat and only drank water when I was insistent.

This morning we took a walk together down to the cove. He confided in me that it had been five years this very day since the incident he had fled and he had been hoping to pass it by in a drunken stupor.

The irony was not lost on me and I imagine cut even closer to the bone for him.

He sobbed in my arms, wondering what had become of those he had left behind. I told him it was not too late to find out.

'Clearly it is,' he said. 'Look at me.'

'I see a man whose guilt and pain have overwhelmed him. But no more.' I looked him in the eye. 'No more.'

He stared at me and I held his gaze. He put his right hand over his left chest. 'My promise to you,' he said. 'I'll never take another sip.'

'No,' I said. 'Promise me you will somehow make right your wrong. For whatever reason, you and I have been given this second chance together. Do not waste it. Do not get to the end of your life and look back and not see any good.'

He nodded.

I have returned home this afternoon to shower and will head back to the boatshed once I have finished this letter. I believe he will be okay, but I must make sure.

Oh, my love, what will happen if he succumbs again?

Time is creeping by. Today and what is left of mine. Time. There it is again.

I will leave you here, my darling, and check on Charlie.

Take care, my sweet. Till we see each other again.

Forever yours,

Ivy

A chill tingled up Nicole's spine. She had sat in the same chair Ivy had and kept watch over Charlie.

Thunder boomed across the peninsula and lightning burst across the darkening sky. As a morning storm rolled in, an almighty crack shook the cottage and heavy rain began to fall.

Nicole put Charlie's letter on the mantle inside and lit a fire the way Danny had shown her. The weather app on the phone suggested the storm would clear later in the day. She could go back and check on Charlie then.

Snuggled on the sofa in front of the fire, Nicole opened Ivy's next letter.

3rd July, 1974
Thomas Wilson,
I do not know why you never told me. Were you worried how I would react?

I have been visiting Joan every week for the last month as her health failed drastically. Cancer, the doctor said. She has had few visitors – hardly surprising. In Peggy's absence I felt someone ought to be there for her.

We were all expecting her to pass weeks ago, but the stubborn woman hung on. Not surprising, I suppose. That woman would have no qualms telling God Himself off if she did not agree with his plans to take her. When I arrived this morning she lay in her bed, gaunt as always, more grey than usual. She had a photo clutched to her chest.

It was a photo of you. You and Joan together. She did not want me to see it, but I had to give her her medicine and she was too weak to stop me.

I recognised your suit. It was the one you were wearing the night we met, the night of the Spring Dance. I also recognised Joan's dress. Did you go to the dance that night with her?

Nicole opened her Ivy folder and pulled out the newspaper clipping with the photo of the Spring Dance. Joan, Ivy, Thomas, their story now complete.

I asked Joan about the picture. She touched the photo and whispered something I could not quite make out, before succumbing to a coughing fit and falling out of consciousness.

Her breathing became very shallow and I called Doctor Johnson Junior. He said all he could do was make her comfortable. We sat together by her side and watched over her.

As dusk crept upon us, she sat up and grabbed my hand. She looked me in the eye and smiled at me. The first time ever, I believe, that woman has graced me with a genuine smile. 'I'm sorry,' she whispered, and raised her frail hand to my cheek.

An hour later she took her last breath. I do not suppose there will be many to farewell her. She had few friends and so many of us are now gone. The burden of living to this wretched age, I suppose, when funerals replace weddings and wakes replace baby showers, and we mark the years with ever fewer Christmas cards.

My head is heavy tonight.

I must sleep.

Ivy

Nicole opened her notebook and outlined a scene. The feeling that surged through her as she wrote again was thrilling.

The rain began to slow and black storm clouds dissipated as the sun forced its way through. Nicole put down her pen and picked up Charlie's second letter.

When she returned from town she headed straight for the boatshed and knocked lightly on the old wooden door.

'What?' came the weak bark from behind.

Nicole entered and the air caught in her chest. She made her way to Charlie's sleeping area and found him sitting in the chair shivering.

'You're going to freeze to death.' She chided as she ripped his quilt off the bed and wrapped him tightly in it.

There was a packet of cup-a-soup on the sink and she boiled the jug.

'Drink this.' She handed him the hot mug.

'I'm fine.' He grumbled.

'You can keep telling yourself that, but I don't believe you.'

Eventually Nicole convinced Charlie to climb into bed. Once he was there, it didn't take long for him to drift off to sleep. She took the opportunity and ran back to the cottage to gather a few supplies – a blanket for herself, a casserole she had in the fridge, some paracetamol.

The day melted into night and Nicole kept vigil.

Despite the medicine she'd given him, his temperature stayed high.

Charlie grabbed her arm.

'I can't get them out . . . the flames are too big . . . I can't . . .'

He fell back on the pillow.

Nicole rinsed the washcloth with fresh cold water and lay it gently across his forehead.

Somewhere around two in the morning, Charlie's fever broke. Relief washed over Nicole.

A few hours later, as sunlight filtered through the portal window of the boatshed, Charlie stirred.

'Are you here again?' Charlie sat up, clearly weak, but the colour had returned to his skin.

'I didn't want you to miss me.'

'I can't miss you if you never leave.'

Nicole laughed.

'You can go. I'm fine.'

Nicole raised an eyebrow.

'If I promise to let Doctor Johnson check me over, will you leave me in peace?'

Nicole made the call and as the doctor arrived, she left.

'I'll be back,' she called.

'I'm sure you will be.'

Walking up the path to the cottage, Nicole stopped and stood at her front gate, admiring the garden and lawn that was now settling nicely. She was in awe of the job Jack had done. She really ought to do something special to thank him.

Danny had been going quietly about replacing and repairing rotting wood around the verandah. A little one day, a little more the next. Their conversations were becoming easier, lighter since that night she'd told him about Mark and her past.

All that was left of the renovation was the back garden, which could be tackled at any point really, and a few, small cosmetic touches in the two bedrooms. And the painting outside. That was the task that would make all the difference now. The cottage would look finished, show everyone who passed how much it was loved, be the pride and joy of the cove once more, perhaps. The transformation complete. And then she'd have to give it up.

'Hot pink and lime green.'

Nicole jumped and turned to see Danny's smiling face. 'Sorry?'

'Colours. For the outside. Hot pink and lime green. She'd really stand out then. Passing ships could use her as a beacon.'

'I will if you will.' Nicole grinned.

'Or subtle greys, perhaps, or beige.'

'It was originally blue and white.' Nicole turned back and looked at the cottage again.

'Will you stick with that?'

'Maybe. Maybe a slightly different shade or tone. Definitely steering away from pink though.'

'Brunch?' He held up some shopping bags. They headed into the kitchen and Danny made himself at home, opening cupboards and drawers as he prepared them each a plate of lamb roast rolls with gravy.

'A girl could get used to this,' Nicole said.

'Nah, this is a one-off.' Danny grinned. 'It's really the only hit in my cooking repertoire, so I usually keep it in reserve till I need it, but I figured, well, with everything that's happened, I wanted to do something nice for you.'

'You're forgetting pancakes,' said Nicole. 'You make pretty mean pancakes.' She swore he blushed a little.

'True. Next time it's your turn, though, seeing I've got nothing else.'

'Then you might want to have a few extra helpings.' Nicole laughed. 'You are familiar with my lack of cooking skills?'

Danny nodded gravely and served himself another slice of lamb. 'I hear they are improving, though.'

'Slowly.'

'How's Charlie?'

'He's back to his usual grumpy self again, so much better. Doctor Johnson is with him now.'

When they finished eating, they washed up the dishes together and Nicole walked him to the door.

'See you.' He swayed on his heels for a second and then turned and left.

Thirty-three

$\mathcal{N}$icole spent the evening on the floor of the spare room applying the last coat of gloss to the skirting board. Danny had texted her about an hour ago with a simple 'Goodnight', but it was enough to give her hope. She knew she had to be patient and that was okay.

Hope was a pretty powerful force. Ivy had taught her that.

She flipped open the wood box and took out Ivy's next letter.

30th November, 1975
My Dearest Tom,
Today is the last Sunday of the month and we had yet another lovely picnic. The sun was glorious and shining, but not too hot. The wind we have been having for the past few days stayed away and the entire town seemed to be spread across my lawn on brightly coloured picnic blankets with baskets full of food. I cannot believe how it has grown over time, but I relish in it. We have not missed a month since the first picnic with Father Anthony.

He brings the Sunday School kids each time and now William Tucker brings the football team. It is wonderful seeing all those people running on my lawn barefoot, enjoying themselves. Carole's little girl, Amanda, seemed to like tearing up the grass and putting it in her mouth.

Nicole couldn't suppress a giggle, picturing a tiny, redheaded Mandy eating Ivy's lawn.

Some of the children play elastics. Some of them have races. The grown-ups seem to have just as much fun. Some of them have races too.

Everyone has it down to a fine art now, setting themselves up comfortably for the afternoon. I always have a few tables with drinks and a selection of salads and some fruit. I decorate the tables with bright flowers from the garden in tall vases and short vases, round and square, glass and ceramic.

Charlie stayed a little longer than usual after helping me set up today. Perhaps he was concerned about my fatigue this morning. But once everyone arrived I was fine, and he soon disappeared.

I have decided what to do with this place, my love, when my time comes as it inevitably will. I am astute enough to know my body slowly fails me, as age dictates it must. I hope you do not disapprove of my plans. Charlie has shown no further relapse and I believe when my time comes he will feel it keenly. So, I have decided to leave him the cottage and the boatshed. Did Mother just turn in her grave? It may just keep him going and he is the only family I am left with.

Charlie owned the cottage. Her suspicions were confirmed.

I spoke with the lawyers on Friday and it is arranged. They couriered the paperwork to me and I sent it straight back signed. The courier was a nice young man. I served him some tea. I must buy some more. It is very expensive these days, but one cannot live without.

I am thoroughly exhausted tonight. But I shall sleep with an easy mind and light heart knowing this is now taken care of.

The courier's name was Tom. Can you believe it?

Forever yours,

Ivy

PS The Royal has a new owner. A funny little Italian man. I am enjoying his pasta on a Friday night. It is not as good as Fabricio's mother's, but it is delicious. I should give Charlie my pasta maker. Or perhaps donate it to the church. I am sure someone will make better use of it than I.

Nicole paced the living room. There was no long-lost cousin from Sydney. It was Charlie all along. Charlie and Ivy's story was now complete.

She replaced the letter and touched the next one in the box. It was terribly thin. She pulled it out. The usually beautiful script was shaky and Nicole's heart started to race.

29th January, 1976

My Dearest Tom,

I write this with desperate haste.

I have called for Doctor Johnson, my love. He will be here soon. I could not leave without saying goodbye and I must return your letters to their hiding place before he arrives.

My time is here, it seems. I do not wish to go. What if I cannot find you? I want to stay here with my picnics, with Charlie. He needs me.

I am coming to you, my dearest. Will you be waiting?

It is time.

Ivy

Nicole's hands shook slightly. She looked in the box for the next letter. There had to be another. 11th January, 1941 – the first one. She frantically filed through the envelopes, hoping she'd missed one; put one out of order. There had to be more.

But there wasn't.

An image of Ivy lying on the hearth having returned the box to its hiding place in the fireplace just in time, close to her beloved Thomas, came to Nicole's mind and she let the tears flow unhindered.

Thirty-four

*C*harlie was waiting for her on the bench seat when Nicole arrived at the boatshed the next morning.

She hesitated then sat beside him. He didn't bark at her to get up.

The day was already warm, but Charlie sat beneath his rug.

'What's that?' He looked at the carved wooden box in Nicole's hands.

'Actually, it's for you.'

'What do I want with a box?' he asked. He looked at it more closely. 'This looks like one I gave away many years ago, if I'm not mistaken.' His eyes widened. 'I made this for Ivy after she helped me . . . . What are you doing with it?'

'I found it in the cottage.'

'Where?'

'Behind the fireplace,' Nicole said, and Charlie narrowed his eyes in suspicion.

'What the hell are you talking about?'

'I found it not long after I moved in.'

She opened the lid, revealing its contents, the stories that had kept her company these past months.

'What are they?' His voice was low.

'Letters. From Ivy to Thomas. She didn't want them found by her mother, or anyone else, I guess,' Nicole said.

'Then why have you got them now?'

'Well, I started reading them. They're beautiful. They deserve to be shared. They detail her life from the time Tom died to when she did.'

Charlie became very still. 'What's in them exactly?'

'All sorts of things. Stories about Joan Wetherby, Lucy, the picnics, meeting you,' Nicole said the last words slowly.

'What right have you to go through someone's private memories? You nosy girl. Give them to me.' He held out his hand. 'Let me burn them.'

Nicole took Charlie's hand gently and squeezed it.

'There is no way I'm letting you burn them,' she said calmly. 'I love these letters and I love Ivy. But I did bring them here for you to read, if you can promise not to destroy them.'

'Don't want to read them. Rubbish letters.' He shook his head.

'Charlie.' Nicole looked him in his fright-filled eyes. 'Whatever is in your past, she didn't reveal it here. She was truly your friend and I thought you might like to know that.'

Charlie stared at her.

'The Charlie I care about is here, now. Not in the past.'

'If you knew my past, you wouldn't care.' He cast his eyes downward.

'Ivy did.' Nicole shrugged.

'She was an angel on Earth.'

'You saved her life.'

He looked up sharply. 'She saved mine.'

'And you both helped me find mine again. I think you should read them.' Nicole held the box out to him.

He hesitated, then took it, running his fingers over the carved shells, and Nicole noticed the despair in his eyes. He turned his head and took a few deep breaths.

'Shall we play today?' Nicole asked, changing the subject. 'Just a quick game. Or should I let you rest?'

'Play.' He took Ivy's box inside and returned with the Scrabble board.

'. . . And e, e, m.' Charlie laid down his tiles. 'Redeem, on a double word score, means . . . means I win.'

He smiled a smile Nicole hadn't seen before. Nervous? Worried?

'So, fifteen to six,' Nicole said. 'Tomorrow is my comeback.'

'Tomorrow you will taste the bitterness of defeat once more.' Charlie shrugged.

'Your cockiness will be your downfall, you know?' Nicole packed away the board and carried it to the boatshed door, leaving it with him there.

౦౨

Charlie watched her go and shook his head. No amount of good manners would get him past St Peter. But he'd made peace with that a long time ago.

Inside he sat on his bed, the pile of letters beside him. He didn't want to read them, face what was inside. But maybe he was supposed to – his final penance.

It was easy, at first, reading about his beloved Ivy. Easy until he got to the letter he'd been dreading. From the date he knew what was coming and he hoped Nicole was right and that Ivy had treated the story of his arrival, of his past, with delicacy. Not that she owed him that, but he hoped nonetheless.

As he read her next letter his heart began to ache, and as he continued with the next, and the one after that, melancholy swept over him.

He read until the dawning hour of morning broke sunlight over the ocean and into the portal window, sending golden rays into the boatshed.

Carefully, he put all the letters back into the box and stroked the lid as he closed it. He felt close to Ivy once more – a gift he would never have hoped for, but one he cherished.

There was one last task. He knew what he had to do next.

As he shuffled towards the cottage, Charlie's pulse quickened. Every new beginning means something has to end.

He was okay with that. Not happy, but content. It was how it was meant to be.

Nicole was outside painting one of the verandah supports. Good. He wouldn't have to knock on the door. He wouldn't have to go in. He could never go in when Ivy was there. To go in now would be a betrayal.

As he pushed open the gate, Nicole turned around and walked down the verandah steps to meet him and he handed her Ivy's box.

'Thank you for sharing these with me.' He hugged her. Tightly. Quickly. Then he pulled away.

'If I'd known they'd turn you into a marshmallow, I'd have given them to you long ago.'

'No need for that,' he grumbled.

'Will you come in for a cuppa?'

'No, thank you,' he said, and shook his head.

'At least sit down and tell me more about her.'

'What's in there is pretty much her. She was one special lady. Not perfect, but an angel to me. Keep them safe.' He tapped on the box.

'I will. Are you sure you don't want a cuppa?'

'I'm sure. You can make yourself useful though.'

'What do you need?' she asked.

'Send this. Today. By courier.'

'Yes, sir.' She saluted. 'Any more and I'll have to start charging you a service fee.'

'Please.' He smiled. He owed her so much, but a smile would have to do.

At least for today.

'I'll do it at lunch.'

'Thank you,' he whispered. *For more than you will ever know.*

He gave her the envelope and pressed it in her hands.

She was a good girl. This letter would mean he'd finally have a chance at doing something right with his life.

'You're welcome.' Nicole tilted her head slightly.

'Place looks good.' He turned to leave.

'Do you like the colour?'

'Prefer the original, but it'll pass. I suppose. Don't give up your day job, though.'

'Don't have one.'

'Yes, you do,' he said, giving her a pointed look. And Nicole frowned.

Thirty-five

$\mathcal{N}$icole headed into town, the sun warming her skin, the gentle breeze teasing her hair. Charlie had been insistent that the letter get posted today and with the only task on her list for the day – painting the verandah supports – now finished a stroll in the midday sun was perfect.

She paid Jacqui for the postage and had a cuddle with Amy.

'My, she's growing,' she noted, cooing at the baby perched on the post office counter.

'They make a habit of it.' Jacqui smiled. 'Do you want to take her out for a bit? Give her some fresh air?'

'Oh, no . . . I couldn't. I can't. I —'

'She's been fed and changed and there's really nowhere you can go where you can't get back here in about fifteen seconds if you need to.'

Jacqui looked so tired Nicole couldn't ignore her plea for help. She gave in, and pushed down the little voice of fear inside. She put on the baby pouch and Jacqui helped her position Amy, who seemed very happy in her new spot, where she could face the big wide world.

'Thanks,' Jacqui said with a sigh, laying her head on the counter.

'No dramas. We'll go buy some lunch for Aunty Nicole and visit Aunty Mandy, and . . .'

Nicole gently closed the post office door, pulling down the small blind that covered the glass panel and turning over the open sign to read 'back in ten'.

Nicole walked down High Street and passed Bill Tucker. He was faring well, but his arthritis was playing up a bit. He was looking forward to the grand final on Saturday, though. Jim was off to a job fixing old Grandma Cartwright's loo, which had nothing wrong with it, the old duck just liked the company. He wouldn't charge for the visit. You'd think the family would pop in and see her some time, but they were always too busy. Greg Telford was on his lunch break, and was thinking of getting something healthy, like a salad. He couldn't have a carb-blowout before the most important match in Ranger history. His dad would have something at the store for him.

Grinning broadly, Nicole headed to the hardware shop. As she arrived she waved at Trevor, who was helping Mr Greene jam a mower into his car boot. Amy blew spit bubbles in greeting.

Cheryl and Mandy rushed over and happily made a fuss over the baby, taking it in turns to hold her with one arm, all the while continuing to man the counter and scan nails, painting tape, and wooden stakes with the other, chatting to Amy in between serving customers.

When Nicole started to leave she was met with cries of protest. 'Can't you stay longer?' Cheryl pleaded. 'Playing with this little sweetie sure beats counting screws any day.'

'Sorry, but I'd better get her back.' Nicole slipped Amy back into the pouch. 'She's been so good; I'm afraid my luck's going to run out.'

Mandy came out from behind the counter. 'One last kiss before you go, cutie pie.'

'Mandy,' Nicole fanned herself with her free hand, 'I never knew you felt that way.' She raised her cheek for a peck.

'Ha, ha.' Mandy bent down and kissed Amy on the forehead.

'Oh,' Nicole said, turning back before leaving the shop. 'What do you reckon about post-match celebrations at my place on Sunday?'

'I reckon great.'

'I reckon you're pretty confident they'll win.' Cheryl laughed.

'If not, it will be a commiserations party instead.' Nicole smiled.

By the time she got back to the post office, Jacqui was awake and looking much brighter.

'Thank you,' she said as she took Amy back.

Meandering up Wilson's Road, Nicole began to sweat, yet the day had cooled. A goanna walked beside her in the gravel, its head bowed, and her stomach churned, her pulse quickened.

A sudden gust of wind made the branches of the gums sag, the burden of their leaves too much to bear under such force. The tiny hairs on the back of her neck tingled. She looked around. No one was following her.

She walked straight past her cottage, something telling her to keep going down the path to the boatshed. Her chest tightened and she picked up her pace, breaking into a jog. With every step she got faster. She ran straight past the open boatshed door to the side of the small building.

Charlie was sitting on the bench, face turned towards the sky, his head resting on the wall behind him, one shoulder dipped down.

Nicole stopped.

She took three deep breaths and walked slowly towards him, squatting beside the bench. She checked his neck and wrist and placed her hand close to his mouth and nose to feel for breath. A futile gesture, she knew. She'd noticed his sunken cheeks, ashen skin and open mouth the second she saw him, and she knew.

She leaned her head against his knee, held his cold hands. 'Oh, Charlie.' Great gulps of tears burst forth and she let them come. 'Goodbye, friend.'

What a powerful word. Friend. What an inadequate word.

She sucked in great gulps of air.

He'd have hated such a display of emotion. A wry smile touched her lips.

Thirty-six

Mandy and Trevor had come right over as soon as Nicole called to tell them the news, and now she was sitting at her dining table with a cold cup of tea in front of her. Mandy fussed about in the sink, washing Nicole's breakfast dishes. Trevor stood beside the fridge, hands in his pockets.

'Don't suppose you feel much like eating?' Mandy asked.

'I should have insisted he go to hospital.'

'None of us could have made Charlie do anything he didn't want to. You know that,' Mandy said as she sat beside her.

'I should have been there. Stayed twenty-four seven till he got better.'

'Oh, he would have just loved that.' Mandy laughed. 'He wasn't going to get better, honey,' she said. 'Charlie's been a lot sicker than most people realise for a long time now. Doctor Johnson's been treating him a while. Cancer. I think they were at what you call the palliative stage. Just keeping him comfortable. Besides, what could you have done if you had been there?'

'Held his hand. Let him know he wasn't alone.'

'He probably preferred it this way.' Mandy put her arm round Nicole's shaking shoulders.

He was sick, he got better, he got her to send one more letter, then he died. A thought occurred to Nicole.

'Do you think people can choose when they die? You know, when they're sick or hurt. Can they pick the exact moment?'

'Maybe. I don't know. But it's a compelling thought.'

'But he was alone,' Nicole sighed.

'He may have died alone, but because of you, he didn't live alone. And that's far more important. You were his friend. You made a difference.'

'The whole thing sucks.' Nicole slammed her hand down on the table.

'Yep.'

'The question now,' Trevor moved towards the table, 'is whether there's anyone who needs to be told. Any long-lost family.'

'Mr Dixon!' Nicole shouted.

'Sorry?' asked Mandy, startled.

'For a few weeks Charlie was getting me to send letters to a Mr Dixon in Sydney. I think there were three altogether. They were going to a business address.'

'Do you think it could be a relative?' Trevor asked.

'Give me a minute.' Mandy started pacing the floor. 'Dixon and Dodge.' She slapped Trevor on the shoulder.

'Ouch.'

'Doyle.' Nicole stood up, seeing the address in her mind. 'Dixon and Doyle. Why didn't I put two and two together?'

Nicole ran into the living room and returned with a file and pulled out the lease for the cottage.

'Dixon and Doyle.' She slammed the document on the table. She'd only paid scant attention when she'd signed it and all her dealings had been with some office junior.

'The bigwigs in Sydney who handled Ivy's estate?' Mandy raised her eyebrows. 'They were sniffing around here not long before you arrived, when we all thought the cottage was going on the market.'

'Charlie's estate now, I guess.' Nicole shrugged.

Mandy stood up. 'What?'

'Ivy left everything to him when she died. The boatshed, the cottage, the land, her money, too, I suppose. She wasn't all that specific.'

'Hang on.' Mandy spun round. '*She* wasn't all that specific? She, as in Ivy?'

Nicole nodded. She would have to explain that later.

Her phone rang.

'Yes, this is she,' answered Nicole. 'No. He passed. This morning, actually. Oh. Okay. Of course.'

She listened for some time without speaking.

'What? Are you sure? I . . . um . . . okay. Thank you. Sure.'

She hung up.

'Sit down.' Mandy guided her to a seat. 'You've gone very pale.'

'That was Mr Dixon. Charlie's solicitor. He got a letter from Charlie saying he knew his time was up and he wanted to sort everything out. Dixon rang to see if he was still with us.'

'Oh my.' Mandy exhaled.

'Why ring you?' Trevor asked.

'I'm named as his executor.' A tear fell down Nicole's cheek.

Mandy's mouth dropped, but no words came out.

'I'm confused.' Trevor shook his head.

'Mr Dixon said someone will be paying a visit in a few days.' Nicole continued.

'To un-confuse me?' Trevor asked.

Mandy shook her head. 'I need a drink.'

Trevor picked up her cup.

'A real one,' she said.

Trevor poured two glasses of red from the bottle on the kitchen bench.

'Someone will come and go through his will with me, I guess.'

'And what about the other letters?'

'What are you talking about, Trev?' Mandy snapped. 'We've far more important things to worry about than a letter.'

'Nicole said Dixon said he got *a* letter, singular. But Nicole sent three letters. If the first letter has created this much drama, what's in the other two?'

'Oh, yeah.' Mandy gasped. She narrowed her gaze. 'He's a secret kazillionaire and he left it all to you.'

'I doubt that.' Nicole smiled. 'I only sent the third one today, so who knows what's in that one.'

'I guess we'll find out when Dixon sends his man.' Trevor collected the teacups and put them in the sink.

'I guess.' Nicole put her glass down.

'And, until then,' Mandy looked at Nicole with raised eyebrows, 'there are some other gaps that could do with some filling in.'

Trevor headed home, leaving the two women to talk and Nicole told Mandy all about the letters, all about Ivy.

'Hang on.' Mandy put her hand up. 'You knew Charlie was behind this crazy rental-reno deal?'

'I only knew for sure when I read the second-last letter. I was going to ask him about it, but . . .'

'Oh dear. Well, whatever happens from here, there's always a home for you with us.'

'Thank you.' Nicole knew now that she would stay in Rosella Cove. Once she spoke with Charlie's lawyers, she'd figure out how. There was too much to think about right now, and not enough information.

'Will you be all right, if I head?' Mandy asked.

'Of course. Thank you for coming over.'

They hugged and Mandy went home.

All alone, the afternoon hours dragged on relentlessly for Nicole. She thought about walking to the boatshed, but couldn't bring herself to do it. Instead she wandered aimlessly through her cottage, running her hands over walls and furniture until the sun set and the evening air took on a slight chill.

Though the night brought no rest, it had felt good to tell Mandy about Ivy, to share with her the stories of the old lady, how special the letters were. Somehow it made the grief of losing Charlie just a little more bearable.

'You here, Nicole?' A warm, familiar voice called from the verandah.

Nicole went to the front door.

'Hey.' She allowed a small smile to cross her face as she opened the screen door.

Danny came inside and as soon as he did, Nicole's bottom lip started to quiver and a tear fell down her cheek. Then another. And another.

He scooped her up into his arms and she sobbed into his chest.

'Shh.' He stroked her hair. 'It's okay. I know what he meant to you.'

'And to you,' she whispered.

He nodded. 'I wonder what will happen to this place now he's gone.'

'We won't know till the lawyers come.' Nicole frowned. 'Hang on a minute. You knew? You knew Charlie owned the cottage?'

Danny cast his eyes down. 'He made me promise not to say anything to anyone.'

'That's why you helped out with the renovations so much?'

'He asked me to help out a bit. I did as much as I did because I liked spending time with you.' He grinned. 'Sorry I didn't tell you.'

'Will you make me a promise, Danny Temple?'

'If I can.'

'Promise me, that no matter what happens between us, we won't keep things from one another again.'

He touched his forehead to hers. 'I promise. Total honesty. And in the interests of that I need to tell you this. I don't know what anything that's happened means for us, Nicole. Long term. Or short. I just know that when I'm this close to you, I don't ever want to leave.'

Nicole gulped. 'I don't want you to resent me down the track, Danny. And I know how you feel about having kids.'

He stood up and walked around the room, running his hands through his hair.

'I saw Charlie yesterday. He stopped me as I was going past and said something I haven't been able to shake since. "Danny, lad, the things you regret when you're my age, are the things you didn't do anything about but could have." I know what he means now.' He pulled her into his embrace.

'But . . .'

'Nicole, I can't do anything about the fertility challenges we'll face, if we ever get to that point. But I can do something about the way the way I feel about you. There are other options for us if we decide we want to have children and we can figure that out later. Together.'

He took her lips in his and kissed her firmly.

Heat enveloped her entire body and she pressed into him. His hands reached beneath her shirt and slid it over her head. In a smooth movement he lifted Nicole and carried her into the bedroom.

The next morning, Nicole woke alone in the bed. On the pillow next to her was a note.

'Go into the kitchen.'

She pulled her dressing-gown on and followed the note's instructions.

On the kitchen bench was another note.

'Open the oven door.'

Inside the oven was a tray of ham and cheese croissants warming on a low heat.

'Check the fridge.' Another note scribbled on the baking paper.

Freshly squeezed orange juice sat chilled in the refrigerator, another note stuck to the glass.

'Last chance footy training this morning. See you at the game, xo.'

Nicole ate breakfast and felt warmed by Danny's gestures, even though she had no idea what any of this meant. And maybe that was okay. Maybe she wasn't supposed to know.

Thirty-seven

The morning rain had stopped, but the mud and the puddles were causing havoc for both teams. Men were slipping and sliding and the ball was being dropped by usually safe hands.

The hooter blew at half-time with the scores locked at six each. The teams gathered in two huddles, desperately trying to find a way to breach the other's defences.

Nicole wrapped her black and white scarf firmly around her neck and went with Mandy to buy a hot drink. A cool southerly had blown in overnight, dropping temperatures.

On Woodville's home turf there were no markets, but the smell of onions on the barbecue was irresistible.

'Two sausage sandwiches,' Nicole ordered. She gave one to Mandy, who handed her a hot chocolate.

Arm in arm, the two ladies walked back to the sideline and joined the sea of black and white stripes.

A stranger wouldn't have been able to pick who had the home ground advantage that day. So many cove supporters had made the journey to the match, Nicole doubted there was anybody left back home.

The ref blew time on and Nicole's heart quickened.

Trevor was going hoarse on the sideline, and Mandy and Nicole jumped up and down whenever the Rangers made any kind of break or good tackle. Nicole finally understood what people meant when they said they played every ball with their team. It was exhausting.

The minutes ticked down. The game was messy and muddy and sluggish. Woodville scored a try and converted. Danny tried to rally his troops with shouts and fist pumps. He looked up at Nicole, who smiled at him and he clapped his hands to rev up his teammates.

Greg crossed for a try with five minutes to spare.

Danny missed the equaliser. Oh, God, was this her fault?

She started biting her nails – something she hadn't done since high school. Mandy rocked back and forth and flailed her arms about, willing the boys forward. Jack screamed at the top of his voice. Jacqui almost dropped Amy with each pass.

Bill Tucker got up from his chair and stood, silently watching every move.

Woodville started to count down.

Greg was awarded a penalty, took a shot at goal, and the score was tied.

A magnificent intercept from Jason as play resumed, and a run half the length of the field roused a cheer from the cove supporters, which swelled in volume as he offloaded to Matt, then collapsed from the effort.

Matt passed the ball to Danny.

Danny set himself for a field goal.

Nicole held her breath.

'C'mon!' The roar went up from the Rangers supporters as the ball sailed over the black dot.

The hooter sounded.

Mandy and Nicole hugged each other and then everyone around them. Wives and girlfriends ran to kiss their mud-covered heroes. Mandy dashed over to embrace Trevor. Danny, swamped by the crowd, looked at Nicole. She smiled at him and he smiled back before being swallowed by junior Rangers who piled on to him.

Back in town, The Royal was packed and draped in black and white streamers and balloons that hung from every possible hook, beam and light fixture. The jukebox was on continuous rotation with everyone joining in when 'We Are the Champions' played.

George and his two bartenders were sweating profusely behind the bar trying to keep the beer flowing, and Greg and Jason jumped back there to lend a hand. The younger kids and teenagers danced on the make-do dance floor created once a few tables had been moved.

Saluted with song and skulling, Danny was the first to be hoisted on to the bar. He was followed by Trevor and then Jason. Eventually, the whole team were celebrated with every player praised, even old Craig, who'd spent the entire eighty minutes on the sideline injured. Then it was Nicole's turn.

'Our lucky socks,' shouted Trevor.

Nicole leaned over to George and asked for sparkling apple juice instead of beer, figuring no one would notice in all the excitement. She climbed up on the cedar bar top and smiled warmly as the entire establishment raised their voices.

'Here's to Nicole, she's true blue . . .'

She swiftly and easily downed her drink, raising her glass in triumph at the end.

Danny helped her down, the press of the crowd keeping them pinned together.

'That goal will become town legend,' Nicole said, his body close to hers.

'The match will.' He smiled. 'As will our lucky charm.'

'Ah yes, every girl's dream, to be forever remembered as a pair of socks.' She laughed.

Danny smiled and raised his hand, brushing her fringe from her face.

'Hey, Cap'n. Great goal.' Matt bumped into them and put his arm round Danny. 'Another round.' He slurred and pushed Danny towards the bar.

Come midnight the celebration showed no sign of easing up, and Danny no sign of being free, so Nicole quietly slipped out and walked home. She had a lot to do before the picnic tomorrow and wanted to get an early start.

The black velvet sky sparkled with stars, the crescent moon smiled on its side, and a few wispy clouds painted her way home.

In the morning Nicole frantically ran around her kitchen, trying to get everything made in time. She chopped tomatoes and cucumbers, stirred pasta, blended pesto, cut up potato wedges and hulled strawberries. All according to the rules Mandy had given her during their cooking lessons. She kept checking the clock. The long, narrow hands appeared to be moving at an increasingly accelerated speed.

Surely no one would be early; more likely late, given the previous evening's festivities. But she wanted to be ready on time anyway. She owed the boys at least that.

Trevor was bringing over his barbecue and Mandy had assured Nicole that everyone would bring their own meat and drinks. But she was the host and that meant ensuring there was enough food for people to walk away happy and full. She had big shoes to fill – it was the first town picnic in decades, and it was taking place once more on Ivy's lawn.

She wiped her forehead, leaving a trail of green pesto above her left eyebrow. No time to stop. She hadn't even set up the tables yet.

'Hello?' A voice called from the front door.

Nicole looked up at the clock. There was still half an hour before anyone was supposed to arrive. She wiped her hands on her apron and rushed to the door.

'I thought you might need a hand,' Danny said with warmth as she opened the screen door.

'You're a godsend.' She sighed.

'That's a good look.'

'Sorry?'

He gently wiped the pesto from her face.

'Oh. Thanks.' She laughed. 'As you can see, I'm quite literally in a mess. I'm so glad you've come early.'

He took her food-stained hands. 'Relax. This is supposed to be a fun afternoon. For everyone. Breathe.'

She looked at the chaos spread across the kitchen bench.

'Breathe,' Danny said again. 'People will bring their own stuff, and if there's not enough we'll get Telford to raid the store.'

Nicole squeezed his hands, which still had a firm grip on her.

'That's better. Now, what can I do?'

'Can you set up the tables for me? Here are some tablecloths.'

'Of course.' He nodded.

Nicole had no idea what spending the night before last together meant. He was leaving for his annual trip to Bangladesh tonight and there was every chance that by the time he got back he'd have changed his mind about her. All she could do was go with it and see what happened.

While Danny took care of the outside, Nicole went back to work in the kitchen. When she was satisfied all her bowls and platters were complete, she carried vases and plates and cutlery into the front yard.

Danny helped her place them on the tables and she walked around the garden picking various flowers to put in the vases. Danny returned from inside with the packets of pink and purple and yellow and green paper napkins she'd left on the dining table. And after Nicole set them on the two tables under the shade of the tall gum at the centre of her expansive yard, she stood back and looked at the effect.

'It feels happy, right?' she asked.

'It looks amazing,' Mandy said as she came through the gate. 'Vaguely familiar.' She winked.

'Thanks.'

'She'd be proud. You can tell it's been done with love.' She hugged Nicole.

'Now, before anyone else arrives, we've got something for you. Well, for the cottage.'

Trevor and Danny completed the circle around Nicole.

'We wanted to give you something to finish off the renovations,' Mandy said.

'You've restored this place to its former glory and I know how connected you feel to Ivy, and, well, I hope this is okay.'

Trevor handed her a piece of wood wrapped in a blue and white bow.

'Made it myself.'

Looking at the house plaque, Nicole breathed in deeply. Into the dark wood, bordered by leaves and vines etched to different depths, 'Ivy Cottage' was carved.

'It's perfect.' She wrapped them all in a group hug.

'I'll hang it now if you like?' Trevor offered.

'Yes, please.'

Trevor headed back to his truck to fetch his tools.

'You keep an eye on that,' he said to Danny, pointing at the barbecue.

Mandy turned to Nicole. 'You go freshen up. People are coming up the road.'

It took a few minutes to compose herself. Nicole splashed her face with water – happy tears were no different from sad, making her skin red and blotchy. As she headed back out on the verandah she took in the scene before her.

On the lawn, groups of people sat on picnic blankets or around portable tables on fold-up chairs. Each blanket and table was laden with bowls and plates of food. Some people stood, talking and laughing with glasses in their hands. Others were at Nicole's salad table dishing themselves up pasta or greens. Half-a-dozen men, including Jason and Bill Tucker, joined Danny and Trevor at the barbecue, and they all took turns turning sausages and steaks before plating them up to ferry back to their family groups. Bill saw Nicole and tipped his peaked cap to her.

She waved at him in greeting.

Little children were running around playing tip, and the older ones had started a game of soccer. Nicole leaned against the post and watched them for a moment before shifting her gaze.

Jacqui and Mandy were in lively discussion on a bright, orange blanket next to the metal brolga perched on the lawn. Cheryl and

Jim were talking with Jack over by the roses he had planted. Jim appeared to be asking Jack questions, but the poor lad was distracted, stealing glances at Katie Lewis, who was entertaining a crawling Amy. George was handing out cans of soft drink from the two eskies he'd brought with him from the pub.

Kicking off her sandals, Nicole laughed and stepped down on the grass with bare feet – the only fitting way to freely enjoy the day. She headed over to grab a plate and fill it up.

Mandy joined her. 'What a turn-out. Half the town is here.' She spooned noodle salad on to her plate.

'It's amazing.'

'Nice send-off for Danny, too,' Mandy said. 'He flies out tomorrow, doesn't he?'

'You know he does.' Nicole noticed Mandy's smirk. 'Giving so much time to that school is amazing.' Nicole shook her head.

'You know,' Mandy said and Nicole turned to face her friend, recognising the conspiratorial tone of voice. 'He doesn't just work at the school.'

'Oh?'

'He built it. And I don't just mean physically with his hands, which is also true. I mean he funded it. He went backpacking after he finished school with some mates and stumbled across the area and fell in love with the place. And, well, after Caitlyn, he used the money his grandfather left him and went back and built them a school. Been going back ever since.'

'You know you don't have to sell him to me anymore,' she said.

'Just making sure.' Mandy grinned.

'Touché.'

A sudden loud whistle from Trevor silenced the entire gathering. 'Thanks everyone for coming along today,' he shouted.

Everyone turned to face him.

'It's great to be able to celebrate yesterday's glorious win with you all.'

'Carn the mighty Rangers!' Greg called out.

'And can we thank our generous host? Nicole!'

Trevor waited for the next round of cheering and clapping to subside.

'While this weekend is about winning . . .'

Another cheer.

'. . . the cove also lost, well, one of its icons, I guess, this week. Nicole, would you mind saying a few words about Charlie?'

Nicole was not at all prepared. But all eyes were on her. Including the pair belonging to a tall stranger who'd just come through the gate.

'I gather most of you didn't know Charlie too well.' She searched for fitting words. 'A lot of you were even frightened of him, I hear.'

A few people shuffled their feet in discomfort.

'But, I did know him, as well as he let me, and he was a kind, intelligent man, who was a good friend to me at a time in my life when, well, I didn't have too many friends.' She looked to Mandy, who tilted her head to the side and raised an eyebrow. 'Something I've come to learn about the people of Rosella Cove is how special they are. Their generosity of spirit is boundless, their friendship is genuine, and I can tell you all that Charlie truly was part of this town. From what I can gather, there are a few among you who also saw glimpses of that in him.'

Mandy was next up and told everyone how Charlie had helped her with her mum, leaving out the more intimate details of her mum's undignified fall into dementia. Danny told of his encounter in the bush. One by one, half-a-dozen people also came forward and recounted personal moments that painted Charlie in a very different light from that of his reputation.

Nicole smiled broadly and raised her glass.

'To two fine examples of our wonderful community: to the mighty Rangers and to Charlie.'

The crowd echoed the toast.

'That was lovely,' Mandy said. 'He'd have hated it, but it was really nice.'

The tall stranger picked his way through the pockets of happy people until he was standing in front of Nicole and Mandy.

'Excuse me,' he said. 'Sorry to crash your party. You must be Nicole Miller.' He extended his hand. 'Mr Dixon said I'd find you here.'

'Oh, hi.' Nicole shook his hand, his grip firm. 'That's dedication for you. Working on a Sunday.'

'Working?' Confusion read across his face.

'Mr Dixon sent you. From Dixon and Doyle. Charlie's lawyers.'

'Oh, no.' The man shook his head. 'I mean yes. They are Charlie's lawyers. But I'm not.'

'You're not?'

'No. Sorry.' He took a deep breath. 'I should start again. My name's Dr James Baker. I'm Charlie's son.'

Thirty-eight

Nicole dropped her glass.

'Sorry?'

Thank goodness for Mandy, who bent down and cleaned up the mess, as Nicole was unable to move.

'I wasn't expecting . . . I didn't know . . . his son?' She took a deep breath. 'I don't even know where to begin.'

'Yeah. I shouldn't have just turned up unannounced like this.' He ran his hand through greying hair. 'But as soon as I found out, I had to come. All these years I never knew he was alive.'

'No, that's fine,' Nicole said. 'I guess we need to have a long chat.'

'I can come back when it's more convenient.'

'No. Stay. Please. Have something to eat. Once this is done we can sit down properly.' She looked into his eyes – the same grey eyes as Charlie's.

Danny came over and placed an arm around Nicole's shoulder briefly. 'Come and I'll fetch you something off the barbie,' he said.

'Thanks. Oh . . .' James turned back to Nicole. 'Is Ivy here?'

'Ivy?'

'Ivy Wilson.'

Nicole and Mandy shared a glance.

'Ivy was the woman who owned the cottage originally. But she's been dead more than forty years.'

'Oh.' James looked surprised. 'But you've been living here?'

'Yes.'

'Then I guess this is for you.' He handed her an envelope. 'Mr Dixon couriered this to me yesterday. It came with instructions for me to deliver it personally.'

Nicole looked down at the envelope.

Ivy Wilson

The Carved Shell Box

Wilson's Rd

Rosella Cove

She looked up at him with wide eyes.

'This is the only house on the road and I didn't see a shell box out front.' James shrugged. 'So I came through the gate.'

'No. The box is . . . We'll talk about that too.' She smiled.

James turned and followed Danny, refusing the beer on offer but taking a squash instead, and Mandy steered Nicole inside.

My sweet Ivy,

I hope this letter finds its way back to you. If it does, then it means the wrongs of the past have started their long journey towards redemption.

I've done what you asked of me. I've tried to make right. I'd let the whole thing go to pot after you passed – the cottage, the boatshed, myself. You'd have been pretty damn disappointed. But I never did touch the drink again. Not a drop. That's one promise that didn't take four decades to fulfil. I've done nothing to be proud of in my life, but I hope you'll be proud of my final few breaths.

Nicole has done a pretty good job fixing up the neglect I imposed on your house. I couldn't touch the place after you left and couldn't bear the thought of anyone else in it. But my time's been coming a while now, and I knew I had to make good on my promise to you. Perhaps you had a hand in bringing her here. I'd like to believe that. She's a lot like you. Smart, feisty, insolent, pushy. Like you, she is a gem amongst the stones. She's made these last few months waiting for death bearable.

My son survived. I found him. I don't know what became of my Hannah, my sweet Hannah. I will carry the guilt of that night with me into the next life.

I've been watching James, watching him from afar and he's a fine man, not at all taking after his father, thank goodness.

I'm leaving him the cottage and the boatshed. They must stay together.

It doesn't change what I did and it can hardly make up for it, but, perhaps it is a gesture that can, in some inadequately small way, say I'm sorry. There is a little bit of money over from what you left me. I hope it is okay that I give it to Nicole.

I also sent James a letter. I don't know what Hannah would have told him about me, if she ever had the chance, but I figure I owe him the truth. When we leave this world what else is there left?

I hope he can forgive me, though I doubt I could if roles were reversed. I am a coward. James will not have the chance to ask me questions, or to get angry with me, or hate me, or hit me, or look on at me with pity. I've robbed him of that, too afraid to face him in person. My only hope is that he is a better man than I and will find a way to deal with the truth.

I hope you made it back into your Thomas's arms. I imagine
where I'm heading now, no friendly smile will greet me. Only flames.
The irony of that is not lost on me. I will conjure your beautiful face
in my mind to comfort me.

Thank you for saving me, Ivy.

Charlie

Nicole read the letter out loud, her voice breaking.

'Bugger me.' Mandy let out a long breath.

Trevor knocked on the doorframe to the kitchen. 'Sorry to interrupt, girls, but a few people are starting to leave and I thought you might want to say goodbye.'

'Thanks, honey,' Mandy said. 'We'll be right out.'

The women stood up and fixed their hair, splashed their faces with water and headed back outside.

'I'll join you in a sec,' Nicole said as Mandy opened the screen door.

She went into her bedroom and opened Ivy's box, now on display in the middle of her dresser. She put Charlie's letter in the back and closed the lid, her fingers lingering on the top just briefly.

Nicole's friends had welcomed James like she knew they would. Everyone had left now except those that were closest to her, and the small group sat around the table under the tall gum. The sun had dropped low towards the horizon and the air was filled with love and gentle laughter.

Nicole could see James beginning to relax and she hoped he would feel comfortable among them. He'd mentioned little about himself, other than he was from Sydney, had a young family there and worked as a burns specialist at Westmead. There were, no doubt, some difficult questions he was here to ask. All she knew of Charlie's past was what she had gleaned from Ivy's letters, and his own letter now. Snippets only. Of drink and guilt, of a night that maybe not everyone survived. Whatever the past held, whatever James was here to discover, it was unlikely pleasant. But she would make it as easy as she could. Later, when everyone was gone and they were alone, she'd show him Charlie's letter. A place to start.

'So,' Danny whispered in her ear. 'James is going to stay with you for a bit?'

'Yeah. He wants to learn everything he can about his father. It didn't seem right him staying at The Royal. It is technically his house.'

'Pretty good-looking.' Danny glanced over at him.

'Hadn't noticed, really.' Nicole couldn't stop the cheeky grin that teased the corners of her mouth.

She had noticed, though. James looked a lot like Nicole might imagine Charlie had looked at the same age.

'A bit old for me, though. He must be in his fifties. Turns out I like men born in the same decade as me.'

Danny blushed but held her gaze.

'What time are you flying tomorrow?' Jacqui leaned over and asked Danny.

'The flight's first thing. Actually, I should probably get going. Start the drive to Sydney and get to the airport motel before it gets too late.' He shook the men's hands and kissed Mandy, Cheryl and Jacqui on their cheeks.

Nicole walked him to the gate.

'Have a safe trip.' She took one step towards him. He didn't step back.

'Thanks.'

'I'm going to miss you.'

He closed the gap between them. The hint of orange and cinnamon on his neck filled Nicole's head with desire. He reached his arm behind her neck, pulling her into him, their bodies pressed tightly together.

Danny brushed her hair behind her ear and cupped her face in his strong hands.

He pressed his mouth to hers and she melted into him. The soft touch of his lips moved slowly at first and then quickened, opening her mouth further, his tongue searching for hers. She moaned softly. A tingle spread up her spine and her breath caught. He slowed his lips, releasing her mouth, taking it again.

'Don't forget, I'm coming back,' Danny whispered.

'I couldn't possibly forget that.'

Thirty-nine

*N*icole and James stood outside the boatshed.

'You ready?' she asked.

'No. You?' He smiled.

He held the old wooden door open.

Nicole hadn't been able to bring herself to enter Charlie's home after his death, but it seemed somehow fitting now with James beside her.

She'd shared everything she could with him over the past week. Everything she knew about Charlie from her own experience of him. Everything in Ivy's letters. And he'd asked questions that she'd answered as best she could. He'd taken in everything she'd told him, and Nicole could tell he'd had trouble processing the information, forming it into a coherent picture of his father.

She'd enjoyed James's quiet company. Enjoyed having someone to eat meals with, someone to talk to about Charlie and Ivy, both of whom she missed terribly.

On James's second-last day at the cove, it was only right that they visit the boatshed together.

Dusty boxes crowded the entry and the two of them twisted to slip through the narrow gaps.

'Does that say Ivy?' James brushed decades of grime from the top of one of the cartons.

Nicole leaned forward.

The few times she'd been in when Charlie was sick, she hadn't noticed anything other than Charlie.

'Yeah. I think so.'

They looked at each box. 'Ivy kitchen', 'Ivy books', 'Ivy linen'.

'She must have left him all this, and he hung on to it.' Nicole moved from cardboard relic to cardboard relic.

'For a really long time.' James whistled.

'What do we do with it now?'

James shrugged.

'You're his son. It's yours, I guess.'

'But these are Ivy's. I kind of feel it should all be yours.'

'We don't have to decide today.' Nicole shook her head.

They moved further in, to where Charlie did his living. On the bed was the Scrabble box with a small piece of paper attached.

'For Nicole', it read. She turned the note over. 'Now you'll never beat me.'

She laughed out loud. 'He was a formidable opponent, you know.'

'Something we have in common, then.'

'Really? Maybe we can play sometime.'

Underneath the Scrabble game was a well-read copy of *Tide* and Nicole let out a gasp. She opened the cover.

'Don't give up your day job.' She read Charlie's inscription to her, a tear sliding down her cheek.

James sat on the bed and comforted her with soft words. She looked up and saw the picture hanging above the bed.

'Ivy.' She nodded towards the beauty of her barefoot friend. 'And look at that.'

She stood up. On the small table beside the bed was a tiny polished silver frame. A striking blonde girl with long curly hair and sad dark eyes sat with a young boy in her lap. Nicole didn't remember seeing it the last time she was in here. Where had he been keeping it?

'That's me. And mum. Before . . .' James took the photo in his trembling hands.

'This isn't easy, I know.' Nicole tried to comfort him with a smile.

'No. But I want to put it all together. His story.' His voice cracked. 'I have to.'

'Shall we get some fresh air?' Nicole suggested.

On the way out Nicole saw a single dust-free book among the untouched novels and tattered volumes of encyclopaedia that lined the shelves. She reached out and touched it and then picked up the old copy of *David Copperfield*, Ivy's beloved novel that had once belonged to her father. The inside cover was inscribed.

'Charlie, you have found your home. Ivy.'

Nicole handed it to James, but he pressed it into her chest.

'This one is definitely for you.'

Together they sat on Charlie and Ivy's bench and watched the ocean kiss the shore and retreat in rhythmic repetition.

'Before I go home, I think maybe you should read this.' James handed Nicole his letter from Charlie.

'It's not exactly light reading.' His smile was warm, his cheekbones strong, his grey eyes intelligent, just like his father's. 'But, if I'm ever going to reconcile any of this, total disclosure is best.'

Nicole stared at the letter. 'I'm not sure about this.' She shook her head.

'From what I've learned this week, you knew him best, and he trusted you. And one thing I am sure of is that if he did trust you, well, then that means something. Somehow you and I have to put all the pieces of the puzzle together.'

He pressed the letter into her hands, squeezing them tightly.

The pain in Nicole's chest threatened to double her over as she slowly took in every word of Charlie's confession. If it wasn't in his own handwriting, she'd never have believed it. Beside her James played with the collar of his linen shirt. He'd been in Rosella Cove for a week now and every day he'd worn a collared shirt.

As he pushed it up and down she saw a scar.

'Is that . . .?'

He sat still and let her look.

Dr James Baker, burns specialist. Charlie's letter. The scars. All the fragments of information started to take shape.

'Surely he didn't burn it down . . .' She looked into James's eyes. 'I mean, not deliberately . . . with you guys inside . . .'

James shrugged and Nicole went back over Charlie's letter.

'I just can't believe . . . it had to be an accident.' Though Charlie's words were clear. In a drunken rage he'd set fire to his house, wife and child trapped inside.

'I'm still trying to figure it all out. Alcohol can do funny things to people. Turns you into someone you're not. It had a hold of him good, that much I know. I also know he pulled me out of the flames. There was nothing left of the house. My mum, Hannah, she never blamed him, you know. She tried to find him once. But she was weak. The firefighters managed to get her out, but her lungs were never the same. It wasn't long after that that she died.'

His voice wavered. Nicole held his hand.

'I was so young. All I've got to go on is in here, really.' He took back the letter and folded it carefully. 'And what you've told me.'

Nicole breathed out and shook her head, thinking of the three different Charlies now unmasked. The guilt-ridden exile who'd saved Ivy's life and had been her loyal companion, the man in her letters; the angry, violent drunk described in his own words; the gentle recluse Nicole herself knew and loved.

Over dinner that night, James was particularly quiet. 'Nicole. I've been thinking. About the cottage. My life is in Sydney and until I figure out what any of this Charlie stuff means, it doesn't feel right to sell this place. Would you be interested in renting it for another twelve months?'

Nicole had to stop herself from launching across the table to hug him.

'I would love that, very much.'

James nodded.

The next day Nicole helped him load his suitcase into his car. 'See you in a few weeks.'

'Next time, I'll stay longer. Organise a proper replacement at the hospital.' He squeezed her hand.

'Oh, please do. And study that dictionary of yours. Scrabble match first night you're back.'

'Will do,' he said. 'Would you mind if I bring my family next time? You can meet the kids.'

'I'd really like that.'

Days faded into weeks, and spring melted into summer.

Nicole sat at her desk with a cup of tea. On his last visit, James had helped her move it into the boatshed, under the portal window that looked out to sea. She and Mandy had cleared out the old building, sorting through Ivy and Charlie's things. Trevor had built shelves and cupboards around the walls and it was starting to feel like a proper study.

She finished the email she'd been composing and hoped with all her heart Jane would respond. Mandy had put her up to it. Now that she was settled in Rosella Cove, was there anything else in her past she wanted to lay to rest? Nicole had told her about Jane last night over dinner.

'Don't text her, though.' Mandy had encouraged her. 'What if she's changed her number? You did when you came here. Besides, texts are so impersonal and short. Maybe writing to her will give you both the space to say what needs to be said.'

The space to say what needs to be said. So much had happened to Nicole in the year and a half since she'd spoken with Jane. So much Jane didn't know, even before they stopped speaking.

A plethora of alternative scenarios around their history had suddenly become apparent to Nicole. She didn't know if reaching out like this would work, but she had to try.

She hit send on the email and hoped. Hoped Jane's old email address was still in use. Hoped she would reply.

She pulled out her notes and research and sat them next to Ivy's box. The information about Ivy's parents she'd sourced from the university the past few weeks had been interesting. More than interesting. Ivy's mother's money was very old, aristocrat old, and when she'd married Ivy's father it had caused quite a stir. Having James help her navigate the massive library archives had certainly proved fruitful.

On the shelf behind her sat the Scrabble box and Charlie's copy of *David Copperfield*. The picture of Ivy dancing barefoot in the grass hung where it always had, watching over Nicole, inspiring her.

Danny's latest letter from Bangladesh sat with the plane ticket he had sent her. In one week she'd be joining him.

She looked at the writing pad in front of her and picked up her favourite pen.

Chapter One

Ivy fidgeted with the pink bow in her hair. She hated bows. She hated pink too, but Mother had insisted she wear it. Top to toe. She pulled at her hair, wishing it could be free from its coiffed constraints. Her feet ached in the ridiculous heels Mother forced her to wear. Her bright, green eyes darted around the room.

The cute boy with the wavy brown locks and warm, dark eyes was looking at her again. The girl he'd arrived with, the one with black hair, was nowhere to be seen. She hoped he would ask her to dance before the girl returned, before Ivy tore the pink bow from her hair and caused a scene, before Mother forced her into the arms of the Fitzgerald lad, Hubert.

Mother didn't approve of young people going to dances, even when Father insisted. It was for a good cause he'd said. Ivy had begged Mother to let her go. She was never allowed to do anything remotely resembling fun. But neither of these forces could sway Mother. It was only when she heard the Fitzgeralds would be there, including their pimply letch of a son with his extremely healthy trust fund in tow, that she changed her mind.

All evening Mother had been working the Fitzgeralds over by the punch bowl at the back of the hall. If she hadn't been so terrified of dancing with Hubert, Ivy might have found Mother's talents impressive.

She could see from the smile on Mother's face that an agreement had been reached. She turned to escape.

'Excuse me.'

She felt a tap on her shoulder.

'I hope you aren't leaving.'

Ivy turned to face those warm, dark eyes that had enchanted her from the moment she saw them.

'Would you like to dance?' he asked.

'Yes.' She smiled.

'Very pleased to meet you,' he said, extending his hand to escort her on to the floor. 'I'm Thomas Wilson.'

Acknowledgements

Thank you to Joel Naoum of Critical Mass Consulting for helping massage an earlier version of *The Cottage at Rosella Cove* and for giving me direction with this story. Your insight and knowledge is second to none.

Jan Wallace Dickinson, thank you for lending your expertise on postwar Italian tourism to this project. Your willingness to help when I reached out to you is why I love the writing community.

To my wonderful writing buddies, Shell, Max, Georgie, El and Benison, thank you for your continued support and being there throughout this process. Thanks also to Anne S and Adrienne M for your ninja moves in bookshops.

Dianne Blacklock, you are the best unofficially adopted mentor a girl could hope for. Thank you for your wise counsel, for talking me off the editing ledge (more than once), and for helping me navigate the world of being a published author. Every writer needs a Di in their life, and I'm so grateful I have you.

Thank you to my amazing beta readers – Mishell Currie for being my staunch cheerleader, for loving this story before I did, and for your amazing support throughout (how many copies of *The Kookaburra Creek Café* do you own?!); Jennifer Johnson for your unwavering support, your willingness to read *yet another* version of *Rosella Cove* at the eleventh hour, and your beautiful texts that keep me going.

Léonie Kelsall, my wonderful critique partner, thank you for the oh-so-many late night messenger conversations about writing, publishing, family, editing and all the stressors that come with this journey and for being such an integral part of *Rosella Cove*. Thank you for flying across the country to be with me when *The Kookaburra Creek Café* came out. You are awesome.

Thank you, Kimberley Atkins, for taking a chance on me and my little stories about small towns with big hearts. I am forever grateful.

To my team at Penguin Random House – Ali, Elena and Emily – thank you for all you do to bring my stories to life and get them into the hands of readers. Thank you for your patience (especially you, Elena) as we wrangled this story into what it was meant to be. Thank you, Laura, for your beautiful cover designs. Everywhere I go people comment on how stunning they are.

To my in-law family, thank you for all your support, from buying books and travelling to events to spreading the word.

To my mum, Irene, thank you for tying down every single bowls player on the entire mid-north coast and forcing them to buy *The Kookaburra Creek Café*. Are you ready to do it again with *Rosella Cove*?

To my sister, Karen, thank you for all your support and for loving Ivy and Nicole and Charlie from the very start. This is the one that brought us back together. This one is for you.

To my husband, Chris, for ensuring I have the time and space to follow this dream, thank you. Sorry for screaming at you when the edits weren't going well, but if you can't scream at the one you love, who can you scream at?

My beautiful daughter, Emily, every day you amaze me with your strength and determination. I hope you know what an inspiration you are to me.

And finally, to the booksellers and librarians and my readers, thank you all for your support!

Book Club Questions

1. Do you think Nicky is justified in her desire to start her life over again in a whole new place?
2. Nicky believes that Mark loves her 'in his way'. Is this ever enough?
3. Rosella Cove is a tight-knit, supportive community. What are the pros and cons of living in a small town like this?
4. In what ways do Ivy and Nicole's stories mirror each other?
5. What does Ivy mean when she says of Lucy: 'In each other's company, neither of us need put on the brave face we do with others to protect those around us from our grief'?
6. Charlie says, 'The less you're seen, the more you see.' Explain.
7. In what ways is the renovation of the cottage physically and symbolically significant to Nicole's journey?
8. At the end of the novel, despite trying to make amends for his past, does Charlie find redemption?
9. What is it that finally gives Nicole the strength to say no to Mark?

10. Discuss the issue of gaslighting and why we seem to hear more about it these days.

11. Danny leaves for Bangladesh, but do you think Nicole and Danny's relationship will continue?

12. What similarities can you find between this novel and the author's first book, *The Kookaburra Creek Café*?

Welcome to the Kookaburra Creek Café

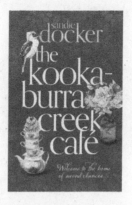

THE PAST

For Hattie, the café has been her refuge for the last fifty years – her second chance at a happy ending after her dreams of being a star were shattered. But will the ghosts of her past succeed in destroying everything she's worked so hard to build?

THE PRESENT

For Alice, the café is her livelihood. After Hattie took her in as a teenager, Alice has slowly forged a quiet life as the café's manager (and chief cupcake baker). But with so many tragedies behind her, is it too late for Alice's story to have a happy ending?

THE FUTURE

For Becca, a teenager in trouble, the café could be the new start she yearns for. That is, if she can be persuaded to stop running from her secrets. Can Becca find a way to believe in the kindness of strangers, and accept that this small town could be the place where she finally belongs?

One small town. Three lost women. And a lifetime of secrets.

Read on for a taste . . .

An excerpt from *The Kookaburra Creek Café*

Prologue

Kookaburra Creek, 2010

*S*he ran as fast as she could.

'Where are you?' she screamed, her voice cracking.

Her throat hurt. Every gasp for air was difficult. She couldn't see very far through the thick black smoke, but she was sure she was close now. She had to be.

Angry orange flames danced across the tops of the gum trees behind her, chasing her down. But she wouldn't stop. She wouldn't leave him out here alone.

Be brave.

She coughed. No air.

'Are you here?' she rasped.

Trees cracked beside her. Branches exploded, sending hot black shards into the air. She ducked. She weaved.

Be brave.

There in the clearing she could see a quiet shadow.

'There you are. Silly boy, running off. It's okay. I'm here now. But we have to go.' She could see fear in his eyes. 'Are you hurt? Can you walk?'

He whimpered. She fell to her knees and ran her hands through his thick coat.

Tears started to fall down her face, before evaporating into the hot, dry air. 'It's okay. I'm here.' She coughed again. Each breath was harder than the last.

'We'll be okay,' she said, as she lay down in the dirt beside her best friend. He nuzzled into her arm. 'We can rest a little bit, then we have to go.'

She closed her eyes, coughing, wheezing. A minute was all she dared rest.

One

Kookaburra Creek, 2018

Alice Pond opened the door to the Kookaburra Creek Café and the brass bell hanging from the entrance frame didn't clang.

Most people entering the café wouldn't have noticed the absence of the bell's ring, but for the last fourteen years every morning of Alice's life had been exactly the same. Nearly every morning. And that meant Alice certainly did notice.

The oven timer's discordant buzz, in contrasting harmony with the door chimes, should have assaulted her ears as she opened the door. But there was only silence.

The smell of freshly cooked bread left to bake overnight should have greeted her. But there was no delicious doughy aroma wafting through the room.

Something was wrong.

Alice looked above her head to see the bracket holding the bell to the door frame was slightly bent. Her eyes darted around the room. Everything else seemed to be in place. The green gingham curtains were drawn shut, the piles of serviettes were on the counter where she'd left them the night before, the chairs were still atop the tables.

Then her gaze fell on the counter. The register was open.

Alice's stomach tightened as she moved slowly through the dining room.

Carefully she inched open the white shutters that divided the dining room and kitchen. The oven was off. She frowned. The pantry door was slightly ajar and she picked up the rolling pin as she tiptoed past the bench. Not that it would do her any good against a band of thieves, or even one thief if they were serious. But false confidence was better than none.

She stepped towards the pantry door. The sound of something hitting the floor, a lid perhaps, made Alice jump. The buggers better not be into her flour. Surely no one would think to look in there for her stashed savings. Well, whoever they were, they picked the wrong café to break into.

She pushed the slatted door open. A crumpled mess of grey spun round to face her.

'Ha-ya!' Alice screamed out, adopting her fiercest ninja pose, rolling pin poised for attack.

'What the —?' The grey mess jumped back and grabbed the closest object to its flailing hands – a tin of beetroot.

The hand holding the beetroot tin was very small and there was a slight curve beneath the grey hoodie. Alice's thief was a girl. A young girl with pieces of half-cooked bread crumbs caught in the folds of her tattered jumper. At least that explained what had happened to her baking.

'The door was open. I didn't break in,' the girl said at once, stepping back and forth looking for a way past her captor.

'What are you doing here?' Alice asked, trying to control her breathing. It was just a child. 'If you put back whatever you've taken, I won't call the police.'

'Don't you dare call the cops.' The girl pushed her greasy black hair behind her ears and raised her eyes to Alice in defiance.

From Alice's trembling hand the rolling pin crashed to the floor, a resounding thud echoing through the silent café, and she gasped.

Those two piercing blue eyes.

The girl shoved past her and sprinted through the café.

'Sorry.' Alice ran after her. 'Wait. I just . . .'

But the girl rushed past, out the café and into the trees across the large grass clearing that stretched in front of the café before Alice got to the bottom of the steps.

Alice sat on the deck that wrapped around the café and tried to calm her racing thoughts. It wasn't the first time she'd seen his eyes gazing back at her from a stranger's face. It wasn't the second or third. There was a time when she saw those eyes in every male she met. In the stare of the postie who'd delivered her bills; the mischievous gazes of the boys in the pub who were probably too young to drink; every second customer that came into the café when she first arrived in Kookaburra Creek. No, it wasn't the first time she'd seen Dean McRae's eyes in another. But only once before had she seen his eyes in a young girl, and that was so long ago, in a life no longer hers.

It was several minutes before Alice felt calm enough to rise on shaky legs and head back inside. Fractured images from her past fought for attention, but she blocked them out. She had a café to open. She couldn't dwell on wasted memories.

She stood in her kitchen, her heart beating fast, not sure where to start. It was too late to make more bread. Betty would be upset, no doubt. So would Claudine. They loved her homemade loaves. But they'd forgive her, just like they had that time a town-wide blackout had turned the oven off in the small hours of the morning. She'd make up some excuse or other. Joey would be able to bring over a few loaves from the bakery if she texted him now, and he'd be popping by for his coffee in about twenty minutes anyway.

Coffee! She hadn't put her coffee on. Nothing could be achieved before that ritual was taken care of. The drip of the Colombian blend falling into her favourite yellow mug was just the tonic she needed. She switched on the coffee machine to heat up and freshly ground the beans. She'd make enough for two.

She took down the wooden chairs, each a different colour – blue, pink, red, orange, purple, green – from the round white tables they perched on overnight. She rearranged them in new combinations, as she did each morning. Except Joey's chair. He liked the aqua and he liked it beside the east-facing window. He was her best customer, after all, even if his motives weren't altogether benign, so she kept his favourite spot for him, just the way he liked it.

As her coffee cooled she wiped down the tables and set them with the salt and pepper shakers collected from around the world: Babushka dolls, English phone booths, an Eiffel Tower set. Every time someone from town travelled overseas, they brought shakers back from their trip as a gift for Alice. Joey had started the tradition with the Leaning Tower of Pisa set and Betty had continued it with the two camels from Dubai. One day, on the table in the middle of the café, Alice would place a set she brought back herself.

She hoped the young thief was all right, that she hadn't been too frightened. Alice knew a little something about being discovered where you shouldn't be. She could never forget those early days when scared, alone and afraid, she'd stumbled upon the neglected café in the tiny town of Kookaburra Creek nestled in the hills in the middle of nowhere and somewhere.

As always, the routine of setting up the café soothed Alice completely, and she slowly sipped her coffee in front of good old Sylvia while waiting for inspiration to strike.

Sylvia always provided an answer, of course. Her warm expression and kind eyes looked down on Alice from her framed place on the wall above the oven, her grey hair collected in a white cotton bonnet. At least they were the colours Alice imagined behind the sepia tones of the picture. Sylvia wasn't her real name, though there was no reason it couldn't have been. Alice had simply called her that all those years ago when she first stepped into the kitchen and looked up in wide-eyed terror, wondering how on earth she'd ended up in this town.

Sylvia had told her that day, by way of the recipe that fell to the bench when Alice reached up to touch the picture hanging on the wall, to bake chocolate fudge cupcakes. So she had. It was the first cake of any description she'd ever made and the world stilled. It was as if everything around her had quieted. It was the first time in Alice's life she'd been able to switch off the constant thoughts in her head. The first time she'd been able to forget the scars and bruises collected in her life and enter The Silence. And so it had been that way ever since.

Alice looked into Sylvia's eyes and waited, asking her silently what to bake today. The answer came at once: strawberry and white chocolate.

Alice lowered her cup, her heart pounding, and stared hard at Sylvia. 'What?'

Sylvia gazed straight back, her eyes giving nothing away.

With shaking hands Alice pulled out the red and white polka-dotted patty cases from the pantry and lined the cupcake tin. She hesitantly reached for her bowls, beaters and measuring cups. Sylvia had never been wrong before. But strawberry and white chocolate?

Alice closed her eyes and, when she opened them again, the morning chorus of magpies and lyrebird no longer floated through the open window, the constant, gentle buzz of the old fridge could not be heard: The Silence.

Her hands steadied as she hulled the strawberries, chopped them into small pieces and folded them into the batter. She pushed a square of white chocolate into the centre of each waiting cupcake and her breathing quickened. Strawberries and white chocolate was not a combination she'd ever used before. Or ever wanted to use. Strawberries, yes. White chocolate, yes. But never together. Memories of that night so long ago teased the edges of Alice's mind. How could Sylvia have known?

Alice slid the tray on to the oven shelf and shut the glass door. She cranked up the music on the radio and moved her hips in time with the beat as she cleaned down the bench and started washing up.

The three-tiered cupcake stand on the counter was Alice's very favourite thing in the room. After the photo of Sylvia, her favourite thing in the whole café. In itself it was nothing special – plain white ceramic that you could probably pick up in any homeware store in any town. But it was the same stand she'd displayed her first batch of cakes on and each batch since, and she always felt such pride every time she loaded the tiers with creations she'd made on her own from scratch.

This particular morning was different, though. Her hands were unsteady as she arranged the strawberry and white chocolate cakes. She shook her head. *Stop being so silly*. It was a coincidence, that's all. How could Sylvia possibly have known the significance of strawberry and white chocolate and that night so very long ago? She was an inanimate object, for goodness' sake. And how could she possibly have known the girl with Dean McRae's eyes would be in Alice's pantry that same morning? She couldn't have. That's right.

'They look good.' A deep voice startled Alice from her thoughts of the past and she dropped the last cupcake, frosting down, on her bright blue bench. 'Sorry, Alice. I'll take that one with my coffee.'

'Good morning, Joey. The usual?' she asked, handing him the double espresso she'd started making before he'd even turned up.

Monday was Joey's only day off from his bakery, and at 9 a.m. Mrs Harris, the reverend's wife, started her shift in Moretti's Bread House. Every Monday Joey then made the walk to the Kookaburra Creek Café and 9.06 on the dot he arrived for his double espresso and cupcake after a long morning baking.

'I got your text. Here are those loaves you wanted.' He put one white, one wholemeal and one tomato and olive loaf on the bench. 'What happened this time?' He asked fondly. 'Or do you finally concede your bread will never be as good as mine?'

'Haha. I just, um . . . I forgot to set the timer. Silly me.' Alice couldn't tell him the truth. He'd only worry if he found out the café had been broken into.

Joey shook his head. 'How long have we known each other, Alice? I can always tell when you're lying. Something's got you rattled.'

He reached across the bench and took her hand, his gentle touch warm, yet hesitant. Still. After all these years.

She started to tug her hand away and he immediately released it, frowning.

'I'd better head.' He nodded and Alice watched him leave. His old dog, Shadow, waited patiently at the bottom of the deck, big eyes staring up, ever hopeful Alice would let him back into the place he once knew as home. But she couldn't.

Despite the morning's disarray, the day passed without much note. As Alice closed the blinds of the café that evening, her thoughts turned to the girl with Dean McRae's eyes, then to the strawberry and white chocolate cupcakes. Surely it was just a coincidence.

Alice was too on edge to head up the external staircase to her apartment and call it a night. Instead, she made her way along the ambling creek that ran past two sides of the café, wrapping its way from the back around to the side before meandering off to the right to cut the town in half about half a kilometre downstream. The single bridge there, joining the east and west banks, was one of Alice's favourite parts of town.

The grass by the creek edge was long this time of year and Alice slipped off her shoes to feel the soft blades between her toes. The fields of Massey's farm to her left had been turned. Planting would begin soon. To the north she could see the lights of town blinking on as the sun began to set. She would only walk as far as the bridge, as far as Dandelion Dell this evening. With little chance of running into anyone, she could stop in her special place. She could sit on the bench hugged by dandelions and run her hands along the wood, like she often did when her thoughts were a mess, and draw on the sense of calm that always washed over her there.

She followed the creek as it curved to the right, stopping just before Dandelion Dell. Curled up on the white bench was the girl in grey.

'You didn't get very far,' Alice said gently, stepping forward.

The girl sat up, and Alice's breath caught as the familiar blue eyes pierced right through her.

The Banksia Bay Beach Shack

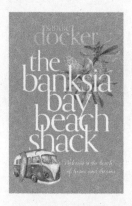

A year is a long time in the memory of a small town. Stories get twisted, truths become warped, history is rewritten.

MYSTERIES

When Laura discovers an old photo of her grandmother, Lillian, with an intriguing inscription on the back, she heads to the sleepy seaside town of Banksia Bay to learn the truth about Lillian's past. But when she arrives, Laura finds a community where everyone seems to be hiding something.

SECRETS

Virginia, owner of the iconic Beach Shack café, has kept her past buried for sixty years. As Laura slowly uncovers the tragic fragments of that summer so long ago, Virginia must decide whether to hold on to her secrets or set the truth free.

LIES

Young Gigi and Lily come from different worlds but forge an unbreakable bond – the 'Sisters of Summer'. But in 1961 a chain of events is set off that reaches far into the future. One lie told. One lie to set someone free. One lie that changes the course of so many lives.

Welcome to the Banksia Bay Beach Shack, where first love is found and last chances are taken.